QUEEN OF THE SKOUR

Book Two of *The Bloodstone Dagger*

K.E. BARRON

Queen of the Skour

K. E. Barron

Published in North America by Bear Hill Publishing.
www.bearhillbooks.com

Cover artwork by Tyson Villeneuve / www.crownnation.com
Cover design © 2021 Bear Hill Books

Paperback ISBN 978-1-989071-05-2

Hardcover ISBN 978-1-989071-06-9

Ebook ISBN 978-1-989071-07-6

To my nana, who is my biggest fan as I am hers.

By K. E. Barron

The Eye of Verishten
'Repudium' (Featured in *The Beginning and
End of All Things: Stories of Man*)

THE BLOODSTONE DAGGER SERIES

*The Immortal Serpent
Queen of the Skour*

Praise for *Queen of the Skour*

"Who will rise? Who will fall? And who will ultimately survive? *Queen of the Skour* is fun, high stakes, big stage fantasy at its best."

—*Manhattan Book Review*

Praise for *The Immortal Serpent*

"A sensual and savage but nuanced epic fantasy tale."

—*Kirkus Reviews*

"K.E Barron's *The Immortal Serpent* is a thrilling high fantasy novel, filled with romance, clever plot twists and an intricate magical world in which readers can get lost."

—*IndieReader*

"Branded as in the style of George R. R. Martin and Brandon Sanderson, *[The] Immortal Serpent* does duty to these two epic fantasy writers with a compelling story, good writing, interesting characters, and an intriguing world."

—*Manhattan Book Review*

Praise for *The Eye of Verishten*

"A gripping tale of intrigue, with a fresh new take on a magical world."

—*Booklist, Starred Review*

Winner of the 2018 silver Independant Publisher Book Award (IPPY) for best sci-fi/fantasy/horror ebook.

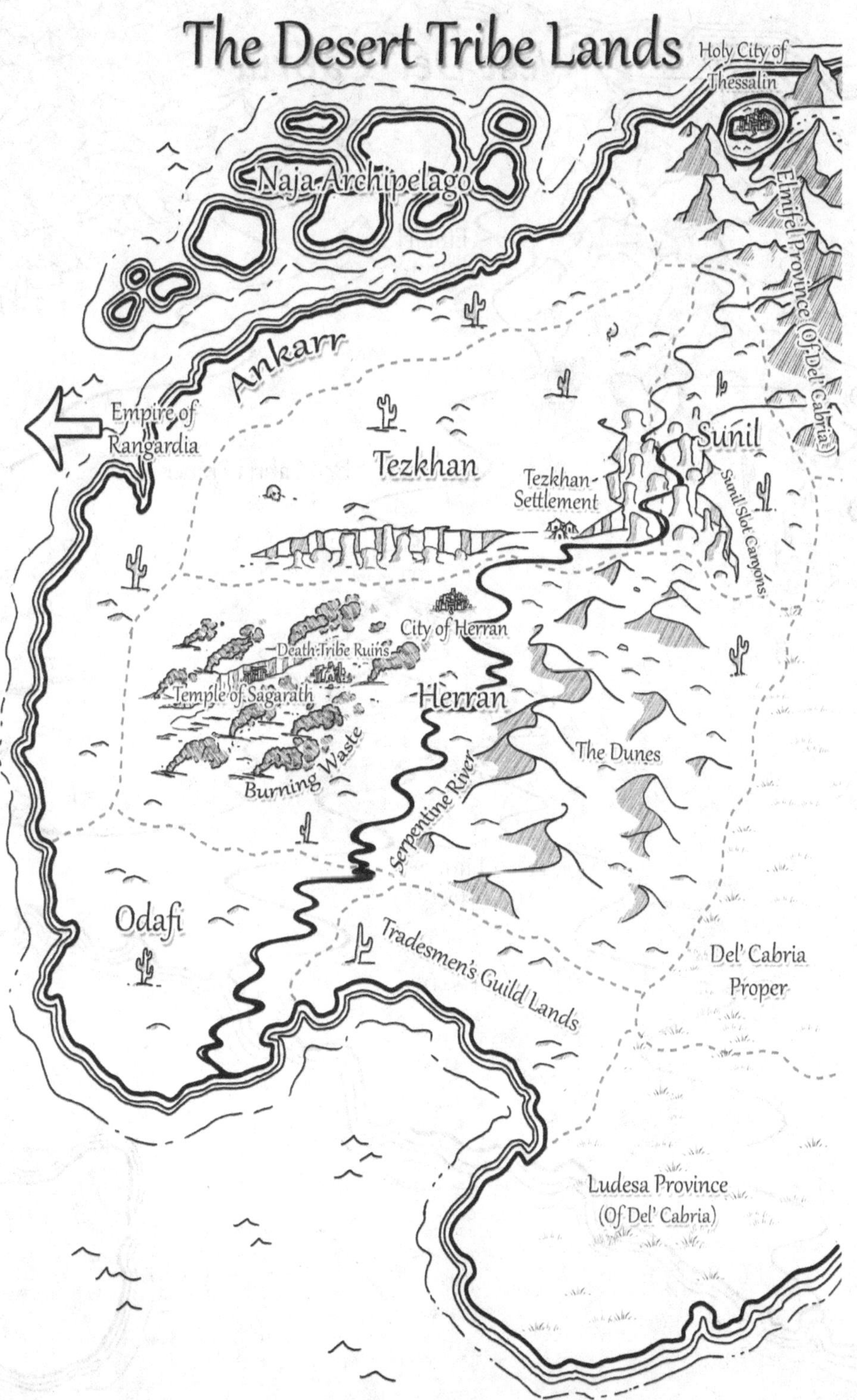

The Desert Tribe Lands
Holy City of Thessalin
Naja Archipelago
Ankarr
Empire of Rangardia
Tezkhan
Tezkhan Settlement
Sunil
Elmifel Province (Of Del' Cabria)
Sunil Slot Canyons
Death Tribe Ruins
City of Herran
Temple of Sagarath
Herran
Burning Waste
The Dunes
Serpentine River
Odafi
Tradesmen's Guild Lands
Del' Cabria Proper
Ludesa Province (Of Del' Cabria)

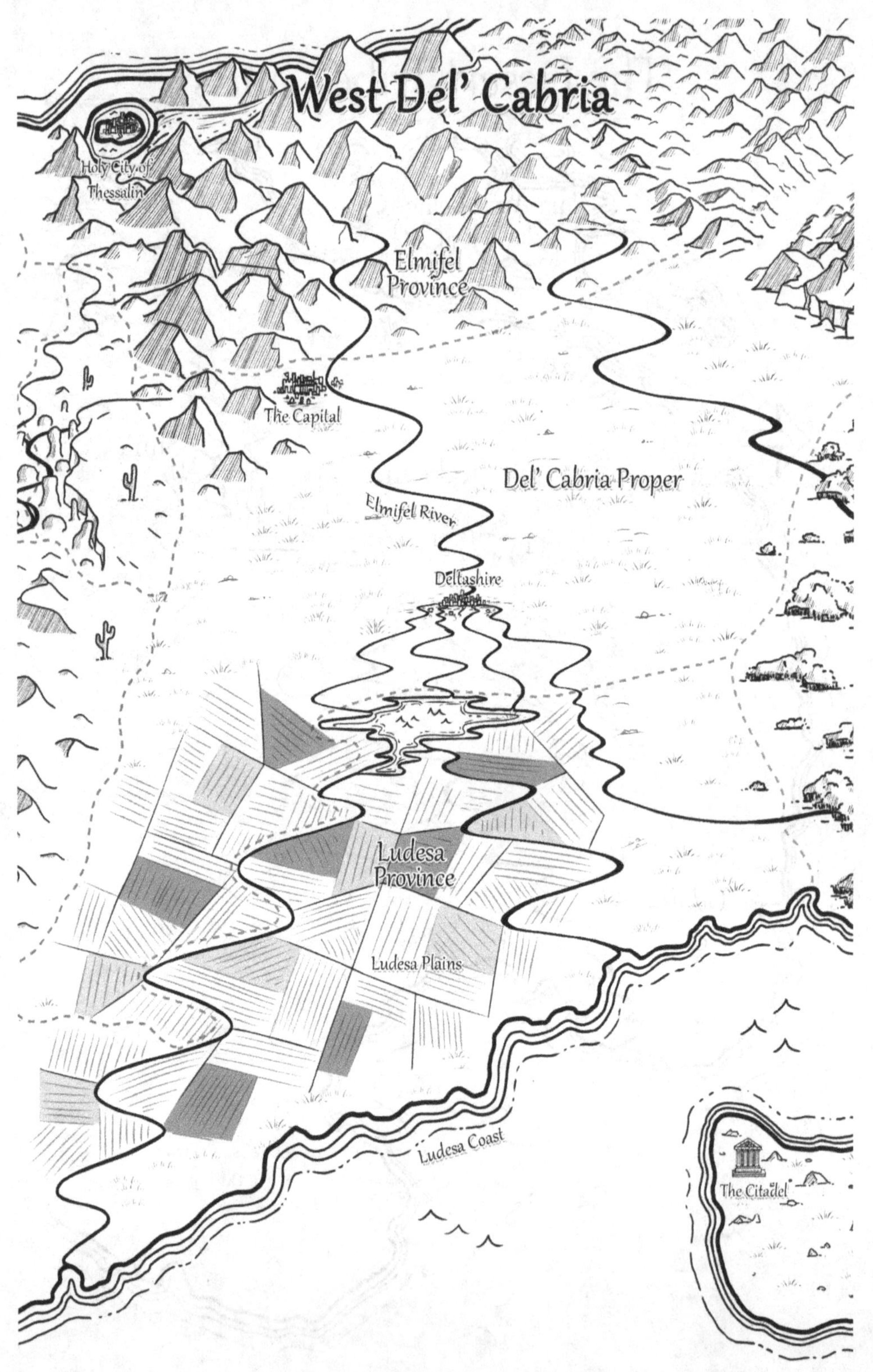

West Del' Cabria
Holy City of Thessalin
Elmifel Province
The Capital
Elmifel River
Del' Cabria Proper
Deltashire
Ludesa Province
Ludesa Plains
Ludesa Coast
The Citadel

East Del' Cabria

The Balance is the duality between the Pure and the Primitive.

Only through penance can one maintain it.

– Saint Orester of Del'Cabria

I

Second Condition

A glistening blue stream drifted up against the black, reaching for something unseen. An image splashed into focus. The Overlord of Herran stood at the base of the throne steps, his form an undulating visage before the King. Skeletal tattoos shimmered sapphire blue in a distorted sunbeam, streaking through the arched window panes. His charcoal-tinted armor, wide-legged pants, and headscarf were still dusted with fine flecks of sand from the desert.

When he opened his mouth to speak, the words sounded hollow as if underwater. "No soldier of yours will take up arms against any warrior of mine, lest our nations return to war."

King Tiberius took a steady, even breath. His pulse, slow but strong. It was the urling way to keep one's nerves in check, and Tiberius never failed in doing so—not even when face to face with the Immortal Serpent.

His calm, emphatic voice rebounded off the high ceilings of his throne room. "You've succeeded in driving my armies out of your tribe lands, but that does not award you the right to dictate the terms of this treaty. The men you've defeated make up only a fraction of our forces. You will find the bulk of them here, prepared to defend their home. Del'Cabria has faced far more dire threats than you, and still, it stands, stronger for having done so." Tiberius's tone hardened. "Empires of chaos, such as yours, do not last long."

The Overlord's serpent eyes blinked sideways as he gave a subtle smirk. "You may be right, Your Majesty, but as new empires rise, ancient ones fade. Yours can continue for many more years to come.

Peaceful co-existence with Herran is the only hope your kingdom has for a future."

Tiberius tapped his fingers on his throne's armrest, sending watery ripples through the air, then exchanged a serious glance with the Captain of the Royal Guard standing silent and steadfast at his left. "You murder one of our most accomplished senators, draw us into war, and now you bring your reptile hordes to our doorstep, all for peaceful co-existence?"

"Peace"—the immortal Mage nodded—"provided my conditions are met: First, my warriors require unrestricted access to Fae'ren Province for the duration of our siege at the Ingleheim borderlands. Second—"

The King held up a hand. "Your attempt to invade those mountain ranges will be the last invasion you ever plan."

Seemingly unperturbed, Nas'Gavarr ambled toward the windows and stared out of them thoughtfully. "Your warning is appreciated but unnecessary. Concern yourself with the lives of your citizens as I reveal to you my second condition." He turned back to Tiberius, his unnerving, reptilian stare causing the King's heart rate to spike.

He stood up from his throne, his liquid surroundings parting before him. "Your immortality makes you believe you are unstoppable, but the Deities are on our side." He took purposeful steps down to the Mage's level. "Threaten my kingdom all you want, but the Serpentine has been and always will be a Conduit of death. No matter how hard you try to change its image to one of equality and freedom, you, along with your false gods, can be killed. Keep *that* in mind when you make your second request." This was Tiberius's kingdom, his throne room. These negotiations were on his terms. He would treat the foreign warlord's 'conditions' as nothing more than mere requests. Ones he would surely dismiss.

The Overlord met the King's eye.

Dong! Splunk!

A wax candle splashed over Nas'Gavarr's grin, sending waves throughout the throne room.

Princess Zephira broke from her scry, gasping for air as her consciousness sharply surfaced in the castle chapel. The nun's harmonious songs rushed back into her ears to replace the surging water in her mind. She was still kneeling before Saint Orester's effigy, intricately carved out of an egg stone pillar. Zephira's candle had somehow fallen into her brass water dish, which had tipped over on its side, the sacred liquid dripping off the altar step and wetting the ends of her gown.

"Oops. Sorry, Zephira . . ." said a lanky boy, his pale cheeks reddening as he cowered on the steps in front of her.

"Rubin?" *That wicked little brat!* She schooled her emotions, suppressing the urge to snatch him by the long ears and tug him off the step. Instead, she remained seated, knowing full well she could never act on such primitive impulses in a holy house of penance.

Pulling her gown away from the creeping puddle, she said in a calm yet assertive tone. "This side of the chapel is for women only. Leave here at once."

"I want to pray too," the scrawny prince whined. "But there are no lit candles in the men's area . . . you weren't supposed to see me."

And what would you possibly be praying for? You still worship your toys! Zephira cleared her throat, shoving away the unwanted burst of emotion. "If you require assistance, find an altar boy. Now, get down from there before you anger the Deities further."

Rubin did as he was told, his shoulders slumping. He clutched his right hand tight to his chest.

"What do you have? Give it here." Zephira held out her palm. *You may get away with swiping trinkets from my room, but I'll be damned if I let you steal from the Deities themselves,* she thought.

Rubin hesitantly showed her the knuckles on his right hand. They were blistering red.

"You've burned yourself." She instantly forgot her previous mental accusation.

"I can put water on it." He pulled out of her grasp and ran to the basin a few feet away, but Zephira snatched up his arm in a flash.

"*That* is water from the Sacred Spring of Elmifel, utilized only for prayer, not for silly boys who burn themselves."

"But it hurts," Rubin moaned.

"Good," Zephira said. "Let the pain be penance for your sinful conduct."

Tears welled up in his large blue eyes; his bottom lip began to quiver. *Oh, no, don't do this here, not now!* Zephira silently pleaded.

Just then, a woman's shrill voice rang off the chapel walls. "Rubin! You are not to be in here."

Queen Henriette's heeled shoes clacked upon the blue and white checkered tile with each rushed step. Like Zephira, she wore a modest high-waisted gown, cinched at the bust and buttoned up to her neck with lace netting over her chest, appropriately modest for visiting a chapel.

She had promised Zephira earlier that she'd watch Rubin, but as always, the princeling snuck away to make his sister's day all the more infuriating.

"The candle burned me, Mummy." Rubin held out his hand.

"No, he burned *himself* on the candle," Zephira corrected.

Henriette bent over to inspect the injury in question. "Oh, Precious"—she kissed her son's knuckles—"let's get you something for it."

Zephira clutched her gown in irritation. "Please ensure he stays on the men's side. If one of the sisters had caught him, he would wish for the candle's flame." She knew better than anyone what a strap wielded by a Sister of the Unnamed felt like, and she had done a lot less to deserve such whippings. She could still feel the sting between her shoulder blades from the last time she had voiced a petty human thought in earshot of the headmistress.

"Zephira, have a little compassion. He's a child," said Henriette.

"He's almost twelve, older than I was when I started tutelage at the Holy City."

"You were always more mature than most children your age. Rubin's time will come. There's no need to rush these things."

"I suppose not." Zephira bit her lip.

It was the law that Rubin would take the throne ahead of Zephira simply because he was the male heir, but it was clear to her that only she possessed the urling resolve required to lead the Kingdom after their father. She prayed that Rubin would abdicate the throne when the time came in recognition of his older sister's worthiness. Such a thing was unlikely, however, since it would require him to take a vow of celibacy in service of the Faith or live in exile.

"Let's go, my Prince." Henriette placed her hand behind Rubin's back and started to lead him away.

"I want to pray with Zephira!" he protested.

"Oh hush, I'm taking you to the infirmary and then straight home." she cooed as the two disappeared down the basement stairs.

Sure her pesky little brother was gone, Zephira rushed back to her prayer space, eager to return to her father's deliberations with the Overlord of Herran. A pang of guilt grew in her chest, making her pause. Not only was she scrying her father under the pretense of prayer, but she had promised him she wouldn't. *'There are things you are not yet prepared to see, my dear,'* he would say. *'Elmifel bestowed upon you a sacred gift. It shall not be used to spy on your kin.'*

With a sigh, she admitted there was no justifiable reason for her to scry any further. The Overlord could never break her father's resolve. No one could. Instead, she refilled the bowl with sacred spring water from the basin and returned to a kneeling position before the altar of Saint Orester. The statue held a long candle, its faint light overwhelmed by the afternoon sun's rays streaming in from the windows thirty feet above.

Despite the time of day, the air inside the chapel was frigid. She raised her hood over her blonde hair, leaned forward, and pressed her forehead to the chilly stone step. "I implore thee, Deities That Cannot Be Named, to watch over our noble King while he is in our enemy's presence."

She unpinned the cameo brooch from her cloak and traced her fingertips over the ancient queen's features, sculpted out of white sardonyx shell and fastened to a velvet backing. She carefully placed it beside the water dish and said, "To Queen Orester, merciful saint, may you grant him your wisdom so he may do what is right in the face of evil."

Zephira dipped her hands into the water, cold to the touch, even to her normally icy fingers. "And to the Spirit of Elmifel, source of all life, may you cleanse his mind and heart of primitive fears so that he may overcome the serpent's deceptions."

Clasping her wet hands together, she closed her eyes tight, willing the icy tendrils of anxiety to cease their climb up her spine. *What could the Overlord's second request be?* Zephira's thoughts spun.

No longer able to help herself, she wet her left hand again and traced the *Veil of Elmifel* on her forehead, customary in prayers involving the Sacred Spirit and vital for scrying. Besides, she reasoned, she would need to learn all she could about the Overlord of Herran in case she ever did become Queen.

She focused all her attention on the dampness on her forehead. Droplets of water lifted off her skin, forming a clear vapor that condensed into tiny phantom streams suspended in the air. A nun refilled the water basin nearby, paying the princess no mind. To her, it would look like Zephira was only praying; no one was able to see the water the way she could.

There were always three streams: One for her mother, a thinner one for her brother, and the largest for her father. The more she used a stream, the more prominent it became.

Hands still clasped together, Zephira pushed her mind toward the largest stream. The Sisters of the Unnamed's voices became muffled by the sound of rushing water filling her ears, and the phantom stream cast her up toward the vaulted ceilings and out of the chapel. Her consciousness moved at such inconceivable speed, the world around her liquified, engulfing her in pure fluid energy.

The brightness of the castle throne room splashed into existence, the chapel now a distant memory. She once again saw through her father's eyes and listened through his ears. An underwater spectator within a body over which she had no control.

Tiberius stood next to Nas'Gavarr, both staring out the window, but now, where the Overlord appeared satisfied, her father struggled to keep himself from shaking with rage. What could Nas'Gavarr have said to upset her father so? "Long before I became known as the Immortal Serpent, I was just a simple Fire Mage," said Nas'Gavarr. "No matter how many essences I've mastered since, I never forgot where it all began."

The reason for the King's dismay soon revealed itself as his wide-eyed gaze fell first to the western city gates, then the north, then the east . . . to the black smoke billowing from every exit point in the city.

Nas'Gavarr's brow furrowed, deep in concentration, like an artist locked in the mania of the creative process. "Fire is the most misunderstood essence, which is why, apart from life force, it is the most difficult to manipulate. Its aura is virtually invisible to the Mage. It can only be felt"—the Overlord placed his forefingers to his temple—"like the throbbing rhythm of blood coursing through veins. Many Mages believe, as with other essences, once one senses the aura, they can learn to control it. But that's where fire differs. Only by understanding its *uncontrollable* nature can a Mage uncover its secrets."

Before Tiberius could utter a word, there was a reverberating pop, and more black smoke to follow, much closer to the castle. So close, he could feel its heat radiating around him, the smoke suffocating . . . but how? Tiberius was safe in the throne room behind glass . . . unless it wasn't Tiberius feeling it at all.

"My family is down there!" The King's heart froze in his chest.

"Then they have nothing to fear. For what safer place than in the house of the Deities who you've assured me are 'on your side.'"

A hand came down hard on Zephira's shoulder, yanking her from her scry. Nuns' shouts bounced off the chapel ceiling. "FIRE, FIRE!"

"Princess, this way!" Sir Kendall, her personal guard, pulled her to her feet.

Smoke stung her nostrils, and she blinked furiously as she followed her guard out the rear exit. They came to the courtyard, gasping. Lines of mulberry bushes and great willow trees erupted in flames. A blazing ring surrounded them, blocking every escape route.

"Back inside!" Kendall waved Zephira back toward the door as rising flames chased them with unnatural speed.

Zephira choked on the smoke that now filled the chapel. The front entrance had become engulfed in a fiery blaze in the few moments they had been outside. *It's too fast!* Flames skirted across the rugs and climbed up the banners and tapestries on the walls.

Sir Allard emerged, coughing through the stifling haze to meet Kendall and Zephira. His charges, her mother and brother, trailed behind him, looking around the chapel in panic.

"Mother, why are you still here?"

"The front courtyard is completely engulfed," the Queen's guard replied in her stead.

"Mummy," Rubin cried. "What's happening?"

His mother coughed into her shoulder while pressing the young prince tightly against her as if her body were a fireproof cloak of protection.

A shrieking nun, her wimple ablaze, careened past the royal family and doused herself in the sacred spring water. Zephira rushed to the basin, wet her hands, and rapidly traced the *Veil* on her forehead. *Father, please just give him what he wants, whatever it is!*

"Stop this at once!" Tiberius bellowed. Zephira had never experienced him yell with such force before. Below the throne room, flames coated the yard and danced up the vines clinging to the stone towers.

"Wildfire." Nas'Gavarr grinned. "Wind and fire essence working as one. The easiest to master combined with one of the most difficult, creating something virtually unstoppable. I can maneuver the flames wherever I wish, even where there is nothing to burn."

"Put it out!" Tiberius said through gritted teeth.

"It likely won't be the flames that kill them," Nas'Gavarr continued. "The smoke will suffocate them first. It will feel like drowning. Some believe that is a more merciful death . . . but I am not so sure. It is one of the few deaths I have never experienced."

"You ask for what I cannot give. My child . . . my legacy!"

Nas'Gavarr raised one arm, and the infernal pillars surrounding the Capital grew higher, rivaling the height of the walls themselves. Tiberius's body was frozen in place, but his insides twisted in knots, helplessly watching his people in the distance scurry to evacuate and finding nowhere to go.

Beside him, Nas'Gavarr smiled out the corner of his mouth, real teeth forming a double layer with the teeth tattooed on his lips. "In a month and a half, the moons will join as one. As my people celebrate their freedom, yours will be rebuilding their homes and mourning their dead. That is, of course, if you continue to deny me. One way or another, I will have what I'm after."

Henriette's face appeared suddenly, dry and well-defined among the watery surroundings. Wiping off Zephira's forehead, the Queen pulled her back to the burning chapel. "Zephira, stop that. We must hurry!"

The princess blinked to full awareness then looked straight at her little brother clutching his mother's skirts. *Rubin* . . . Her heart froze despite the heat.

"To the men's side, quickly," ordered Allard.

Kendall took Zephira's other arm and tugged her away from the basin. Smoke rose to the ceiling, completely obscuring the decorative carvings as they ran into the men's chapel.

As they arrived, windows shattered and glass sprinkled down. More flames blew in, igniting every banner. Their fiery fingers wrapped around the stairwells and proceeded to jump across the upper balconies. "The entire building is surrounded!" a priest cried in panic. Others flung themselves over the balustrades of the second floor to escape the blaze pushing in through the broken windows.

"By the Deities, where do we go?" Henriette coughed. She tore off her wig of blonde ringlets and dabbed at the sweat pouring from her brow.

Zephira loosed her own hair from her circlet and pressed the garment to her nose and mouth. It didn't seem to help much; each breath was still a hot iron scraping the back of her throat.

"The downward stairwells are clear." Kendall pointed to the sweeping staircase to their left before hacking into his arm. "The basement is our best chance."

They descended to the chapel's lower level, and the air cooled considerably, but hot orange waves rippled across the low ceiling in relentless pursuit.

Zephira panted, dragging hot air into her lungs. Flames blocked their way ahead, and they had to turn around. More flames raced up behind them.

The guards threw themselves against a locked door to their right, fire already licking the walls around them. It flung open, and they rushed into a dark dormitory. A lone nun was curled up underneath her bed, praying in terrified murmurs.

Allard spun around to inspect the room. "There are no windows. Blast these old structures!"

He went to close the door, but the blaze burst in from the hallway. He cursed and scurried back, pressing everyone against the far wall.

"Keep low!" Kendall placed both hands on Zephira's shoulders, forcing her into a crouch. The others followed suit, priests and nuns spreading out flat on their bellies.

Tears mixed with sweat streamed down Henriette's face. "You did all you could, brave sirs." The royal family huddled close together as blinding smoke filled the room. Bright flames closed in, the heat overwhelming, the smell of burning bedspreads nauseating.

Zephira grasped for her brooch to find it missing. Her heart sank even deeper into her gut upon realizing she had left it upstairs. She prayed to the wise saint anyway: "Deliver us . . . may Father find the resolve to strike down the serpent where he stands." Zephira's eyes stung, the smoke so thick, she could barely see those right next to her.

Then, as if a brisk wind blew out of the room, the smoke and fire receded, hovering just outside the door. The immediate threat of burning alive seemed to be over, but Zephira knew Nas'Gavarr was not about to let them leave, which meant the King had made his decision or the decision had been made for him.

"The Overlord," Zephira croaked. "He's going to take Rubin."

"What?" Henriette choked.

"How do you know that?" Allard asked, sweat pouring down his salt and pepper stubble.

"Mummy," Rubin cried through violent coughs.

"It will be all right, Precious."

Zephira's core shook with rage watching her eleven-year-old brother, trembling in his mother's arms, awaiting his dreadful fate. She vowed in that moment that when she became Queen, the Immortal Serpent would pay dearly for this. His desert barbarians would never dare set foot on Del'Cabrian soil again, and she would bring Rubin home. The Kingdom's honor would be restored at all costs.

The smoke eventually cleared, revealing a way out of the sweltering dormitory. Heavy footsteps sounded from the basement hallway, growing louder as they neared the room.

"The fire's going out," said Allard, rising to his feet. "I will secure an escape route."

"No." Zephira grabbed hold of his pant leg. "He's coming."

Kendall, too, rose to his feet. Both guards unsheathed their swords. "Who's coming?"

"The Overlord of Herran." Zephira took her brother by the shoulders and pulled him from his mother's grasp.

Henriette gasped, "Zephira wha—?"

She ignored her mother's pleas and looked straight into her brother's bloodshot eyes. "Listen to me, Rubin. He's coming to take you away for a while."

"Why?" he cried. "Mummy?"

With a firm shake, Zephira captured his attention. "You won't be hurt, do you hear me? The Deities are with you, always."

"I won't go!"

"You will, little brother, but I promise to watch out for you, wherever you go," she assured him, brushing stray hairs off his sweaty brow. "Just remember, you are the Crown Prince of Del'Cabria. You must be strong."

"My Prince!" Henriette wrapped her arms around him and Zephira both. "You're not going anywhere. I will not let that heathen touch you!"

"And neither shall we," said Allard, exchanging a grim nod with Kendall.

At that moment, the smoke parted, and Nas'Gavarr stepped through. He stared down the two guards with his demonic serpent eyes.

"You will come no closer," shouted Allard, voice quavering.

"Step aside, by order of your King," Nas'Gavarr replied calmly.

The guards held their ground, swords outstretched.

Nas'Gavarr took a step forward, and Allard attacked. With barely a glance, the Overlord caught his sword in his bare hand, grabbed Allard by the neck, and flung him, the crack of his bones echoing off the stone walls of the small room. The guard collapsed like a limp mass on the floor as Nas'Gavarr's sliced hand sealed before their eyes.

"Do not come any closer," ordered Kendall, darting his eyes back and forth between the Overlord and his brother-in-arms slumped against the wall, motionless.

"Stay back, vile snake!" Henriette screamed, squeezing Rubin's head tighter against her breast.

Zephira rose to her feet and stepped in front of her mother and brother. "What do you want with the prince?" Her voice came out as a terrified mouse trapped within her burning throat.

The Overlord's head swayed to the side like an advancing cobra, not taking his eyes off Zephira. "It's not him I came for."

She felt her chest collapse as she fought to breathe. Below, her mother and brother rocked back and forth, arms clasped around each other.

Nas'Gavarr moved aside, exposing the doorway. "Come with me, Princess, and I will leave your steadfast protector unharmed." He gazed pointedly at Kendall, who was rapidly pulling the Queen and prince to their feet and ushering them out of the room.

Henriette took Zephira by the arm. "Come, sweetheart!"

Numb, Zephira wouldn't budge. "If I don't go with him, he will burn the Capital and everyone in it."

"Zephira!" her mother screeched, ignoring her daughter's reasoning. Rubin's high-pitched wails filled her head, along with the murmurings of the nun, still under the bed.

With a determined roar, Kendall advanced with his sword held high.

"Sir Kendall!" Zephira cried, but her loyal guard didn't deter. The Overlord effortlessly dodged his blade, then grabbed hold of his head in two large hands and crushed his skull like an eggshell.

Zephira's breath seized, staring at the handsome urling man who had been at her side since she was ten, crumpled and broken at her feet. Her legs, like two gelatinous masses, gave way beneath her. Henriette tried with all her might to drag her daughter away from the advancing sorcerer, but Zephira could not peel her eyes from her guard's crushed skull. She didn't even notice the priests and nuns having fled the room, leaving the royal family to face the demon Mage alone.

Now, he was looming over her. He took her by the bicep and pulled her to her feet with hardly an ounce of effort.

"Get your hands off her!" The Queen pulled Zephira's other arm until it felt like it would snap right off.

Tiberius rushed into the room, out of breath, followed by the Captain of the Royal Guard. "Henriette, release her and come to me. Now!"

"Tiberius. You must stop him."

"Let her go," he said again, his voice deflated.

"Tiberius, she hasn't yet reached marrying age. This heathen will add her to his harem. Please, don't do this. She's our little girl!"

Without another word, Tiberius marched over and forcefully yanked his wife away from Zephira and the Mage clutching her.

Henriette shrieked, fighting against her husband's grasp while reaching for her daughter, but she soon collapsed to the scorched floor in hysterics, soot staining her gown. Rubin stood flat against the wall, wide-eyed and trembling in pure terror.

The King turned to his captain and nodded toward his son. "Take him away from here." The prince was unresponsive to the captain's approach, too fixated on his big sister in the Overlord's unrelenting grip. The captain had to scoop him up and carry him out of the room as if he were a helpless toddler.

Nas'Gavarr released Zephira's arm and grabbed her head with both hands, forcing her to face him. She stood paralyzed as her mind buzzed. The sounds of her mother's cries, her brother's squeals down the hall, and the sole nun's frightened murmurs melded into a petrifying hum. There were no phantom rivers to take her away; any water left on her skin had long since evaporated.

"Don't be afraid, Zephira." her father's calm voice cut through the noise. "This is what is best for the Kingdom." The same sentiments she had just uttered to her brother didn't bring her any degree of comfort, only caused the dreadful chasm in her stomach to open wider. But it didn't matter how she felt; they were all primitive human emotions that had to be buried and the earth salted.

Her gaze stayed rooted on Nas'Gavarr's serpent eyes, but it was her father she responded to, a quote from King Cornelius II coming to mind automatically: "Fear does not serve in times of need. Only duty.'"

"And you will fulfill that duty," expressed Nas'Gavarr with a knowing smirk. "You will be Queen."

He waved his hand in front of her eyes, and the world faded to black.

2

No Friend of Womankind

(Seven and a half months later)

Vidya caught her breath, rainfall soaking through her wrap-around shirt and flattening her frizzy hair. Four prison guards lay crumpled at her feet. The oldest among them groaned, prompting her to give him an extra kick to the head with the heel of her worn boot.

"Alright, Vidi, you made your point," said Phrea. "Are you going to fly us out of here or what?"

The other prisoners stood as still as stone pillars in the downpour, transfixed by the winged woman who had just pummeled four armed guards into the gravel. Footsteps thundered from inside the prison structure, growing louder as they neared the gates to the yard. Several of the prisoners glanced behind them, biting their lips in anxiety.

Vidya, on the other hand, had never felt so tranquil.

"I didn't just come for you and Daph." She picked up a guard's wooden baton and tossed it to Phrea, then turned to the rest of the women. "You've only witnessed a tiny fraction of what a harpy can do." She kicked another fallen baton over to Daphne. "I came here today to share that power with you all. But first"—the gates flung open with a groan, and a dozen more guards poured into the yard—"punish the men who abused you here, then we will punish the sirens that *put* you here."

Vidya funneled the wind and rain toward the advance with a mighty flap of her wings, knocking the first line of guards into the row behind. Two prisoners grabbed the last of the weapons off the ground and took battle stances.

"You heard her, ladies!" Phrea tapped her thick wooden baton against her palm. "You want wings? Fight for them!" With a sidelong grin, she rushed a young male guard attempting to return to his feet. She belted him back down into the gravel and didn't let up until he ceased to move.

Daphne and the rest of the prisoners swiftly took advantage of the guards' shock. The inmates' frenzy exploded into battle cries as they rushed their jailers.

A wave of shaven heads and plain cotton smocks took down the leather-clad guards with such fervor, Vidya worried the skirmish would end too soon. She grazed her fingertips over the bone hilt of the Bloodstone Dagger at her hip. *I may have to visit the men's prison to find a worthy sacrifice.* For one man to give rise to over thirty harpies at a time, he needed to be stronger than anyone she'd seen so far.

More prison guards pushed their way through the gates, shoving the women back into the rain. Vidya flapped her wings, tripping the advancing guards with storm winds once again. There were more guards than prisoners in the yard; they needed to free the rest and fast.

"Take it inside," Vidya roared. She barreled through the line of guards clogging the gates, clearing a path for the women to flood in.

On the top floor, Vidya surveyed the tri-level cell block, searching for the maximum-security area. Rows of guards ran up the spiral staircases, batons at the ready. She thought about taking them out first lest they quell her burgeoning riot. Then, a winged shadow formed at the railing next to her. *"You need only free one prisoner, and our harpy revolution can truly begin,"* it tittered. Vidya swore she saw the creature smile, an eerie grin that stretched across the entirety of its dark, ethereal face.

"Keys! I have keys!" a prisoner cheered, jingling them above her head for the other ladies to see. She ran to the nearest cell door, casting it open and releasing the four inmates locked within. Vidya smiled, already proud of who these women were becoming. *Good, now for what I really came for.*

Spreading her wings, Vidya vaulted over the railing and glided down the cylindrical cell block until she found the thick iron doors on the ground level's south side. She lifted the metal flap of the first door she came upon and looked inside the cell. *No, not her.* Second: *Nope.* Third and fourth: *Empty.* She peered through the shutter of the fifth door. A thin wisp of a woman hunched in the corner, graying black hair hanging in front of her face and pale, yellow wings plastered to her bony back. *That's got to be her.*

"Stop where you are!" A man barked, a pistol cocking behind Vidya. "Turn around and slowly."

She did so, holding her hands at head-level. The warden pointed a flintlock pistol at her face, and he had a second one waiting in the holster at his side.

"Since when do wardens get to carry firearms?" she asked.

"Don't move." His unarmed hand fiddled with a ring of keys, which he used to open the fourth cell door. With the pistol still aimed at Vidya, the warden bobbed his head to the side. "Get in . . . now." He gave her a wide berth to walk past him and into the empty cell, but she was not about to comply.

Vidya stepped forward. "That's a good girl," the warden smirked and straightened his back.

She shook with indignation. *"Girl?"* With a sharp flap of her wings, she shot up to the ceiling. The warden fired, but the round chipped the wall behind her. He fumbled with the pistol in his other holster, giving Vidya ample time to drop down and slam her elbow into his head, knocking him unconscious. "I'm no girl."

She took his keys and unlocked the iron latch of the fifth door.

The woman inside snapped her head up, glaring as Vidya strode into the grimy cell. Her big eyes, bright and blue, were lined with wrinkles. She looked to be in her seventh decade, but Vidya thought she should be younger than that. Her imprisonment had aged her.

A metal grating shrouded the bottom half of her face, and a leather mouthpiece smothered her call of surprise.

The woman stood up on bony legs and took hesitant steps toward Vidya, her filthy, bare feet shuffling along the floor. Clipped yellow wings, like crumpled papyrus, unfolded, their hollow bones popping. She held out her caged hands, appearing as iron stumps.

Vidya carefully reached around the woman's head to remove the mask, grunting as the latches snapped apart.

The siren lurched forward, gagging on the air and breathing in deep rasps between fits of laughter. She scratched her chin maniacally, her liberated jaw much paler than the rest of her face.

"You're Cosima, former Mistress of Sciences, is that correct?" Vidya severed the straps around the woman's biceps, freeing the heavy chains that secured her iron gauntlets.

"You're not like any siren I've ever seen before." She stared into Vidya as if trying to see her through a thick haze with a barely perceptible smile tugging at her scabbed lips.

Vidya scowled at the notion. "I'm a harpy and the daughter of Sarta." The gauntlets dropped to the cell floor with a clank.

The scientist laughed, a sound like a cat being strangled. "Oh, I know who *you* are." She pointed a bony talon-like finger at the ceiling. "A little birdy told me—tweet-tweeting outside my door. All the birds chirp about you. The Republic's new great mistake."

"How flattering," Vidya said dryly. "Tell me, why did you attempt to poison the entire Mothers' Assembly, including the Archon? They say you influenced their breeders, even some of their husbands and sons, to carry it out for you." Vidya stared into the former councilor's eyes, gauging her reaction. "What possessed you to abuse the Siren's power like that?" The first steps in Vidya's plan to take back Credence from the Council depended on this traitorous and legendary siren. She wondered how close Cosima's motivations were to her own.

Cosima cocked her head to the side like a buzzard. "The Assembly kept voting her in, over and over, not caring about the unspeakable things she did to get there. They had grown as complacent as the men they touch, blinded by the shimmer of her flaxen wings."

"You speak of Xenith?" Vidya raised an eyebrow.

"Xenith . . ." She spat the name as if it were a foul thing in her mouth. "Am I to assume she still sits in the Archon's seat?"

Vidya's hand danced over the bone grip of her dagger. "Not if I have anything to say about it." She hoped the shadow harpy would tell her what Xenith had done, but it remained silent, as it always did when it came to the evil deeds of women. It didn't mean they didn't deserve punishment all the same.

Cosima displayed her rotting teeth once again. However putrid her breath, it didn't bother Vidya. After the vermin she had regurgitated in the Spirit Chamber a few weeks back, nothing short of the maltreatment of women disgusted her now.

"Sarta's eldest is out for blood, I see," Cosima purred.

"I'm out for more than that. I need an army, and you are going to help me build it, starting today."

The siren's features twisted as if in pain. "Oh no. I couldn't!"

In an instant, her previous look melted off to reveal a sudden surprise. ". . . You *do* know that the Harpy shall never rule Credence again, don't you?" She poked Vidya in the chest with her gnarled finger, the nails worn to cracked stumps. "That's her punishment for bringing such suffering to humanity, for reaching beyond what was rightfully hers. Had it not been for the Siren, those urling misogynists would have taken everything from us."

"One could argue the Harpy deserved her punishment back then." Vidya heard a bitter scoff from the shadow in the cell's corner, but she continued, "Now, she must punish the Siren for her cowardice, for selling our island to the serpent who killed my mother and dares to believe men should stand as equals with women."

Cosima pushed her long greasy hair off her face and scowled. "Xenith is no friend of womankind and never has been."

"Join me," said Vidya. "And witness a harpy do what a siren could not."

The former councilor bit her lip then grinned in such a way that the hairs on the back of Vidya's neck stood on end. "If it involves dethroning Xenith in the most painful way imaginable, you may use me however you wish."

With a grim nod, Vidya said, "First, I'll need you to dust off those vocal cords."

She turned on her heel and walked back into the rioting cell block with Cosima tip-toeing daintily behind her. Most of the prisoners were out of their cells, creating an all-out war on every level. "Stay here," Vidya said, then flew into the air.

Hovering in the middle of the cell block, she surveyed the fight all around her. A monstrous guard blocked the second level walkway, his reach so long, no woman in his path could escape his swinging club. *He will do nicely.*

Launching herself toward her target, Vidya dropped onto the guard's massive shoulders and clasped her hands over his ears. She shouted to the recently freed siren waiting patiently on the ground floor. "Cosima! Now!"

The siren took a deep breath and belted a note so coarse and out of tune, everyone recoiled, halting the riot for a brief moment. Vidya's heart sank. The large man beneath her tried to shake her off, but she held on fast.

"Apologies," Cosima said with a cough. "A little rusty." Clearing her throat, she walked forward and lifted her hand to the rioters like they were an audience at her theatrical debut. Her lungs expanded with a great heap of air, and she opened her mouth. Through the gravel, emerged a siren's song like no other. It wafted effortlessly over all three levels. No man could escape, except the guard whose ears Vidya's grasped. She needed him to be in his right mind for what she wanted to do.

The male guards released their struggling captives, dropped their weapons at their feet, some even fell to their knees in awe of the most dangerous siren in Credence. The female guards stood maligned in shock, wholly outnumbered with no choice but to submit.

Once the song ended, Vidya lifted the giant guard and flew him down to the ground floor in the center of the cell block. "Gather round, inmates and guards. I present to you this fine warrior who has volunteered to prove his worth to the Harpy."

The man's giant lips molded into an immovable grimace, and he cracked his knuckles in his palm. Vidya beckoned him toward her with a wave of her fingers. "May she guide your fists."

He tightened his scraggly hairtail and snapped a punch straight at Vidya's head. She backed away just in time, blinking at the sheer force whistling past her face.

She pivoted around him, dodging his strikes. His nostrils flared in frustration.

With his next attack, she planted her feet, letting the hit land. After all, he needed to prove he was worthy. A gigantic fist hammered her into the cold stone floor, her shoulder buckled on impact, and she bit back a grin.

He was on her in an instant, the back of his hand colliding with her cheek and sending her flailing to the side. She spat out blood from her bitten tongue then turned over, baring her bloody teeth for her female audience. *Now that's a hit worthy of a Harplite!*

Women gasped as they watched the giant guard grab Vidya by the wing and drag her across the floor. She twirled around on the ground and kicked him away, but he kicked her right back down. His pillar of a foot on her chest pressed her into the unrelenting stone. Enough was enough. Vidya grabbed the guard's massive leather boot and muttered through her blood-stained teeth, "The Harpy thanks you for your sacrifice."

The man scrunched his prominent brow ridge in confusion and Vidya used the strength of three men to lift his foot from her chest and roll out from beneath it.

Growling, he tried to stomp on her again, but she caught his tree trunk calf, breaking the bone with a palm strike. The man's bellows echoed across all three levels, matched only by the thunder vibrating the cell block's rock walls. He faltered to one knee, panting in rasping gulps.

Vidya clutched his breastplate, unsheathed the Bloodstone Dagger, and lodged it into the bulk between his neck and shoulder. She slowly rose to her feet as the tiny red spots in the green stone expanded, soaking up his blood and multiplying it a hundredfold. The giant man made a weak attempt to yank her arm off him, but Vidya snatched his fingers and bent them back until they snapped.

As the dagger continued to drain him, his arms dropped to his sides, and he slumped back on his heels. His eyes rolled into his skull; flashes of lightning through the barred windows casting his skin in a pale gray hue.

Satisfied that she had enough blood for her demonstration, she kicked the hulking guard down on his back, the dagger ripping from his neck and spraying blood over the nearest onlookers.

She held up the now red dagger for all to see. Over a hundred women's faces stared down at her, mouths agape. "It takes three men to create one harpy," she shouted, her face breaking into a wild grin, "or it used to anyway."

Daphne's aqua doe eyes glistened with awe from the second level staircase.

Vidya pointed to the large guard bleeding out on the ground. "Because of the dagger I hold, this man's blood, along with two others like him, will create one hundred harpies."

Holding the dagger point down, she squeezed the stone grip, allowing the blood to spill from the magic stone and splatter on the floor at her feet. Prisoners on the ground floor edged closer, morbidly entranced by the continuous stream of blood pouring from the knife's tip.

Phrea rushed down the stairs. "Don't waste it. We need that!"

Vidya twirled the dagger right side up, halting the flow. "Not to worry, my future sisters. There's plenty for everyone."

She took to one knee and stabbed the dead guard's heart to take what was left. The prisoners clambered down to the ground floor, adding to the amassing crowd. Phrea and Daphne pushed their way through them so they could stand at Vidya's side. "Those siren cunts are going down," said Phrea.

Cosima, the lone siren with her cloud of mesmerized guards congregating around her, gleefully clapped her bony hands while giggling through her cracked, discolored teeth.

As the large man's heart drained into the dagger in Vidya's hand, her own swelled with sweet anticipation for all the punishments she'd soon inflict.

3
Best be Cautious

(One year later)

"Jethro, Jethro, I found some!" Ellion waved a bundle of long green leaves above his head as he skipped over the foliage near Lanore's east road. He stumbled over a ground root and fell face first. Jeth interrupted his own foraging to help the four-year-old back to his feet.

"Careful there, wee lad."

The fae boy sprang up without complaint and handed Jeth the leaves he carried.

Right away, Jeth knew they weren't what they were looking for. "Close, but . . ." He showed Ellion the vera leaves he had already collected. "Vera is long and rubbery, see?" He took Ellion's hand and grazed his fingers over the leaf. "You think you can find leaves that feel like that?"

"Aye!" The boy nodded eagerly and dashed back into the bush.

Jeth smiled and returned to the vera bush at his feet, breaking the remaining leaves off then tossing them in his open satchel.

He didn't usually volunteer to collect wild plants for the commune healer—making arrows, training fighters, and hunting kept him busy enough—but if he didn't do something to help her, they would never have any time together during the spring planting season.

What he didn't expect was to have to take her son along. Sure, it got him out of her hair and satisfied the kid's incessant need for adventure. And Jeth was happy to take him out and teach him a few things—even if he couldn't get him to stop calling him 'Jethro'—but the more time he spent with him, the more his heart ached for what could never be. *What would it be like doing this with your own son . . . the one who still remains nameless?*

Ellion ran up to him again. "Jethro, what about this?" He held out another plant that resembled a clover with elongated leaves.

"No, that's not . . ." The savory scent was unmistakable: Fae grass, a substance that Jeth rarely turned down the opportunity to smoke. "Whoa, wait . . . where'd you find those?"

The boy took Jeth's hand and led him to a modest patch behind a dead oak.

"Great find, little lad. Let's pack some of this up."

"Will it help mommy heal people?"

"In a way." Jeth chuckled as he and Ellion pulled the fragrant plants out by the stems and plunked them in the satchel with the vera leaves. The bag now bulging, Jeth walked Ellion out of the woods and back to the road where his dapple-gray waited patiently with her lead tied to a low hanging branch.

After he secured the satchel around the horse's neck, Jeth said, "Time to go." He hoisted the four-year-old onto Torrent's soft suede saddle pad and prepared to climb up behind him.

"Can I ride Tor by myself?"

"Hah." Jeth shook his head as Torrent expelled a puff of air from her nostrils. "Tor's not a kid's horse."

"Pleeeeeeeease."

"Tell you what. You can ride one of the ponies in the corral at home."

"But I want to ride Tor! She's the best horse and my favorite, please, I can do it. Like you." Ellion's pleading blue eyes grew three sizes bigger, just the way his mother's had done when she begged Jeth to take the kid out foraging in the first place. There was no refusing him now.

Jeth rubbed the back of his neck as Torrent munched the long grass along the path. She was well-behaved overall . . . provided Jeth was with her . . . most of the time.

With a leery sigh, Jeth said, "Alright, but do exactly as I say."

Ellion wriggled with excitement, making Torrent raise her head and start dancing side to side.

Jeth quickly tightened his hold on her lead. "Which is *don't* fidget." He put a hand on Ellion's leg. "Don't give her a reason to buck you off, now."

Jeth took Ellion's hands and placed them onto the thin rope that weaved throughout the mare's gray mane. "Hold on tight, and no matter what, do not let go." He gave his little leg a pat. "Stretch those legs down, so you don't slide off."

Ellion nodded keenly and did what he was told. Once Jeth felt satisfied the boy was secure, he clicked his tongue over the back of his teeth and led Torrent forward, keeping his palm against the side of her neck. She bobbed her head up and down a few times but otherwise was calm. Ever since Jeth decided to stay in Fae'ren, his Tezkhan steed had taken to the tranquil forests rather well. This place had been good for both of them.

"Look, Jethro, I'm doing it, I'm doing it!"

"Yeah, you're doing great up there."

Jeth kept his senses honed as they continued their plodding pace toward Lanore.

"Can we go faster?"

"If you let me up there with you, I'll show you how fast this girl can go."

"Yeah! Faster, faster." Ellion's thick brown mop of curls bounced back and forth over his pointed ears, longer than most fae's due to his half urling heritage.

"Alright, alright." He brought Torrent to a stop, then, with lead in hand, sidled up to her in preparation to mount. A distant rustling in the bushes stilled Jeth for a moment, but Torrent's ears didn't turn toward it. Too far away for her to hear, perhaps. Then came a sharp metallic clang.

Her ears jerked up, and she tottered backward. "Whoa, girl," he murmured reassuringly.

The horse let out a low nicker before settling down.

A flash of gold and silver fur shot out of the woods and bolted across the path right in front of his anxious horse.

Torrent jolted violently and took off at a dead run. Her lead rope ripped out of Jeth's grasp, burning his entire left palm before sending him face down into the dirt. When he lifted his head, the dapple-gray was galloping full speed down the path, the screeching child hanging on for dear life.

"Hold on, Ell!" Jeth scrambled to his feet and broke into a sprint.

No other horses could keep pace with a Tezkhan bred steed, but Jeth was not a horse, and this was his home turf. He sped forward until the forest blurred into a collage of greens and browns. He kept his heightened vision trained on the mare ahead.

Torrent turned sharply, following a deer path into the woods. Jeth's heart leaped into his throat at the sight of Ellion's little body bouncing over her back. *Please stay on, little lad, please stay on.*

With another burst of speed, Jeth reached for her tail, but she zigzagged just out of his grasp. He whistled, but the sound was lost in the trees, not that she would respond in her panicked state.

She broke into a grassy clearing, spooking several unsuspecting deer and scattering them across the field. Jeth took advantage of the open space to push himself harder, enough to reach Torrent's left flank. "Ell, let go."

"I can't." His little knuckles were white, his eyes clamped shut.

"I'll catch you."

Torrent took a hard left, spinning toward Jeth. He flailed back, nearly colliding with a frightened stag. Fighting to regain his balance, he dove forward as Ellion slipped off Torrent's left side with a screech. He caught the boy, twisting in mid-air, so he hit the ground on his back with Ellion on top of him.

The two lay in the moss, breathing hard. As Torrent's hoofbeats faded into the underbrush, the little boy's heartbeat drummed strongly in Jeth's honed ears, indicating he was alive and well. *'Is he okay . . . ? Please, Jeth . . . Jethril?'* He could still hear Anwarr's desperate cries and the cavernous silence of her womb that came with them. *Two lives you failed to save that day.*

"Again! I want to go again!" Ellion giggled until he snorted.

"Oh no, we're going straight home. And you are never to speak of this to your mother, you hear me?"

"Aww, why?"

"Because she'll dismember me, that's why."

"What's dismember mean?" Ellion scrunched his face.

"Something too horrible for a wee lad like you to be learning about." Jeth brushed a few leaves from the boy's fluffy hair.

"I won't let anything bad happen to you, Jethro." Ellion beamed up at him and took his hand, the terror of a disaster since averted melting away.

Jeth couldn't help but grin wide despite his exhaustion. "Thanks for having my back. Now help me sniff out our steed, aye?"

He put his nose to the air and took in sharp breaths, with Ellion emulating his every move. He locked onto the runaway mare's scent straight away, and the two continued north across the field.

Before they reached the tree line, Jeth's ears picked up on someone approaching. "Hey!" An adolescent boy, wearing a foxtail hat, jogged toward them from the west with a silver and gold wolf at his heels. "Jeth," he panted. "I thought I saw you back there." The boy, Tomas, stopped short and stood silent before Jeth as if expecting him to continue the exchange.

"Uh . . . yeah, that was us. Mind telling me what your wolf was doing out there, Tom? He scared Tor halfway to Ingleheim." Jeth raised his red and peeling hand, the skin broken at his finger joints.

Tomas lifted up a dead rabbit by its long hind feet, not seeming to make the connection between Jeth's account of a spooked mare and his rope burn. "I was trapping, and Pup got overexcited, as he does."

"Guess we both have trouble taming our beasts," Jeth grumbled.

The young Fae'ren snapped back. "Pup's no beast. He meant no harm."

Jeth lacked the energy to coax down the adolescent's defenses. He flashed him a wry glare and sighed. "Don't worry about it, lad. Just try not to trap so close to the road next time, aye?"

Tomas's cheeks flushed as he hung his head. "Right. I-I'll get to skinning then." He wiped his nose with his sleeve of animal hides then looked about the field as if he had somewhere to be. "Bye."

Tomas and his wolf scurried back into the bushes before Jeth could say anything. *What was that? No apology?* he thought, but quickly dismissed his harsh judgment of the lad. Tomas had spent most of his childhood fending for himself in the woods until recently arriving at Lanore. All he'd had before that was an abandoned wolf pup that hardly left his side. Jeth remembered what it was like to be that isolated when he was his age, and he'd wager that fairies were better at teaching basic social skills than a wolf.

It took almost an hour for Jeth and Ellion to locate Torrent, who had been drinking her fill from a creek calm as could be. He spent a few minutes soothing her even though he wanted nothing more than to whip her silly for taking off like that. He took a vera leaf from the satchel and squeezed the clear jelly onto his red, raw palm to help it heal faster.

"Can we race again?" Ellion jumped up and down.

"How about we get you home in one piece instead?"

Later that afternoon, with Ellion secure in front of him, Jeth rode into the Commune of Lanore.

"Aye, Jeth!" An archer waved at him from the watch post, built high up in the sprawling oak branches where he could see the entire eastern road.

"Aye, Leif," Jeth and Ellion waved back as they made their way into the forest village. Once the site of a bloody naja brawl, it had returned to its former peaceful state, only with one crucial difference. Its population had ballooned from a mere seventy to well over a hundred. Orphans from all over the province migrated to Lanore, many of them having arrived the same day Jeth survived what had since been coined the Battle of the Deep Wood.

He handed his steed off to the stable boy, Finn. Then, with Ellion and their satchel of the day's pickings, he headed to the healer's cabin, nestled between two sizable oaks on the commune's east side.

Henna leaned against the doorframe, arms crossed and tongue pushing out the inside of her cheek. Jeth instantly began to sweat. To him, there was no other woman who could simultaneously freeze the blood in his veins and warm his heart with a single look. She was nearly unrecognizable from the scared orphan mother he had helped on the muddy streets of Fairieshome.

"Remember, Ell"—he bent down and whispered in his ear—"don't say anything about your little ride, aye?"

Not hearing a word from Jeth's mouth, the boy sprinted full tilt toward his mother and wrapped his arms around her woven skirt. Her dour expression transformed into a beaming smile in the blink of an eye. "There you are, Pumpkin." She laid a loud smooch on the top of his head. "Did you find lots of vera for mum?"

"We found this much!" Ellion stretched out both arms as long as they could go.

Jeth handed her the sack, and she took a quick peek. "Great job, boyos, but . . ." She eyed Jeth suspiciously. "I'd expect twice this much by how long you took. I was starting to worry."

"Take another look, Hen." Jeth nodded to the bag. "There's a surprise in there for you."

She rifled through the vera leaves then pulled out a sprig of fae grass. Her face lit up. "I had no idea we had wild grass so close."

"All thanks to your little lad here." Jeth took the bow and quiver off his back and rested them against the cabin's outside wall.

Henna let out a playful grin, swaying side to side. She turned to her son. "Here, Ell. Dump all of this in the bin, the big one by the counter."

"Aye!" He took the sack in both arms and scuttled into the cabin.

When the boy was out of sight, Jeth took Henna by the waist with one hand and, with the other, brushed aside the dark brown locks that had escaped her wool hairnet.

He took her by her chin and leaned in to kiss her. Without missing a beat, Henna snatched his hand off her face and stared at his palm. "Your hand."

Jeth winced and pulled it back. "It's fine."

"What happened?" Her lips pursed, and her blue eyes steeled.

"Uhh . . ." Jeth rubbed the back of his neck. "Tor sort of . . . acted up."

Henna tried to pull him inside. "Come in. I'll get you something for it."

He resisted. "I put vera on it already."

"Is that not your bow hand? At least let me wrap it for you."

"Do what you will with me then." Jeth playfully relented.

Henna led him by the arm into the cabin and placed it over the counter. She tore a strip off a linen roll she kept in her deer hide medicine pouch, grabbed a honey jar from the shelf above the counter, then yanked off the cork.

She had grown to be quite the accomplished healer in such a short time. Since Henna moved to Lanore, Elder Healer Leena was more than happy to take her under her wing.

Creaking hinges distracted Jeth from Henna's full-figured form as Tomas entered the cabin.

"Puppy!" Ellion pointed at the lupine, squeezing his head between the doorframe and his companion's leg.

"Don't let that wolf in here," warned Henna.

"Pup, out!" The wolf bowed his head and shambled away as Tomas continued inside.

"What can I do for you, Tom?" Henna took out a flat wooden stick and dunked it into the honey jar before spinning and stretching the golden-brown blob at its tip.

"I wanted to check on Jeth." Tomas pointed to Jeth's hand. "Will you be up for the hunt tomorrow?"

"You bet, as long as you tell the lads to refrain from the wanking jokes. I do that with my other hand."

Henna snorted as she spread the honey over the linen strip on the table.

"You sure?" Tomas replied, Jeth's quip flying right over his foxtail. "That nasty rope burn might make it painful to hold a bow."

Suppose that's as close to an apology as you're going to get from this lad. "It'll be fine. Right, Hen?" He flashed the healer an endearing grin.

Henna didn't respond, only put down the stick and turned to Tomas. "How do you know about his hand?"

"Uh . . ." Tomas scratched his head under his hat. "Pup and I were trapping, and he spooked Torrent."

"That's not how it happened," said Ellion. "I made her run all by myself."

Henna blinked, looking back and forth between Jeth and Ellion. "What?"

"A wild imagination, this one," Jeth said with a nervous chuckle followed by a severe look to Ellion. It only seemed to urge the boy on.

"Jethro said I could ride all by myself. Tor ran really, really fast, and I held on the whole time just like Jethro said. He raced us, and he almost beat us, and he told me to let go, and I did, and he catched me, then Tor was gone, but we found her with our noses."

Jeth prayed the floor would swallow him.

Tomas cleared his throat. "See you at the hunt, Jeth."

"If he survives the night," Henna said in a low voice that sent chills down Jeth's spine. Tomas was out the door before her full fury rained down on him. "You let Ellion ride Torrent by himself?"

"Not by him—I mean . . . sort of. I was right beside him."

"He's too young to ride, Jeth." Henna crossed her arms. "And you put him on *Torrent* of all beasts."

"She's been good lately. I didn't think she'd react like that."

"How did you expect her to react to a wolf?"

"Alright, I know, it sounds bad, but he's fine, aren't you, little lad?"

Ellion nodded, but his mother was far from calmed. "That's not the point." She turned back to the counter and pulled out a clay flask from the drawer. After tearing a new linen strip, she dumped a hefty dollop of the sharp-smelling contents over it. "If you're going to put my son in danger, at least run it past me first."

She grabbed hold of Jeth's wrist and took in hand the alcohol-soaked fabric. "Hey, what about the honey?" He clenched his fist.

"I've decided you need something stronger."

"Hen, come on—"

"Do you want that burn to fester?"

You don't stand a chance, just take what she gives you. Jeth sighed and opened his palm up to her, ready to weather the sting of Del'Cabria's number one cure-all. He winced as Henna wrapped his hand tight.

"You're right," Jeth rasped as she tied off the bandage. "It was reckless, and it won't happen again."

"You're damn right it won't."

"No!" Ellion's pitched wail made Jeth's sensitive ears ring. "I want to ride horsies with Jethro!"

"That's enough, Ellion." Henna snapped.

The boy's bottom lip quivered as tears trickled down his small cheeks. "He said I could. It's not fair." He threw open the cabin door and sprinted away.

"Ell!" Henna called after him. She stopped by the doorway and watched him run toward the cottage they shared next door.

He was circumvented by three of the commune's teenage girls. "Oh, little Ell, what has you all in a fuss?" said Jule as she kneeled down to dry his tears.

"I'm not allowed to ride horsies anymore," he blubbered.

"Oh dear, let's get you all washed up. How does that sound?" Two of the girls took each of his hands and walked him toward the well.

Jeth cautiously approached Henna from behind and put his arms around her. "I'm sorry, I should have told you."

"If only you knew what I had to go through to keep that boy alive for this long." She rested her head back on Jeth's shoulder, finally disarmed. *Mother Oak be praised.*

"You know I wouldn't let anything happen to him."

He kissed her small pointed ear, and she nodded. "I know."

At that moment, the third and tallest of the girls, Silese, walked up to the cabin carrying a short bow and quiver over her lithe shoulder. "Jeth, I've been waiting for over an hour. Now, I can see why."

He immediately let go of Henna. "Shit, was that today?"

The blonde girl nodded with a knowing sneer.

"What's today?" Henna asked.

"My archery lesson," Silese replied.

Grabbing his bow and quiver, he kissed Henna's cheek. "See you later tonight. Unless you're still planning to rake me over the coals. Not that I wouldn't enjoy that, but the lads are going to need me at my best for the hunt."

Henna twisted her lips in an attempt to hide her smile, which only made Jeth grin wider. She always strived to maintain a serious demeanor, while Jeth liked to make that as difficult for her as possible. There was something irresistible about that face she made; it presented a challenge as exhilarating as the day he tamed his untamable steed.

"Suppose I'll let you live. This time." She cast him a devilish look, eyes smiling where her mouth would not. "Just don't be too long."

The arrow wobbled in the air, tilting down just as it hit the dirt under the target where three other arrows lay scattered.

Silese huffed. "I can't get any lift. Should I angle it higher?"

"No, no. Here," Jeth cautioned the fourteen-year-old. "You're not following through. Let your wrist continue back as you release." He nocked one of his own arrows and demonstrated, exaggerating the flick of his wrist as the arrow was loosed. Despite the soreness of his injured hand around the bow, his arrow found the center of the target with ease. "That should give you the lift you need."

The archery training area was the first project Jeth had undertaken after deciding to remain in Lanore. He had erected targets on tree stumps, hung them from branches, and nailed them to trunks, dispersed around the deep pits that had once housed a naja contingent a year ago.

Silese and her brother, a woodcutter, lived nearby, and after months of her watching Jeth train some of the other orphans, she insisted that he let her try as well. She adjusted the bundle of blonde locks atop her head and pulled another arrow from the quiver. This time, her shot gained the necessary height, sailing right over the target.

"That's it!" Jeth cheered.

"But I still didn't hit the target," she whined.

"That'll come with practice. Don't try so hard to hit it, or you never will."

"*Don't* try to hit the target?" She raised an eyebrow in disbelief.

"I know it sounds strange, but yes. Trust your form; it'll get you there."

With a sigh akin to a horse's snort, Silese pulled out another arrow. While she practiced, Jeth shot a few of his own, aiming for the targets hidden amongst the trees on the far side of the field. The sound of Dayne chopping wood a few feet away echoed off the bark. That and the steady thunk of Tomas's throwing knives piercing the target next to Silese's brought Jeth into a meditative state before each release. In this one fleeting moment he felt truly whole, and nothing could hurt him or anyone he loved. But then, the arrow would launch out of his fingertips, and the pangs of loss and grief would cloud around him to fill the space.

Thwang! Silese dropped her bow and shot her arms up into the air. "I did it!" Her arrow quavered on the outer edge of the triple ring.

Jeth clapped. "Great shot, Sil."

Tomas paused his knife throwing, something that could be construed as a grin crossing his face, but as soon as Jeth caught his eye, he turned around and continued his activity. Jeth scratched his beard, trying to recall if he'd ever seen the boy use the archery grounds before. *Looks like the lad is growing a little more comfortable around us. That's good.*

"Dayne, look!" Silese called for her brother.

The towering Fae'ren wiped the sweat from his brow and let his axe down. He labored up the grassy slope to join Jeth and Silese. "Not bad, Sis."

"Can I come on the hunt tomorrow?"

"You'll need to hit a few more of these standing targets before you can hit moving ones," said Jeth.

"I won't use my bow at first. I just want to see how you boys do it."

Dayne shook his head. "Too dangerous."

"I'll stay in the trees the entire time."

"Midwives shouldn't be out hunting."

Silese threw down her bow, crossing her arms, and stepped up to her brother, almost reaching his height even though she was six years younger. "I can be a midwife and a huntress at the same time."

Dayne stretched his axe arm over his head. "Midwifery always comes first, you know that. No point in hunting if there are no future mouths to feed."

"Daynerel!"

He shrugged. "What do you want me to say?"

The girl growled and stormed off, leaving Dayne shaking his head of long, blond fairy locks. Jeth had always been entranced by them. His own had been burnt off on the left side of his head, so he shaved the other to even it out, keeping the top intact enough to form a long tail down his back. As it turned out, everyone liked the style, so he decided to keep it for the rest of the year.

"She doesn't *have* to be a midwife," said Jeth.

Dayne sighed. "Trust me, she'll want to when she sees the value in it. She was too young when our mother died and doesn't remember how influential she was. Sil has the potential to be so much more than I ever will."

"Del'Cabrians approaching!" an archer shouted from the south watch post.

Immediately, dozens of cottage doors swung open, filling the air with a ruckus of creaking hinges and shuffling feet. The elders emerged from their homes and made way for the large hut at the commune's west end.

As Commune Protector, Jeth needed to gather the fighters, just in case anything escalated. *You never know with Del'Cabrians.*

"Dayne, mind collecting the arrows for me?" Jeth called over his shoulder.

"Aye."

Jeth thanked him and marched down the hill. His archer captaen, Gern, jogged over to him. "They're noblemen. Elder Abel's going to meet them at the well. We'll keep watch from here."

"No soldiers?"

Gern shook his head. "No blue coats. The driver wields a sword; the two horsemen, spears."

A foul taste filled Jeth's mouth at the mention of spearmen. "Military trained, no doubt. Best be cautious. Keep your weapons out of sight. Don't let them feel threatened but be ready to defend if necessary."

"Nobles don't strut around here often," Gern said, running his hand over his scruffy beard. "What could they possibly want?"

The Desert War Traitor? Jeth wondered, although if that were the case, he'd expect an officer or two, but perhaps they didn't want to risk tipping anyone off.

A black stagecoach with varnished wood panels trundled up the road toward the commune's central well. Elder Abel stood in wait, gray locks so long they nearly touched the ground.

"Alright, disperse," ordered Jeth.

"Aye." Gern signaled to the archers to take their positions. Dayne returned to his woodcutting, his body angled so he would have a view of the well. Jeth casually trod toward the stables.

The driver halted the four shining bays pulling the coach, stepped down, and opened the door. A middle-aged gentleman, wearing a brown wig so bountiful it nearly covered his long pointy ears, stepped out. He tugged on the lapels of his dark violet frock coat, sunlight glinting off his silver-embroidered cuffs and his polished riding boots.

The spearmen in their matching burgundy tailcoats dismounted and tied their horses outside the nearby tavern hall. As the nobleman and Abel conversed, the spearmen wandered around, studying the surrounding men and women as they went about their work. They definitely seemed to be searching for someone specific.

It was only a matter of time before the rumors of Jethril of the Deep Wood would hit Del'Cabrian ears, allowing them to put two and two together. In that event, Jeth would hide out with the fairies until their suspicions wore off, and the Del'Cabrians could go back to believing him dead.

Jeth slipped inside the barn, collecting Torrent's saddle pad and bridle. His cottage was on the other side of the corral just east of the stable. He could collect what he needed from home and slip away before anyone noticed. Tilting his head, he directed his hearing toward the center of the commune.

"Please, Sir, let's discuss this further in the Elders' Hut," said Abel.

"You will address me as *lord*," said the urling, drawling over the word with a stiff eloquence.

During his stint in the Del'Cabrian forces, Jeth had learned the proper honorific terms in addressing nobility. 'Lord' was reserved for dukes, governors, and the like. However, regular noblemen insisted the peasantry address them as such, even though 'Sir' was perfectly acceptable.

"Forgive me, my lord," Abel said. "As an Elder of Lanore, I speak for all who live here. As soon as you tell me what business you have with our healer, I can arrange a meeting, but her welfare is our primary concern."

Wait. Healer? Jeth's pulse pounded against his ears.

"Very well. Take me to your . . . *hut*," the nobleman sneered, "but do not presume to waste my time. Tell Henna that Count Radley awaits her there and to bring her son forthwith."

4
Bears, Counts, and Overlords

Jeth dropped the saddle pad and ran to the healer's cabin to find Henna.

She glanced at Jeth briefly before returning to preparing the vera leaves for storage. "Lesson's over already?"

"A Count Radley is here," he panted, raising a questioning eyebrow. "And he's looking for you."

The color drained from Henna's face as she slowly sank onto the stool by the counter. "Ell."

"You told me his father was some rich urling banker in Fairieshome." Jeth put his hand on her shoulder, coaxing her to face him.

"He is." She shook her head, barking a short burst of rueful laughter. "So rich, in fact, he earned himself the title of count a couple years ago. I was his cleaning woman before then."

"Any idea what he wants with Ell?"

Henna's eyelashes fluttered. "When he found out I was carrying his child, he cast me out. He said it was his wife's idea, but I know it was because he didn't want a bastard running around, rivaling his true-born son for inheritance. I can't imagine why he'd choose *now* to take an interest in him." She put a quivering hand to her forehead, smoothing out the stray frizz that escaped her kerchief.

Jeth drew her close to him. "He's just asking to see him. Let's not assume the worst." Although, assuming the worst was all Jeth could do at that moment.

"I don't want to keep Ell in the dark about his father, but . . . something's not right."

Jeth's own stomach did somersaults, imagining what an urling noble would want from a fae boy. He could only imagine what Henna was feeling. "Want me to go get him?"

Henna opened her mouth to respond, but her gaze caught something past his shoulder. Abel appeared in the doorway. "Henna, love, you and Ellion are needed in the Elders' Hut. You should come as well, Jethril."

"We'll be right there," said Henna. She quickly composed herself and looked to Jeth. "Go with him. I'll fetch Ell."

Jeth gave Henna's shoulder a reassuring squeeze and followed Abel to the Elders' Hut. He hadn't felt this nervous since the first time he'd been brought to the large thatched structure over a year ago. Back then, he'd been bound and deposited on his knees in front of Nas'Gavarr. It had turned out to be Snake Eye disguised as the Immortal Serpent, much to Jeth's overwhelming relief. He could only pray for that kind of relief now.

Abel nodded to the two spearmen posted outside and strolled in. Jeth rested his bow and quiver against the outside wall and did the same.

Inside, the count and his swordsman sat on stools customarily reserved for the senior elders who had more trouble getting up from the ground. The elders instead sat on burlap mats, craning their necks to look up at the count like gray-haired children expecting a story from their esteemed patriarch.

The image made Jeth cringe, and he only half-listened to what the nobleman was telling them: ". . . insist on meeting in this strange hovel?"

"My lord," Twilla, the Elder Midwife, said with a light, careful air. "Communal decisions are made in huts much like this one all over Fae'ren. It is our tradition. I understand that in Fairieshome, things are done a little differently now."

Radley harrumphed. "Yes, and for good reason."

Jeth made his way inside and sat down cross-legged on an open mat, close to the clay fire pit in the center of the room.

Radley flicked his finger toward him. "Who is this young man? He's not an elder."

Twilla replied, "He is Lanore's protector, my lord."

"And what exactly does he protect you from?" he huffed, a bushy eyebrow raised.

Jeth took it upon himself to answer. "Communes as isolated as this are vulnerable to many threats, my lord. Foreign invaders being one example."

"Well." Radley cleared his throat and smoothed his mustache with his fingertips. "I assure you, your services will not be needed here today, for I have my own men." He indicated to the swordsman next to him. "Perhaps there is a bear somewhere you can fend off instead."

The mood in the hut turned sour. Nobody made a sound. *Bears, counts, and overlords. All in a day's work,* Jeth thought. He wished he could say the words aloud, but the count didn't seem like the type to take a hint or step down, despite being outnumbered in a foreign village.

"You misunderstand, my lord," said Abel. "Our protector has as much right as everyone else in this hut to partake in Elders' gatherings. Just as there is an elder to represent the midwives, healers, farmers, builders, and hunters, Jethril fulfills the role of Elder Protector as we've never had use of one before."

"Is that so?" Radley said dryly. "Then, as Protector, you may be interested to know that the plague has spread farther throughout the southern communes."

"We've been aware for over a year now, my lord," said Jeth.

"Yes, but this time, the disease is far deadlier than the ones that came before. It's said to be infecting Del'Cabrians with as much veracity as it infected your lot."

Every eye in the hut widened. Radley cleared his throat, clarifying. "Not urlings, of course, but the human loss is mounting fast. That's why we had to put the communes to flame, so we could stop the spread from reaching Fairieshome."

"Mother, help us all," Leena gasped. The elders squeezed their fairy locks in silent prayer.

"It may be too late," continued Radley. "Droves of supposedly uninfected fae demand to be allowed through the barricade. There's no telling how many among them are diseased." He turned up his nose in disgust.

Abel took a steadying breath. "We don't have much here, but Lanore will accommodate as many of the survivors as we can."

"I'm sure that won't be necessary. Lanore is reviled by Fae'ren people everywhere, or so I hear. They are calling you the *Cursed* Commune. Is it true you allow orphans to live among you?"

"It is," Twilla said without pause. "And it has served us well. Lanore stands as proof that orphans are in no way cursed."

Jeth swallowed. Despite all the progress his people had made in moving Fae'ren away from its devastating superstitions, this new plague could just as easily be blamed on the rising numbers of orphans among them as it was in previous bouts.

"Now, where is this son of mine? What's taking so long?" Radley griped.

"We're here," Henna said from the entryway, holding Ellion by the shoulders.

He pointed to Jeth and waved with his whole body. "Hi, Jethro!"

Jeth smiled and waved back.

Henna curtsied. "My lord, this is Ellion."

Radley rose to his feet with a groaning effort. "Come here, Son, let me get a look at you."

Ellion looked up at his mother. She bit her lip, then urged him forward. "Go ahead, Pumpkin."

Radley bent down as Ellion approached. "My, my, your ears are much longer than I imagined. That is good."

The boy touched his pointed ears and scrunched his face.

Radley ran his hand through his curly brown mop. "Hair's a little on the wild side, but nothing a good comb and trim can't work out. I'm pleased. He should pass well."

"Pass for what?" Henna peeped.

"As my heir." He straightened and looked at Henna as though what he said were the most obvious thing in the world. "I must ensure my holdings in this province are passed down through my line. With him handling business here, I can retire in Deltashire with the peace of mind that every man strives for."

"Y-you want Ellion to inherit your business?" Henna blinked. "I don't understand. What of your legitimate heir?"

"Ah." Radley clasped his hands behind his back, showcasing the protruding paunch beneath his velvet waistcoat. His eyes were crestfallen as he stepped closer to Henna and spoke quietly. "My son would have been a fine banker. He took pride in every aspect of the profession. So much, in fact, he would travel the province, personally collecting payments. Alas, he had always been a rather sickly boy, and although it appeared not to follow him into adulthood, he . . . fell ill and is now deceased."

Henna put her hand to her mouth. "Sir Radley, I'm so . . . that's awful."

"We are truly sorry for your loss, my lord," added Abel.

"As I have no other sons, the next in line is my bastard."

"But you have a daughter," Henna said. "Surely something can be arranged for her to—"

"Del'Cabrian law does not permit women to own property, and any potential husband of hers will not suffice. I wish only for my wealth to pass down to the next available male heir." Radley looked to Ellion, now clutching his mother's side. "As long as this boy shares my blood, he will have a claim to my estate regardless of whom I award it to. I don't see there being an issue. Unless, of course, you'd rather him grow up in this squalor than in the luxuries of Deltashire."

"Deltashire?"

"Yes." Radley nodded. "There, he will receive his education in high finance and everything else a boy of his station needs until he is ready to take his place in Fairieshome."

"That's too far away," Henna protested, hugging Ellion close to her leg. "If you wish to be a part of his life, I can't stop you. Send your tutors, teach him in the way of finance and decorum, whatever you need to do, but I will not have him taken from me."

Radley balked. "Sweet Deity, no. I wouldn't dream of it. You've done well caring for him thus far."

Henna's jaw steeled at the comment.

No thanks to you. Jeth clenched his fists.

"I'd permit you to come along," Radley offered graciously. "You'd both be safe from the impending outbreak, and you could serve as his nurse until he reaches the age of independence."

"Nurse? I am his mother!"

"Do understand. You will always be the one who birthed him, but if I'm to legitimize him, his mother on paper must be my wife."

Henna blinked profusely, her expression dumbfounded. "I-I see."

"Then it is settled." He tousled his son's hair once again. "I'll enroll the boy in school as soon as possible. When travel arrangements are made, I will send for you both. Thank you, Elders, for accommodating me, but I must be off."

The count and his swordsman breezed out of the hut, leaving everyone else in shocked silence.

Jeth's cheeks were overcome with a sudden heat. "Who does that wighead think he is? I'm going to tell him to find another bastard." He sprung to his feet and marched towards the door.

"Jeth, wait!" Henna grabbed his sleeve.

"You're not seriously thinking about going with him, are you?" Jeth said heatedly. "The man abused you, and he'll likely do it again if you consent to live under his roof. How do you think his wife is going to treat you when you get there? Her son is dead, and now her husband wants to replace him. And Ell being part fae will only make it worse."

A couple tears descended from Henna's cheek, and she quickly wiped them away. "I know that. It's just . . . I remember what my father said—about providing for your children what you never had yourself."

Ellion pulled on his mother's apron. "Mommy, is he going to take me away?" Tears welled in his eyes, and he buried his face in his mother's apron.

Henna bent down and cupped his face with both hands. "No, Pumpkin." She looked up to Jeth then the elders.

Elder Leena stepped forward and put her hand on her protege's shoulder. "What we can provide him here far outweighs any of the so-called luxuries in Deltashire."

"But he's his father—"

"And he has more than a dozen fathers here to choose from, lass," said Abel. "Ones far more fit than that pompous fool."

Henna looked straight at Jeth and exhaled slowly. "Please, Hen," he whispered, shaking his head. "Don't go."

"I don't want to go away, Mommy," Ellion cried.

"You're not going anywhere, Pumpkin. Stay with Jeth. I'll be right back."

The boy took Jeth's hand and watched his mother storm out of the hut. Everyone else followed but kept a modest distance.

Radley was about to step into his stagecoach when Henna called out, "We are far from settled, Count Radley!"

He turned, surprised. "I beg your pardon?"

"I do not consent to me or my son leaving this commune. He belongs here with the people who love him."

Radley bristled, lifting a hand and waving a finger toward Henna like a father about to give his bratty child the what for. "I am doing what is in his best interest."

"You cast us out! All those times you drove through Fairieshome in your lofty coach, did you not see us there, begging in the streets? Were you thinking of our son's best interest then?"

Radley's nostrils flared. Other members of the commune began to congregate around them. Dayne hefted his axe over his shoulder as half a dozen other fighters crept closer, ready to spring into action.

The count continued, "That was regrettable, I admit, but it does not change the fact that to live with me is what is best for him now."

"He is *my* son, and he will stay here until he is old enough to choose for himself." Henna crossed her arms, her feet rooted like solid oak.

The count's face reddened. He took another step toward Henna, looming over her, but she didn't budge an inch. Jeth couldn't be prouder of her in that moment. "On the day he bears my name, *I* will decide his future, not you. If you wish to have any part in it, you will reconsider my offer, which I assure you will provide him a far better life than a half-fae can ever hope to get. If you cannot see that, then I can have you deemed unfit to care for him."

An electric rage radiated through Jeth's body. He quietly passed Ellion to Twilla and picked up his bow and quiver.

"You do not have the right!" Henna snapped.

Radley grabbed her arm and jerked her toward him. "You dare raise your voice to me, savage? I've a mind to—"

Jeth drew back his bowstring with an arrow aimed straight at Radley. "Lay one hand on the wee lad and see how far you get."

Eyes darting to Jeth, Radley flinched, releasing Henna's arm. "Do you have any idea what you're doing, boy?"

"What *all* of us are doing, you mean?" He bobbed his head toward Gern and the other archers, their bows raised and arrows nocked as well. Dayne tapped his axe against his palm. Tomas drew a throwing knife, and Pup's growl rumbled deep in his throat.

"Jeth, please. Put down the bow," Henna's voice shook.

One of the spearmen whispered in Radley's ear, "It's not worth it, Sir." He eyed Jeth warily. "We should take our leave."

The count nodded once and turned back to Henna. "Think hard about my offer, and I hope you make the right decision for *our* son. Good day."

Count Radley ducked inside his coach, and his men mounted their steeds. Nobody lowered their bows until the carriage had passed out of sight down the southern road.

5
This Time Feels Different

With a sleepy smile, Henna pressed her smooth backside flush against Jeth's hips. Her breathing hastened, her blood throbbing loudly in her jugular vein, keeping rhythm with his own.

He kept the pace slow and his movements deliberate as he savored her. His lips trailed down the warmth of her neck, while his hands moved along her ample hips, across the softness of her navel, and cupped the fullness of her breasts. He kissed the back of her neck and behind her ear.

"Yes, yes, like that," she moaned, her fingers reaching around and entwining with his hair. With a gasp, her whole body tensed, the waves of her climax tightening around him.

She relaxed in his arms, languorous and yielding. Her head turned, and she pressed her lips to his.

Overcome with his mounting desire, Jeth pulled out and flipped her onto her back. With a salacious grin, she trapped him between her generous thighs, inviting every inch of him back inside her.

She ran her fingers along the shaven sides of his head before grabbing his locks and pulling him down to her lips once again.

He lost himself in her scent of herbs and the earth itself—she smelled like home. There was nowhere else he'd rather be in that moment.

Remnants of a sweet aroma that he only wanted to forget crept in from the dark recesses of his memory. Flashes of silken white hair, a sultry giggle . . . . *No, don't think of her.* Jeth forced himself to look into Henna's blue eyes, begging his mind to stay with her, but every time he blinked, omnipresent eyes of frost looked back at him.

He nestled his head at the crook of her neck and thrust vigorously until the carnal pressure in his loins capsized.

Jeth pulled out with great effort and spilled his seed on Henna's stomach before collapsing breathlessly beside her. After a moment to catch his breath, he kissed her one more time and retrieved a cloth to wipe her stomach.

"You know, I wouldn't mind if . . ." Henna paused and looked away. "Forget it."

"What is it?" Jeth tossed the cloth in the bin, and she snuggled up next to him.

She ran her fingers over his chest hair before replying. "It'd be fine if you . . . finished inside me sometimes."

"I know you got your herbs and that, but they're not the most reliable."

"That's not what I'm getting at . . ." Her big blue eyes rose to meet his, and she bit her lip.

Jeth sat up with a start. "You're saying you *want* to get pregnant?"

She twisted the bedsheets on her lap. "There's no rush or anything, but . . . yes. Don't you?"

"Eventually," he muttered as he laid back down, mind reeling.

Henna nestled back into his arms. "We've been sharing a bed for the better half of a year. We've both been clear we hold no desire to sleep anywhere else. What other reason for a pairing like ours if not to have children? It's time, isn't it?"

He ran his fingers over the thin white lines decorating her abdomen, relics of her first pregnancy. "You know a pairing like ours—the unmarried sort—is technically against Del'Cabrian law."

"We don't need a parchment blessed by a priest to be with the ones we love. That was imposed on us. You've never paid mind to stuffy urling laws anyway." She wrapped one of his locks playfully around her finger.

Jeth snorted. "*Urling* laws? Try *any* laws. I'm still a wanted man, remember?"

"They think you're dead."

"Unconfirmed." He then continued more seriously, "But, Hen, are you sure you want another kid right now?"

"I never dreamed I'd be doing anything other than fighting for mine and Ell's survival. All I hoped for was that he'd have a chance at a better life, even if it meant I'd have to give him up."

"You did the right thing, Hen." Jeth paused as that old familiar knot formed in his gut. *Henna made the right choice, but you know it's not over.*

"That's what I'm saying. Ell has a chance at a wonderful life here. And none of that would be possible were it not for what you did in the Deep Wood."

"I barely did anything," Jeth muttered.

"No"—Henna's eyes ignited with a fluttering reverence—"it was *everything*."

He let her go and rose from the bed. "I'm surprised you're even able to think about babes with everything so uncertain."

Laying on her side, head propped up with her hand, Henna replied, "Radley has no right to Ell, and he knows it. He assumed he'd come upon the passive fae he deals with in Fairieshome, but he was sorely mistaken. If he returns, you'll be waiting in the trees. Is that not what you've been training the lads for?"

During the last year, he taught the arriving orphans how to handle a blade or shoot an arrow. Dayne told of centuries-old accounts from his northern commune describing Fae'ren fighting tactics. The most effective among them were surprise attacks, camouflaged in the trees. Jeth wondered if the Fae'ren could have beaten back the Del'Cabrians in those days had it not been The First Wave that invaded with them, reducing their numbers to a mere fraction of what they had been.

"We can fight off a thousand Radleys, but stealth tactics won't work against a plague," he said, climbing into his forest green trousers. He put his arms through the sleeves of a cream shirt that had been laid out the night before. "The count said it himself: The Third Wave is in full swing. We have to focus on making sure this commune isn't reduced to ash like in the South." He pulled the shirt over his head and tugged open his dresser drawer.

Henna moved to her stomach, her ankles crossed in the air. "And like the First and Second Waves before it, Lanore will be left untouched."

Rummaging in the drawer for a belt and not finding one, he searched the clothing in the bin. "Listen, Hen, for the first time in both our lives, we found a place that not only accepts us but depends on us. At any time, it can be taken away. I can't bring another child into this world until I know it's safe." His hand finally felt the soft yet firm boar hide belt within the pile of clothes and pulled it out.

Henna sighed. "What happened to your son was not your fault."

"This isn't about him. I've come to realize that he was never meant for this world." *If he were, you'd be able to think of a name. . . .* Jeth picked up his suede vest from the floor, sniffed it, and recoiled at the odor. "You forgot I nearly killed yours yesterday."

She dismissed his comment with a wave of her hand. "I've been nearly killing him his whole life. You tried to teach him something. Gave him a memory he'll think of fondly for the rest of his life." She looked down at her hands bashfully. "Maybe I shouldn't push this on you. It's just . . . you're more of a father to Ell than anyone has ever cared to be. Call me selfish, but I want you to father the rest of my children."

"I want to, Hen, but—" The words caught in his throat. He didn't know what to say to the beautiful fae woman lying in his bed, partly covered by his sheets.

"But I'm not Anwarr," she murmured.

"No," Jeth said with a start. "No, you're not, and I'd never ask you to be." He sat down beside her on the bed and rubbed a hand over her bare back. "She was never the woman for me."

"You still keep her in your heart."

Jeth sighed. "She's gone. So, it shouldn't matter where I keep her." He reached for his boots on the floor beside the bed and pulled them on before getting back up.

"I upset you." Henna sat up on the bed.

"There's nothing you can do to upset me, Hen." Jeth kissed her forehead before heading for the bedroom door. "I got to take Tor for a run."

She rose to her feet. "She ran enough yesterday. Don't you have the hunt today?"

"At dusk."

Henna went to the drawers to find some clothing. "Let me make you some breakfast."

"If I leave right now, I can be back by noon. Got arrowheads to whittle and that."

"You're going to the Deep Wood, aren't you?" Henna guessed. "Fine, I'll have lunch waiting instead, so don't be late."

He turned around and patted the bedroom door frame. "Aye."

Jeth felt a twinge in his heart as he left the room. When he peered into Ellion's and looked upon the boy, sleeping soundly in his bed, the pain in his chest only increased in severity. *You need to clear your head, Jethro. Just be back for lunch.*

Jeth rode bareback through the tight trees of the Deep Wood, weaving along the narrow path the fairies maintained, guiding him straight to the Grove of the Crannabeatha. Only a year ago, the place had burned to the dirt. Every forest pixie, wood nymph, and water sprite had worked day and night to bring it back to its former splendor. His skin still prickled at the memory of the scalding flames that almost claimed his entire left side.

"Hello, Jeth," Serra's cheerful voice sounded from behind him.

He slipped off Torrent and turned around to find no one there. "Ser?" She didn't reply, but he did get a whiff of her pungent pixie aroma. "You can't hide from this nose, you know that." He pushed aside a large fern. There was a *swoosh* and, as expected, nothing.

Serra giggled from somewhere up in the Crannabeatha's bounty of leaves. "You are way off."

Jeth felt like a little boy again, endlessly chasing Serra and the other fairies around the grove. They had taunted him from every direction, then just when he was sure he had them cornered, they sped to another location in a blink of an eye. It had hardly been fair, yet he'd never been able to resist playing with them.

"Come on, Ser, I need to talk to you."

"You loved to do this all the time before," Serra said, her voice now emanating from the creek to the east. Jeth and Torrent made their way toward it.

"I was eight." He ducked beneath a low branch and came upon the peaceful stream that surrounded the ancient oak.

Serra was nowhere to be seen, but now that he was here, he found himself overcome with thirst. He took to his hands and knees and slurped up the fresh spring water. Two enormous blue eyes appeared, glaring up at him from under the water. He yelped as a blue-haired woman burst from the surface and spewed water onto his face from her mouth. "Hey!" Torrent whinnied and danced away from the water's edge.

"Put your face in my stream, I'll put my stream in your face," she trilled, raising the fin-like appendages on her arms.

Jeth blew the water out his nose and wiped his face. "Long time no see, Sky." She sank back under the water, and Jeth muttered under his breath, "Damn water sprites."

Serra's raucous cackle betrayed her hiding spot behind a moss-covered boulder. She sprang up holding her stomach, laughing loud enough for Torrent's ears to flatten against her head. "Oh, they are definitely the worst."

"Hey!" Sky surfaced again. "Try growing your plants without us, Pixie." She stuck out a blue-tinged tongue, then swam away in a barrage of twinkling blue sparks.

Serra plunked down on the boulder and folded her iridescent wings against her back. They appeared as stems embedded in her shoulder blades like a tree's roots sprouting from the earth.

"It has been quite a while," Serra said with a blink of her long dark eyelashes.

"The commune keeps me busy these days." Jeth stretched and rested his back against a protruding root. "I hardly have time to think."

"So, you had to come all the way out here?" She hugged her vine-entwined legs to her chest.

Jeth watched Torrent munch on a clover patch. "It's the only place the others won't follow."

"Ah." Serra gave a knowing nod. "Humans irritating you? Now you know why we fairies hide away in these woods."

"Hey now, it's not that." Jeth rubbed his hand down his bearded face. "It's just . . ."

"They expect a lot from you," Serra finished for him.

"Don't mind, really. We orphans need to join together if we're going to survive what's to . . ." He turned back to the pixie and met her prodding green gaze. "The day I came to you with my plan to stop Nas'Gavarr, you said things would get harder for my people. Is that still true?"

Serra fiddled with a clump of her green locks and nodded. "The Crannabeatha still whispers her warning to stay vigilant. That means the Fae'ren people's plight is far from over."

Jeth gulped. "The plague's making a third round."

"Lanore was spared twice before."

"That's what everyone keeps saying, but this time . . . I don't know. This time feels different."

Serra sighed and continued to play with her hair. "I wish I could tell you exactly what's to come. It could be another plague; it could be something else entirely. Either way, you're going to be needed."

Jeth stood up and walked to his horse. "I can't protect them all."

Serra stood up as well. "Are you not teaching them how to protect themselves?"

"From Del'Cabrians and whoever else, yeah. And they're coming along, mind, especially Gern and Dayne, but I'm starting to think it won't be enough. We need the whole province to come together. Still too many think we're cursed." Jeth picked at the leaves, buds, and pollens tangled in Torrent's mane. "If they can't see past that, we'll never stand strong enough to challenge what will inevitably come. I don't know what to do."

"Why must it fall solely on your shoulders?" Serra said, picking up a handful of clover to feed Torrent with.

"They chose me as their protector. I'm the Champion," said Jeth.

"Champion doesn't mean savior," the fairy corrected him.

"Didn't you just say that they're going to need me?"

"Of course, they need you, but you need them too."

"I need them to stand on their own, but they all keep—" Jeth swallowed, unsure of what he was trying to say. "It's how they look at me. Like they see . . ." he sighed and turned away to collect his thoughts.

"What do they see?"

He turned back around. "A hero. Their last bloody hope. As if I'm literally Gershlon Reborn. And no matter how many times I tell them, they'll never understand how close I came to letting them down. Nas'Gavarr beat me. And somehow, they still put all their faith in me."

"Well, when you put it that way, maybe you are destined to fail." Serra shrugged.

"What?"

She brushed her hands off after Torrent ate the last of the vegetation. "Other Champions certainly have over the ages. Their *Way* takes them down one path, and once that's complete, there's not much left for them."

"That's not very encouraging."

Holding her hands behind her back, Serra continued, "Maybe it's time for you to finally be happy for once. Make little humans that grow up to be just like you."

Jeth's heart flipped, echoes of that morning's disagreement with Henna rocking him.

"Must be worth doing because for some reason, you humans keep doing it, despite everything out there that can kill you."

"Mother Oak, Ser!"

"And there are a lot of things that can kill you—I mean, *a lot*. How do you keep track?"

"Alright, already, I get it."

"You do? Good." She blinked. "Because I forgot where I was going with that."

"I shouldn't be worrying about what I can't control. I *should* be getting home, though. Hen will be right furious if I don't make it back for lunch."

"Then you better hurry," said Serra, already waving him along.

"It'll be fine. I sort of like it when she's angry." Jeth hopped on the back of Torrent.

"Why?" Serra scrunched her nose.

Jeth shrugged. "I seem to be one of the few who can make her that way. Makes a fella feel special, I guess."

Serra scoffed. "Aren't you special enough already?"

Jeth chuckled as he pressed one leg to Torrent's side and gently tugged the thin ropes in her mane to turn her around. "A different sort of special. You wouldn't get it."

She shook her head. "I'll never understand humans."

"You and me both."

6
Take Back What is Ours

Waiting high in the trees of Lanore's northern wood, Jeth honed his ears for cloven hoof beats and disgruntled oinks.

Tomas stood below with his tamed wolf and pointed down the path. "Pup, go find." The lupine bounded through the underbrush.

"We should be sending you out there, Jeth." Dayne stood perched on a broad oak root under Jeth's branch. "You smell just as good."

"Thanks for noticing." Jeth chortled. "I did bathe yesterday, just for you lads."

The six-foot-tall Fae'ren laughed, tossing a few matted long, blond locks over his shoulder.

"Pup doesn't need the help," Tomas's face soured.

"Aye, but we're hunting northern boars, not the wee piglets you get down south," said Dayne, scratching his angular chin.

Tomas puffed out his scrawny chest, aided by the layers of pelts made from the wild game he had skinned. "He can take down stags all by himself."

Jeth cringed at the boy's scowling demeanor. The whole 'Nothing can offend a Fae'ren' stereotype didn't seem to apply to him. And where Pup was concerned, almost everything offended him.

Jeth smiled down at Tomas. "He's a fine animal, Tom. You've trained him well." Everyone else nodded, and the red slowly drained from Tomas's face.

Moments later, a panting Pup returned, and his master took up the long wooden horn hanging from his neck. "That was quick. Sounder must be close."

"Let 'em hear it," said Jeth.

Tomas blew into the mouthpiece to sound a low drone simulating the hogs' mating call.

Within minutes, Jeth heard frenzied oinks from the east, followed by galloping hooves. A sharp stench of urine mixed with oily residue shot up his nostrils, and he reeled back, suppressing his sense of smell. The wolf dashed into the bush to herd the boars toward them as his human companion scuttled up the nearest tree.

"Get ready." Jeth nocked an arrow, taken from his quiver at his lower back. Gern followed suit, and Dayne crouched further into the nook between the branch and trunk.

"Dayne, you sure you don't want to be higher up?" Gern asked, keeping his attention firmly east.

"No, I prefer to fight nearer to the ground. I'll save the trees for you shorties."

"Are you afraid we'll be able to look up your skirt?" Jeth snorted.

"It's not a skirt. It's—"

Tomas's second horn blast interrupted Dayne's rebuttal.

Gern stared down the shaft of his arrow. "They're coming."

Brown and gray stripes sped down the path into Jeth's field of vision. Time slowed as he activated his speed, giving him a full view of a sow ripe for the picking. He released his arrow, sending it right between the ears. The beast collapsed in the dirt with hardly a squeak as the rest of the sounder rushed through the foliage to avoid it.

"One more." Gern loosed an arrow at a young spotted hog, but it struck a root, and the animal hopped over it. "Shit!"

Dayne threw his axe, embedding it in a tree trunk just above his target. The young hog squealed and dashed off the path.

"Mother Oak!" Dayne cursed.

"I got it." Tomas readied a knife and shuffled down the length of his branch to find an optimal angle for throwing. Once the thinner end of the branch bore his full weight, it snapped in half, and Tomas fell straight down onto the path with a thump, dropping his blade.

"You all right, lad?" Gern called down.

Jeth felt the earth vibrate under his tree. The boar stampede hadn't passed them yet. "Get up, Tom!"

Before the boy could react, a large straggler hurtled down the path at full tilt. Tomas grabbed another knife from his scabbard as the boar charged straight for him.

Pup burst from the bushes and sank his teeth into the beast's hairy neck. The boar shook off the wolf, nearly embedding its tusk into his side. Pup growled and bared his fangs to draw the snorting hog's attention.

The boar charged for the wolf, and he dashed into the bush. "Pup!"

The wild boar jerked at Tomas's call, spinning in a frenzied semi-circle. The young trapper scurried backward as the massive hog careened for him.

Time slowed once again, and Jeth shot two arrows into its skull simultaneously. The animal fell mid-stride, sliding headfirst into the moss at Tomas's feet.

No longer sensing hogs trampling down the path, Jeth and Gern descended from the trees.

"We got our two kills, but that was a reckless way to go about it," Dayne griped as he ripped his weapon out from the tree trunk.

Tomas, still wide-eyed, bolted to his feet and ran into the bush, whistling for his runaway wolf.

Dayne stared after him. "Think he'll thank us later?"

"In his own strange way in his own good time." Jeth patted Dayne's shoulder, and all three men started cutting down branches and arranging them to build their sledges.

"Got any twine up that skirt of yours, Dayne?" Gern asked with a sidelong grin.

"For the last time, it's not a skirt. It's a *lein-croich*."

Jeth lifted his head to see the skirt-sporting man stooped over the branches across from him. "More like *I-see-crotch*."

The lofty Fae'ren flushed and stood up straight with a snap.

Gern sniggered as Dayne took two rolls of twine from his fur pouch and tossed one to Jeth and the other to Gern. "Don't mock the *lein-croich*. Fae'ren fighters used to wear them into battle." He spun in a circle to showcase his ensemble. "Easy to move around in, like wearing nothing at all."

"I bet." Gern tied his corner of the sledge together. Jeth eyed the ridiculous sheet of woven plant fibers, worn off one shoulder, and belted at the hip to form a knee-length skirt. Perhaps it was good for sleeping or sitting around the house. But not for hunting. *Wouldn't you feel exposed?*

"Maybe you'll know this, Jeth." Dayne began to chop down branches for the second sledge. "How do Del'Cabrians wear those tight trousers all day without getting everything bunched up in there? Can't be healthy."

"They don't seem too bothered by it." He absent-mindedly pulled at his own crotch.

Dayne dropped a few more branches beside the other men. "Well I, for one, need to *breathe*."

"Just get bigger trousers like the rest of us," Gern said.

Jeth thought longingly of the flowing Herrani pants he used to don, but the modern Fae'ren garb—loose trousers that tapered below the knee and breezy shirts under suede vests—still offered plenty of comfort.

"They don't make trousers big enough for me," Dayne said with a wink.

Gern rolled his eyes but laughed all the same.

"Then, you should take a trip to Ingleheim," said Jeth. "You'll be swimming in their clothes."

"So, Jeth. How did you not drown while you were there then?" The captaen slapped his knee as he dropped his corner of the completed sledge.

"I can stay afloat, don't you worry." The two chuckled.

"Hey," Dayne said. "Are we still talking about our willies?"

Jeth and Gern stared at each other for a moment, blinked, then shrugged.

The three men erupted in guffaws as Tomas returned with Pup, both panting.

"Glad to have you back, lad." Dayne pointed at the pig. "Help me get this fat bugger loaded up, will you?"

"Aye-ah." Tomas bent over and helped lug the heavy carcass onto the sledge. The pig flopped over with a squelch. Unfazed, the boy took out his hunting dagger and began carving out the left tusk.

Jeth and Gern shared a curious expression then left Tomas to it. They moved to assemble the second sledge by the first boar they killed.

"You know"—Dayne took the rope he had been wearing crossways over his shoulder and started tying the hog—"when the Ingles came to take our land during the Golem Wars, it was Fae'ren fighters, led by the Great Gershlon, wearing *lein-croiches*, that held them off."

"And you know this because?" Jeth wound the roll of twine over the first corner of the next sledge.

"My great grandfather fought at Gershlon's side. Yours probably did too. He drew fighters from every commune, mounting the largest force Fae'ren has ever known."

"Not large enough," Gern muttered.

"Well, unlike most of you, I was orphaned shortly after birth," Jeth reminded them. "So, I can't tell you anything about my *father*, let alone my great grandfather."

Behind him, Tomas finally wrenched the boar's tusk from its snout with a loud crack. He waved it around to get his wolf's attention before tossing it into the air. Pup sprang up and caught it within his powerful jaws, then laid down to chew it.

"But weren't *lein-croiches* banned after Gershlon's rebellion?" Gern asked.

Dayne snorted. "All the more reason to start wearing them again."

"Aye." Jeth nodded. "We have to take back what is ours, one little piece at a time, no matter how insignificant." The phrase tumbled easily from his lips; he'd spouted it so many times this last year. But today, it gnawed at his stomach, much like how the wolf's fangs scraped against the boar's tusk. *Taking back what is ours is one thing, defending it is another.*

"Sorry," Gern said, standing up. "But you aren't getting me to wear that."

"Tell him, Jeth." Dayne smacked the big boar's hide having finally secured it to the sledge. "If we don't rediscover our identities, we'll surely lose them for good. I'm wearing part of that identity, and you'd all best do the same, I'm telling you."

"Alright, it's settled." Jeth walked over to the sow and yanked his arrow from its forehead. "*Lein-croiches* for everyone!"

Dayne lifted the sow by its back legs and Jeth the front. "I'll have Sil and the girls sew up a bunch when we get back."

The men huffed and puffed, carrying the heavy hog onto the empty sledge. As they tied the hog with the remaining rope, the cogs in Jeth's mind started to turn. There was no sturdier wood than the mighty oaks of Fae'ren Province and no stronger twine than the braided flax made by the fae bowyers. Something was coming, Serra had told him as much, but he still didn't know what. All he knew was that it was up to him to protect the commune.

"Hey, you know those old naja pits?" Jeth said, tightening the rope around the animal's neck. "What if we extended them around the entire commune? We could build collapsible bridges over them, cover them with dirt and moss."

Tomas perked up. "You mean like a trap?"

Jeth nodded and held up the left-over roll of twine. "We might be able to suspend nets made of this. It can entangle all manner of man and beast, I reckon."

Dayne snorted. "You don't think we can handle one nobleman and a few guards on our own?"

"It's not just them. It's everyone else. We're the Cursed Commune, and with the plague's resurgence . . . there's going to be a backlash. We have to be ready."

Everyone exchanged silent glances, then Dayne, Gern, and Tomas nodded in agreement. "You can count me in, Jeth, Protector of Lanore," said Gern. "Just tell me where to aim, and I'll shoot."

"I'll round up some woodcutters and get to chopping," Dayne agreed.

Tomas rubbed his hands together, gray eyes glinting with excitement for the first time since Jeth had known him. "And I'll design a rig for the bridges."

"Good. Now let's get back before we lose any more light." The knot in his gut was finally starting to unravel a little. "Tonight, we feast. Tomorrow, we dig."

The sun had sunk below the trees by the time the hunting party crested the northern hill, Lanore coming into view. A blonde girl sprinted up the incline toward them, waving her arms above her head. "Hey, it's Sil." Tomas's pulse quickened noticeably in Jeth's honed ears.

Once she reached them, she doubled over to catch her breath. "Thank Mother Oak, you're back," she wheezed.

The men dropped their sledges, and Dayne took Silese by the arms. "Hey, it's all right. We bit off a tad more than we could chew." He cast a glance at the big boar behind him. "But we're here now. Have them prepare the fires, and we can—"

Silese shook her head, still out of breath. "Forget the boars, Dayne. . . ." She brushed her brother aside and looked straight at Jeth. "Don't come home, Jeth."

"Why?" he asked.

"Soldiers." Her green eyes darted between each of the men. "More than I've ever seen in one place before."

Jeth's pulse hastened. "How did he bring so many men from Fairieshome in one day?"

"Who?" asked Dayne.

"Count Radley."

Silese shook her head. "It's not Radley. They're looking for *you.*"

First Radley and now the Del'Cabrian army? Why now? Jeth's mind buzzed.

"Alright," Dayne said. "We prepared for this. Tom, take Jeth to your place, get him some food and water then head for the Deep Wood. You'll be his only contact with Lanore until it's safe to return."

Tomas nodded and took his place next to Jeth.

"And when will that be?" Silese's voice quavered. "They sound pretty sure we're harboring him."

"Sil's right." Jeth shook his head. "They wouldn't bring a large force to every commune just to ask questions. They must know I'm here."

"Doesn't matter. We stick with the plan," Dayne insisted.

Gern trudged ahead. "I'll rally the fighters. If the Del'Cabrians make a move, it will be their last."

"Right behind you," Dayne turned to his sister. "You and the girls secure an escape route for the women and youngins if things go sideways."

Jeth couldn't help but be proud watching his fellow Fae'ren take charge. It was only a year ago that the very mention of a Del'Cabrian soldier in their midst had them running scared. Now they would face them head-on . . . all to protect him.

But now that the time had come, Jeth couldn't imagine going through with the plan. How could he cower in the woods while his people fought and died for his freedom? There was so much more at stake now.

Dayne placed a hand on Jeth's shoulder. "Go with Tom. We got this."

"What about Hen . . . ?"

"I'll take care of her and Ellion. Promise."

Silese hugged Jeth. "Be careful, both of you."

"We will." Tomas whistled for Pup. "Let's go."

As if an outside force had taken control of Jeth's limbs, he waved goodbye to his loyal fighters and followed Tomas and Pup back through the woods.

Tomas's abode was a wooden shack built as an extension of a hollowed-out oak. The boy wasn't much of a builder, but it served in providing shelter and the seclusion he was accustomed to.

The heavy lump in Jeth's stomach grew so big he could choke on it. *How did they find out you're alive?* He couldn't shake the feeling that Radley's visit the day before had something to do with it.

"Wait here," Tomas said as he opened his rickety door.

"I can't do this." Jeth backed away from the boy.

"Do what?"

"This isn't right. Ell. . . ." Jeth looked southwest toward the commune he was about to leave behind. All he could see were the glowing spheres of torchlight in the dark. Through his honed ears, he could hear faint murmurings of male voices and distant horse whinnies.

"He'll be fine. Dayne said—"

"I'm not leaving without them," Jeth snapped, then took a breath. "They aren't safe in Lanore anymore."

"If they see you, they'll have all of our necks." Tomas's eyes began to dart around the woods as if something might pop out at them any second.

"They won't see me. Stay here and prepare for when we get back." Not waiting for further objections, Jeth turned and burst into a sprint toward Lanore.

He arrived to find the commune swarming with blue tailcoats. A soldier was posted at every cottage, and there were more than enough to outnumber the Fae'ren's small fighting force. The Del'Cabrians were looking for a fight either way. *You can't let that happen.*

Jeth snuck along the outskirts of the commune, keeping himself in the shadows and away from the lit braziers. He ducked behind a chicken coop and peered around the edge. A man wearing a feathered tricorn and a colonel's crest on his lapel marched down his line of soldiers. Elder Abel, backed up by Dayne, Gern, and the rest of the Fae'ren fighters, stood before them.

"We know the Desert War Traitor resides here. Refusing to hand him over makes you all implicit in his crimes," the colonel exclaimed. "Give him to us, and there won't be cause for trouble."

"What was his name again?" Abel asked, playing a man far feebler than he actually was. "Jethril? Never heard it before." All the fighters shook their heads and shrugged.

"We have a witness who reported a man living here by that name just yesterday. Playing ignorant will only increase the severity of your sentences."

Someone here yesterday? Which one of those pointy-ear bastards knew you by name? He had to get to Henna and Ellion now.

Through his honed vision, Jeth saw the front door of the healer's cabin bolted shut, but a window in his cottage was alight. He crept along the hedges and ducked below the open window.

Voices muttered inside, one of them haughty and refined. "Hunting at night, you say?"

"Yes, boars are nocturnal," Henna replied. "He may not return until the morning if he returns at all. Wild boars have been known to gore many a man to death."

Jeth could hear Henna's rapid heartbeat in her chest. Floorboards creaked as the soldier walked around the room, pausing by the window where Jeth hid below. "You seem quite cavalier in regards to the safety of your husband. Do you not wish for him to return?"

"All I'm saying is, don't expect him home anytime soon. Now, will you tell me why you think my husband is this Desert War Traitor?"

Floorboards creaked again, this time from the other side of the house . . . from Ellion's room.

A high-pitched screech impaled Jeth's sharpened ears, making him cry out.

"Mommy!"

"Ell?" Henna screamed.

No longer concerned with being seen, Jeth dashed to the other side of the house. A man in a tricorn hat appeared at the open window with Ellion under his right arm and a spear in his left hand.

Jeth met the man face to face. "Let me help you there, mate." He grabbed his burgundy lapels and pulled both the man and boy out the window as the spear fell to the bedroom floor.

"That's my son!" Henna shrieked from inside.

The kidnapper landed on his back, Ellion on top of him. The boy wriggled free as Jeth pulled the man to his feet and slammed him against the cottage's stone and mud wall.

The man was not a soldier, but Jeth had seen him before. *Radley's spearman!*

"Did *you* bring these soldiers here?"

"No," he rasped. "You did. The moment you aimed your arrow at my lordship and your woman uttered your name."

"Who are you?"

The spearman spit in his face. "I trained with Sirs Tobin and Baird. And now I will bring their murderer to justice."

"Justice?" Jeth bashed him against the wall once more. "You're abducting a child!"

"Ell!" Henna ran around the house and stopped dead. "Jeth, where did you—?"

"Mommy!" Ellion ran to his mother, and she promptly scooped him up into her arms.

Jeth shoved the spearman into the stone again, hard enough that he collapsed in a dazed heap.

The Del'Cabrian soldier appeared behind Henna and grabbed her arms. "Miss, get back inside."

"Hands off her!" Jeth growled. He didn't give the soldier a chance to comply before he dashed behind him, wrapped his arm around his neck, and squeezed.

Bringing the soldier to the ground, kicking and flailing, Jeth held fast for a few more moments until the man lost consciousness. The spearman groaned and lifted his head. Jeth and Henna ran into the garden behind the healer's cabin and hid between the rows of pea trellises.

"Mommy, is the bad man gone?" Ellion clutched his mother's locks with quivering hands.

"Take him to Tom's place," Jeth said. "He can hide you both until it's safe."

"You're coming with us, right?"

Not too far away, he heard the crunch of grass and twigs underfoot of someone in pursuit.

He shook his head. "Not yet." He kissed her forehead then touched Ellion's face. "Take care of your mum, aye?"

With trembling lips, he murmured, "Aye."

Henna grabbed his arm, digging her nails into the skin. "Don't you dare leave us."

He yanked himself out of her grasp. "There's no time to argue. I have to make sure everyone is all right. Get to Tom's now!"

Her eyes filled with tears and her mouth formed a scowl. Only Henna could show anger and devastation all in one expression. "If you don't catch up with us, I'll never forgive you."

Jeth heard the ragged breathing of Radley's spearman, now in the garden with them. "Go. Now!"

Henna picked her son up and gave Jeth one last anguished look before scurrying off into the night.

Jeth crept between the plant rows, tracking the man with his nose. He cleared his throat to expose his position, then crouched in wait behind the bushing potato plants.

A spear cut through the air at Jeth's right side, and he rolled out of the way just in time. Still crouched low, he kicked out the spearman's feet and straddled him. He clobbered him, fists blurring as he struck in rapid succession until the man was out completely.

Jeth checked the urling's pulse. *Still alive. Good. No sense adding another murdered spearman to your charges.*

Satisfied the man wouldn't be able to follow Henna, Jeth left him unconscious in the garden and ran back to the center of the commune. He had to make sure everyone else would be all right. They were his responsibility.

Fae'ren and Del'Cabrians stood on opposite sides of the well, bowstrings and handheld weapons drawn.

The colonel called out, "Put down your weapons, or we will deem this an open rebellion against the Crown."

Nobody moved a muscle.

Jeth had faith in his men's training. There was little doubt in his mind that his fighters would be victorious, but the death toll on their side would be far too high without the element of surprise. There was only one way Jeth would allow this to end. *You know what you have to do.*

He dashed between the two lines of men and put his hands up. "Stop! I'm the Desert War Traitor!"

The Fae'ren behind him gasped.

Del'Cabrian archers pivoted, aiming straight at Jeth.

He gulped. There were enough arrows that dodging them all would be impossible, even if he wanted to. "If you wish to bring me to justice, then you can do so. But do not spill a drop of Fae'ren blood."

Gern yelled from behind him, "Jeth, don't!"

He turned to face his fighters while still addressing the soldiers. "I never asked my people to fight for my freedom. Only to stand up for their own. Take me and spare them."

"That is for His Majesty the King to decide," replied the colonel. He sheathed his sword and told two soldiers to restrain Jeth.

They forced him to his knees as his people looked on, horrified.

Dayne rushed forward. "We can fight. You don't have to go with them!" A soldier stepped up to him and pointed a spear to his throat, halting him in his tracks.

"I won't let you all die for my crimes." Jeth couldn't look his friend in the eye. "There are more important things to do. You're Lanore's protector now."

Dayne shook his head, his face contorting with grief. Another soldier clamped a pair of manacles over Jeth's wrists.

The colonel spouted, "Jethril of Fae'ren, you are hereby under arrest for murder and treason." He waved a hand. "Take him."

As the soldiers led him away, Jeth met eyes with Gern, Twilla, Abel, Finn, every Fae'ren he could find to let them know it was going to be all right. He only wished he could tell Henna how sorry he was. She may not forgive him, but at least she and Ell would be safe.

Two coaches sat at the southern entrance, one for prisoners, the other for high-status military officers. Outside it stood a familiar swordsman in a burgundy tailcoat.

Jeth's skin erupted in a cold sweat. *Where's the other spearman? Where's Radley?*

He pulled against the soldiers leading him, frantically looking all around.

"No, stop!" Henna's cry carried across the commune, stabbing an icy tendril into Jeth's heart.

The second spearman appeared, running toward the carriage with a shrieking Ellion in his arms. *You idiot! You should have beat him into the dirt like his compatriot.*

Radley stepped out of the coach and reached for him. "There's my boy."

"You can't take him!" Henna screamed, sprinting for the count.

After handing the boy to Radley, the spearman spun around and swung his spear low, tripping her. Two soldiers rushed toward her and held her down.

"Hen!" Jeth roared.

He writhed within the grasps of the two soldiers holding him. Another one pelted him in the skull with the pommel of his sword.

Jeth's spark ignited instantly, keeping him conscious despite the blow to the head that threatened to pull him under. "Give him back, Radley!"

The count turned to Jeth, several feet away. He scoffed before securing a squirming Ellion inside his coach.

When he stepped back out, Radley held a rolled-up parchment, which he showed to Henna. "I have my certificate of paternity right here. Ellion, son of Radley of Del'Cabria Proper." Jeth couldn't believe his ears. He had that certificate the whole time, no doubt. The soldiers must have been standing by a few miles out, waiting for confirmation that the Desert War Traitor was here, and Radley was more than happy to give it to them for a chance to abduct his son while the authorities looked the other way. "He no longer belongs to you, fae whore."

Henna gnashed her teeth like a mother bear about to claw through the beast that stood between her and her cub, but unlike a bear, she was powerless in the clutches of the men who held her.

"Henna!" Jeth screamed again, desperately tugging against the now three soldiers dragging him backward.

She turned toward him with bloodshot eyes, her skin ghostly white. She couldn't utter a single word. Neither could he.

What could he say? *I'm sorry? I love you? This is why I shouldn't be the one to father your future children?* Jeth could only watch Henna crumble into unrelenting grief as he moved farther away from her. It broke his heart to see her so helpless; that image of the battered and desperate fae woman in Fairieshome, uselessly fending off Herrani thugs, begging for mercy and receiving none. Jeth was there for her then, but he could never be again. Perhaps he was wrong. Maybe they couldn't stand on their own. They weren't ready. *You failed her . . . you failed them all.*

A burlap sack, forced over his head and tied at the neck, cut off his vision of her—his home, everything he had fought to protect for the last year. The soldiers threw him in the back of the prison cart. The barred doors clanked shut, and he knew right then it was all over.

7
Final Straw

The light of the two full moons shone down into Jeth's cell beneath the streets of the Capital's troubled west side.

Horse-drawn carts rumbled above, loosening dirt from the ceiling. Drunkards, out in force, barked obscenities outside the various taverns and whorehouses that littered the thoroughfare. Jeth couldn't tell if the stench of human waste originated from the street above or down in his cell. It permeated every inch of his surroundings, and he couldn't escape it no matter how much he disengaged his senses.

A dirty urling boy peeked through the grimy metal grating above and pointed at Jeth, nine feet below. "Oi, they got a fae down there. Wonder what he did?"

A couple of human boys joined him. "Probably fucked a goat or something," one of the humans lisped. He grinned at his wit, revealing his lack of front teeth.

"Let me see." The third boy shoved his friend aside and kneeled down to look for himself. "Hey, fae, bet you feel right at home down there, huh?"

"Only the finest accommodations here at the Capital," added the urling boy with a punch on the arm to the toothless friend next to him. All three wore ragged clothing with patched up coats and pants that fit either too small or too large.

Street urchins, Jeth thought, although he didn't have any sympathy for these particular ones at the moment.

"Smells better than your mother's place." Jeth tossed a pebble at the grating, and it smacked against the bars with a loud dong.

The boys jumped up with a start but returned to continue their taunts. "Hey, my mum would never touch a dirty fae like you, and she's a two del prossy!"

"She's a what?"

"How about I fix that smell problem for you." The toothless boy squatted down and dropped his frayed trousers around his ankles.

Jeth recoiled into the corner as far from the grating as possible. He held his nose and helplessly witnessed the boy defecate in amounts that should not have been possible for someone of his size. Retching violently, Jeth struggled to keep down the contents of his grumbling stomach.

The street urchins rolled about the street in guffaws until a prison guard finally made his rounds. "Move it along, wretches!"

They picked themselves up and yelled down to Jeth before running off. "Eat up, goat fucker!"

Jeth contended with the putrid stench of feces for the rest of the night until the morning rains attempted to wash it away. The water liquefied it into puddles between the uneven stone, forcing Jeth to stand flat against the far wall to avoid the brown streams trickling down to the small center drain.

He hadn't drunk anything since the day before, but he couldn't bring himself to drink the rain falling through the shit covered bars. *How long can you go before you have to?*

In the far corner of his cell, Jeth shivered in a crouch, waiting for the rains to pass and his empty stomach to stop cramping. When it finally let up in the afternoon, a buzzing, raucous crowd formed in the streets above, drowning out the flies buzzing about his cell. It grew from disgruntled jabber to a howling mob in only a few minutes. Enraged chants shuddered down the grating, bouncing off the walls around him and ringing in his ears. Too exhausted to listen, he covered his head, scaling his hearing back until the voices melded together into a throbbing drone.

Jeth barely detected the heavy iron door of his cell opening a few hours later. A guard, holding a rag to his nose, nodded for him to get up. Rising from his crouch with stiff legs, Jeth shambled through the puddles that he couldn't entirely avoid on his way to the corridor beyond his confines.

"Is it time for my trial?" he croaked.

"Not yet. You have a visitor."

The hefty guard led Jeth down the underground hallways and into a room with a caged partition. He made him sit on a bench and chained his ankles against the wall. The guard left Jeth there to stare at the bars and fidget for what felt like a quarter-hour.

Finally, the door on the other side of the bars opened. "He's in there," the guard muttered, then took a seat on a bench in the corner.

"Thank you, kindly," said a man with a familiar Ludesan twang. A red-mustached soldier, wearing a blue buttoned tailcoat and tricorn hat, ambled in.

Jeth stood up, teetering on shackled ankles. "Oli?"

The bowman stopped a foot from the bars, hands behind his back for the guard's benefit. He looked Jeth up and down like a buyer inspecting cattle for auction. Finally, he met his eyes. "So, it really *is* you."

"It is," Jeth replied.

"You smell like shit."

Jeth groaned inwardly, still fuming about the boys from last night. "Do me a favor. If you come across a gap-toothed street brat, put your foot up his arse for me. So . . . How've you been?"

With a good-natured sigh, he replied, "Well, got some dels to my name now. A wife."

"You married that Ludesan girl?"

"Sure did. Patrice."

"Glad to hear it." Jeth sat back down, exhausted from standing there in his heavy irons. "How'd you find out I was here?"

Olivier snorted. "The news of the Desert War Traitor's capture has reached every square yard of the Kingdom." He crossed his arms. "I heard from a fellow bowman who heard that a former spearman saw you in Lanore. I didn't believe it. How by the Unnamed are you sitting here right now?"

"A Flesh Mage healed me. Otherwise, I would never have left those woods."

"But Nas'Gavarr did. It's a real shame too because had you defeated him, a heroic tale like that could really work in your favor at trial."

"Not sure it would." Jeth shook his head. "Del'Cabria doesn't mind killing its heroes as long as they're Fae'ren."

He swallowed a bitter lump in his throat. Even if he could tell all of Del'Cabria the truth about the Overlord's death, who would believe him? All it would take is Melikheil showing up in Nas'Gavarr's skin to make Jeth a liar, not to mention, what little stability the desert tribes currently had would be torn asunder if the truth came out. He owed Snake Eye at least that much.

Olivier removed his hat and ran his hand through his thinning red hair. "For what it's worth, I'm still willing to testify to your benefit, but right now, you stand a better chance of marrying an urling gal than receiving a merciful verdict."

"I know." Jeth bowed his head, unable to think of a witty quip to lighten the mood. "I should have honored the agreement, but I had a responsibility to my people."

"People you didn't have a year ago," said Olivier.

Jeth lifted his heavy hands to his face and scratched under his eye. He had nothing more to say.

"Listen, I get it," continued Olivier. "If I had a mob of Fae'ren wailing my name out there"—he gestured in the direction of the street—"the last thing I'd want to do is volunteer to hang for some stupid mistake I made years ago."

"Mob?" Jeth's whole body twitched.

Olivier nodded. "Yeah, I almost couldn't get through them to see you. City Watch put up a barricade around the street cells, but I'd hate to see what'll happen if they decide to jump over it."

Why did they come for you? They should have stayed to protect the commune. Jeth clenched his fists and released. A shuddering breath escaped him. He rose to his feet again and walked toward the bars until his chain was taut. The guard glared at Jeth a moment, then returned to picking at his teeth with his dirty fingernails. "H-how many are there?"

"Too many to count. Men, women, elderly, even some kids. It's a real circus."

Jeth pushed out his cheek with his tongue. *Could it be? Could there be more than just Lanore out there?*

". . . not that I think of Fae'ren as circus people." Olivier sputtered. "Not that there's anything wrong with circus people. . . ." The man's freckled face burned red, making Jeth chuckle at his old friend.

"Oli, I appreciate your offer to defend me, but we both know it won't do any good. There is something else I need from you."

"Does it have anything to do with kicking a street kid in the keister?"

Jeth snickered. "No, I need you to find a fae woman for me. Her name is Henna."

Olivier clicked his tongue over his teeth and shook his head. "Yet another lady getting you in trouble, I see."

"She's the one in trouble. Her wee lad was recently abducted by a Count Radley and taken to Deltashire. She needs a professional advocate to get him back. He's only four . . . and you told me once you had a cousin practicing there."

"I'll do what I can for her." Olivier nodded. "Which is about as much as I can do for you." Jeth nodded solemnly, knowing it was a long shot, but Henna's options were thin, to say the least. "Know where I can find this fae lady?"

"Look for the tall, blond, skirt-wearing Fae'ren in the crowd."

Olivier lifted his brow. "She sounds like quite the looker."

"No, that's my man, Daynerel. He'll get you in touch with Henna. But yes, he too, is a looker."

"Come to think of it, I might've seen a man matching that description on the way in."

"Thanks," Jeth said, wishing he could reach through the bars to pat his friend on the arm—hug him even.

"I'll see you at your trial in three days."

Jeth shifted his weight, the chains around his ankles clanking. "Do you know what I can expect? Besides a guilty verdict followed by a noose around my neck."

"You'll come before the Royal Magistrate who will read you your charges before a public court. Then, you will be given an opportunity to defend yourself, followed by witness testimony."

"Who are the other witnesses?"

"Faron, Master Loche, and some soldiers who fought you in a tavern in Fairieshome."

"I suppose none of them will be coming out in favor of me," Jeth grimaced.

"They'll tell the truth, nothing more."

That fact did nothing to alleviate the knob of dread in Jeth's gut. "Great," he said with false levity. "Then I have nothing to worry about."

Olivier simply put his hat back on and looked away. "I'm sorry, Jeth. You don't deserve this."

"Sure, I do."

"A club to the head, maybe."

Jeth blew out a sharp breath through his nose. "I've had my fair share of those already. Didn't help."

The bowman gripped a bar with his right hand, tense and hesitant like he wanted to stick his hand through and touch him. Jeth's chain ensured he would never reach. The guard eyed the bowman, watching to see if he might try to pass something off to the prisoner.

"See you soon, alright?" Olivier shook the bar a bit before turning and heading for the exit. The husky guard rose with a groan and opened the door for him.

"Hey, Oli," Jeth called after him.

He turned around expectantly.

"Your bow's at my cottage in Lanore. You can have it back if you like."

"Got a new one. Let your woman keep it." With that, Olivier gave Jeth a closed mouth smile before stepping out the door.

Jeth was then returned to his cell. In his absence, the Fae'ren crowds had grown twice as loud. He wished he could climb up to the grating and see for himself how many there were. Was the entire province really out there for him? *Maybe you had more influence than you thought.*

His heart wrenched in his chest, imagining all of them watching him demeaned and hanged in front of hissing spectators. Then what next? Go back to their normal lives under urling oppression? Back to shunning orphans? Or would they be stronger than ever, able to weather the plague or anything else that threatened them?

Perhaps this was the push they needed all along; he could do one last thing for them. He could be their final straw. It was all they had left now. Nas'Gavarr's words echoed through his mind. *'Sometimes it's the meaning of our death that gives meaning to our life.'*

The more Jeth thought about his execution, the lighter he felt. Like the painful knot in his gut had finally unraveled, and he was free— shackled in a shit-smeared cell, more afraid than he'd ever been, but free nonetheless. His people could finally stand strong, take back their culture, and cultivate a new one in his memory. He could give them far more as a martyr than as a fugitive.

It would be enough. It had to be.

Early the next morning, the guard kicked Jeth's foot and barked, "Wake up, traitor."

"Huh . . . ?" Jeth squinted, the sunlight forming shadow lines over the guard's face. "Has it been three days already?"

"You've been summoned"—the man reached down and forced him up on his feet—"by His Majesty the King."

"I think there's been a mistake. What would the King want with me?" Jeth asked as the guard led him out the door.

"Not my place to know. I reckon it may have something to do with the pack of fae howling outside."

Jeth bit his tongue, following the guard down the long tunnels that linked every street cell together. They finally reached a staircase that took them up inside a large building in a less run-down part of town. It was the prison itself, where they had brought Jeth for initial processing. They entered a locked room where the husky human pointed to a bucket and sponge. "Start scrubbing."

Jeth didn't hesitate in stripping down and taking the sponge to his sweat-stained skin. He dunked his locks into the soapy water, lathering them vigorously. The guard smirked as Jeth took his time washing each individual strand.

"We don't have all day, you know."

"You want me to come before His Majesty smelling like Del'Cabria's arsehole?"

The guard rolled his eyes and tossed him a towel. "There's no amount of soap in the Kingdom that will change that. Now, dry off. The King awaits you in the warden's office."

Jeth swallowed any further retorts and jumped into a clean set of prison rags, waiting for him on the shelf. After the guard refitted him with shackles around his wrists and ankles, he escorted him out of the room and down a more pristine hallway, his chains clanking against the bare stone tile as he went.

Two spear-toting guards stood at each side of the double oak doors wearing fine red tunics belted at the waist with tall velvet hats held on by chin straps. Jeth's spine tautened at the sight of them. *Those men guard the bloody King of Del'Cabria*, he gulped, *who you're about to meet.*

He broke into a cold sweat as the heavy-set prison guard knocked on the door. The two royal guards stood statue-still, eying him from their peripheries.

The doors swung open, revealing a muscular urling man with a dark mustache. He wore a deep red military jacket with shoulder tassels and gold chains sweeping across his chest. Cream pants, belted high on the waist, with a red stripe down each leg, made his bottom half appear unnaturally long.

"The Captain of the Royal Guard will take the prisoner from here, thank you," a stiff and eloquent voice sounded from the back of the room.

The captain took Jeth by the arm and led him to a single chair before a wide, polished oak desk. The King sat on the opposite side, unconcernedly scrawling on parchments with a quill. The captain shoved Jeth into his seat and stepped aside, hovering at the edge of the room.

King Tiberius continued to write for several minutes as Jeth's hands fidgeted within his manacles. He knew enough about Del'Cabrian etiquette that he didn't dare make a peep until the man of higher standing—make that the highest standing in the land—spoke first.

His appearance was more youthful than Jeth had expected for a man of his years, even with the snow-white wig on his head and indented creases lining the corners of his eyes. Underneath it all was an almost frail creature, pale skin with visible blue veins and not a speck of facial hair outside of powdery eyebrows. His long ears stretched majestically in front of his wig, a golden crown perched on top.

As urling stock went, the royal family was as pure as it got. They resembled their ashray ancestors with wide-set eyes and small lips. At first glance, the man was anything but threatening. However, as soon as he placed his quill back in its well and met Jeth's eyes with a cold blue stare, a tremor coursed up his spine. There was no doubt this man could crush Jeth with a single wave of his delicate hand.

Jeth turned his head away, trying to escape the King's scrutinizing gaze. He only found the equally stiff-mannered captain staring down at him as if he were a fly in the King's presence he'd like to swat.

In a disarmingly temperate voice, Tiberius finally spoke. "I understand your discomfort. A king having words with a traitor, days before his trial, is a rather uncommon practice."

Now that Jeth was free to speak, he had to do everything to force the words out. "I-I wouldn't know, Your Grace."

Tiberius's facial features remained unchanged. "Hmm, I suppose you wouldn't." He sat back in his chair and crossed his dainty hands over his lap, resting his elbows on large armrests. "I forgot how young you'd be."

"I don't suppose my youth will persuade you to let me off with a firm warning, Your Majesty?" Jeth let out a nervous chuckle.

Tiberius stared right through him, unaffected by Jeth's attempt at levity. "Despite what your people may believe, I garner no enjoyment in signing death warrants. I'd much prefer there be no need for such things."

"We all do what we have to, Your Grace. I made my choice, so there's no use in lecturing me or whatever it is you brought me up here to do. Doesn't matter how sorry I am for what I did. It all ends with me on the hangman's noose, now doesn't it?"

The faintest of smiles appeared on the King's face. "I'm beginning to see how you eluded capture for so long. You're wiser than you appear."

Jeth raised an eyebrow and leaned back in his seat. "More quick on my feet, maybe."

"So, I've heard." Tiberius pushed himself out of his chair and walked around to the front of the desk. He cast aside his fine golden cloak, revealing a thin yet doughy physique commonly seen among urling men past their prime, but he carried himself with youthful grace.

He lifted a leg to sit on the corner of the desk, showcasing golden trousers cinched at the knee to accommodate white stockings. "I've heard many rumors about you, Jethril of Fae'ren. You are considered cursed by your people, and yet droves of them rally outside for your release. You stood guard at the Crannabeatha; you fought side by side with some of my finest soldiers. They say you died there, but here you are, reborn."

"It was sort of a confusing time for all of us, Your Grace," Jeth murmured.

Tiberius nodded. "Yes. The name Gershlon Reborn is being spoken across the Kingdom. I even heard rumors that you had something to do with the fall of the Heinrich Regime in Ingleheim, but that's more ridiculous than Gershlon himself returning to life."

Jeth pushed his tongue against the side of his cheek and snorted. "That ol' rumor mill keeps on churning, doesn't it?"

Tiberius stood up straight, putting his hands behind his back. "It is one particular rumor from the Desert Tribe Lands that interests me the most. I'm hoping you can shed light on it before your sentence is carried out."

"What rumor needs clearing up so badly that His Majesty would drag the Desert War Traitor from his cell?" Jeth struggled to hold back a more sardonic inquiry. *Tell me, Your Grace, how can I be of service before*

I'm hanged from the neck until dead?

"The Rangardian Armada attacked Odafi without any regard for the Overlord's retaliation. They are claiming he died"—Tiberius made a stiff and slight turn of the head—"in the Deep Wood where you supposedly did. Care to elaborate on what transpired that day?"

How would Rangardians know about that? Jeth quickly remembered who had ties to that empire. Vidya. His guts twisted, and he forced out a laugh to compensate. "No Rangarder was anywhere near the Deep Wood that day. I don't see why they'd assume Nas'Gavarr is dead. I reckon he'll tear them all apart before the year is up."

"During the war, our men heard of a Fae'ren outlaw who tried to rob his Serpentine temple twice and lived to tell the tale. Surviving two altercations is unusual enough, and now a third?"

"That's the way of it."

Tiberius tilted his head. "The Herrani appear to be unaware of their Overlord's demise—many speak of sightings as recently as two months ago. One thing is for certain: The tribes are at war, and their leader has done nothing. Dead or alive, he is undoubtedly absent."

Snake Eye had told Jeth that he would keep the death of his brother secret to prevent those less scrupulous from taking power. Perhaps the ashipu was ready to make his move, but he had promised he would send word to Jeth if that ever happened. *How much is safe for you to tell? What would the King of Del'Cabria do with this revelation? Rekindle the Desert War and take the tribes out from under Snake Eye?*

Jeth honed his sight and hearing, searching for any physical indicator of Tiberius's intentions, but the man was a fortress. "If Nas'Gavarr did die in the Deep Wood, that would make you the last man to see him alive." He clasped his hands together and pointed his intertwined index fingers at Jeth in his chair. "I'll ask you this once. Did you kill Nas'Gavarr or otherwise witness his demise?"

Jeth swallowed hard before replying. "No and no, Your Grace."

The King's lips made a subtle twitch. He stood firm as a bulwark, but his pupils dilated so suddenly, Jeth's pulse quickened in response. For a man with such a rigid countenance, every meager tic in his features appeared as outright contortions to Jeth's sharp eyes.

"Well . . ." Tiberius walked around his desk and sat back down, heart thudding like a war drum under his embroidered waistcoat despite the rigidness of his demeanor. "Captain Hamill, do fetch me a glass of water if you please." The King massaged his temples. Jeth thought that he saw his fingers quiver slightly.

"Right away, Sire." The captain went to a small table where a pitcher of water sat. He poured a glass and handed it to the King.

Tiberius took two reserved sips, then held it still, lost in thought.

"May I ask what the matter is, Your Grace?"

Tiberius continued to stare into the glass as he spoke. "My kingdom violated the terms of the treaty that day by opposing Nas'Gavarr at the Deep Wood. If he survived, then why has he not sought retribution?" He put the glass down. "I must know what became of him, or I fear our nations will return to war." The King's blue eyes bored through Jeth in his chair, severe and unyielding. "How do you wish history to look upon you? As a traitor protecting the enemy yet again, or as a man redeemed in the eyes of the Deities?"

Jeth leaned back in his chair, honing his hearing further. The King's blood thrashed violently in his veins. "I think it's more than that." Many people had wondered what possessed the most powerful nation in the world to lay down its arms and make a treaty with Herran after only a few defeats. Jeth had suspected Del'Cabria benefited from it somehow. Why else would they allow Herrani warriors to walk into Fae'ren Province, uproot Fae'ren lives, and hand over the Ingle borderlands unless they were getting something in return? Whatever it was, the King did not want this treaty broken, Overlord, or no Overlord. "Something about the treaty has you right shaken, Your Grace."

"You dare question the King's resolve, traitor?" Hamill barked.

Tiberius put up his palm to silence the captain but did not remove his cold gaze from the chained man before him.

"Then you know he has my daughter," he said in a low voice.

"Whoa, wait." Jeth sputtered. "The princess?" *Alright, wasn't expecting that.*

Tiberius nodded. "As a condition of our treaty. He promised not to kill her. He made no such promise not to hurt her, but she'd get to live. Part of our agreement also involved allowing him and his armies full access to Del'Cabrian lands."

"Fae'ren lands." Jeth clenched his fists.

"As long as our men didn't take up arms against his and made no attempts to look for the princess, he would return her when he was finished. In what state . . ." Tiberius took down the rest of his water and swallowed audibly "I cannot be certain."

Behind him, Jeth heard the quiet cracking of Hamill's white knuckles as he gripped the pommel of his sheathed sword.

"If Nas'Gavarr is dead, then this poses a problem. Will whoever succeed him honor the treaty? Do they still require my daughter for something? Did they kill her, or did she escape? If I send men to find out, then I violate the treaty, which may or may not exist. Either way, I chance never seeing her again."

"Have you tried speaking to one of his sons? Surely someone has been in charge all this time," Jeth offered.

Tiberius sighed. "Our ambassadors have had no luck in contacting any of them. Chaos reigns supreme in the desert. All that matters to me now is bringing my daughter home."

The pain of losing his own son compelled Jeth to alleviate the King's suffering. "The Overlord of Herran is, in fact, dead, Your Grace."

Despite the King's stiff countenance, Jeth could see the glisten of sweat blanching his forehead just under his wig line. He made a soft grunt, contemplating what Jeth said. "See, now I think you're telling me what I wish to hear." He waved a finger. "I left something out of my synopsis earlier. My men did not witness the Overlord leaving the Deep Wood, but several Fae'ren spotted him traveling west. How do you account for that?"

"It wasn't Nas'Gavarr they saw, but the Mage you tasked with killing him in the first place."

"The Raven Sorcerer?" The King's heart skipped a beat, distinct in Jeth's ear.

"When Melikhcil died, his spirit lay in wait within Nas'Gavarr's body until he could take over the empty vessel."

"Then who emptied the vessel?"

Jeth looked down at his hands as he gathered his thoughts. *No use mentioning Vidya right now.* He raised his eyes to meet Tiberius's. "I did, Your Grace."

"Lies," he dismissed.

"I survived him twice before that day. You don't think I learned a few things about him in the process? I consulted his enemies, uncovered his weaknesses. I found out what he knew, what his plans were, and I used that knowledge to defeat him."

"Then why keep it a secret? I'd think a man of your lowly stature wouldn't hesitate in letting the world know of such impossible heroics."

"I made a promise to a friend not to let the world know. But I suppose the cat's out of the bag now."

"Tell me everything you know as it relates to my daughter."

Jeth's mouth clamped shut. *You know nothing, but as soon as you admit that, it's to the gallows with you.* Although, this whole situation made him wonder. What could Nas'Gavarr have wanted with the Princess of Del'Cabria? Could it be the same thing he wanted from Jeth, Vidya, and Siegfried of Ingleheim? A chill ran through him as he realized for the first time since the Great Gershlon, a Fae'ren had something the Crown needed, albeit only the perception of something, but that might just be enough.

"Speak," Tiberius demanded.

This is your only chance. He needs his daughter back; your people need their independence. "Until I can talk to my Herrani contacts and investigate further, I can't tell you anything more. But it'll be hard given my present situation." He held up his wrist restraints.

The King sighed. "I wondered when it would come to this. Frankly, I'm surprised you'd reveal so much before asking for something in return. It seems you possess something of a conscience." He took his pen out of the ink well then flipped a blank page down in front of him. "I assume you desire a pardon? All you need do is tell me everything you know of Nas'Gavarr's plans with my daughter——"

"That's it?"

"And you will get in touch with your so-called Herrani contacts and use those thieving skills I've heard so much about to steal the princess back. Only then will I pardon you for the crimes you've committed."

"So . . . I do all that and return to Fae'ren a free man?"

The King nodded, his quill tip a hair away from the ink.

Any relief Jeth felt from Tiberius's offer was soon replaced with a new type of dread. *If only that were enough.*

"So, I go free, and then what?" Jeth clenched his jaw. "Wait until the next time a noble prick decides to have his way with my woman or steal her babe right out from her arms? Death doesn't scare me, Your Grace. You should spend a few days in my home province. You'll see there are fates far worse than death."

Tiberius's eyelashes fluttered, but he recovered from his shock quickly and tipped his quill in the ink. "Ah, you want a chance to escape the squalor of your home province. How many dels will it take to loosen your tongue?"

Jeth leaned forward in his chair, closing the wide gap between them. "No dels . . . a woman's child returned home safe."

Tiberius looked up from his parchment. "What of this woman and child?"

Jeth recounted Henna's situation with Count Radley.

Tiberius put down the quill, sat back in his desk chair, and placed his forefingers to his chin. "You ask only that a child be returned to his mother, and you'll do everything I ask?"

"That will get me to tell you what I know. For actually going out to find your daughter, however, I want mine *and* my people's freedom." Jeth's palms grew sweaty, and his heart pounded. *You should have stopped at your own freedom; he'll never go for all of Fae'ren . . . but with his flesh and blood on the line?*

The King shook his head. "I'm not about to grant independence to people who've fostered rebellion in the past. The deal is one life for another—yours for my daughter's, no one else's. If you are successful, perhaps we can talk about the mother and child, but I make no promises. Take the deal as it is or hang."

Jeth's heart sank. *Take the freedom, you git. Figure out another way to get Ell back.* But such action would likely make not only himself but Henna a fugitive, their whole family forever on the run. What good was risking his life to find the princess, earn his freedom, return home, only to eventually find himself at odds with Del'Cabria all over again? The vicious cycle would never end. This was his only chance for real change. If he could show that he was willing to die for the cause, the King would have to settle for some kind of deal beyond just a pardon. Either that or never see his daughter again.

Jeth shrugged. "Then I hang."

"You're a fool."

"I'll hang, and all the knowledge about Nas'Gavarr and the princess dies with me. Also, you'll have to deal with my people out there." He nodded toward the window where crowds still hollered several blocks away. "The first Gershlon caused quite the uproar when he was executed, but I'm not so sure it'll quiet down as easily the second time around."

"A boy thief who kills his brothers in arms to dally with an enemy woman is a far cry from a war hero turned insurrectionist. Any unrest caused by your death will be quelled in the time it takes to cut down your body," Tiberius growled. "You don't have the courage he did."

"And yet they choose to call me by his name." Jeth shrugged, hoping the King would buy his bluff.

Tiberius folded his hands over his desk, studying Jeth. "I think you already told me everything you know. It may be true you were involved in Nas'Gavarr's machinations, perhaps even killed him, but I don't think you have a clue where my daughter is." He waved his hand down in dismissal. "Take the martyr's path, if that's what you choose."

Hamill grabbed Jeth's bicep, shooting cold panic down his spine. *He's faking, he hopes you will cave and spill everything, then he won't have to free you, help Henna, or do anything for your people.* He had counted too much on the King's desperation; he didn't expect he'd go back on the whole deal.

"You need me, Your Grace." Jeth broke away from Hamill and slammed his manacled hands on the desk, demanding Tiberius's attention. "I'm the only one who can find her because I'm the only one who knows what he wanted with her."

The King looked up for only an instant. "Take him back to his cell." He then returned to his papers. "His trial will be waived."

Jeth felt the blood drain from his face. "You can't . . ."

"It would be a pity to delay his martyrdom any more than we must. The trial would only serve as a formality at this point. I decree it be replaced with his execution."

Hamill took Jeth by the arm and pulled him toward the door.

"Think of your daughter, Your Grace," he cried, but the King's gaze remained fixed on his parchments. Jeth was a dead man to him now.

"Your Grace!"

Hamill threw Jeth into the prison guard's grasp outside the room and slammed the double doors shut.

8
Last Words

The clang of bells from the Del'Roche Cathedral reverberated in Jeth's ears as the prison cart bobbled over cobblestones. Several other prisoners, also heading for the execution grounds, grunted and groaned over each bump. At least two of them looked like they'd hurl all over their soiled smocks.

Jeth had spent three more nights in the street cell. The unruly people outside had only grown louder, keeping him from sleep. Not that he could have slept much anyway. Jeth had hoped the King would change his mind and agree to his conditions before the three days were up, but he had not been summoned a second time. He had thought of asking the guard for one last chance to speak to the King, but he had stubbornly kept his mouth shut, and now it was too late. *Just as well. You knew it would end this way eventually.*

Urling noblemen and working-class humans hissed and jeered at the caged criminals passing them by. Rocks struck the bars. One small stone hit a fellow Fae'ren prisoner in the forehead. He grumbled and nursed his fresh welt but could do nothing in retaliation.

Two more rocks whisked through the bars, and Jeth dodged them easily. The other prisoners looked moderately impressed with his speed until foul-smelling water splashed over his head. An old woman cackled from a balcony above, holding her chamber pot upside down.

"For Mother's sake," he growled.

"She's lucky we're locked up in here," said the wet man beside him. "I used to kill old crones like her for less cause than that."

Jeth wiped his face with his filthy sleeve and subtly edged away from the old-crone killer as far as the cramped cage would allow.

The cart trundled under a grand archway and into Del'Roche's plaza, encased within the confines of the cathedral's outer structure. They came to a halt beside the gallows, erected at the center of the square for execution day.

Hundreds of proper Del'Cabrians filled the square. The Fae'ren gathered behind a makeshift barricade on the west side of the grounds, surrounded by a dozen officers from the City Watch.

"Get back to your post," a watchman yelled. The severity of his tone caused Jeth to crane his neck to see who it was. "Don't take your eyes off a single fae!"

Jeth couldn't believe his eyes or ears. Faron, once a major in the Del'Cabrian army, was dressed in the long gray tunic and round hat of the City Watch. The hard-faced urling marched down the length of the barricade, favoring his left leg.

Faron's rank had depended on bringing the Desert War Traitor to justice. He hadn't. Instead, it appeared that he had taken the fall for his men at the Battle of the Deep Wood.

Jeth felt the urge to slump down to avoid catching his former major's eye. *Why hide? He's going to see your sorry mug hanging from that noose anyhow.*

Once the caged cart came to a halt, a thin priest in dark blue robes and a shoulder cape stepped up to the raised podium beside the gallows' stage. His hair was close-cropped and his chin as pointy as his ears. "Good citizens of the Capital, please welcome His Eminence Archbishop Eccles." The priest stepped aside to accommodate an older and much rounder man in white robes and blue doublet, his miter a towering spire atop his head.

The citizens put their palms together and bowed in respect for the head of the Del'Cabrian Faith as he shuffled up to the podium, leaning heavily on his brass staff.

He cleared his throat, his jowls jiggling in its wake. "Six men stand condemned before six Deities That Cannot Be Named, by whom they will receive final judgment. I will now speak unto the Deities, who through their infinite wisdom, will free these men from their primitive states, and perhaps they may find forgiveness in the Spirit Realm." The archbishop lifted his palm to the sky and bowed his head before rambling off the incoherent babble that was the ancient urling tongue.

Jeth's stomach lurched when the gallows crew ushered the prisoners out of the cart. They formed a shackled line at the bottom of the north staircase, leading up to the wooden stage ten feet above them.

With a nod from the priest, the crewmen pushed the line of criminals up the steps. Jeth's knees threatened to give out until one crewman held up his arm to prevent him from continuing. He grabbed the two men behind Jeth, the last being the other Fae'ren. The young man looked back and gave him a knowing nod before the crewman pushed him up the steps, leaving Jeth at the bottom.

"Leaving the best for last, I see," he muttered, legs still shaking.

"You're the traitor, right? That means, His Majesty gets the final say, and he has yet to arrive. So, relax and enjoy the proceedings," the crewman said with a sly smirk.

The hangman, wearing a long black frock coat, tricorn hat, and a red scarf tucked into his black vest, climbed onto the stage from the other side. When the archbishop's prayer was complete, the hangman opened the leather-bound book he had tucked under his arm then took out a monocle to read from it. "Your Eminence Eccles, and the people of the Capital, I will read the charges for these men."

He proceeded to list off the names, crimes, and sentences of each: Murder, rape and murder, two robberies, and for the young Fae'ren, repeated indecent relations with an urling woman. The fact that he wasn't convicted of rape suggested the relations were proven consensual, but for a Fae'ren male, that didn't matter much where the abstinence laws were concerned. Jeth could only bow his head and bite the inside of his cheek.

Eccles gave his final verbal blessing, "By will of the Deities That Cannot Be Named, those sentenced shall be hanged by the neck until dead."

The hangman placed nooses over the heads of all five men.

The priest carried a brass dish onto the stage. He dipped his long bony forefingers into the liquid contained within and drew an upside-down 'U' with dots on either side onto the grimy forehead of the first criminal. "May you find Balance in the Spirit Realm," he whispered, then went to do the same to the next man.

The hangman grabbed the wooden lever behind the first prisoner. "Last words?"

The young human, appearing no older than twenty, trembled. "I-I'm sorry, Momma."

In expected stone-faced urling fashion, the hangman pulled the lever, causing the floor panel to drop out beneath the man's feet. He fell straight through the hole and came to a neck-snapping halt six feet below the stage.

Jeth swallowed the putrid lump in his throat as the hangman moved on to the next lever.

"Last words?" he asked the second criminal.

The hefty, bearded human bared his rotting teeth and growled, "Get on with it, you urling ponce, before I rip free from this here noose, crack your skull in half, and shit down your——"

The hangman didn't wait for him to finish and pulled the lever. The fat around the criminal's neck ensured that it didn't break from the fall. His body jerked and stiffened. Spittle dribbled down his bulbous chin, and the blue veins in his forehead bulged.

Hisses and cheers from the crowd grew so loud Jeth scaled back his hearing, numbing the experience further.

The two robbers hanged before the second criminal's body finally stilled.

The breeze carried the stench of evacuated bowels eastward. It was a struggle for Jeth to keep down his last meal.

Jeth gulped as the hangman approached the Fae'ren's lever. He wondered if he, too, were an orphan, if he could have found a home in Lanore instead of succumbing to this cruel fate. *Doesn't matter where we go, they'll find us wherever we are.* For his final statement, the Fae'ren lifted his head and looked to someone in the crowd. "I regret nothing! I love you, Lady Nora."

Hearing the young Fae'ren say the woman's name made Jeth think briefly of Lady Hanalei and how foolish he'd been to think he'd earn the right to marry her upon his triumphant return from war, and she was a human. The poor lad was marked for death the moment he fell for an urling.

The man's floor gave out, and he died as quickly as the rest. Jeth heard a woman's wail right before the crowd erupted in hisses and boos for the supposed degenerate swinging stiffly side to side. They were immediately drowned out by the Fae'ren people farther back, hollering with righteous fury. Jeth, on the other hand, hung his head and closed his eyes. *Don't you dare let them down.*

His heart was a battering ram within his chest as the gallows crew cut down the five dead men. They cleared the bodies away and strung up a lone noose. Jeth stood in a cold sweat at the foot of the stairs for what seemed like hours.

The crowd started to grow impatient, including the Fae'ren. They railed against the barricade, earning a couple of wallops from the watchmen. Faron remained planted, keeping his attention away from the gallows and firmly on the rowdy pack.

At last, the archbishop's voice rang out, "Make way for Their Majesties King Tiberius and Queen Henriette."

A parade of mounted Royal Guard rode in from the north entrance, bisecting the crowd to accommodate a brilliant white and gold stagecoach, pulled by blindingly white horses.

Captain Hamill dismounted and opened the doors, allowing King Tiberius to step out in full cape and crown. Around him, nobles bowed or lifted their skirts to curtsy low. All the lower classes took to one knee.

The crewman kicked Jeth's feet and pushed him down to his knees as well. *Is this even necessary?* Jeth glared back at him, but his attention was now on His Majesty.

Tiberius circled around to assist the Queen. She unfurled from the coach in a gown of dark blue silk over a grotesquely wide hoop skirt. Her corset cinched her waist to a blade of grass, blonde ringlets lay bundled atop of her head nearly as tall as the archbishop's miter. Tiberius extended his elbow to her, and she hastily took it.

The royal pair joined Eccles on the podium platform where priests had planted two small thrones for them to sit. Guards took various tactical positions around them. Jeth even spotted a few bowmen above the high lancets and vaulted rooftops overlooking the plaza.

Before sitting down, the King cleared his throat and announced, "Hangman, you may proceed with the final execution of the day."

"Your Majesty." The hangman bowed.

The crewman nudged Jeth up the stairs. He walked up them, floating above his body.

From up on the stage, he could see the audience's pale, angry faces in perfect clarity. Despite how high he stood above them, he still felt small. He could taste their hatred, see the contempt in their eyes. None worse than the Queen herself, an uneasy ire in her blue gaze, piercing him through her dark facial netting.

Jeth looked away from her and to the barricade beyond.

Tomas climbed one of the posts, his fox tail flapping in the breeze. Dayne was just as easy to find, blond locks towering above the rest with Silese beside him. Gern and the other archers were there too, as well as Abel, Twilla, and countless fae he didn't recognize. It did appear as if all of Fae'ren Province and its diaspora came to see their Gershlon Reborn hang.

His thoughts turned to Henna, the only face he couldn't find. With a quivering breath, he willed his heart not to break at the thought of how he had left things with her. *Hopefully, she won't hate you forever.*

The hangman read from his book. "Here stands Jethril of Fae'ren, the Desert War Traitor, and murderer of Sirs Baird and Tobin of Del'Cabria Proper."

The audience erupted in snarls and taunts. Radley's spearman stood right up front, two black eyes fuming. Count Radley wasn't with him, but Jeth supposed he was too busy with his new son in Deltashire.

Oliver, out of uniform, stood quietly in the crowd, staring solemnly up at Jeth.

The hangman continued, "He has waived his right to trial and confessed his crimes to His Majesty the King. He is sentenced to hang by the neck until dead. Are the Deities in favor of this punishment?"

From his podium, Eccles waved his hands to the sky. "By will of the Deities That Cannot Be Named, this traitor shall hang." He then turned to the royal couple sitting on their thrones next to him. "However, as this man has trespassed against you, Gracious Majesty, his fate rests in your hands."

Tiberius stood, backed by the towering cathedral and its six-petaled rose window, like the six Deities themselves staring back at Jeth with their divine judgment.

"As this man has waived his trial, I will offer him one last chance to claim his innocence before the good citizens of Del'Cabria. Perhaps a modicum of mercy can be found."

There it is—a second chance!

The audience hissed at the idea. The Fae'ren continued to scream for Jeth's release. "Tell them what you did for us!" Dayne yelled.

"Jethril of Fae'ren," Tiberius addressed him directly. "Do you deny betraying your king and country?"

The crowd quieted down to a dull buzz. Jeth met eyes with Dayne, who gave him an encouraging nod. *Sorry, Dayne, but you all didn't come here to watch a Fae'ren grovel for the King's mercy.* He looked straight at Tiberius and said in the loudest and clearest voice he could muster, "I deny it."

Many in the audience donned looks of confusion. The King cocked his head to the side before Jeth continued, "I can't betray a country that I'm not truly part of. I was born on Del'Cabrian land, fought in a Del'Cabrian war, but I'm not a Del'Cabrian. You all made sure of that when you gave up our home to Herrani invaders, allowed them to mar and uproot our communes. You stripped us of our way of life while excluding us from taking part in yours. As long as the word 'fae' is spoken with vitriolic intent, I and others like me will never be Del'Cabrian citizens. You execute me unlawfully, Your Grace." Jeth ended his tirade with a disingenuous bow.

The King's jaw steeled. "Have you no remorse for the lives you've taken?"

Again, Jeth looked into Tiberius's eyes and said, "I'm remorseful for many things, Your Grace. But not that."

"Fae scum!" The audience roared obscenities to such a degree the King and archbishop both raised their arms to remind them whose presence they were in.

"I did what I believed to be just at the time, and I'd do it again."

Olivier looked away as the crowd erupted in rage.

"I won't stand by and watch injustices carried out in your name, be it against Del'Cabrians, Herrani, or Fae'ren. If you must hang me for that, then so be it. But it will *not* be for treason!"

Fae'ren roared, and Del'Cabrians hissed. Tiberius raised his hand to quell the hysterical crowd once more. "Is that your final statement?"

"It is."

The King didn't move. A chilling hush fell over the crowd as the breeze whistled over the gallows, the wood creaking in its wake. With a stiff nod, Tiberius sat back down. He then waved his hand for the execution to commence.

The hangman placed the noose over Jeth's head. The jeering crowd faded behind his blurred vision. A new panic rushed over him at the sensation of the rope tightening around his neck. *He called your bluff. Say something. Tell him you know where the princess is, you killed Nas'Gavarr, anything. You're going to die. This is it. This is it. This is it!*

Jeth froze, his mouth dry. His fingers twitched as the priest stepped up and traced his wet finger over his forehead. "May you find Balance in the Spirit Realm."

The hangman took his position at the lever. Looking down at his feet, Jeth tracked the outline of the panel that would soon disappear beneath him.

A sudden breeze like icy tendrils rifled through his locks and wrapped around his body. He squeezed his eyes tight.

The Fae'ren people's cries rang louder in his ears. If he were going to take the King's deal—if he were going to live, it had to be now, but something sick and twisted in his core kept him stationary. It was like being stuck in the temple floor again with the Bloodstone Dagger about to penetrate his flesh. But this time he almost welcomed it . . . he was ready.

This is your Way.

"Wait!"

Jeth's head snapped up, his nerves a clanging bell toll.

The King stood, and his arm extended toward the hangman who let go of the lever and stepped back.

"Your Majesty?" Eccles sputtered.

The Queen glared at her husband.

Relief crashed against Jeth's body like ocean waves, nearly dropping him to his knees.

"It is plain to see this Fae'ren has inspired the loyalty of many like him," said Tiberius. "For the safety of our citizens here today, I rule it unwise to hang this man."

He sat back down as the crowd exchanged confused glances. Their befuddled mutterings quickly transformed into screeches of disapproval.

Eccles's flabby chin shook with his next words. "The traitor has confessed everything, Your Majesty. The Deities have since condemned him to death."

The audience roared in agreement.

"He will not hang," Tiberius insisted.

"What?" Jeth murmured under his breath. *Did he just cave? Did you just win?*

"If his life will not be offered as penance, then there must be some other form of atonement," said Eccles, glancing at the jeering crowd. "The good people of Del'Cabria deserve to see justice served, at least for the murder charges."

"I have every intention of bringing this man to justice, Your Eminence." Tiberius nodded. "As penance, I decree he receive the death sentence equivalent in lashes, followed by lifetime imprisonment."

"Lashes?" Jeth muttered. "How many—how many is that?"

"One hundred," whispered the hangman as he hastily took the noose from around his neck.

Out of the frying pan and into the fire. Jeth gulped.

The hangman led him by the arm off the stage. He pushed through the crowd toward the pillory at the north end of the square, directly across from the archbishop's podium.

"Traitorous dog!" a woman hissed as he passed.

"Pig fucker!" A man spat in his face.

Crewmen swarmed around Jeth and the hangman, escorting them safely to the pillory.

The hangman pulled Jeth onto the stage. One crewman climbed up after them and unlocked his manacles. Jeth rubbed his sore wrists gratefully before the man forced those wrists onto one of the wooden stocks, clamped the panel down, and locked him in place.

"Where's the flogger?" the hangman called.

"Here." A lithe urling man, wearing the same black frock coat and red scarf as the other, stepped up onto the pillory stage.

"Good," said the hangman. "Get on with it."

The flogger immediately ordered one of the guards to cut away Jeth's shirt while he unraveled a sinister-looking cat-o-nine-tails, glee in his slate eyes.

"Careful now, you could really hurt someone with that thing," Jeth said, fighting his nerves with false bravado.

The flogger smirked and turned to one of the crewmen. "I can't get a clear view of his back. Shear off his hair."

"H-hey, why not just tie it up?" Jeth pulled against the stocks.

"Shut your gob," the crewman grumbled, grabbing a handful of Jeth's locks at the top of his head.

"You know how long it took me to grow these? The sentence was one hundred lashes, not a shaved head!"

The flogger laughed. "Be grateful that you're only losing hair and skin today, traitor."

The crewman yanked Jeth's strands, snipping them one by one with the same shears he had used to cut off his shirt. As each mat dropped to the stage floor, Jeth shook with indignation, helplessly watching his connection to the forest, to the Mother Oak, and his fairy heritage, all fall away one by one. The Fae'ren behind the fence wailed for his loss.

The breeze chilled Jeth's shorn scalp. *At least they'll let you keep your beard.* The crewman took out a knife from his coat pocket and pressed it to Jeth's face. "Oh, come on," he groaned. Several clumsy cuts later, the crewman crudely hacked away Jeth's facial hair, leaving a red-raw patch job in its place.

The flogger lifted his scarf around his nose and mouth before taking position.

"Just be gentle," Jeth quipped with his last shred of dignity. He heard a few chuckles from the audience. *That's something at least.*

He clenched his jaw in anticipation of the reverberating crack. Nine knotted thongs hit squarely between his shoulder blades, bringing with them a sharp sting, but not as painful as he had imagined. *Right then, just ninety-nine of these to go. You can do it,* he thought, knowing full well how wrong he was.

The agony of each subsequent lash mounted. Jeth found no respite between each biting strike. He ground his teeth so hard, his jaw ached. By the twentieth lash, he could smell his own blood.

Twenty-one, twenty-two, twenty-three—each one broke new skin. Pain throbbed across the entirety of his shoulders and upper back, and radiated down the length of his spine.

By thirty-five, Jeth's legs gave out, and he was on his knees. Blood streamed down to the small of his back as more skin tore away. His vision blurred, the mob's shouts blending into one homogenous drum.

The flogger continued to wail upon his back, releasing satisfied grunts with each go. The thongs bit deeper into his flesh, coming that much closer to the bone beneath. *You've been through worse pain than this . . . just keep it together. Sixty more to go.*

Fifty lashes in, the flogger paused to stretch his arm. "Salt!" The crewman opened a burlap sack and scooped up some white granules into a tin cup. Without mercy, he tossed the contents on Jeth's open back.

He screamed through gritted teeth. The salt dug into his wound like invisible fingers prying deep inside and opening the gashes wider. "Mother Oak, please!" he moaned, tears trickling down his cold, shaven face.

The flogger put the cat-o-nine-tails into his other hand and continued his assault. The next strike activated Jeth's spark. It brought his focus away from the burning pain, giving him a burst of energy to fight back. He railed against the stocks so hard he thought he'd snap his wrists. *Just get out of these and run. Don't look back!* He barely noticed the next twenty lashes until more salt showered his back.

Jeth screamed curses, his strength rapidly depleting.

At about seventy-five lashes, the flogger slowed. The crowd's jeers deepened, their movements sluggish. He had activated his speed by accident, but the stocks held him in place, arms and wrists numb. He couldn't run—no way to escape the excruciatingly slow lashes scraping against his welted flesh like electrical bolts zapping him over and over again. He could no longer distinguish the audience's cries from his own.

His flagging vision caught the men and women behind the barricade, standing in silence. His hope to inspire his people to fight for themselves had backfired. And life in prison would make it impossible to make it up to them. *Your people will gain nothing from seeing you like this. You failed them for the last time. And they will never forget it.*

Jeth lost track of how many lashes there were to go.

It didn't matter; his grasp on reality was fading fast.

Vines wound up his arms, foliage cradled his torso, roots protected him from the fiery whip. And yet still more blood sprayed over him, a slippery, coppery stink. *Crack.* Melikheil's skin torn from his mutilated form. *Crack.* Anwarr slipped out of his blood-slick grasp. Falling . . . so far out of reach.

Jeth let out a weak cry. *I should have named you. You deserved a name . . . you deserved a name.*

Time sped up, his spark gone. Leather thongs belted harder, faster. The audience, rabid with bloodlust, counted each strike.

"Ninety-one!" *Crack* "Ninety-two!" *Crack.* The silence between each count was an excruciating harbinger for the next wallop, bringing him closer to death.

Jeth wheezed in the chilled air, tasting his own blood within it.

He was drowning, blood pulling him down and under.

Jeth came to, face down on an operating table in a cold torchlit room. His throat rattled in pain as something moved on his back.

It's still happening! Mother Oak, please make it stop. . . . He was too weak to move, too weak to even cry out. His vision was blurry, like he was trapped in a nightmare he couldn't fully wake from.

"Why would His Majesty order one hundred lashes if he wants him to survive the night?" said a woman with a Ludesan twang from behind him.

He heard a snip, then the splat of a piece of bloody meat falling into a brass dish at the woman's feet. Nausea rose into his throat as he realized that flesh came from him, but he somehow couldn't feel it.

"The salt keeps away the rot. He should make it through."

Jeth strained to see the man at his head, wiping his bloody hands over his already blood-stained apron.

"Oh, I get it now," Jeth croaked. "Throwing salt on the wound was for my *benefit*."

The woman gasped. "He's awake!"

"That's a good sign." The man put his fingers to Jeth's weedy pulse. "I'll send for the King."

He removed his apron, washed his hands in a sink across the room, then left. The nurse proceeded to lay bandages in horizontal strips over Jeth's gashes, each piece of fabric stinging like another crack of the lash. He clenched and unclenched his fists repeatedly to cope with a pain that seemed worse now than it was on the pillory.

His vision faded in and out until the door creaked open. The King, still wearing his fancy suit from the execution, sauntered in with his walking stick.

"Your Grace." The nurse turned around and curtsied low.

"Do continue." He pulled up a chair and sat down, gazing over Jeth's wounds, his lip curling in disgust. Once the nurse finished laying the bandages, he sent her away.

Jeth tilted his weak head, centering Tiberius in his vision. "I'd bow, Your Grace, but I'm not sure I'll be able to bend anymore."

Tiberius stared down at him with his cool blue eyes. The left side of his pale face glowed red in the torchlight, shadow draping over the right side, making him look more creature than man. "Had you cooperated with me from the beginning, you would have gone to trial, and the fact of Saf'Raisha's mistaken identity could have cast doubt on your guilt."

"You—you knew about that?"

That mistaken identity was Anwarr, posing as the daughter of Nas'Gavarr on her way to her Tezkhan betrothed. Had his major listened to him then, Jeth may never have killed those spearmen, Anwarr would still be alive, living large with her band of thieves, and Jeth would not be bloody and in pain on this table.

"It didn't take long to uncover the truth during Major Faron's manhunt. Your actions, however inadvertent, prevented a Tezkhan-Herrani alliance but also prevented Meister Melikheil from battling the

Overlord as planned. Now you tell me the Ingle Mage had intended to steal his body to do who knows what with. That could have given me a plausible reason to pardon you. But you wanted to be a martyr instead." He gracefully crossed one leg over the other. "So, I played along. Many a 'brave' human's resolve wains when that noose tightens around his neck. All you had to do was repent before the people, plead your innocence, say anything to garner a shred of mercy from me. Your belligerence had me sparing the life of a man my citizens would much rather see drawn and quartered."

"Perhaps you should have given them what they wanted," Jeth muttered.

"Mark me, Jethril of Fae'ren. You are no martyr. Just a broken man who longs to be released from this world. Dare I say, unexpected for someone without remorse for the lives he's taken."

"You'll have to forgive me, Your Grace," said Jeth. "But it's been my experience that nothing good comes from trusting urlings. Our fate has been decided by people like you for centuries, just like you had mine decided the moment you summoned me from my cell. I tasted freedom in the desert, and I'll die before accepting anything less for my people."

Tiberius tapped his fingers over the pearl knob of his walking stick. "But you won't die"—his voice took on a frightening severity—"precisely *because* I decide your fate. What you've suffered today can easily be made an annual tradition to warn others of what happens when they insult the Crown. How would your people's morale fare upon witnessing the one they admire so much, subjected to every manner of public humiliation over and over again? All I need do is imagine what I desire to inflict on the man who took my daughter and make you his proxy. As long as you hold onto the information I need to bring her back, you are no different than him to me."

"I see you are more than willing to cause pain and suffering to get your daughter back, but you won't consider alleviating it for the same result," Jeth cringed as a surge of pain went through him. "I wasn't lying. I can find her, but not for nothing."

"Is your life nothing?"

"If it means that I and everyone I care about has to live under the rule of men who hate our way of life, steal babes from their mother's arms, and hang those for loving as they please, then it might as well be."

Tiberius's eyes drifted away from Jeth's and settled on his cane. His voice softened considerably. "Rumors have painted many contradictory pictures of you. One, a murderous thief using the people who once cast him out to hide from the hand of justice. The other, a hero who stood up against the enemy to protect those people. Your choice today helped prove the latter, but it also proved how pig-headed you are."

Jeth raised his eyebrow. "We prefer to say boar-headed, Your Grace."

The King huffed through his nose. "I am not an overlord, nor am I a führer. I am a monarch beholden to the law. To do what you ask will require both Senate approval and the Clergy's blessing, something neither would ever grant. The stability of the Kingdom is more important than any one province. I risk that stability by even searching for my daughter. Until we know for sure whether the treaty is invalid, she's likely better off where she is. To bargain with her life for Fae'ren independence is a remarkably foolish undertaking. And even stupider to martyr yourself for it." He sat back in the chair. "Though, I do admire your devotion to your people. For them to lose you to such an impossible dream would be sheer folly. But urling gratitude for bringing our princess home could help your people more than one man's death ever could."

Jeth winced as he propped himself up on his elbows. "And what exactly would your gratitude bring us, Your Grace?"

Tiberius leaned forward and placed a hand over Jeth's tender wrist. "Upon my daughter's safe return, my gratitude may go as far as ensuring Fae'ren safety and individual liberty, provided more primitive aspects of your way of life are left behind. The only way to Fae'ren prosperity is complete cooperation with the rest of Del'Cabria, not living like animals and fearing civilization."

Jeth clenched his fists, red hot anger rising in his temples. *You're outmatched here. Why did you think you could win a battle of wills with the bloody King of Del'Cabria?*

"And if she's already dead or otherwise unable to come home," Jeth rasped. "What of your gratitude then?"

Tiberius let go of Jeth's wrist as he cleared his throat. "Unlike King Cornelius II to the Great Gershlon, I do not make promises I don't intend to keep. Regardless of the outcome, if I'm satisfied you've done all you can to find her, you will have your freedom. Refuse or otherwise abandon the mission, and you will rot under the streets of the Capital and your people will suffer with you one way or another. . . ."

Shivers coursed down Jeth's bruised spine at the King's last words.

"You'd let me go, even if your citizens want me drawn and quartered?" Jeth's fingers twitched in agitation with every throb of his back.

Tiberius scratched softly at his pale face. "We'll think of something to justify your release. Perhaps inform the people you were the one who killed Nas'Gavarr. If that won't make them forget your trespasses, nothing will. Until the word comes out of *my* mouth, however, nobody will believe it."

Jeth stared at his bloodied fingernails folded in front of him. *The royal wighead is right, you are no martyr.* The lump in his throat choked him. How quickly he had accepted his fate. He almost died for nothing. He thought of poor Ellion and how Radley could never lawfully do what he did in an independent Fae'ren. Now, that dream was even farther off than it had been before. Jeth had to settle for the next best thing. *The King's bloody gratitude.*

He ground his teeth and held out a shaky hand to Tiberius. "You have a deal, Your Majesty."

Tiberius took Jeth's hand and shook it firmly. "Good." A thin smile graced his lips, the most genuine emotion Jeth had seen in him yet.

9
Laws of Succession

(One year and eight months ago)

Princess Zephira forced her heavy eyelids open and blinked to bring her surroundings into focus.

She was in a carriage. Rays of sunlight pierced through the half-drawn shades, and lush vineyards lined the road outside. The sound of rushing water urged her mind to clear.

Elmifel River, she realized. She must be in Elmifel Province, heading north on the Holy Road.

Zephira was nine years old the last time she traveled this road on her way to the Holy City of Thessalin. She could still remember that first day when she had let her emotions get the better of her, and the fiery sting of the headmistress's strap raked across her bare shoulder blades:

"The pain you feel now, my dear, is paltry in comparison to the sheer agony your spirit will suffer when you allow the Primitive Force to manifest."

Thwack!

Zephira bit her cheek as the pain of the strap spread over her back like razor blades bursting out from under her skin.

"Wisdom comes at a cost, and it's a cost you and all royals must bear. Destroy the violence in your own heart before it destroys you."

Thwack!

"Surrender to it only once, and it will overtake you. Our ability to overcome it is what separates us from the humans. If you can't manage this, then you are unfit to lead them."

Zephira shook her groggy head and shifted herself in the carriage seat. "W-why am I back here?" she mumbled.

"You shouldn't be awake yet," said a man with a Herrani dialect next to her.

Turning her heavy head to the side, the blurred image of a skeleton face and serpent eyes came into focus. A jolt ran up her spine, but her lethargy kept her stationary. The searing flames, the suffocating smoke, and her mother's hysterical cries came rushing back.

"What's happening . . . ?" It took all her strength to move her arm, appearing as an indistinct blob attached to her side.

"You've been in a spiritual slumber for a few days," said Nas'Gavarr.

"Where are we going?"

Instead of answering, Nas'Gavarr suddenly lunged for her. She gasped and jerked away, but it was impossible to avoid him. He grabbed her by the face and forced a canteen to her lips. "Drink."

The cold liquid hit her tongue, igniting a desperate thirst. She let it flow down her throat until it flooded into her windpipe. She choked, spewing some of it onto her dress—the same smokey gown she wore in the chapel. *He didn't undress me,* she thought with some relief.

After drinking her fill, she took several deep, quivering breaths. The Mage put the canteen back under his belt sash.

"Where are you taking me?" she asked again.

"Thessalin," he replied, glancing out the carriage window.

"You can't. Only royalty is allowed inside. And if you think you can use me to gain access . . ." She touched her temples, pounding with every bump in the road.

"I have my own way in."

"How is that possible?"

"Your great grandfather granted me permission to seek tutelage there. He thought it would make me sympathetic to Del'Cabrian ideals—easier to ally with."

"Clearly, he was unsuccessful," she said with contempt.

"I wouldn't say that." Nas'Gavarr unfurled his headscarf, revealing his bald head and the *Veil of Elmifel* branded on his forehead.

Zephira gulped. Only ashray monks had that mark, and it sickened her to know that they gave it to a reptilian-blooded human when they had stopped giving it to urling kings over a century ago.

"You must have been most pious to have earned that mark," she said.

He turned his head away in silence before the carriage sharply veered off the road and lumbered across uneven, grassy terrain. A short distance away, a small waterfall tumbled over a rocky cliff, wet mist fogging the windows.

The carriage came to a halt at the rushing river. Without a word, Nas'Gavarr stepped out. She heard him muttering to the driver, "We can't leave the carriage here. Take it back to the Capital." He snapped his fingers. "You, you're coming with us."

"Yes, Master," two male voices said in unison.

A moment later, he opened the door on Zephira's side. Her heart leaped in her chest as he reached for her. "Do not touch me!"

He placed his palm to her forehead and said, "Get out."

Her head kicked back with a jolt at his touch, but slowly, the energy in her limbs returned, and her mind fog dissipated. Nas'Gavarr walked away, and Zephira stepped onto the riverbank. Her heels wedged between the rocks, nearly tripping her.

As she steadied herself against the carriage door, two men dressed in black and gray robes with similar skeletal tattoos took two bags from the trunk at the back of the carriage and brought them to their master. After a few hushed words with the Overlord, the driver climbed back onto his seat and, with a sharp whistle to the draft horses, turned the carriage around and trundled back toward the road.

"He's leaving us here?"

"Rest for a moment, then we continue on," Nas'Gavarr said before turning to collect the bags left on the ground. Zephira stared at him while his back was to her. *Just tell me your intentions!* she screamed within her mind, but she wasn't sure she wanted to know.

Instead, she turned to the falls, one of the many that flowed from the Sacred Spring of Elmifel. Lifting her heavy skirts, she hobbled across the rocks. She knelt down and submerged her hands into the freezing glacier stream. A shiver ran through her as she traced the *Veil of Elmifel* over her forehead and clasped her wet hands together in prayer.

She watched the three phantom streams branch out from her forehead as always, inviting her mind to dive in and follow them. As soon as she emerged in the royal study, an overwhelming rage threatened to burst from her skull.

Tiberius picked up a swan-shaped paperweight on his desk. He would often let Zephira play with it while he worked. He fondled it between each hand as he focused on his racing heart and willed it to slow. Even in moments of great strife, the King of Del'Cabria commanded his emotions as stridently as Captain Hamill commanded the Royal Guard.

Lord Fratwell cleared his throat from across the King's desk. "Your Majesty, I know this is dire, but you made the right decision. It buys time for us to rethink our strategy. The prince is unharmed, which means—"

"How did he know?" the King muttered under his breath, not able to face the Royal Advisor.

"Pardon me, Sire?"

Tiberius put down the swan and opened a drawer in his desk. He pulled out a pile of documents with ink markings all over the typeset. The title 'Laws of Royal Succession' stood out at the top of the first page. He put the pile on the desk for Fratwell to look at.

The advisor placed a monocle over his right eye and began to read, his jaw falling open as he looked back at the King. "You never told me you were working on this."

"I wanted to wait until Rubin completed his tutelage before seeking your counsel. Thessalin may prepare him for the throne, or it may not, but Zephira is the eldest and wise beyond her years. I never told a soul about this idea, and yet the Overlord bypassed the opportunity to take my lawful heir for *her.* How did he know how important she is to me?"

"Perhaps he bypassed the prince out of fear you'd refuse to meet his demands. Or . . . his motivations are of a baser nature." Fratwell cast his eyes down. "He wishes to solidify the treaty through marriage."

"No." the King ran his hand over his receding gray hair, free of its usual wig. "He made it clear that he does not intend to add her to his harem. He wants her for something else."

"For what, dare I ask?" said a hoarse-voiced woman, standing at the north doorway in nothing more than a lounging robe. Her blonde wig was unkempt and disheveled.

"Henriette?" Tiberius jumped to his feet and strode around the desk.

Hamill appeared right next to the Queen. "Apologies, Sire. I told her you would not be disturbed, but she was insistent."

"Not to worry, Captain, you may return to your duties."

Hamill nodded curtly and left as Henriette approached her husband. "Tell me what you think that desert demon wants with our baby girl if not to defile her?"

"Darling, you should be resting." Tiberius took her hands in his.

She jerked them away. "How can I rest after my husband sells our only daughter to our enemy behind closed doors?"

"You and I will discuss this later." Tiberius attempted to escort her outside the room, but she remained planted.

"Tell me what you and that Mage talked about? Tell me why my baby is gone?"

Tiberius grabbed his wife's arm and squeezed tight, making her wince. "Command your emotions, woman!"

A bracing smack reverberated off Tiberius's cheek.

He grabbed her by both arms and shook her. "You are not of Ludesa Province anymore. You live among the highest of urlings here!"

"Have you no soul?" she snapped back.

Tiberius took a deep breath and released her. "Perhaps you should tend to the child we have left. I'm certain he needs your comfort now more than ever."

She looked up at her husband with a quivering lip, tears streaming down her cheeks. "Zephira idolizes you. I wonder if she feels that way still." Henriette spun on her heels and stormed out of the study.

Fratwell stood unobtrusively in the corner, lips tight.

The King eyed the crystal paperweight. A violent rage boiled into his temples. He snatched it and heaved it against the wall with incredible force. It shattered into thousands of tiny iridescent fragments, raining jagged shards into the rug's violet fibers.

Zephira sharply pulled her hands apart and broke from her scry. "Father . . ." She was shocked by his outburst, but more than that, she was surprised by what he had been working on before her abduction. He meant to amend the laws of succession . . . to make her first in line for the throne before her brother. *I could actually be Queen someday.* That thought brought the Overlord's words to mind, right before she lost consciousness in the chapel, *'You will be Queen.'*

She swallowed the lump in her throat, cupping her hands in the water once more to take a drink. She tried to ignore the triple streams and their sweet promises to take her home; it wasn't real. She had to do everything in her power to return home in person. It was her duty to maintain her resolve no matter what. She was Del'Cabria's future ruler.

When she finished slurping up the pure spring water from her hands, Zephira noticed something strange coming off her forehead. The thinnest of streams separated from the rest, then several more. Endless strands of water, like iridescent sewing threads, wove between one another in the air. *Where do those lead?*

"Are you finished?" Nas'Gavarr's shadow loomed over her, and she jumped.

She wiped her forehead with her sleeve, the phantom streams dissipating. Zephira opened her mouth to reply, but he walked away before she could.

He waded through the shallow water to the waterfall and let it splash against his open palm. The falls split down the middle as if the water fell on either side of an invisible pillar, a large tunnel appearing behind it.

Zephira slowly stood as Nas'Gavarr beckoned. "Come." He entered the tunnel with one bag over his shoulder, followed by his subordinate with the other.

Her gaze swiveled south. The closest vineyard was only a few miles away. *That's less than a day on foot.* With a deep breath, she turned to run, but her legs wouldn't budge. Her body stood frozen in place. *Run. Go, before he—*

Zephira's head turned against her will. Nas'Gavarr stared at her from the mouth of the cave. Reaching an arm out toward her, he curled a single finger. Her leg jerked forward. Then the other, moving her closer, defying every effort to run in the opposite direction.

When she came an arm's length from Nas'Gavarr, he said, "While you were asleep, I ingested your flesh and blood. I can control it if I must. However, it would be easier for both of us if you do as I say and follow where I lead."

A putrid taste filled her mouth. "How?"

"I healed you afterward, so you did not have to suffer a wound on our journey. Now, will you follow me of your own accord, or should we continue on this way?"

Zephira nodded, unable to release a single breath. Never had she felt so violated. She wanted to jump into the river and scrub herself to the bone. *What part of me did he ingest?*

The Mage turned, and she collapsed to her knees.

"Keep up," his voice echoed off the surrounding stone.

She pulled herself to her shaking feet and hurried to do as he said.

Nas'Gavarr led the way through the uneven tunnels, his robed companion in the rear. She tripped numerous times on the rocks.

"Take off your shoes," the Overlord suggested. They waited a moment for her to do so, and she continued in stockinged feet. Although her toes ached, she felt more assured in her steps.

They ventured along a high ledge, the tunnels opening into a wide cavern of sparkling blue quartz and an underground river flowing through it.

The water vapors blanketed her, making her hair frizz and skin pucker. The water's purity tempted her to scry again. She couldn't resist retracing the *Veil* with a damp finger and watching the three waterways condense in front of her with little need for her to concentrate. *If my body can't escape, at least, my mind can,* she thought. She let her mind slip through the moisture in the air, this time following her mother's stream.

The Queen lay in Zephira's bed, clutching a pillow soaked with tears.

Soft knocks sounded on the chamber doors. Rubin's high voice followed. "Mother, Mummy, are you in there?"

His distressed cries made Henriette's heart wrench in her chest, her teeth grinding together painfully. She made no move to let her son in, only pulled the pillow over her ears to drown out the noise.

Zephira quickly yanked herself back into the tunnels. *I'm sorry, Mother, I just can't . . .*

Unrelenting guilt tugged at Zephira's insides after her brief encounter with her mother's experience. It was a challenge to scry her mother—the woman refused to regulate her emotions even in the best of times. Now, she had every reason to be in pain, but Zephira simply couldn't bear it. Her guilt gave way to frustration and anger at the Mage marshaling her.

She wiped the *Veil* off her forehead and said in the most commanding tone she could muster, "Why did you take me and not my brother?"

Nas'Gavarr didn't bother looking back at her. "Because it can only be you."

She exhaled heavily. "You told my father you do not wish to add me to your harem, which I appreciate, but my mother believes otherwise. I know I'm powerless to stop you from taking my body, but you will never possess my spirit, Gavarr. You will not break me."

The Overlord stopped abruptly and spun, so his face was inches from hers. "Understand this"—his serpent eyes blinked sideways—"it is not what you have between your legs that I desire, but what flows through your veins."

A coldness filled her chest. "Then my father is right. You want me for something else, some profane ritual?"

Gavarr's eyes narrowed. "When did your father speak of this with you?"

Zephira cast her eyes down. She had to be careful not to reveal her abilities to him lest he magically control them too.

"Of course. I should have realized back at the riverbank." Gavarr continued onward, and Zephira promptly followed, her curiosity piqued.

"Realized what at the riverbank?"

"You were connecting to your father, yes? As the ashray do with one another?" He shifted his bag to the other shoulder.

"I don't know what you're talking about."

"The connection is similar to a spiritual rapport between a Mage and subject, only there is no need for priming."

"Priming?"

"Making the subject's mind vulnerable in order to form a permanent connection with it. A Spirit Mage, even one as experienced as me, cannot simply enter a mind without priming it first. This can be done easily if the Mage is related to the subject, be it by blood or devotion."

Zephira's fear of Gavarr discovering her abilities was soon replaced by a fascination to learn more about them. "So, it is spirit magic then. I don't have to prime my family's mind because of our blood relation."

"No." Gavarr put a finger up in the air. "I can sense from here that you are no Spirit Mage. Your abilities derive from Elmifel itself, like the ashray."

"Tell me what you know of ashray abilities," Zephira demanded. All she'd learned was that a few of her ancestors had been able to scry, one of them rumored to have been Saint Orester herself. Zephira reflexively touched the top of her breast, expecting her brooch to be there. The absence of the saint's blessing made her heart feel weak and vulnerable.

Gavarr jogged up a steep incline and took Zephira by the arm to pull her up alongside him. "The ashray share a consciousness over hundreds of bodies, all birthed from the Sacred Spring of Elmifel."

"Yes, I know that," she said. "So, you're saying I'm sharing consciousness with my parents?"

"Spiritual rapports, like what I share with some of my children, allow a Spirit Mage to reach out to their subjects and see briefly what they see. To do this, I must purposely establish a tiny remnant of my spirit within my children, typically done while they are young and only by spending adequate time with them."

Zephira tried to conjure the image of the immortal, tattooed Mage rocking infants or bouncing kids upon his knee, but the picture refused to come to mind.

Gavarr went on, "Ashray, on the other hand, live in a constant state of oneness from the moment they come into existence. They experience every move, every breath of one another. They cannot read thoughts, but that matters not for they all share the same thoughts."

"Because they are all one spirit?"

"Yes and no. They have individual spirits, but they all operate under a more powerful one, like raindrops swallowed by the ocean."

"The Spirit of Elmifel," Zephira guessed.

Gavarr nodded as the caverns widened to accommodate two more canals where the underground river split off. "Yes, similar to how the Spirit Realm births new spirits into physical vessels and reabsorbs them when those vessels are destroyed."

"That's where the water comes in," she said. "Elmifel's spirit exists in water and is at its strongest in the Sacred Spring."

The Overlord turned to smile at her for just a moment, like an instructor proud of his pupil. "The spring is its mind and the rivers its body. As long as the ashray are near water, be it in the ground or in the air, pieces of their spirits can roam wherever they please. As can yours."

"Why are you telling me this? Surely you haven't taken me all this way to familiarize me with my ashray heritage." Zephira slipped on a rock but caught a protrusion against the wall to steady herself.

"It's not your *ashray* roots I mean to reconnect you with." They turned a tight corner and came to a blue quartz wall blocking their path. Gavarr placed his hand on it, and the rock vibrated with such force, Zephira nearly fell backward into the man coming up behind her. The wall bent and liquefied before pouring over the edge and splashing into the water below as re-solidified rock. Up the steep incline Gavarr revealed, Zephira strained to keep pace as her feet bled through her torn stockings.

A massive granite ring appeared before them at the top of the incline, lodged in an alcove. "A warping gate!" Zephira gasped. "I read that the only gates left in existence are in Credence and Rangardia."

"I've built my own," Gavarr stated. "Now that your father has allowed me access to Fae'ren lands, I plan to build another one there."

"Why are you telling me all this? Do you not intend for me to survive whatever it is you have planned?"

"Stay right there," he ordered as he walked up the steps onto the gate's base.

Zephira continued from below, "What makes you think I won't pass this information along to my father through our connection? He could have heard this entire conversation already and is deploying his men to retrieve me."

Gavarr put down his sack and rifled through it. "Your connection only goes one way."

"He has just as much ashray blood as I do, if not more."

Taking out a yellow, vase-sized gem from the bag, Gavarr placed it in the cubby hole at the base's center. He then went to the large handle sticking out from the ring. "Ashray blood or no, *you* are the only one with the blood of a Champion." He pushed the giant ring around, angling it in a direction that only he knew.

"You mean the Champion of Elmifel? Preposterous," she scoffed.

Satisfied, Gavarr stepped away from the handle. "When did these abilities manifest in you?"

"I don't know. . . ."

"You do." He narrowed his serpent gaze at her. "It was two years ago, wasn't it?"

She looked down at her blistered feet. "H-how do you know that?"

"That would be around the time I started excavating these tunnels to build this gate. Elmifel has sensed the danger to its sacred city and thus activated its Champion to protect it. Champion activation is an automatic process that the Conduits don't seem completely aware of. I believe the Deities themselves are responsible for it." He then turned to his robed helper, grabbing the second bag from him. "Create a pathway and man this gate until I send someone to relieve you."

"Yes, Master." He went to the crankshaft at the other side of the ring and started spinning it with great force, the warp stone's chimes echoing throughout the narrow passage.

Zephira yelled over the noise, "Why threaten a Conduit just to activate me?"

"I intend to activate all the Champions, but you will be the most valuable among them."

"Because I am to become Queen," she guessed. "How did you know my father intended to change the laws of succession?"

"I didn't." Gavarr watched the spinning stone below. "But it is about time."

"Then . . . why did you say I will be Queen?" It then dawned on Zephira what such a thing would mean. "Is your plan to kill my father and brother and put me on the throne?"

Before he could respond, the warp stone's liquid energy sprang forth and splashed within the confines of the granite ring. A distorted vision of a dark place existed beyond.

He turned to her with a wry glare. "You believe it's Del'Cabria you are to rule over? Silly girl, there will be no Del'Cabria after I am finished. There will only be one place, one people. You will be Queen of them all."

"And I suppose you will be King," Zephira said, swallowing down the terror and nausea rising in her throat.

Shaking his head, Gavarr stepped aside, his expression grim. "Not King; servant." He made a sweeping motion with his arm, prompting Zephira to walk up the base. "This way."

He expects me to believe he'd be subservient to me when he controls my very flesh and blood? Sensing she would get no more details from the mad Mage, she lifted her skirts and climbed up the granite steps. She schooled her face into a façade of courage and strode past Gavarr, waiting beside the swirling energy.

And at that moment, she left the glistening caverns and her life behind and stepped into the all-devouring darkness.

10
Delicate Feathers

(A year and one month later)

Hiding her hair and wings under a cloak, Vidya strolled past a line of Citadel guards, standing steadfast, their spears vertical and shields raised. One of them nodded to her. She gave him a tight-lipped smile and continued into the crowd. Heavy clouds obscured the sun, the island winds whistled between the marble pillars. She couldn't hope for better weather on a day like today.

The Siren Council stood in a line between the Harpy and Siren effigies, their voices melding together with the sound of ocean waves rolling over the nearby shoreline. Even Vidya couldn't deny the exquisite beauty of the siren's song.

She weaved through the droves of women, husbands, and breeders in her attempt to get as close to the Grand Altar as a woman of her status was permitted. The closest and most comfortable vantage points were reserved for sirens, Mothers and now Fathers of the Assembly, and prominent grandmothers. Everyone else found whatever empty space in the plaza that was available, most of them filling the white marble stands erected off the surrounding buildings. She spotted the other hooded women in the crowd, all in their places and waiting for her signal.

By the powerful beat of the Archon's flaxen wings, the people's rejoicing hushed. "Mothers and Fathers. Women and men. One thousand years ago today, the Harpy received her punishment. This ended her cruel reign and cultivated peace between the Daughters of Yasharra ever since. We present the Harpy with the year's most dishonorable men. We appease her, we remember her, and we satiate her wrath on this historic day."

Unlike the ritual that made Vidya into a winged carrier of vengeance, the annual sacrifice was a time for all Credes to come together to pay tribute to Yasharra's most feared daughter. After the resulting rain washed away the blood, Credence returned to suppressing the Harpy within all womankind for the remainder of the year.

Xenith gathered her breathy blue gown and stepped toward the first sacrifice, chained to the Harpy's effigy and naked save a linen cloth over his pelvic region. "This man shall confess his crimes and face the Harpy's Punishment."

Xenith lifted the prisoner's chin to the audience, influencing him to tell the truth of his crimes with her touch, as the Mistress of Law and Order had done during his trial to ensure no man would be convicted of a crime he did not commit.

"Confess," Xenith demanded.

Complete silence enveloped the audience as they awaited the criminal's reply.

"I . . . I've killed . . ." the sacrifice said, his voice deep and coarse.

"Killed whom?"

"Women. Five of them."

"And?"

"And I enjoyed it!" His throat rattled with ferocity.

Incensed gasps and angry cries rumbled through Vidya's eardrums. "Punish him, punish him, punish him!"

Vidya smiled. It was time.

She looked to the cloudy gray skies, willing the wind to spin them around, faster and faster into an ominous cyclone.

One of the young sirens on the altar unsheathed her sacrificial dagger and slowly approached the prisoner. The man stared defiantly at the glistening dagger about to open his femoral arteries.

A flash of lightning cracked, followed by a low rumble of thunder. The wind blew through women's hair and ruffled sirens' feathers as they looked to the sky and gasped at the spinning maelstrom above.

The young siren stilled her blade.

"Do not fear," said Xenith. "The Harpy is eager to punish this heinous criminal. This is the day we give unto her what she wills."

"Punish him, punish him, punish him."

Vidya let down her hood and undid the ties holding her long cloak on. Her cramped wings unfurled, knocking back the men and women surrounding her. They screamed as Vidya sprang into the air, spinning in time with the funnel cloud forming dangerously close to the plaza.

She flew up to meet it, channeling the winds around her body. One with the cyclone, she rode the wind over the Assembly and landed firmly on the altar between the two effigies and directly in front of the Archon.

Pushing the whirling column of wind outward, she extinguished the surrounding torches, covering the plaza in dust and embers. The councilors covered their faces, and sirens in the audience screamed.

Vidya stilled the winds, allowing her to walk out from the dust to face the stunned audience.

Nobody made a sound as the cyclone continued to whirl above the plaza, preventing anyone with wings from flying away.

"Blessed Yasharra!" Her sister Demeter took a few steps back, mouth agape and shaking her head in horror. Her natural dark brown ringlets bounced off her pale olive cheeks. She resembled their mother more than ever. *Damn her.*

Vidya turned back to the sea of shocked expressions. "People of Credence. I, Vidya, daughter of Sarta, have returned."

Xenith stepped forward. "You are barred from this island. Your very presence here violates the treaty."

Vidya scoffed. "The treaty is as dead as the Mage you made it with."

The Archon's eyelashes fluttered, but her arms remained stiff at her sides. "What do you mean?"

"What I just said," Vidya blared. "I killed the Overlord of Herran."

Sirens' jaws dropped in unison; confused chatter fell over the crowd.

"You lie!" Xenith hissed.

Vidya raised the Bloodstone Dagger above her head for all to see. "I took this from the Overlord after I killed him. The treaty is over. Credence no longer needs Herran's protection, and the Siren need not rule here any longer!"

"Guards! Seize her!" Xenith wailed.

Citadel guards from every direction marched up the altar steps, spears and shields in hand.

Vidya held her breath as a bead of sweat trickled down the back of her neck. Her entire plan hinged on this moment.

The guards rushed right past Vidya and formed a tight circle around the councilors, forcing them back into a unified clump beside their own effigy.

Vidya exhaled.

"What is the meaning of this?" exclaimed Calisto, Mistress of Treasures.

The guards raised their spears high, aiming for the sirens' throats. More formed impassable phalanxes at every exit to the plaza.

The swirling winds above picked up speed. A few sirens in front took flight toward the exits, but the air pushed them back down.

The Archon took a deep breath and sang, "Seize the harpy." Her graceful voice was known to render the most intelligent man's mind to mush, but this time, it had no effect.

A haunting melody drifted from the crowd, the voice of a siren, unseen. The expressions of men in the audience dampened at the glorious sound. Xenith's hard gray eyes transformed into fragile glass. A hooded woman in a flowing red dress floated up the altar steps, and the song stopped. She let her hood down, revealing black hair held up in a golden band, a silver strand hanging down one side of her face. "They won't succumb to your song, Xenith."

"Cosima," Xenith breathed. "How did you . . . ?" She gulped down the rest of her words, already knowing the answer.

Vidya shouted across the plaza, "Six and a half months ago, your elected leaders made a deal with our enemy. Without a single thought to you, they submitted to a two-hundred-year-old *man*. They believed his false promises of peace and equality."

"We have peace!" a Mother exclaimed from the audience. People in her vicinity threw their fists up in agreement.

"We can vote!" called a man.

Vidya ignored them, continuing with her declaration, "Yasharra gave this island to all womankind, not just those who bear children or are lucky enough to be born a siren. This land, this *world* belongs to every Crede woman. It is time to take it back. For the Harpy within us all!"

The whirlwind widened over the plaza. More frightened sirens lifted off, only to get flung around and sent back down to the ground.

"These weak-willed women don't care about the rest of us." She pointed to the councilors. "The wingless, the childless, you do not get a vote. You have no say in the future of this republic. Under the treaty, a siren's *husband* gets to vote before you do. How is that just?"

"Do not listen to this treacherous creature!" Xenith brayed. "Know your history. Know what happened when the Harpy ruled here. She robbed this land of its resources and rained destruction down on its people. She brought the wrath of Del'Cabria upon us. They've continued to threaten our sovereignty ever since!"

"Is that why you did it, Xenith?" Vidya turned to the Archon. "Is that why you ordered the deaths of tens of thousands?"

"What?"

"She speaks the truth." Cosima flounced toward the huddled councilors. "After I was elected Mistress of Sciences, I found something in the laboratory of my predecessor, something you thought you could hide."

"Stay back, murderess!" Calisto hissed.

"Oh, shut up, you old bat!" snapped Cosima. "You approved of its funding through the treasury."

"What did you fund?" Penelope, Mistress of Markets, asked Calisto.

"Tell them, *O Archon,*" Cosima dared in a mocking tone. "Tell the new ladies on the Council your part in the creation of *femena mortum!*"

A soft hush draped over the crowd immediately followed by faint murmurs. "That can't be."

"The *disease?*"

"All those women . . ."

Vidya continued, "Admit to your people the role you played in the deaths and infertility of Rangardia's women."

"That's impossible," cried Althea, Mistress of Law and Order. "Archon, please tell these traitors that they're wrong."

Xenith redonned her stoic countenance. "We had no choice! Del'Cabria was determined to bring our republic under their backward rule. Their forces outnumbered ours twenty to one. Rangardia was this close"—she squeezed the air between her thumb and forefinger—"to siding with them in return for trade deals beyond what we could maintain. What would you have done?"

"Used the siren's touch like with every aggressor before," Cosima replied, running her hand across one of the guard's shoulder plates.

"Del'Cabria had become wise to our ways long ago, which only amplified their desire to knock us off our perch. They would have enslaved us all and used our ally to help them do it. It was them or us!"

"Hear that, Credence?" Vidya shouted to the crowd. "She took from Rangardia what they valued most and offered them the solution:

Healthy wombs. Women were the one thing she knew we had that Del'Cabria would never give." The crowd's confused mutters increased to frightened and angered ramblings. "Now, Rangardia protects us from the other male-ruled nations . . . that is until she sold us to desert snakes! Was Rangardia threatening to betray us again, Xenith? Did Herran make them a better offer? Did we whore ourselves to foreign men in vain?"

"Your mother was part of this, too," Xenith grated. "She was the first woman and only siren to honor the Procreation Agreement on behalf of us all. She believed it to be for the best, as it is for all first-born, wingless daughters. It was our duty to the Republic, something I don't expect *you* to understand."

Vidya's rage boiled over her temples. She clenched her fists so tight around the dagger's bone hilt, drops of blood dripped out and splattered upon the altar. *How dare she try to deflect her monstrous actions onto Mother. What does she know of duty? I fulfilled mine!*

She spun back around to face the audience once more. "Women of Credence, are you tired of selling your wingless daughters to would-be betrayers? Are you sick of following women who cower behind men?" A significant number of women cried out their agreement—at least one hundred of them were former prisoners she had helped smuggle into the crowd.

Cosima signaled to a few of the Citadel guards she had under her control to bring in buckets of water filled hours before.

"No longer shall we cater to the whims of the male-ruled nations for fear they will devour us. The Harpy will devour *them!*" The guards poured out their buckets into the pool at the Harpy's base. Once it reached the desired level, all Vidya had to do was add enough blood from the dagger to equal that of three men.

"It is *she* who makes us strong. It is *she* who will set us free, not a death-worshipping Mage." She stepped to the edge of the partially filled pool, held her dagger over it, and squeezed the bone grip. As the blood from her prison kill six and a half months ago streamed into the water, she continued her rousing speech, "Through the blood of one sacrifice, I invoke the Harpy to make thirty-three sisters this night. Wingless ones, childless ones who cannot vote, even mothers and grandmothers whose voices were never heard, this is your chance." Phrea and Daphne pushed through the crowd and climbed the altar steps.

Keeping one hand on the dagger, Vidya turned from the pool to face the audience. "I cannot promise you that the experience will not be frightening or painful. But after the wings sprout from your back, you will come to know power beyond your wildest imagination. Give the Harpy her right to rule once again and watch as rival nations bow before us, not with a siren's touch that wears off in time, but by their own recognition of harpy superiority!"

A few of the female prisoners put down their hoods and took determined steps toward the altar as planned. Even some women Vidya didn't recognize from the prison hesitantly stepped forward as their relatives reached for them, begging them to reconsider.

"Make me into a harpy," yelled Malantha, a former prisoner.

"Me too!" said another named Theoni.

Several more female voices rang out their support. "Make me a harpy."

"I want to be a harpy!"

Cosima clapped her hands and grinned wide, showing her brown teeth.

"Vidya, stop this madness," Demeter begged. "How do you expect to rule Credence after this? By killing us all?"

Vidya handed Phrea the dagger to continue pouring it into the pool while she turned to her sister. "Harpies need feathers, don't they?"

Cosima picked up her gown and twirled between the sirens. "Ooh, which one would like to donate first?" She ran her hand over Calisto's magnificent golden primaries. "So ancient and glamorous, these ones." Then to Althea's silver-tipped tertials. "Mmm, mmm, these would look gorgeous at sunset."

As Cosima came closer, Xenith lunged forward and grabbed the unattended spear of the nearest guard. Before she could drive it through the treacherous siren, the guard dove in front of her, his own spear tip impaling him through the gap in his armor. He fell to the ground in a heap, and Cosima jumped back.

Xenith held out the bloody spear. "You want my wings? Try and take them."

The female prisoners wailed for the Archon's demise. "Punish her, punish her, punish her!"

Vidya pointed to the spear. "Are you sure you know how to use that?"

"Never you mind. Where are your blades?"

Vidya looked to her bare arms. "With my banishment, it's been difficult to find weapons to my liking, but my fists have served me well in the interim."

"You believe the Siren is too weak to rule? Well, this is your chance to prove it."

With a powerful beat of her wings, Xenith launched herself into the air, keeping low enough to avoid the whirlwinds above. She careened for Vidya, jabbing her spear at her head, but Vidya dodged it easily. She ducked, evading another strike, then swooped underneath and kicked the siren backward, expelling air violently from her lungs. Xenith bared her teeth and threw her spear with all her might. Sniggering, Vidya caught it and snapped the shaft over her knee. "It's futile to fight me, Xenith."

"The people have chosen me to lead them. What am I to do but fight?" She dove for Vidya with a determined roar.

The two-winged women crashed together in the air. Vidya grabbed both the Archon's shoulders and shoved her hard, hurling her against the Siren statue. The harp's white marble strings shattered on impact, and Xenith dropped to the altar floor with a dull thwack.

All the other sirens, except Cosima, clutched their chests in despair. They watched their Archon's flaxen wings flutter in her struggle to get up.

Vidya floated back to the ground. "Guards, spread her."

Cosima nodded to her men, and they picked the disoriented Archon up by the wings. *Snap!* Xenith cried in agony as they forcibly stretched out her injured left wing.

"Let go!" Xenith clutched the guard's bare thigh, hoping beyond hope he would comply with her pleas, but Cosima's hold on him was far too great.

"Chain her to the Siren," Vidya ordered.

Phrea handed the dagger back to Vidya. "The pool is filled."

"Free the sacrifices." She slotted it back into its scabbard.

The two young sirens had already fled into the crowd along with their prisoners, leaving only the one chained to the Harpy. Vidya wasn't keen on letting a confessed woman-killer go, but she figured there would be other days to punish evil men under her new rule.

She called the winds, increasing their severity until they thrashed against the marble walls of the Citadel.

"All those who wish to be harpies, there is only one thing left in your way," she bellowed. "Kill the sirens where you see them and take from them what you need!"

The former female prisoners, along with the recently freed sacrifice, dove off the altar and into the crowd. With weapons they had fashioned in the prison or picked up from town in the days prior, Vidya's makeshift army bludgeoned, stabbed, and sliced through the Mothers' Assembly. An eruption of screams and cries filled the plaza, a tranquil song in Vidya's ears.

Men and women scrambled out of the stands, falling from balconies, while others chased them down, drove them through with swords, cut their wings, and plucked their feathers.

"When should I give the order?" Cosima asked, seemingly bored.

Vidya turned back to what remained of the Council, still trapped behind a circle of pointed spears. "You won't. Tell your men to step aside and let them go."

"What? But-but they are all complicit." Cosima whined.

"I said for your men to let them go. I never said I would. Just watch my sister while I deal with the rest." *I have waited too long for this day to let the glory of the kill go to some brainwashed thugs.*

Cosima beckoned her guards to put down their spears and move away from all the councilors except Demeter.

As Vidya approached the huddled flock, they scattered. Vidya, Phrea, and Daphne split off in pursuit.

Phrea tackled the spindly Mistress of Law and Order to the ground and climbed up her back. "I sentence *you* to a life of winglessness, bitch!" With the dagger she had pilfered from a prison guard, Phrea hacked mercilessly at Althea's flapping silver wings. She shrieked in agony before the former spy forever silenced her with a stab to the back of her neck.

The Mistress of Markets flapped her lilac wings furiously across the altar, but her hefty frame didn't grant her much lift. Daphne made a running leap, grabbed her by the ankle, and brought her down hard on her stomach. "No!" the siren bellowed.

"Sorry, Mistress. The market has spoken." With a handful of Penelope's hair in hand, Daphne smashed her face into the marble tile, the siren's blood splattered, teeth shooting out in every direction.

Vidya watched in awe, pleased by her friends' ruthlessness, especially the usually unaffected Daphne. She could hardly fathom the agony of having her wings ripped from her back, especially after all the suffering endured to obtain them. They deserved this revenge as much as she did.

Vidya launched into the air in pursuit of the other councilors flapping furiously against the storm winds. She took the Mistress of Agriculture by the ankles and bashed her frail body against the outstretched bronze wing of the Harpy statue, then catapulted toward the Mistress of Treasures. She grabbed hold of her golden wings from behind, leveraged her boot between them, and tore the feathered appendages out of her back. The grand old siren fell to the earth, screaming incoherent curses as she slipped through the sacrificial crevasse and split apart upon the jagged rocks of the shore below.

Vidya turned back to see the Mistress of Infrastructure tumbling down the right stairwell, blood pouring from her throat as Phrea marched after her, knife in hand, and Daphne fired her pistol, shooting down the Mistress of Sciences.

Demeter kicked one of the guards surrounding her in the knee and escaped their grasp. *Suppose my little sister learned something watching her breeders fight all this time.* She ran for the left stairwell, but Vidya landed directly in her path. "Don't go running off now, Demi."

Demeter slid to a halt and attempted to dart down an open path to the left, but Vidya yanked her by the wing and flung her to the ground. She rolled a few paces, sobbing breathlessly. "Vidya, please don't do this. Think of what Mother would say!"

"I know what Mother would say. She understood more than anyone the Harpy's value within womankind, but not enough to stop the Siren from completely suppressing her. That oversight was her undoing, as it will be yours."

The guards surrounded Demeter as Cosima came up beside Vidya and handed her the broken end of Xenith's spear. "I know she's the only family you have left, so I suggest you make it quick."

Taking it in hand, she replied, "I appreciate the encouragement, Cosima, but you cannot be the only siren left alive on this island. We will need many more harpies after today, which means we'll need a constant supply of feathers. Unless you think yours will suffice?"

"These old things?" She scoffed at the paltry wings hidden under her cloak. "I see your point. What would you have done with her in the meantime?"

Vidya caught her sister's pleading, tearful gaze. She knew all too well not to fall for her field mouse façade. "Whatever you see fit, just don't kill her . . . yet."

Demeter's bloodshot eyes blackened, her carefully crafted veneer cracking in an instant. "It was *me* who convinced the Archon to let you keep your wings!" she spat, wringing her gown in her hands. "We should have ripped them from your back alongside your harpy spawn!"

And there she is.

Vidya remained stone-faced as she watched Cosima's men drag her sister away, cursing. *Now, to finish this.*

She walked back to the Siren statue.

Rusty iron hooks that had once been used on Daphne and Phrea pierced crudely through the tips of Xenith's wings, leaving most of the fine feathers intact. "You're a fool!" the Archon rasped. "This day will mark the end of our republic. Do you understand that?"

"This republic was dead the moment you let that serpent slither into her inner sanctum."

Xenith lunged for her, chains jerking taut. "The Harpy. Shall never. Rule Cred—"

Vidya sank the spear tip through Xenith's diaphragm. Blood gurgled from her mouth in place of her last words—words Vidya had gotten all too sick of hearing.

She pushed the spear deeper, Xenith's ribs snapped and popped, satisfying a long-overdue desire to see her punished. Mirroring the words spoken to Vidya on the day Xenith sold her to the enemy, she said in a grim voice, "We can and we must. Your actions have left us no other alternative."

She yanked the spear out with a sickening slurp and the Republic's longest governing Archon hung limp by each wing. Rich red blood leaked out the front of her sky-blue gown and dripped onto the pristine tile below the Siren's effigy.

Vidya's hand trembled as she squeezed the spear shaft, made slick with warm blood. The coppery smell brought her right back to the night she became a harpy on this very altar. *A siren's blood smells the same as any man's.* She gazed out at what was left of them. Women and men splayed across the ground. Feathers—so many delicate feathers swirled through the air, falling like fluffy pollen, to be soiled by the crimson pools trickling into the mortar.

Something ethereal stood in the middle of it all. Not quite a shadow, not fully corporeal. Dark gray wings like storm clouds unfurled, revealing a skeletal form with dark pitted sockets and a demented grin creeping across its face. *"Thank you, Daughter . . ."* the winged creature rasped in a voice that Vidya had come to know more than her own mother's. It wrapped its wings around itself then dissipated in a burst of shadowy feathers.

Hundreds of women scrambled up the altar steps, holding out blood-drenched plumes and disembodied wings as offerings to their goddess.

Vidya nodded to Daphne to enter the pool of blood. "Let us begin."

I I

The Pure and the Primitive

(Seven months later)

"Sit," said the Captain of the Royal Guard after he ushered Jeth into the King's study. The captain took his place by the door as the officer who had accompanied Jeth from the prison infirmary saluted and left.

Jeth sat on one of the blue velvet sofas, sinking into it like a soft bed of moss. "My arse could get used to this." He bounced up and down on the plush cushions before his attention drifted to the clear glass table in front of him, loaded with shimmering silver salvers. His reflection peered back at him in the perfectly polished platter. He lifted the dish to get a better look at his new self.

It irked him to see his fairy locks and beard absent from his reflection. Only a scrawny Del'Cabrian boy, dwarfed by the dark green tricorn hat and powdered wig, stared back at him. Jeth tugged at the small hairtail itching the nape of his neck, cursing the costume that helped him blend in on his trip to the castle. *Did you always have such a tiny head?*

"Do put that down, my boy." An older urling gentleman with a cascading gray wig and purple velvet tailcoat strode into the room. The King was not far behind.

"Uh . . . sorry." Jeth carefully placed the platter back on the table. He jumped up from his seat, pressed his hat to his chest, and bowed. "Your Grace, and my Lord . . . ?"

"Excellency," the man corrected.

Why can't these people decide on one term of address for everyone?

"This is Lord Fratwell, my Royal Advisor," said Tiberius, then nodded to his captain, still standing by the door. "Only the four of us will be privy to the matters discussed here today."

"Great." Jeth wiped his sweaty palms on his new moleskin trousers, and the three men sat in their respective seats: Tiberius in the high-backed chair and Fratwell on the small sofa opposite Jeth.

"You look well, Jethril," The King began. "I assume you were adequately cared for during your recovery."

"I feel a lot better, Your Grace. Thank you." Truthfully, Jeth's back still ached at the slightest movement even though it was now scabbed over. On top of that, he had caught a terrible case of the sweats that turned into delirium. It was a wonder he'd been able to convince the nurse to find a Fae'ren shop and get him the necessary herbs to keep his fever under control. With Del'Cabrian medical ointments and Fae'ren natural remedies combined, Jeth began to feel like his usual self by the third week, albeit exhausted.

"And the clothes are to your liking?"

Jeth adjusted the cuffs of his forest green tailcoat then pulled on his cravat to keep it from strangling him further. The trousers and stockings were constricting, his buckled shoes pinched his toes, and the wig felt like it was crawling with bugs. "Fits like a glove," he said, "although, would either of you mind if I take off this wig, it's scratching me something fierce."

"Well," Fratwell looked to Tiberius. "I suppose in your case . . ."

"Make yourself comfortable," the King finished. "We have much to discuss."

With a sigh of relief, he removed the wig then rubbed down his shaven head. Fratwell scowled with displeasure.

"Don't worry, Your Excellency, they made me bathe and shave before coming here, so I'm clean as a whistle." He continued to stroke the new hairs sprouting from his head. "You should feel how soft this is, you wouldn't believe—"

"Let's talk of my daughter's whereabouts, shall we?" Tiberius cut in with a sharp tone.

Jeth immediately stopped scratching. "In all honesty, Your Grace, I don't know where she is, but I know what Nas'Gavarr wanted with her. I believe she's the Champion of Elmifel."

Tiberius folded his hands together and crossed one leg over the other. "Is that what he told you before he died?"

"He never mentioned her, but he was collecting Champions, so he could use their blood to close down the Conduits."

Fratwell's eyes widened as he looked to his King, but Tiberius only narrowed his gaze at Jeth. "What do *you* know of the Conduits?"

Jeth sheepishly scratched his absent sideburns. "I learned all about them in Thessalin, Your Grace."

"That's preposterous!" Fratwell huffed. "Only the royal family is permitted access to the Holy City."

"A hundred some odd years ago, the Overlord of Herran was given access. I dropped his name, and the ashray told me everything I needed to know."

"The ashray told you Zephira is Elmifel's Champion?"

"No. I came to that conclusion all on my own based on the timing of her disappearance. Being one of them myself, it's the most reasonable explanation."

"You're an ashray?" Fratwell sputtered in disbelief. Jeth gave the advisor a wry look.

"You're the Champion of the Crannabeatha," Tiberius guessed. "That's why you defended the Deep Wood that day."

Jeth nodded. "I've known since the day my blood shut down the Serpentine, creating a forest in the desert in a matter of hours."

"Ah," Fratwell put up his index finger, "the spontaneous oasis. The Herrani are calling it the Gift of Salotaph."

"Impossible," whispered Tiberius.

Jeth relayed the story of the Bloodstone Dagger and the frightening ritual Nas'Gavarr performed to destroy the Serpentine's influence. "He planned to shut down all but one—a sixth Conduit that he said only he knew about. He, uh, died before I could learn more." He swallowed hard at his small deception. *You had the chance to find out, but you weren't exactly in the mood to listen.*

The King leaned forward. "You believe he was going to close off the Crannabeatha with my daughter's blood?"

Fratwell chimed in, "That's why he needed possession of both Zephira and the Ingleheim borderlands as a condition of the treaty."

Jeth shook his head. "You're only half right. He used Vidya, a harpy from Credence. The Champion of Elmifel was supposed to be used to destroy Yasharra, which would have been his next target."

"Then she's in Credence," Tiberius said, sounding hopeful.

"Doubt it." Jeth shook his head again. "You two would know more than me about the ladies who run that island, but I don't peg them as the type to hide Del'Cabrian royalty for over a year without making it known."

Tiberius nodded in contemplation. "Unless they are unaware of her identity. Living as a common woman in Credence would be a safer strategy than hiding in Herran." He turned to Jeth. "Would you be able to contact this Vidya? Perhaps she can be of some assistance."

Jeth scoffed at the idea. "I'm afraid that's not possible. Last I heard, she was banished or some such . . . as a condition of their treaty with Herran. I don't know where she's gone."

"Perhaps it is best to keep Credence out of this, Sire," Fratwell said. "The Siren Republic have gone the way of the former Heinrich Regime and isolated themselves. No word has come from that island in several months. They haven't sent a diplomat since the Desert War, and only then to make it clear they wanted no part in an alliance."

Tiberius continued, "This Rangardian attack on Odafi is concerning as they are Credence's strongest ally. It's as if Credence wants to appear to be upholding the treaty while benefiting from sacking the desert's wealthiest region."

"Well, Vidya didn't speak too highly of Del'Cabria or the desert tribes. I reckon the rest of her nation feels similarly," said Jeth.

"I don't blame them. My forbearers made vigorous attempts to bring them to heel during the Confederation Period, but their siren wiles and Rangardian protection made it difficult."

"So that's why they were spared becoming a province." Jeth shifted in his seat.

A small smile curled the King's lips. "We came close during my father's reign, as it happens. He attempted to ally with Rangardia and put pressure on Credence to submit."

"Until that horrid woman-killing disease put an end to that," Fratwell added.

"I, for one, have no intention of bringing such heathenish people into our fold."

"Wicked women." Fratwell shuddered.

Tiberius nodded. "Ironically, for creatures with the power to bend the hearts of men, sirens do not trust them overly much."

"Just as well, I suppose." Jeth stretched his arms casually along the back of the sofa and ignored the indignant stares from Fratwell. "I don't think Nas'Gavarr would take the princess to Credence."

"Then where?"

"Somewhere far from those who could recognize her or would dare question who she is. Somewhere completely hidden from outside eyes, yet still providing for her every need. If I were an overlord keen on hiding a beautiful maiden in Herran, I know exactly where I would do it." The King's jaw tightened. "Not that *I'd* ever hide a maiden, Your Grace."

"Where?" The question came out blunt as a hammer.

"Harem—" Jeth cleared his throat. "With his harem. When I was in the palace before, I didn't see any urling women, but I wasn't there long."

Fratwell breathed in so sharply he choked on his saliva. "You saw the Overlord's harem? What in good graces were you doing there? On second thought, I do not wish to know."

Jeth smiled out of the corner of his mouth. "My reason for being there isn't important, Your Excellency. All you need know is that my thieving crew and I can gain access easy enough."

"How can we be sure she is still there?" Fratwell asked.

"It's a starting point," said Tiberius.

Jeth nodded. "At the very least, we can get information from the other ladies. His son Ryeem was also in on his plans. If anyone would know the princess's exact whereabouts, it'd be him."

"Do you know him personally?" asked the King.

"We've had a run-in or two," said Jeth, crossing his ankle over his knee.

"He's not a Mage to be trifled with, Sire," the advisor said. "I don't recommend inquiring to him about the princess unless absolutely necessary. He's the most likely candidate for Overlord, and it's imperative that the treaty remains in place for as long as possible. It's obvious they don't wish for the world to know their leader is gone."

"I'd rather not confront him myself if I can help it. Though, I do have a good relationship with his uncle . . . or aunt." Jeth scratched his head while the King and his advisor exchanged glances. "Any goings-on regarding Ryeem, he'd be able to find out."

"Wonderful." Tiberius uncrossed his legs. "But even if you and your . . . *fellow thieves* can gain access to the palace, there remains the matter of ensuring her identity. Another urling woman could lie about being her, or she may not feel safe enough to confirm herself to you."

"Shouldn't be hard," said Jeth. "I'll just need something with her scent on it."

"I beg your pardon?" Fratwell huffed.

Jeth rolled his eyes at himself. "It's not what you think. I have a good sense of smell, so good I can identify people by scent alone."

"Like a hound?" Tiberius asked.

"Aye." Jeth nodded.

The King leaned in to whisper into his advisor's ear. "Can all Fae'ren do that?"

"I-I don't rightly know, Sire."

"No, just me," Jeth said.

Both urlings bristled at his interruption.

"Good hearing, too." He pointed to his left ear.

"Very well then." Tiberius stood up with a sigh. "I will take you to her chambers. Find what you need there, and may we never speak of it again."

"Lead the way, Your Grace."

Princess Zephira's private quarters, located in the castle's west wing, were so far from the study, Jeth was winded by the time they reached it. He hoped he'd be at his full strength when it came time to head out.

A single guard unlocked and opened the double doors, and Jeth and Tiberius stepped inside. Jeth wandered through the expansive drawing room, honing his sense of smell. All he picked up were faint odors of dust on the rows of bookshelves, polish on the pianoforte, and ash from the unlit hearth. Hoping to find more, he went into the next room through a set of heavy drapes. Beyond were rows upon rows of gowns, petticoats, and crinolines, including various other lady's underthings. He immediately drew the curtains closed.

"Is it proper for me to be in here, Your Grace?" he asked, his face reddening.

"Whatever you need to find her, just make it quick." Tiberius swallowed his obvious discomfort and urged Jeth forward with his arm.

He bowed his head and continued into the room of gowns.

As he walked down the aisles of garments, various contradictory aromas passed through his nostrils, none of them signifying a live being having ever worn them.

Urlings possessed a more sterile odor than humans, but they had an odor nonetheless. The only one he sensed was Tiberius standing a few feet away. "Is there any particular garment she wore more than the others?"

"I've never seen her in the same gown twice. The designers make them faster than she can wear them." *Of course*, Jeth thought with a shake of the head. Tiberius pointed to another set of drapes ahead. "Her bed is through there."

Pushing them aside, Jeth came upon another room with a second fireplace and a canopy bed wide enough for an extended family to sleep comfortably. A light perfume permeated from the bed; he heard soft breathing behind the sheer curtains. "Someone's here." He moved them aside and found a blonde urling woman lying on the top of the quilted bedspread.

She gasped and spun around to a seated position. "Guards!"

Tiberius joined Jeth at the bedside then put out his hands to calm the woman. "Do not be afraid, my dear."

"Tiberius?" The Queen shot out of bed. "Why do you bring a stranger to our daughter's private quarters?"

"You shouldn't be in here." Tiberius took hold of his wife's arm.

She jerked out of his grasp. "I go where I please."

Two palace guards rushed into the room. "Is everything all right, Your Highness?"

"Yes, yes, return to your posts," the King snapped, and the guards immediately backed out the way they came. "Continue, Jethril."

Jeth gave a respectful bow. "Sorry to frighten you, Your Highness. I won't be long." He sniffed the bedspread and the canopy curtains, but the only scent he could pick up was the Queen's.

"What is he doing?" she demanded. "Wait, did you say Jethril? The Desert War Traitor? Why is he not locked in his cell?" She began to shoo Jeth away. "Leave here at once! You will not sully the bed of the princess!"

"Henriette, please . . ." Tiberius put his arm out between him and the enraged Queen.

Henriette pushed against it in her attempt to get at Jeth. "If it weren't for you, Nas'Gavarr would have been killed long before that blasted treaty."

"I'm sorry for your loss," he started, "but—"

"Do *not* presume to speak to me, you filthy—"

"Henriette!" Tiberius barked, taking her by both arms.

"First, you overturn his execution. Now you bring him into our home?"

"I can do this later," Jeth said.

"You will do this now," Tiberius insisted, then turned back to his wife. "Darling, there is one man responsible for Zephira's disappearance, and he is dead. If you must place your blame on someone else, let it be me."

"I *already* blame you," she spat.

Jeth raised an eyebrow.

Tiberius took a deep breath. "I will explain everything to you later, but for now, you must allow Jethril to complete his task."

"I'm not leaving this room until you tell me what in Deity's lack of name is going on."

The King matched the volume of his wife's voice. "I've asked him to bring Zephira home!"

The Queen put her hand to her chest as if her heart had stopped.

"I'll do my best, Your Highness. You have my word." Jeth bowed.

"Your word is worthless," she hissed.

Jeth grit his teeth in frustration.

"Jethril is her last hope. He's the only person privy to the Overlord's plans with her."

"Then what do you expect to find in here?"

"Not sure anymore," Jeth said. "There's no scent that doesn't belong to present company."

Henriette replied, "She's been gone for over a year, and everything has been cleaned several times over."

"Even so, I should be able to pick up *something*." He looked around the room. "Is there anything at all precious to her that she wore or handled daily, something you wouldn't think to wash?"

Henriette looked to her husband, who stared at her in turn.

"Dear, do you know something?" he asked. The Queen walked over to a bureau across the room with a sigh, opened a drawer, and pulled out a silver and velvet brooch.

She grazed her hand across a carving of a woman's profile and handed it hesitantly to Jeth. "This was given to her when she was a small child, passed down over a thousand years through our female line. It was blessed by Saint Orester when she was crowned Queen at the end of the Dividing Period."

Jeth took it from her and brought it to his nose. "Smoke?"

"She left it in the chapel that caught fire," said Henriette. "Miraculously, the flames never touched it. I only had to wipe off some soot."

"Zephira was never without it," Tiberius said. "She only took it off to sleep or pray."

Jeth turned it over and sniffed again. He still couldn't get much of an urling scent off it, which was strange. Sure, it had been over a year, but his nose should have been able to sense remnants of her when pushed hard enough. He then noticed words etched into the silver backing. "What does this inscription say?"

Tiberius moved to read over his shoulder, but Henriette spoke first, already knowing it by heart: "'The Balance is the duality between the Pure and the Primitive. Only through penance can one maintain it.'"

"Sweet Mother," Jeth muttered under his breath. "And they say urlings don't know how to have fun."

"What was that, Jethril?" Tiberius asked.

Jeth's face reddened. "Nothing, Your Grace, just"—he turned to the Queen—"is it all right if I take this with me?"

"Absolutely not. You hold a priceless heirloom." Henriette put out her hand, palm up.

"It may be useful in gaining her trust. She might not be in the state to believe a Fae'ren man who claims he wants to take her home," he said.

"Take it," the King said, and his wife dropped her hand with a huff. "Ask her to recite the inscription before seeing it. If she gets it right, then you'll know it is her."

"He'll know her as soon as he sees her," Henriette said. "She looks like a younger me but with eyes of violet. Common among royal bloodlines, but a rare trait overall."

Jeth put the brooch in his inside coat pocket. "I'll make sure she gets it."

Henriette sighed, glancing at Tiberius. "Surely, any of our loyal soldiers would be more qualified for this monumental task."

"None who know the desert tribes like Jethril. Moreover, the Senate and Clergy cannot know about this mission. Any attempt to go back on the treaty will make future peace talks with Herran more difficult. We can't let the desert tribes know that we are aware of their Overlord's death. At least not yet."

"Especially if some of *them* don't know it yet," Jeth added. "Although, the Queen's got a point, Your Grace. Not that I'm ungrateful for your faith in me, but why not just use me for information and send men of your own to do the heavy lifting."

"When I first asked you to find Zephira, I planned to send you in chains with a few good men to chaperone, but now I know you'll put your people's welfare before your own, and that welfare depends on the outcome of this mission. Do not presume to be going alone, however. I will assign a small task force to accompany you."

"That ought to be interesting," Jeth muttered.

"If we're quite done here, we shall return to the study and discuss our plan of action." Tiberius took Jeth around the shoulder to lead him away.

Henriette blocked their path to the doors. "Before you go, I must warn you. As it may be difficult for you Fae'ren men to keep your hands to yourselves . . ." Jeth was taken aback by the audacity of the Queen's comment, but not at all surprised by it. He choked back a sarcastic remark, and she continued, "But if my daughter returns without her virtue fully intact, and I learn it is you who has tarnished it, I will personally see that you are punished in the way Crede women punish their violators!"

"Henriette!" Tiberius warned.

"Not to worry, Your Highness," Jeth said. "I don't much fancy urling ladies."

"I beg your pardon?"

"Ears." He pointed to his own. "They're too big. But I'll be sure to keep your warning in mind at any rate."

Henriette flushed, blue veins bulging in her forehead. Surprisingly, she remained calm. "May the Deities guide you on your journey." She gathered her skirts and stomped out of the room.

"You must forgive the Queen. Our daughter's absence has been . . ."

"Hard," Jeth finished. "I get it."

"You mentioned a woman who lost a son in your commune."

"Aye."

"Upon your return, we shall talk about her as well."

Jeth nodded eagerly as the two walked out of the room.

"For now," Tiberius continued, "we shall discuss who will join you on your quest. They must be battle-trained. However, as this mission will occur outside regular military protocol, they must no longer serve or be willing to promptly end their service. The Senate has agreed to send warships to the Odafi Gulf to assist in their defense. If I were to go behind their backs and send soldiers to search for the princess at the same time . . ." Tiberius closed the doors behind them and nodded to the guard to lock it.

"Right," Jeth said. "The treaty's broken, putting the princess in danger."

"It should go without saying that these men must be loyal to the Crown, meaning they cannot be Fae'ren born."

"Does that mean I can't return to my commune before starting the mission? My bow and horse are all still there as well as a right angry mob waiting to avenge my public humiliation, I reckon."

"Fae'ren is quite out of the way."

"Not since Nas'Gavarr built the warping gate. My crew is manning the one in Herran. They'll let us through."

"Ah, that's right." Tiberius tapped his chin. "Very well, return home and do what you can to quell notions of rebellion. We shall assemble your team as soon as possible. Although I do plan to reward them, they need to be comfortable with following your directives. It may take a while to find men who fit all these criteria."

Scratching his stubbled chin, Jeth thought of the men right away. "If you'll consider them, Your Grace, I may have a few good men in mind."

⌁

Jeth yanked on his bay gelding's reins to keep it from eating the luscious greenery along the road to Fairieshome. "Come on, you git. You've had enough." Clicking his tongue against his teeth, he squeezed the horse forward and found a place alongside Olivier. "I know I said this already, Oli, but thanks for risking your hide for me. Again."

Olivier chuckled atop his flaxen-maned chestnut. "I'm not doing this for you. I've got an all-tuitions paid stint at the medical school of my choosing. Something like that would take ages for me to save up on a military stipend."

"A wife and kids aren't cheap," added Master Loche, riding up behind them on his shaggy, flea-bitten mare. He had hardly said two words since they set out from the Capital six days ago, so Jeth didn't expect him to be listening in. "That's why the old lady and I are going to live the simple life after all this is through. A sturdy fishing vessel to sail the high seas is all I'm asking for."

"Lucky bastards. All I get is the King's gratitude." Jeth said sardonically.

"Don't forget freedom," Olivier added.

". . . however far that gets me."

"At least you get to live out your days more or less in peace."

Jeth wiped his itchy nose with his sleeve. "Sure, right up until the Third Wave hits, but I can always take comfort in knowing it's infecting Del'Cabrians nearly as often as Fae'ren this time around. No offense to you fine gents."

"Well, your people wanted equality," grunted Loche.

Olivier laughed. "Maybe Del'Cabrians will abandon the region, and you'll get your independence by default."

"I sure missed these old talks of ours," Jeth said, picking his teeth of the morning's breakfast and spitting out the remnants.

"Like old times." Olivier chuckled.

"Minus the searing desert heat." Loche removed his tricorn hat before wiping his brow.

"And the stifling uniforms," added Olivier, looking comfortable in his snug sailor's coat and neckerchief.

Jeth scratched beneath his knitted sailor's cap. Because he could easily hide his fairy locks within it, he'd grown fond of wearing them during his ranching days even though he'd never been on a boat in his life. Now it served to keep his shaven head warm. "We're just two spearmen and an Ingle Mage away from having our old team back together."

Faron, riding ahead, piped in, "What of the Ingle Mage?"

Jeth replied, "Oh, you didn't hear? He was torn to pieces by—"

"No, the one who is supposed to join us on *this* mission."

"Right, right. Kaiser Siegfried sent word that she left for the desert, something about rescuing naja. You know, they used to be human beings." Jeth felt a twinge of disappointment in not getting to see Jenn again. It would have been handy to have an Essence and Spirit Mage on the team, but alas, they'd have to make do without.

"We've arrived." Faron pointed to the barricaded commune ahead.

As if you need Fairieshome pointed out to you, Jeth thought in annoyance. He had his doubts about suggesting Faron for this mission, but because he had bravely stood up to Nas'Gavarr with only twenty men for no reason beyond Jeth's word, he was confident of his integrity. What he hadn't expected was for Faron to agree to come along. His present situation must have been worse than Jeth first assumed. While Olivier and Loche dreamed of medical school and sailing ships, Faron's only reward would be reinstatement to Major.

Faron continued, "We are losing daylight. We shall find lodging here tonight."

The team rode up to the gates. The same gatemen were manning their posts from when he came through with a pregnant Anwarr long ago. Their heads were still shaved, to which Jeth could now relate.

Anticipating the man's question, Jeth said with a fake Ludesan twang, "How do you do, good sirs. We're Ludesan traders seeking lodging." He pointed back to the clay jars strapped to their horse's saddles, the contents of which were oil samples from a Ludesan whaling outfit to support their cover.

The guard shook his head. "I can't let you in."

All four men exchanged worried glances from their mounts. "Why ever not?" asked Faron. "We carry no disease if that is what worries you."

"This gate behind me isn't here to keep the diseased out anymore," the man said with a heaviness that caused the lump in Jeth's stomach to churn once again.

"It's to keep them in," Jeth finished.

"You'll only be trading with the dead in these parts," said the gateman. "Many of the healthy fled to the northern and eastern communes. Perhaps try your luck there. You're welcome to spend the night at our encampment." He pointed a thumb to the north side of the barricade.

The men turned their horses away and circled around to the small camp along the outskirts. They sat down by a fire and shared a meal with some of the gatemen on break.

"When did this happen?" Olivier wondered aloud.

The fae man to his right answered between chews. "The story goes, a nobleman refused to go through inspection. He made such a stink, his father threatened to have the man on duty arrested just for doing his job. A couple of weeks later, the son dies, and the father leaves the province."

An older fae woman commented. "Brings the plague into

Fairieshome, then leaves us all to rot in it. I hope his son gave it to him, and he spreads it to the rest of those wigheads."

Jeth almost threw up his broth. *Could they be talking about Radley? Could the illness his son died of be the plague? Could it actually kill urlings?* He reached for a lock to make a silent prayer to the Crannebeatha, but there was only air to grasp. One of the older gatemen gave him a strange look as if he suspected Jeth was actually one of them.

Olivier looked back to the barricade. "Do you have enough medics in there?"

"What do you think?" the younger gateman said.

Olivier sighed and returned to his stew.

After a restless night's sleep, the men thanked their hosts and set off down the northeastern road toward Lanore. Jeth led the way, but eventually, Faron passed him and took the lead position once again. *Still a major at heart,* Jeth shook his head. "Sure, you don't want me to ride up front, Faron?" he asked, still finding it strange to refer to the man who had once been his superior by name.

"I remember the way," he said in a dry monotone.

Jeth didn't press further and left Faron to his position for now. *Hope he'll know how to follow when the time comes . . . and you'll know how to lead.*

"So, Oli," Jeth called back to his friend behind him. "You never told me what your cousin had to say on our way out of Deltashire."

Olivier grimaced. "He sure wasn't keen on going against a count, but he promised he'd look into some legal loopholes. While I'm gone, he'll send word to your lady if he finds anything useful."

"That's all right. If we're successful, the King said he'd intervene, but if we aren't . . ." Jeth lost himself in the thought.

"We may never find the princess," said Faron. "If it's true that Nas'Gavarr is dead, then we must prepare for the possibility that his followers disposed of her."

"Sweet Deity, Faron, can't you be a little more optimistic?" Olivier exclaimed.

"She's a Conduit Champion, just like me," said Jeth. "They'll hang onto her."

"Conduits, Champions," Loche grumbled. "It all sounds like hogwash to me."

"You let me worry about the hogwash, Master Loche," said Jeth. "All you need do is lend us your sword and navigation prowess. Then, you'll have done your duty."

"And if you manage not to run away with a Herrani woman, then you'll have done yours." Loche flashed Jeth a wry look from the corner of his eye.

His words almost knocked Jeth off his saddle. Olivier guffawed. "And the old swordsman comes in with a jab to end all jabs."

Jeth snickered and looked to Faron. He expected him to comment, but he remained silent and stoic as usual.

"Jeth's in charge this time." Olivia chuckled. "If he says it's necessary to run away with Herrani women, who are we to disobey?" He winked at Jeth, who grinned right back.

"If I ever order you fellas to do such a thing, I strongly suggest you mutiny."

12

Curse of the Lash

The task force arrived in Lanore by late afternoon. Jeth's spine tingled with anxiety at the sound of chopping wood and sharpening steel. He trotted ahead. "Urlings, stay behind me and let me make introductions."

The commune was busier than Jeth had ever seen it. Women, children, and elders whom he didn't recognize lined up at the pots for stew while men whittled arrows, sharpened knives, and carried logs over their shoulders. Jeth saw no sores on their skin or heard any coughing. *So far, so good.*

He and Olivier dismounted, leaving their horses in Loche and Faron's care, and walked toward the south entrance. Gern and five other archers met them there.

"What brings you gentlemen to Lanore?" Gern asked in a wary tone.

He glanced at Jeth, then Olivier. Not a glint of recognition appeared in his eyes. Jeth's heart sank despite understanding the reason.

Olivier took his hat off and bowed. "Pleased to make your acquaintance, I'm Olivier of Ludesa—"

"Wait, you're the fella who's helping Hen. Right this way, sir."

"Oh, come on, Gern, you'd recognize him before me?" said Jeth. "I thought we knew each other better than that."

The captaen's head snapped back. His eyes widened like a man seeing a nude woman for the first time. "Mother Oak, Jeth. How did you . . . ? What are you wearing? Aye, who cares? You escaped, you clever bastard." He guffawed and took Jeth into his wiry embrace.

"I knew those wigheads couldn't keep you locked up. Praise the Crannabeatha!"

The rest of the archers clambered around Jeth, patting him affectionately and laughing. Leif lifted him off his feet, reminding him of the scars he now bore. "Ow, mind the back."

"Sorry, mate." Leif deposited him on the ground.

"Who are those urlings over there? Friends of yours?" Gern asked, pointing to Loche and Faron.

"More or less. They traveled far to get me here, so perhaps someone can tend to them."

"I'll see to it." Gern patted him on the shoulder and went to task.

Jeth grinned as he entered the commune he thought he'd never step foot in again. Hugs, pats, and a barrage of questions came at him all at once from all directions. Silese appeared with tears running down her cheeks. She nearly knocked him down with her embrace. "Don't ever leave us again!"

Jeth hugged her for a moment. "Then you will not like what I have to say."

She stepped away and wiped her eyes as her brother strode over.

"Glad to see you standing on two feet." Dayne pulled him into a quick embrace. "How did you get out?"

"Gather the Elders. I'll tell you all about it, and you can tell me what in Mother's good graces is going on around here." He gestured at the flurry of activity around them as he, Dayne, and Olivier broke away from the others.

"We're preparing for war," Dayne said. "The backlash is coming after what happened in the Capital. We will not get caught with our *lein-croiches* down."

"You should be building a barricade. We have to keep the plague out at all costs. Get these extra men on it."

"We need them digging the trenches before the invasion comes."

"There's not going to be an invasion," said Jeth, pointing his finger for emphasis. "The plague's a bigger threat right now."

Dayne swept his long arm around. "These people came from all over Fae'ren. They've either seen or heard what happened to you, and they all joined our cause. It's like you said at the hanging: Orphaned or no, we're all cursed in the eyes of the Del'Cabrians, and we need to band together for once and fight for our home."

As proud as he was to hear Dayne say those words, Jeth's brow furrowed as he looked upon the Fae'ren fighting force, now more than doubled in size.

Dayne took notice. "You don't think it'll be enough, do you? Or is this not what you were willing to die for?"

Jeth put a hand on the taller man's shoulder and stopped walking. "I knew that if I could accomplish one thing in this life, it would be to give all of Fae'ren the will to fight back, but things have changed."

"Ever since Sil and I came here, you told us this day would come. Now you want us to stop? Have you forgotten about little Ell? I assure you, Hen hasn't."

"Where is Hen?" Jeth asked, looking around.

"She spends all her time in her garden." Dayne frowned. "She's beside herself, as you can imagine."

"I have to see her. Make sure my men are fed and rested. Then, we will discuss our new plan with the Elders. Trust me, Dayne."

Dayne bit his lip and nodded. "Alright, go find your woman. Maybe she'll spare you a whipping on account of the King getting there first."

Jeth shook his head and chortled. "You don't know my Hen."

Olivier and Jeth continued past the healer's cabin and down to the herb garden behind it. Henna was there, as Dayne said, crouched down and gathering garlic stalks in her apron. Her overabundance of brown locks threatened to burst through her woolen hair net. Looking at her made Jeth's heart thud in his chest at such a frantic beat he thought he'd faint.

"I'll wait over there," Olivier bobbed his head toward the corral.

Jeth trudged between the rows of wild carrot and garlic. "Hen."

She shot up with a start and dropped the day's pickings on the ground. He pulled off his knitted cap and took a few more cautious steps toward her.

Henna stared at him, shaking with anger. Then her eyes softened and filled with tears. She flung her arms around his neck. "You stupid, stupid man!"

He pulled her in close, but her entire body stiffened in his arms, and she pushed him away. "Hen, I'm sorry."

She turned to pick up the herbs. Jeth bent down to assist, but she yanked the plants away, stood up, and stormed past him.

"Look, I know you're upset, but I have some news that may cheer you up."

Without looking back, she said, "I don't need cheering up. I need my son."

"I know . . . and we're working on it." Jeth rushed after her and put himself in her path, but she plowed right by.

"Yes, I know all about your friend's advocate, but Radley's a count. It won't be that easy."

Jeth followed her into the cabin where Elder Leena stood at the counter, mashing something into powder with a mortar and pestle.

"Come to the Elders' Hut, and you can hear our plan," Jeth continued.

Henna dumped her produce into the bin by the counter. "I'm glad you took the time away from prison to tell us all the good news." She tore each bulb from their spindly chutes and tossed them into a bowl like severed heads piled in a mass grave.

Jeth glanced at Leena. She gave him a knowing nod and left to attend the gathering.

"Hen, please listen to me." He grabbed her arm and coaxed her to face him. "The King of Del'Cabria offered me a deal. I have to go to the desert for a while, find his missing daughter, and in return, he will give me my freedom and security for Fae'ren."

She tugged her arm out of his and crossed them over her chest. "And here I thought you'd be the last person to fall for an urling's deceptions."

Jeth twisted his knitted cap in his hands. "It's the best option we have. I can redeem my good name; the King will be obligated to me. He even said he'd help get Ell back."

"*Don't* use my son to make me all right with this." She wiped her tearing eyes and pushed him aside. "You're doing it again."

"Doing what again?" He tried to get in front of her, but she pivoted out of his path and went for the door.

Henna took off her medicine belt, hung it carelessly on a hook, and left the cabin.

Jeth called after her, but she wouldn't slow. He could dash up to her and make her talk to him, but there was something about her wrath this time that made him keep his distance, something that caused that lump to dig itself a little deeper into his gut. He wasn't sure he was ready to hear what she had to say.

Tucking his cap into his back pocket, he followed Henna past the corral on the way to their cottage.

"Everything good?" Olivier asked as they passed.

"It's fine. I'll just be a few."

"Take your time." Olivier tipped the wide brim of his hat.

In their cottage, Jeth smelled a fire in the hearth not fully put out and food spoiling on the countertop. Henna's clothes were draped haphazardly over the chairs. The beds, including Ellion's, had been left unmade.

Jeth closed the door, shutting away the rest of the commune. Now Henna could blare into him without mercy.

"Do you have any regard for your own life?" she shouted. "You didn't hesitate in giving yourself over to them. You should have stuck with the plan and come with me."

"You know I couldn't hide in the woods like some frightened squirrel. They would have killed every one of you to get to me."

"Then what are you training the lads for?"

"To fight for our home and our freedom, not to fight for me alone."

"Don't you get it? We need you, Jeth. Here, in Lanore, not in a Del'Cabrian prison or searching for lost royals. You went because you don't want to be here." She tore off her hair netting and smoothed down her frizzy locks.

Jeth clenched his fists. "That's not true. I'm Lanore's protector—"

"Then stay and protect it!"

"I turned myself in to keep you all from getting slaughtered for my crimes!"

She shook her head. "I know that's what you want to believe, but you know the truth as well as I do." Jeth opened his mouth to argue, but Henna wasn't done. "You left because it was easier."

"Easier?" Jeth shouted. "You haven't a clue what you're yapping about, woman."

"The others told me what happened. The King offered you mercy, and you dug your heels in."

"You weren't there! Death would have been mercy compared to what I got," he blared.

"And that's exactly what you wanted," she shot back. "To die. It'd be easier than having to see what will become of us."

"You don't know what I know, what could have . . ." Jeth's throat constricted, cutting his argument short.

"You don't think I know how hopeless things have been? That doesn't mean you get to abandon us."

"Is that what you think? Everything I do is for us—for Lanore."

"Then why doesn't it feel like that?" She traced down one of her locks with her fingertips.

"You know what?" Jeth seethed. "I don't need this from you. You didn't bother coming to the execution. You don't know what I felt. You don't know anything. You're just afraid, like every other fae since Gershlon's death."

"Of course, I am!"

"Well, not me." He jabbed a thumb into his chest, feeling his power rising there. "Not anymore. I'm the one risking my life out there, trying to buy you all a chance at a future, when all you can think about is making more mouths to feed."

Henna stepped back as if he had struck her, lashes fluttering. "How foolish of me."

"Where's my bow?"

Henna breathed sharply out of her teeth and marched to the trunk between the bedroom and dining area. She shoved Jeth's bow, strings, and quiver into his chest. "Go then. Do what you must. The rest of us will continue the struggle here without you."

Jeth shook his head and went for the door. *She's wrong! How can she not see that?*

"Wait," Henna called after him. He turned back to her with bated breath. "If you're going back to the desert, take this stupid thing with you." She took the sheathed tulwar from the trunk and roughly tossed it to him.

He caught it by the hilt and stared at it for a moment. He never imagined using this sword again. It felt like some foreign object to him now. He almost fell apart in front of Henna, thinking of the woman that once wielded it. "When I come home, everything will be better, Hen. I promise."

"Save it," she spat. "Dayne's done a fine enough job in your absence. Maybe we don't need you."

Jeth swallowed the lump, willing the heartbroken wrath inside him to stay down where it belonged. "Glad to hear he's got it covered. Goodbye, Henna."

He opened the heavy wooden door and slammed it shut behind him. His sinking heart throbbed painfully in his chest as he plodded toward the stables.

Olivier came up beside him. "Got everything worked out with your little lady?"

"Aye, you know how it is." He looked back to their cottage, hoping Henna would follow him out or at least stand apologetically in the doorway. *Nope.*

"I sure do. I got an earful from Patrice when I told her I agreed to this mission. We were planning on starting a family soon. Then, I told her how we'd get to live anywhere we wanted after my graduation, free of charge. She couldn't get me out the door fast enough."

Jeth chuckled along but only heard half of what the man said, his attention on the little cottage behind him.

"The elders are in that hut," Olivier continued, pointing. "Faron and Loche are there too. We're all waiting on you."

Stopping suddenly, Jeth handed his weapons to Olivier and nodded toward the stables. "Take these to Finn to put with Torrent's things for tomorrow."

"Uh . . . sure."

"Then, go to the hut and get everyone up to speed. I'll be there shortly." He didn't wait for confirmation from Olivier before heading back into the house. Henna sat at the table, eyes red and cheeks blotchy with tears.

She stood but said nothing as Jeth strode over to her, took her by the face, and brought his lips to hers. She braced herself against his chest as they pulled apart. "This doesn't change anything, you know. I'm still furious with you," she whispered.

"I expect nothing less." He pulled her flush against him by her hips and found her lips again. This time, she wrapped her arms around his neck and kissed him back.

She pulled him by the lapels, dragging him toward the table before hopping onto it. Her nimble fingers hurriedly untied the back of her dress while Jeth threw off his coat.

With the ties loosened on Henna's bodice, it was easy for him to pull down, exposing her bouncing breasts to him. He squeezed one in his hand, and his lips trailed down her neck.

She tore off his neckerchief and began unbuttoning his waistcoat.

"Bloody Del'Cabrians wear too many layers," she murmured, the waistcoat falling to the floor.

Henna laid back, her wild locks fanning across the table, and pulled him on top of her. As soon as his lips met hers again, he lost all sense of himself. The desperation to liberate his bulging urgency from his trousers took over all of his faculties.

While he fumbled with the pant buckles, Henna pulled off his shirt then ran her hands up his bare back.

Crack! Jeth cursed. The ever-present bite of the cat-o-nine-tails had him gasping, falling brutally into memories of the pillory.

He pulled away from Henna and sat on the edge of the table. It was as if his spirit had left his body, and he was looking down at the ruined scene around him. He could see his hunched shoulders, the ripple of crisscrossing scars across his back, and Henna's sudden concern.

"Mother, have mercy." Her fingertips gently grazed across the scabs. The sensation in his back fluctuated from numb to screaming with fiery jolts of agony. "They told me how many lashes you received, but I didn't let myself imagine."

"I'll live." He stood and picked up his shirt from the floor.

Holding her bodice to her chest, Henna sat up on the table. "I should have gone with the others."

"It was not a sight you needed to see," he said after putting his shirt back on. "I promise you, we'll get Ell back, but I need you to trust me. Please . . . I can't do this knowing you'd hate me for it."

Henna got off the table and stood in front of him, stopping him from putting his waistcoat back on. "There's nothing you can do that will make me hate you, Jeth. But that doesn't mean I can trust the King to keep his word or that I'm any less scared of you never coming back."

He buried his hand in her locks. "I know it's a risk. That's why I'm trusting the same men who stood at my side to protect the Deep Wood to get me home. They are proof that not all Del'Cabrians aim to stab us in the back. I have to believe the King won't either."

"Alright, but . . . if the King doesn't keep his word, I'm going to get Ell back one way or another. On my own, if I have to."

Jeth pulled her closer to him. "Then I feel sorry for anyone who stands in your way."

"Let me make you some garlic honey to take with you," she said, stroking the stubble sprouting from his chin. "It will ward off the *Curse of the Lash.*"

Jeth rolled his eyes. The *Curse of the Lash* referred to the tales of people falling dead weeks, sometimes months, after a severe flogging, even once the wounds had healed and the fever had gone. Jeth had heard of many Fae'ren, young and old, succumbing to it, but he had always thought it was just another superstition.

"Promise me you'll take it," she said.

"I will."

Henna ran her hand over Jeth's head, her brow lining with sorrow at his missing locks. "It's just hair," he said.

She sniffed back her tears and smiled. Letting her bodice fall to the floor, her left hand joined the right in its caressing, making Jeth moan under his breath. "I don't mind it. It's smooth."

"Take advantage while you can."

Henna pulled his head down and kissed him again, this time slower and more deliberate, coaxing a new arousal to press against his constricting Del'Cabrian trousers.

They made their way into the bedroom.

"I'm about to be pardoned, and you'd have me break the law again, taking an unmarried woman to bed?" Jeth said between kisses.

Henna pulled him onto the bed with her. "I won't tell your Del'Cabrian friends if you don't."

The next morning, Jeth arrived at the stables where his loyal steed waited with the team's other mounts. "Ready to go on another adventure, Tor?" He rubbed her nose then fed her a carrot.

It had taken an hour for him, Olivier, Faron, and Loche to explain the situation to the Elders the day before, but they had agreed that the Fae'ren people would keep their heads down until Jeth returned.

They took the bay Jeth had ridden in on and packed it with extra food and supplies provided by the commune to carry along with their whale oil.

Silese came to the stables with bundles of arrows in her arms. "Gern had these made for you and Oli. I helped with the fletching."

"Thanks a bunch, Sil." He inspected a sample and patted her on the shoulder. "That's some skilled work."

Jeth tied the shafts to the packhorse as Tomas ran up, Pup at his heels. Olivier and the two urlings backed away with their horses.

"It's all right, fellas, he won't bite," said Jeth.

"Unless provoked or hungry . . . or when he hates someone," Tomas corrected.

Jeth cleared his throat. "And what can I do for you, Tom?"

"Are you sure you have to leave so soon? We could use you on the hunt tomorrow."

Silese lit up. "Can I come instead? I can hit the target almost every time now."

Tomas scratched his head under his fur hat. "Uh . . . maybe, I guess if you stay up in the trees."

"You're the boss." She bounced up and down excitedly. Dayne lumbered over, and his sister swatted his chest with the back of her hand. "Guess what? Tom says I can come out on the hunt tomorrow."

"He did, did he?" Dayne cast a disapproving glare over Tomas, who looked down at his feet, face reddening.

Jeth went to tighten Torrent's saddle belts. "I'll let you all hash this out amongst yourselves. I hope you don't mind continuing as Commune Protector for a little while longer, Dayne."

"I'll do what I can."

"And take care of Hen for me, aye?"

"Aye." He nodded, his pale complexion taking on a pinkish hue. "Just make it back in one piece, alright?"

"Jeth!" Henna called from behind him. He spun around to find her holding a burlap sack.

"What is it?"

"You forgot this." She shoved the sack into his chest. It made a distinct clunk against his sternum.

"Ow, what's in here?"

"Garlic honey you promised to take with you."

"Oh, right . . . thanks." Jeth looked at the jar filled with a thick, cloudy liquid. After securing it in his saddlebag, he turned back to give Henna one last kiss. "Don't know what I'd do without you, Hen," he said after coming up for air.

"And I you," she whispered. "Be careful. I can't lose you, too."

"You haven't lost anything yet," Jeth reminded her while stroking her locks. "You'll see Ell again soon. He's the toughest little lad out there."

Henna nodded, her eyelashes fluttering.

"Time to get a move on," Olivier announced, mounting his steed.

"Olivier." Henna stepped around Jeth and offered him her hand. "I can't thank you enough for all that you've done."

"I've not done anything yet, but you're welcome." He kissed the top of her hand like a proper Del'Cabrian gentleman.

"You're a healer, right?"

"A medic, yes."

"Good. Then I know whose head to smash in if Jeth is not returned to me in good health," she said.

"Oh, uh . . ." Olivier cast a look of concern toward Jeth.

"You better believe her, Oli. Don't let me die, whatever you do." Jeth mounted up.

"Drink one mouthful of the honey once a day until it's gone, promise me," Henna called. Jeth nodded and waved to her. She pointed to Olivier. "You make sure he does."

"I will."

Jeth waved to the rest of the commune dwellers as they cheered him off. When the party turned down the east road toward the Deep Wood, the onlookers disappeared behind the tree line.

They reached the warping gate later that afternoon. Awestruck, Olivier looked up at the massive granite structure. "Will you get a load of that?"

"You should have destroyed it," said Faron. "At any moment, desert marauders can pass through here and wreak havoc."

"No one can come through a gate unless someone on the other side lets them in," said Jeth. "The warp stone chimes when someone at another gate points it in this direction and turns their crank. A hermit lives nearby who will hear it and turn the crank on this side to complete the pathway, as I've shown him."

"But what if the people on the other side aren't who you think they are?" Loche asked.

"The risks of instant travel." Jeth shrugged.

Before Snake Eye had returned to Herran, he told Jeth that the first thing he'd do was secure the warping gate with his own army. He warped to Fae'ren soon after to inform Jeth personally of his success. Jeth and a few men then went to the other side to help clear away the rubble from the temple.

A few weeks ago, Fratwell, versed in Herrani script, sent a message via pigeon on Jeth's behalf informing Bing Snake Eye of his team's plan. He could only hope they'd received it and were waiting on the other side to let him through.

Jeth dismounted and walked up the steps to the gate's base. He checked that the warp stone was secure in its cubbyhole and the dais still pointed toward Herran. He then took the crank at the side of the granite ring. "Now, watch this, fellas."

As he turned the crank, the warp stone spun in its cubby, glowing brighter and brighter until it began to chime. He turned the crank for so long he had to switch arms.

Loche grumbled. "I knew this contraption wouldn't work."

"Just give them a chance to respond," Jeth said. Finally, someone on the other side answered the call. The stone's chiming grew louder and picked up pace. Before long, the center of the ring fulminated into wet blue energy.

All three men gaped at the vibrating luminescence encased inside the ring as Jeth massaged his weary arms. *So much for your strength returning.*

He marched back down the steps and readied his mount. Before he could climb into the saddle, his ears picked up a faint rustle in the faraway foliage, followed by repeated swishing noises. Jeth was content to chalk it up to wildlife, but it was rapidly getting closer. A bright green light flashed in his periphery. He grabbed his bow and spun around to face whatever it was.

"We aren't going through until you do, Jeth," Loche said. "So stop mucking about."

Jeth turned his head toward his team and put his finger to his lips. He dragged an arrow out from his quiver and crept closer to the underbrush. The green light vanished, then reappeared at his left, bigger and growing bigger still. With an arrow nocked, he pulled back on the bowstring.

"What is that thing?" Olivier whispered, taking his own bow in hand.

As the light came closer, Jeth could finally make out an outline of a head, then arms and legs. *A fairy? Out here?*

"Serra?" Jeth put his bow down and motioned for Olivier to do the same.

The glowing green fairy zipped through the forest toward them and swarmed around Jeth's head like a dragonfly. The other men pulled their horses back as Jeth swatted instinctively.

"Jeth, Jeth, it's me," Serra exclaimed after finally landing on Torrent's saddle. Her green glow faded as her iridescent wings folded down between her shoulder blades.

Jeth stared at her wide-eyed. "How—why are you so little? I haven't smoked grass in months. I must be dreaming." He bopped himself on the side of the head a few times. "Wake up."

Serra flew up to his face and put her tiny arms out. "No need to bash yourself silly. I've taken a smaller size to conserve my spark while outside of the Deep Wood. You wouldn't want me running low on life force so far from the Crannabeatha, would you?"

"Oh," Jeth said, shaking his head. "You can live among fairies your whole life and still learn something new." He glanced at the other men staring at the miniature hovering woman in shock.

Olivier slowly dismounted and approached Serra, his eyes twinkling with a child-like wonder. "Well, throw me on a skillet and flip me over. It's a real fairy!"

"Pixie, to be specific," Serra said with a proud nod. "And, I'm not about to throw you on a skillet, whatever that is."

"Careful what you say," said Jeth. "Fairies take things rather literally."

"Pretty little thing, isn't she?" Loche said, grinning ear to ear.

"You're familiar with this creature?" Faron asked.

"*Her* name is Serra, and she's my . . ." He scratched the side of his stubbled face. "My uh . . ."

She perched on Jeth's shoulder. "I'm his mother."

"You're not my mother."

"Adoptive mother."

"Nope. Still weird."

"I took care of you, didn't I?"

Jeth cinched his brow, tilting his hand side to side. "Eh."

"A fairy raised you?" Olivier slapped his knee. "That explains a lot."

"No, it doesn't, because she's not my moth—you know what? Think of her as my guardian."

"Why is she here?" Faron asked.

"Yeah, Ser, why are you here?"

"The Crannabeatha sent me. Bad things are coming, and she told me to look out for you once again."

"Did she happen to tell you why this time?"

Serra pursed her lips and shook her head. "Only that the force that almost destroyed her before isn't finished yet."

"Pestilence devours the living," Jeth murmured. Vidya's vicious words came to mind. *I will have my Harplite. Stand in my way, and you will come to know its wrath!*

"The princess is our only priority," Faron reminded him.

"He's right. I have to complete this mission first."

"No need to change your plans." Serra flew back to Torrent's saddle to more easily address all the men. "Your *Way* will guide you. This mission is part of that, and I'm going to help."

"Not the *Way*," Jeth whined. "I thought I was done with that shit."

Faron cleared his throat. "His Majesty made it clear that no Fae'ren may join this task force."

Jeth shrugged. "Said nothing about fairies, though. Not the same thing."

"She'll get in the way."

"How?" Serra protested. "I'm not even a foot tall."

"Come on, Faron," said Loche. "She'll provide some entertainment at least."

"I'll be more than that." Serra flew up and hovered between them. "I have superior senses. I'm immune to spirit manipulation. Not to mention, sparks, flight, and ability to grow plants from anywhere."

"All that sounds like pretty good reasons to let her come along," said Olivier.

"Very well," sighed Faron. "She may accompany us." Everyone stared at the former major. "What?" He rolled his eyes. "Fine. Provided Jeth agrees, of course."

"Why not?" Jeth grinned. "Welcome to the team, Ser."

Serra giggled and flew a few celebratory circles in the air.

"Now, let's get a move on," Loche said, nodding ahead. "Standing here with this strange thing is making me nervous."

"Strange?" Serra turned up her nose. "I'll have you know we fairies had been here thousands of years before you urlings came along."

"I-I was speaking of the warping gate."

"Oh, well, alright then." She flew over to Jeth and plunked down on his shoulder while he mounted his horse.

With Jeth at their head, the task force rode through the warping gate and into Herran's new oasis.

The temple forest had flourished since Jeth had been there last. Long vines wound up every crumbling pillar and draped over thick tree branches. Various plants clawed up the stone walls, surrounding the team with blue-green foliage, unlike anything they had left behind in Fae'ren.

Not a single soul stood there to meet the four-man-one-fairy procession.

Who let us through then? Jeth immediately looked to his left, and a skeletal, tattooed figure jumped off the platform and disappeared into the overgrowth.

Jeth rode Torrent down the steps and honed all his senses. Four distinct heartbeats, his included, thrummed in his ears. More sounded somewhere to his left, or was it straight ahead—*no, everywhere!* "Look alive, men. I'm not sure we have friends here anymore."

Serra fluttered above him. "We're being watched, and whoever it is does not want us here."

"My bets are on the Magi of Sagorath." He gulped. "Have to say, I never thought I'd be dealing with them again."

After Nas'Gavarr's death, Jeth hadn't given a single thought to the fates of his loyal followers. Was it too much to hope that they'd scattered into the desert winds?

"Care to point them out to us, little pixie?" Olivier asked as he nocked an arrow.

Serra pointed a tiny finger straight ahead then spun around in a full circle.

"That'll do," Loche muttered, unsheathing his sword.

"We go back and take the long way." Faron turned his horse around.

Jeth reached out to Faron. "Hold on. We don't know how many there are. Or what they'll do." If they could get around them somehow, it would save them the twelve-day journey from Fae'ren to Herran.

The urling pursed his lips as the other two men readied their weapons and ventured into the cavernous hollow of the ruined temple.

Jeth called out in his fake Ludesan twang, "We don't want any trouble, just passing through." Vines stirred in the southwest. "Show yourselves."

His sharp eyes pinpointed the disturbance in the grass. Then came the smell of air before a lightning storm. "Water Mage, over there." Serra pointed to a crackling light between a tree's branches. "He's charging an attack."

Jeth let an arrow fly. A man grunted, and the light extinguished. "Thanks, Ser."

Leaves shook, and grass shifted all around them. Dozens of magi sprang from the bushes, wielding quarterstaffs.

"Back to Fae'ren!" Faron kicked his horse toward the still-active gate.

Jeth groaned with disappointment but turned to follow along.

A swarm of skeletal faces burst through the underbrush, forming a line between the task force and the gate. Some held fireballs or electrical charges in their palms, ready to release.

There were too many for the five of them to hope to fight on their own. "Everyone, stop!" Jeth commanded too late.

The Fire Mages combined their flames to create a burning wall and pushed it toward the retreating task force. Faron's bay reared, the fire licking its front hooves and making it screech. A sea of black and gray robes closed in, the wall of flame surrounding them.

Jeth struggled to take his spooked mare in hand as she shuddered in terror beneath him. "Where are you, Snake Eye?" he murmured.

Serra hid under Jeth's knitted cap and whispered in his ear. "Not off to a brilliant start, but your *Way* doesn't end here, Jeth."

"That's good to know, but can you say the same for the rest of our team?" Jeth put away his bow and raised both hands in the air. The others stared at him but reluctantly did the same. *There'll be a chance to escape later. Right now, stay alive.*

An elder magus stepped out in front of the rest, carrying a staff made from vertebrae topped with a skull far too small to belong to an adult. In a deep, gravelly voice, he said, "Who dares pass through the Overlord's sacred gate?"

Still with his hands in the air, Jeth replied, "We're Del'Cabrian traders looking to deliver our goods to Odafi."

The magus narrowed his ice-blue eyes. "We guard this gate to prepare for Nas'Gavarr's inevitable return, and you insult him by using it for your profiteering endeavors!"

An oddly familiar magus, among the others, distracted Jeth from the leader's rant. His eyes were dark, with angular bones protruding from his face, resembling a real skeleton. As soon as Jeth made eye contact, the thin magus slipped back into the crowd and disappeared. *Have you seen that one before?*

"Our apologies," said Olivier. "We didn't mean to offend your master. We'll just be on our way."

The older magus raised his voice. "You already offended us when you attacked first." He pointed to the bow at Olivier's side.

Flames edged closer from behind; the horses shook beneath their riders. "We had no choice. He was about to electrocute us," Jeth argued.

The magus dug his bone staff into the soft earth and yelled. "You must die."

"Wait!" cried Jeth.

The fire tightened, pressing them into one another. Soon the jars of oil they carried would catch, and everything, including them, would go up in flames.

"We could really use a Mage of our own right about now," Loche said, unsheathing his sword.

Jeth and Olivier readied their arrows. At least they could pick off an easy dozen between them before they burned alive.

Perfect. You're about to die right out the gate.

13

Broken Marble

(Seven and a half months ago)

A sharp crack shook the air.

The Siren effigy snapped at the ankles as draft horses labored forward. Severed from her magnificent base, the statue tipped. Her left wing met with the altar steps first, shattering, before the body smashed like a giant ornate vase, bursting into pieces across the cold stone. Her head rolled down the steps before settling face up, mouth agape in a perpetual song turned death cry.

The shadow harpy released a rumbling chortle under her breath. *"The Siren's rule has finally come to an end."*

"That it has." Vidya looked to the hunched over creature, perched upon the balustrade of the second-floor balconies overlooking the Grand Altar. Although draped in an uncanny shadow during the light of day, Vidya could make out her hands and feet like gnarled black roots, a protruding spine, and enormous wings tinted blood red. Her gaunt face remained hidden behind long, stringy strands, save her glowing yellow eyes that pierced the air between her and Vidya.

Vidya shuddered under the glare, unnerved and yet comforted by the creature's omnipresence. The shadow harpy had changed drastically since the annual sacrifice two weeks ago, but she was still invisible to everyone but Vidya.

Phrea stepped up to the balustrade next to her as the laborers piled marble pieces onto horse-drawn carts. Her silky black tresses had grown out to her shoulders but were still too short to tie up. Now the breeze sifted through her hair like an affectionate hand.

"You should be resting with the other squabs," said Vidya.

"Forget rest," Phrea scoffed. "I had enough of that the first time around."

Vidya glanced behind Phrea to inspect her feathers. From the tufts sprouting through the skin, she could tell her new black wings would be every bit as spectacular as her first pair. "I've been meaning to come by. How are the others?"

Phrea leaned over the balustrade with her thick forearms. "Oh, they'll get through it, just like we did. I can't believe it's finally happening. In a couple of months, we'll have the deadliest force the world has ever seen."

"We need more." Vidya's eyes were fixed on the horses carrying the carts of broken marble away. "After losing three to Ariston and his rebels . . . and at their most vulnerable." She squeezed the balustrade so hard it cracked. Just two days after the mass ritual, several military men, who had survived the slaughter, organized a massacre of their own at the squab estates. The death toll would have been far more had the attackers known that harpies had three lives each. They had managed to behead only two before their capture.

Phrea laid her hand over Vidya's. "I scheduled Ariston's execution for tomorrow. You may make it as painful as you wish."

A pleasurable chill danced up and down her spine in anticipation of punishing the former supreme commander. "The Harpy will have her due."

"Then we'll plunge the dagger into any one of those traitors and make our numbers an even hundred."

"We need far more than a hundred." Vidya stepped away from the balustrade and made way for the Citadel's south entrance. She had a meeting with Cosima in the War Council Chambers.

"Not to worry." Phrea kept pace. "We have more and more women coming forward every day and a prison full of ex-military men devoted to our cause. Not all men enjoyed living under siren influence, it turns out."

Vidya's knee-high boots clacked loudly over the tile as she walked. "I suppose patience is the virtue of the day. It's a shame I'm not very good at it."

Phrea raised her unibrow and chuckled. "Blessed Yasharra, you've waited this long. At any rate, I also come bearing news of a duller nature." She took out a roll of parchment from her back pocket and placed it in Vidya's hand. "A pigeon brought it to our estate this morning."

Vidya halted her step and stared down at the outline of a bodacious female figure carved into the red seal. "Rangardia." She broke the seal with quivering fingers and unrolled the parchment. Her cheeks went cold—she hadn't seen that handwriting in years. . . .

"This is addressed to the Mistress of Foreign Relations and Trade," Vidya said. A quick scan told her that although it was in Agustin's hand, it was indeed worded by his brother Ricardo. "Rangardia is wondering when their next bevy of brides will arrive."

"Didn't you already decree that no more of our women would have to marry those sex-starved buffoons?" Phrea scowled.

"They don't exactly know that yet," Vidya admitted, shuffling through the blank sheets provided. "And they want a reply soon."

"Until the Harplite can fly, I don't think we should inform them of our recent change in government."

"I agree. But . . ." Vidya rolled up the parchment, tucking it into her bodice. "Don't worry. I'll take care of this. You pick out the strongest three rebels and prepare them for our next sacrifice. They will replace the harpies they killed and then some."

"Right away, Anassa."

Hearing the word 'Anassa' gave Vidya a tingle deep within her chest like she was living a thousand years in the past when the Harpy's rule was absolute. She bid her friend adieu and continued into the War Council Chambers.

She found Cosima sashaying down the line of bronze helmed men and lightly grazing her hand across each of their faces as she passed. "Be extra vigilant, boys. There are traitors afoot who wish to dishonor Yasharra and her most hallowed daughter."

Each man's eyes sparkled with reverence. They nodded, speaking as one: "Yes, O Mistress, we will not let you down."

"Good," she cooed.

Vidya shifted her weight uncomfortably. These men were all who stood between her squabs and those who would avenge the old republic, and they paid fealty to only one siren.

The Citadel guards took to one knee and bowed their heads, spears pointed at the ceiling.

With a light clap, Cosima said, "Now, go man your posts."

"Yes, O Mistress."

The guards marched out of the room, leaving Cosima and Vidya alone. "Mistress . . . it's been so long since anyone's called me that." Cosima gave a sidelong smirk. "Never liked it. I want a new title."

Vidya crossed her arms. "I assumed you might."

"Since *Anassa* is already taken." She stifled a cheeky giggle with her hand. "What about Supreme Commander? I heard there is an opening."

Vidya held back her own chortle. As strange and flighty as the siren was, she could always lighten the mood in a way that Vidya appreciated. "As long as you continue to keep these men in line, you can call yourself whatever you please."

She clapped her hands repeatedly in front of her face. "Ooh, I like this unstructured method of rule. Then, my first act as Supreme Commander will be to show you my old laboratory and a new project we've been working on."

"We?"

Cosima opened a secret door in the room and beckoned Vidya with long, knobby fingers. "I've had a little helper. Come see, come see."

Vidya followed the prancing siren down the winding stone steps to the Citadel's cool, subterranean chambers. The silks of her dark blue gown flowed over each step like a trickling stream at night.

These secret chambers were located just above the mausoleum and insulated from all outside heat. Cool island winds were siphoned through ducts, keeping the area chilled.

Cosima unlocked an unassuming wooden door and entered the laboratory. "Make way for the Anassa of Credence," she sang.

Vidya spotted Daphne hunched over a desk with her nose in a massive text. Her infant wings wrapped in bandages, the wounds on her shoulder blades still red.

"Hi, Vidi," she said, not bothering to look up from the book.

Vidya looked around the gigantic room, unable to process most of what she saw. "So, this was the home of former Councilor Synthi."

"And where *femena mortum* was born," Cosima added.

A high-pitched screech echoed off the stone walls, drawing Vidya's attention to a caged enclosure tucked in the corner.

Four small monkeys scampered side to side. Cosima wiggled her fingers at them through the cage bars. "Hello, Renaldo, you're looking handsome this morning."

"Renaldo?" Vidya raised an eyebrow.

"That's the name on his collar," Daphne said, flipping the page. "They're from Rangardia. They've been infected with *femena mortum*, but as with men, it doesn't harm them. That way, the disease can be incubated and tested through their bloodstream. It's all documented in Synthi's notes that Cosima found. Fascinating, don't you think?"

"For you, I'm sure," commented Vidya.

Renaldo gave Cosima's fingers a sniff.

"I wouldn't touch them," Daphne warned.

"I used to all the time," she huffed. "I've taken the cure long ago; they can't infect me."

"According to Synthi, the cure from your day hasn't worked in over a decade. The disease has split into at least three different strains, and I'm still trying to work out which one each of them has, so . . ."

The siren snapped her finger back. "And that's why I entrust this laboratory to you now. Do treat it well."

"In that case," Vidya turned to Daphne, "your first priority should be to find a cure for the new strains. Then, when you're able to fly, go to Rangardia and test them on infected women there. Be discreet about it, though."

Vidya wondered how she would deal with her children's murderer and Credence's only ally now that she was in charge. She especially wasn't prepared for him to discover the source of the disease currently ravaging their female population.

"I'll do my best," said Daphne, finally standing up from the desk. "But there's something you should see, something developed more recently."

The thin squab beckoned to the other winged women, leading them past the monkey cages, through a set of sliding glass doors, and into a much brighter room. Sunlight seeped through slits near the ceiling, basking them in much-desired warmth. Rows of bird cages hung at shoulder level, filled with a dozen different species native to the island and the mainland.

Daphne stopped at a cage filled with island gulls, squawking obnoxiously. They were pure white with jet black heads and bright orange beaks, a species most commonly found on Credence's infinite coast that migrated north to Fae'ren during the hotter months. They were quite beautiful for such irritating creatures.

"What pathogen do these birds carry?" Vidya asked.

"Only the mainland's worst nightmare," Daphne replied as she opened a small cage door and took one of the birds in hand.

"The plague," Vidya murmured.

Cosima backed away. "Don't take that thing out!"

"Relax," Daphne told the frightened siren. "Harpies have resistance to all known pathogens."

"Oh," she trilled, not relaxed at all. "Then what am *I* worried about?" She continued to amble backward until she was at a comfortable distance from the infected birds.

"Did they really plan on using these gulls to spread the plague to the Herrani?" Vidya asked as she dragged her forefinger over the bird's soft black head.

Daphne fed it pellets from the feeder nearby. "The ones in this cage carry a pathogen most closely resembling the First Wave."

"The one from one hundred years ago? That can't be . . ." Vidya turned to Cosima, raising a questioning eyebrow.

The siren ruffled her wings and shrugged. "Our grandmothers only meant to protect us with a cure in the event of a Del'Cabrian invasion. They didn't invent the disease."

Vidya sighed a small relief. It was painful enough to learn the old republic was responsible for thousands of female deaths in Rangardia, and she didn't want millions of mainlanders added to that number.

"But they did, in a way." Daphne placed the bird back in its cage. "According to their notes, they managed to create a pathogen much milder than its deadly cousin, one that doesn't result in death."

The two women's confused glares urged Daphne onward. "You see, they theorized that the first pathogen derived from birds not unlike these, then somehow jumped to hens, then humans in Ludesa Province likely before the Confederation Period. Over the years, Del'Cabrians developed a natural resistance, so when they eventually invaded Fae'ren . . ."

"The Fae'ren died in droves, yes. We know, Daphne."

"Well, the First Wave ran its course, and the Fae'ren left alive showed a similar tolerance. Our grandmothers learned this and developed that strain, making it weaker. They then infected themselves with it so that they didn't die when exposed to the original."

"So, we have a cure for the First Wave. Big deal."

Daphne's aquamarine eyes lit up. "But the plague should never have returned to those previously infected populations in the Second

Wave . . . or at least not as strongly. Because they had already been infected with the first." Daphne scuttled out of the bird room and back into the laboratory. She flipped through one of the research volumes on her desk.

"But it did return." Vidya closed the sliding doors to the bird room. "Deadlier than ever before."

Daphne nodded. "And it was able to spread easily between traditionally isolated communes, something I always found strange." She pointed to a paragraph dated about twenty years ago. "Look. Right here: 'Fae subjects exhibit symptoms similar to the First Wave. The death rate has doubled and even infects some urling subjects, but at a much lower rate. Strain to cause death in urling populations unsuccessful.'"

"The Second Wave," Vidya gasped, "that was Credence." She snapped her head around to Cosima, nonchalantly perusing the other volumes on the shelves. "Cosima, you must have known this!"

She looked up. "Hmm? Oh, the plague resurgence? Afraid not. That was all Synthi. My hands were quite literally tied at the time." She put up her hands and wiggled her fingers.

Vidya felt a twinge in her gut that she wasn't prepared for. "This has gone on for generations. We infected thousands and sat on the cure to protect ourselves from an imperialist threat that never came."

"What started as a means to protect ourselves from foreign pathogens resulted in the creation of our island's greatest weapon. And here you thought it was harpies." Cosima giggled into her hands again. "Though, I agree, creating a plague to wipe out the entire urling race is a tad overkill."

"That's the understatement for all time," Vidya spat.

"You take issue with casualties on the mainland decades past, but not with the slaughter of our own sisters two weeks ago?" said Cosima, eyelashes fluttering.

"Are you having regrets?" Vidya glared at the siren, arms crossed.

"I think what she means," Daphne chimed, "is who cares about mainlanders?"

"Ah, thank you, Daphne, well put." Cosima smiled and nodded.

Vidya understood where the two women were coming from, and any other time, she'd be right there with them, but her gut continued to twist. And she knew precisely why. Credence was the reason Jeth's parents were dead. The reason hundreds of orphan children were shunned and abandoned at birth. *Yasharra really is the enemy of the Crannebeatha.*

Vidya had hardly thought about that annoying Fae'ren male since she retrieved the dagger. Had he even survived their last altercation?

"He's not your friend. He will always be against us, just like all of Del'Cabria is against us," rasped the shadow harpy, sitting on the counter next to Cosima.

"How can you know that?" she whispered back.

"How can I know what?" Daphne replied in the shadow's stead.

Vidya shook her head. "Nothing, I just wonder if we should destroy those birds. If word of this gets out to the rest of the world, then surely the mainland will have every reason to declare war on us."

"Or we hang onto the diseases and their respective cures," said Daphne. "That way, if anyone attacks for any reason, we have a lethal weapon that can never be used against us."

"We need not resort to disease," Vidya scoffed. "Our Harplite is mere months from being ready."

"The Third Wave has already started. Before my first transition, I had orders from the War Council to test it in the southern Fae'ren communes, remember? It's too late to backtrack."

"Listen to your harpy sister," the shadow whispered in her ear. *"You were not there when Del'Cabria nearly destroyed us. It will happen again if you are not ready. The true power of the Harplite is not brute strength in battle or windstorms in flight, but resistance to all things that devour men from within."*

Tremors traveled up and down Vidya's spine. The shadow harpy had proven time and time again to know the hearts of men, even those miles away. She had to trust her, now more than ever. Vidya gulped before saying, "Very good. Two cures. Each one will have their respective empires eating out of our hands."

"Don't forget the Herrani," the shadow sang in a whisper.

"What about the Herrani?" she asked aloud.

This time, Cosima answered her. "They still believe the Siren Council is in power and have honored the treaty thus far."

"And you were banished from the island and in Nas'Gavarr's custody when you killed him; therefore, you were not acting in Credence's name at the time," added Daphne.

"That's true. Not to mention most of the tribes still believe he's alive, being 'immortal' and everything." Vidya made quotations with her index fingers around the word immortal.

The women's cackles echoed off the cold stone walls, but the shadow harpy made Vidya's laughter catch in her throat. *"Not for long. His son seeks to avenge his father, and he knows you're responsible. He will not be willing to honor the treaty when he realizes his father's murderer rules here now. In fact, he has set out to rebuild his naja army to hunt you down."*

Vidya gulped, turning back to Daphne and Cosima. "Nevertheless, we should perceive them as a potential threat, especially if his son or sister take power. They may want the Bloodstone Dagger back, and under no circumstances can we lose it to them. I say we deal with the desert tribes first."

"I agree. Strike now while they're leaderless," said Cosima.

Daphne nodded, and Vidya took her leave. Discomfort tugged at her gut. They were surrounded by enemies, outside and within. She had to be at her most vigilant until her Harplite was complete. That also meant keeping Rangardia as an ally was paramount.

Upon leaving the Citadel, she flew to the siren estates in the south hills. The massive house Vidya and Demeter had once called home now belonged to Vidya, Phrea, and Daphne. The other homes were occupied by the rest of the squabs, so they could enjoy a life of siren comforts while they waited for their harpy wings to fully form.

She flew through the open terrace window of her house and made her way to the basement levels. She stopped at a locked door.

An ex-prisoner turned guard, stood watch. "O Anassa." He bowed and unlocked the chamber door.

Vidya entered the small living chambers that once belonged to Demeter's breeder Rufios. He had spent most of his nights in his mistress's rooms but had been here the night Vidya and her followers stormed the estate.

His blood still stained the white marble at the foot of the bed where Vidya had no choice but to smash his head in. Hopelessly enthralled by Demeter, the young breeder fought viciously to protect her. Her other breeder Camdus, however, had the good sense to flee.

Closing the door behind her, Vidya walked through the small beam of light shining through the tiny, square window. Chains clinked together and scraped against the floor. Demeter sprang at Vidya from the darkness, but the chains around her neck and ankles jerked her back. She fought and strained, lunging forward again with newfound wrath, her hands locked within Cosima's old iron gauntlets.

Vidya squatted just out of reach of Demeter's blunt metal stumps.

She cocked her head. "Why, Demi, it's only me . . . your sister."

Demeter flapped her clipped wings in vain, their once blue sheen tarnished by black soot from the fireplace. She screeched unintelligible words through the metal gag mask strapped to the bottom half of her face.

"I'm sorry, but I can't hear you through that thing," Vidya continued to taunt.

Tears filled Demeter's eyes as she fell back against the wall in breathless defeat.

"I assure you your family is fine." Vidya stood back up and aimlessly explored the room. "Your son lives with your husband now, and your daughter is with the other young sirens in the northeast sector. It is important to keep them far from the male population until they can learn their place in this new republic." Vidya couldn't abide by the slaughter of children in her rise to power. Besides, a certain number of sirens were needed in the future. If they showed signs of rebelling in their adulthood, they would be dealt with at that time. "I suppose it's not really a republic anymore. What would you call it?" Vidya pursed her lips in thought. "A queendom? Ah, there'll be time to figure that out later."

Demeter glared at her sister through greasy curls plastered to her forehead. She exhaled through her snot-filled nostrils in short, wet bursts. The siren screamed behind the mask until her shoulders slumped in defeat, and she slid down the wall, landing heavily.

Vidya scraped a wooden chair across the floor and straddled it, resting her arms over the back. "I never envisioned things turning out this way, you know."

Demeter mumbled something in response, but Vidya ignored it.

"I just wanted to present Nas'Gavarr's head to the Council, receive my accolades, and allow Mother to rest in peace. Then, I would continue to serve the Republic with my two harpy sisters for the foreseeable future. Who knows? Maybe I would have succumbed to the idea of taking a Crede husband and having the bare minimum of two children. Finally birth something for the island that birthed all of us. Isn't that what you and Mother used to go on about?"

This time, Demeter's reply was a single tear running down her face.

"Hmm, looks like you don't want to talk about Mother today. Oh well . . ." She pulled the parchment out from between her breasts. "I'm here as your Anassa anyway. You received this from the Emperador of

Rangardia." She unrolled the parchment and read it aloud.

She placed one of the blank sheets on the floor in front of Demeter, then got up to find an inkwell in Rufios's desk drawer. Not locating it right away, Vidya grumbled, "Come on, where's the quill? The breeder knew how to write, didn't he?"

Demeter's chest heaved. It had been apparent from her overblown reaction to his death that she held affections for Rufios far beyond what was expected. It wasn't any wonder why her husband stopped living with her soon after the new man arrived, although it wasn't polite society to speak of his absence.

A few moments later, Vidya located the quill in a bottom drawer. "Ah, there it is." She placed the writing implements next to the paper then returned to her seat.

Demeter looked down at the rolled-up parchment then back to Vidya. She shrugged and shook her head.

"Oh, silly me." Vidya got up to unstrap Demeter's right gauntlet.

Demeter stretched her fingers, then scratched her head and face, wherever she could reach.

After a few moments, Vidya said, "Is that better? Now, you will reply to Agustin. Tell him Rangardia will no longer receive Crede brides."

Demeter's eyes widened.

"That's right. Tell him that he and his administrador, and whoever else among his brothers he wishes to bring, shall come to the Citadel to negotiate a new alliance. One stronger than ever before."

Demeter picked up the quill and started writing. Before she could sign off, Vidya inputted. "Oh, and maybe mention that Xenith has passed away suddenly and that at this time, we cannot yet determine who the new Archon will be." She thought it best not to give the Rangarders a chance to refuse the meeting if they had any inkling of what occurred.

Demeter's fingers stiffened over the quill. In a flash, she smacked the ink and paper to the side, spilling the black liquid onto the beige rug.

Vidya sighed. "Now look what you did. It will take you ages to scrub that out."

Her sister stared at the stain, squeezing the quill in her whitened grip—as if suddenly reminded of the horrific events that brought her to her present state.

"Perhaps I should pay a visit to my niece. I imagine she'd be in need of different accommodations," said Vidya. "Do you think the northeast sector is fine, or would the north*west* suit her better?" The northwest part of the city was Credence's most impoverished, populated mostly by single men working as laborers, many of them petty criminals paying their debt to the Republic. Women rarely ventured there on their own volition, and for a siren to go anywhere near it would be unthinkable.

Demeter's whole body shook as more tears poured out, but she made no move to write.

Vidya leaned forward. "You told the Council that I threatened the lives of your children, knowing full well what I went through with mine," she hissed. "At least there is a chance you may see their sweet faces again. Be grateful that I am not the monster you made me out to be."

Demeter blinked a few times, then warily crawled across the rug and picked up the inkwell with a shaking hand. Vidya removed the spoiled parchment and placed a second blank sheet on the floor. "This is the last one, so don't blunder it up."

Careful not to smear ink onto the new page with her stained fingers, Demeter returned to writing.

14

Harpy's Restraint

Demeter strode into the Council Chambers with three Rangarders in tow. She struggled to keep her fake smile on her face as she stopped short of where the podium used to be.

Vidya watched from the hidden stairwell that led to the councilor's exclusive entrance. Phrea, Daphnc, and Cosima waited silently at her back.

Señor Ricardo looked around the empty space. "This place has changed. Where are all the seats?"

"We've taken the opportunity to do some . . . remodeling," Demeter said, primping her red wig.

"Will the rest of the Council be joining us?" Ricardo asked.

Demeter's eyelashes fluttered. "I'm afraid not, Señor."

"Again, Señora Demeter," said a man with a gravelly voice, one that made Vidya's heart lurch in her chest. "The Empire grieves for the loss of your Archon."

"As does all of Credence." Demeter cast her eyes down to the floor.

Ricardo said, "As you may appreciate, we are eager to renegotiate the terms of our alliance. But, since your republic remains leaderless, it may be better to hold off these matters until after an election, yes?"

"That won't be necessary, Señor," said Demeter. "We are far from leaderless. In fact, the reason we are revisiting the alliance now is because of a recent change in our governing structure."

Time to make my entrance, thought Vidya.

She sauntered into her new throne room. She had retired her brown leathers for armor over a long military tunic complete with knee-high boots and armored shin guards. Her bronze half-helm allowed her thick brown curls to fall down her back while keeping the gnarled strands off her face.

Demeter, involved in idle chitchat, spun around with a nervous jolt. "Oh! Emperador, Señors." She made a sweeping motion with her arm. "I'd like to present Vidya, Anassa of Credence." The other three women followed close behind. "These are Commanders Phrea and Daphne of the Harplite and Supreme Commander Cosima."

"Anassa?" Agustin murmured.

"Thank you all for coming here today." Vidya could hardly keep the disdain out of her voice as she eyed all three men in the room, first Jiménez, Ricardo, and finally, after swallowing the lump in her throat, Agustin.

His dark eyes shone in awe of his estranged wife, standing four steps above him, and yet she still broke into a cold sweat under her armored corset.

Like Ricardo, Agustin had aged considerably, though he hid it well. The only signs of his fifty years were the deep lines around his eyes and the gray peppering his fine mustache. His hair—what was left of it—was hidden beneath a wig of silky black ringlets, cascading over a frock coat with red and gold embroidery. He wore a frilly cravat and knee-length breeches that hugged his thighs as thick as horse's hindquarters that briefly reminded Vidya of his other attribute that could be compared to a horse. No matter how muddled the Emperador's memory had become, he never forgot how to dress.

He took out a vial of clear liquid from his inside coat pocket, pulled out a tiny cork, and tipped two drops onto his tongue.

Still taking those, I see. She scowled at him and his weakness.

Rangardian drops were a common pastime among men of the Empire. They believed it enhanced masculine bravado and virility. It was meant to assist in many male activities, from competitive sport to lovemaking. And it also numbed the pain that such things often brought.

She broke eye contact with Agustin and caught the others' gazes instead. Ricardo licked his dry lips while the young Capitán General Jiménez stared up at her wide-eyed as if he were about to bolt out of the room.

Vidya sat down in the Archon's seat, now the sole chair in the chambers. "Apologies for not preparing you in advance for the recent change, but our negotiations are simply too important to wait for the dust to settle."

Ricardo huffed through his narrow nostrils and glared at Demeter. "Was this a change welcomed by you and the Council?"

The siren's wings ruffled. She looked to Vidya, who raised a stern eyebrow, silently reminding her of what would become of her children if she weren't compliant.

"Change is unavoidable," replied Demeter. "But I will leave you to your business. Do give my regards to the rest of your family, Señors."

She put her hand out for Agustin to kiss, but Vidya loudly cleared her throat. "There is no need to touch her. The Siren rules here no longer." Agustin paused as he gave his attention back to his wife. Demeter bit her trembling lip and let her hand down. With a curtsey to the harpies, she took swift steps out of the chambers and into the hands of her guard escorts.

"Vidya," Agustin said in breathless wonderment. "By the Cursed Isle of Cordos, it has been a long time." The Emperador took hastened strides toward her. "There is so much I wish to—"

Vidya shot her palm up. "You are not to approach."

"Do you not miss me as I do you?"

"Our reunion must wait," she said coldly. "I invited you here to act as Rangardia's sovereign, not my husband."

Ricardo placed his hand on Agustin's puffed shoulder. "She's no longer your wife, Brother. She is a harpy, pure in form."

"I don't care," he spat.

"You know what harpies are capable of." Ricardo cast daggers at Vidya with his gaze. "We should leave this place at once."

The adminstrador pulled on his brother's sleeve, but Agustin yanked it away. "First, we shall listen to what she has to say. Do you not care about the Agreement?"

"There is no Agreement . . ." Ricardo lifted his head to meet Vidya's eye. "Is there?"

"No," she stated bluntly. "I'm offering something better." She crossed one leg over the other and leaned on the armrest. "A chance for your empire to regain what it has lost. To have your women elevated to the status they once enjoyed before *femena mortum* ravaged their wombs and stole their lives."

Ricardo gave a disingenuous closed-mouth grin. "I see. You claim to have a cure for all our empire's ills, uh? Let me guess, all you require in return is thousands of our strongest men to sacrifice to your goddess."

At those words, the shadow harpy materialized behind the administrador and placed long clawed fingers over his shoulders. *"Hypocrite. He cares not for his own men and never has. He deceived us before, and he's doing it now."* Vidya recalled her shadow's many warnings of Ricardo. He had played ignorant when she confronted him about Nas'Gavarr taking warp stone from the Venerra District mine. Later on, he had ushered Nas'Gavarr through their central gate and into Credence to make the treaty that saw her banished and her friends de-winged. *Never again!*

Vidya smiled. "For a chance to bring back your female population, I'd think you'd gladly sacrifice as many men as it took."

"You assume I believe you," Ricardo said. "You have not been in power long enough to develop such a cure, and if the Council had it, why would they not bring it forth earlier?"

Vidya straightened in her chair. "Because the Council saw no benefit in Rangardian women returning to good health, only in preventing the disease from infecting our own populace."

All three men stepped back in shock. Ricardo shook his head while rubbing his black goatee. "That can't be true. To allow innocent women to suffer . . ."

Vidya continued, "Believe me, Señor, my harpy blood boils over at their crimes against womankind. We've since punished them severely."

Ricardo shook with indignation. "But not until after the decades of military protection the Agreement bought you."

"The Siren is cowardly, only capable of following her own self-interest, but the Harpy aims to set things right, no matter the cost. Under her rule, we need all wingless women here, to become future harpies, not Rangardian wives."

Jiménez spoke up, his voice soft for such a hardened military man. "Then you will no longer require our military protection, Señora?"

"Until the Harplite reaches adequate numbers, we require Rangardian support in the battles to come."

"What battles?" asked Jiménez. "Did you not carve out peace with the Overlord of Herran and, by extension, Del'Cabria? What has Credence to fear?"

"Nas'Gavarr is dead, and his son Saf'Ryeem is sure to take up his mantle. He and his naja horde have terrorized the desert tribes in desperate attempts to hold power, but the Bahazur of Odafi are in a position to take the Herrani Tribe Lands for the merchants."

"Have you had spies in the desert after the treaty? We know nothing of this." Jiménez narrowed his bulbous eyes on Vidya, then glanced at Ricardo with a questioning gaze.

"I don't require spies, Capitán. The Harpy holds all knowledge of her enemies. We must push the desert back into its chaotic tribal state, and Rangardia will regain her dominance in the region."

"You'd have us declare war on Odafi after nearly four hundred years of peace?" Ricardo exclaimed, his arms making sweeping motions. "You are every manner of vile if you think we will throw that all away for a supposed—"

The back of Agustin's hand smacked Ricardo's cheek so hard his head threw back. He held his face, growing red with mortification.

"That is no way to speak to your Emperatriz!" the Emperador exclaimed.

"Agustin . . ." Ricardo sputtered.

The shadow harpy screeched with laughter. *"Still so devoted. It's as if he doesn't remember what happened to your poor boys."*

Vidya took a deep breath and dug her nails into her palms. "There will be no peace, no trade with Odafi as long as the naja continue to exist. Ryeem is not about to return them to the earth anytime soon. We must destroy him."

"Then fly there and destroy him yourselves. Why do you need us to take Odafi?" asked Jiménez.

Vidya replied, "The Merchant Council will take his place, and their power will only increase as they bring stability to the region. We cannot allow that."

"Odafi is the center of wealth for all desert tribes and could well surpass Del'Cabria in the next century," added Phrea. "If Odafi falls, all tribes fall with it. An invasion will be the best way to draw out those seeking power and show the world that the Immortal Serpent is truly dead."

"Leaving the perfect opportunity for Del'Cabria to gallop in and take advantage of that instability," said the capitán general. "For decades, they've longed to bring those tribes to heel. They will surely challenge us for the ports and be seen as liberators for it."

"Not if it is Rangardia who occupies it," Daphne said. "Del'Cabria will not risk warring against you for fear of a disease that they believe is incurable."

"How do we know you can cure it?" Ricardo pressed more subdued as his brother watched him from the corner of his eye.

"We have a cure for the oldest strain already. Once I have access to some infected women, we will cure the remaining strains before the year is out," said Daphne.

"Give us the first cure now, and we may consider your request," offered Ricardo.

"Oh, Señors," Cosima cooed, sauntering down the stairs to address the Rangarders at their level. "What happened to the passionate empire of old? The one that conquered the twelve islands you call home, most of Odafi, and half of Ankarr? Why push forth for territory of that size if not for the women you used to worship?" She sashayed between Jiménez, then Ricardo until finally stopping in front of Agustin. "Is war not a worthy price for saving the few women you have left?" She looked up at Vidya on her throne, inviting Agustin to do the same.

Ricardo answered for him, "Apologies, Señoras, but we will not agree to such lunacy without more assurances. Cure or no cure, we have a female shortage *now*. We'd sooner maintain our original Agreement at this present time. Come, Brothers." The administrador spun on his heel and went for the doors. Jiménez turned to follow, but Agustin hesitated.

Vidya clenched her teeth, cursing Yasharra for letting it come to this. "There's more."

Ricardo spun around and took heated steps forward. "What more can you offer us besides flying into the sun?"

Vidya rose from her seat and walked down each step with Agustin locked in her gaze.

"Husband?" Vidya's voice softened, intentionally drawing in the worthless cur.

"Yes, my love."

"Our nations should be as one." She swallowed the bile in her throat. "Deploy your armada and take Odafi for me, and I will return to your side. We will rule both Credence and Rangardia together, Yasharra be willing."

"Y-you'd be mine again?"

Vidya put out her hand for him to take. "Yes, Agustin. And your uninfected men will have countless desert widows to marry until the full benefits of the cure are reached, provided they consent, of course."

He bit his lip and looked to Ricardo, who shook his head in warning.

Ignoring his brother's silent pleas, Agustin took Vidya's hand in his. They were cold and sweaty, and she clenched her other fist at her side to keep from scratching out his eyes.

He bowed and put her hand to his lips while focusing his dark, languid gaze upon her. "Thank you for this second chance. I promise to be a more honorable husband to you than I've been in the past. You are good to forgive me as I have forgiven you."

An image of a blood-filled porcelain tub flashed in her mind over and over again. The marble pillars spun around her as she struggled to remain upright. *How could he not remember them?*

"I will do everything in my power to make up for lost time," he continued through her dizzying haze. "Rangardia will fight for Credence."

She slipped her fingers out of his. "And may Rangardia return to her former glory."

As much as Vidya loathed the idea of sharing an island with her children's murderer, she put up the Emperador and his brothers in the guesthouse her mother reserved for foreign diplomats. They had much to discuss in the days to come.

At sunset, the Anassa and her commanders retired in their own estate. They all sat under a great gazebo with harpy squabs sparring in the courtyard beyond. Attractive male servants wandered back and forth with trays of fruit and sweets. All those sirenless breeders needed to make themselves useful somehow.

Vidya waved away a bunch of grapes offered to her, lost in her own thoughts. Her attention settled on Demeter a few feet away. She watched her scrub the gazebo tiles. Her feathers had been plucked almost bare in preparation for the upcoming sacrifice that would bring her Harplite to an even hundred. Then it would be time to fill her dagger with another three body's worth of blood. *If only the three Rangarders in that guest house could serve as such.* She immediately shook her head at the thought, despite every beat of her heart urging her in that direction.

Phrea flopped down on the lounge next to Vidya, chewing on cured pork. "I applaud you, Vidi," she said with her mouth full. "The way you had the Emperador melting in your palm . . ."

"The passion in that man's eyes," tittered Cosima, wringing out her wet hair upon returning from her splash in the fountains. "I didn't know you had it in you, frankly."

"Had what in me?" Vidya asked with a scowl.

Phrea nudged her with her elbow. "She means you must be as wild as a Rangarder in the bedroom."

Vidya's cheeks burned, but she forced a wry grin on her face anyway. *If only they knew how difficult it was to face him today. They'd be praising me even more . . . or perhaps they'd think I'm as out of touch as he is.*

She accidentally met Demeter's eyes. She thought she noticed a look of sympathy, but Demeter immediately turned her head back down to her cleaning.

Cosima splayed herself out on a plush chair. She selected a handful of grapes from the passing breeder, but not before lustfully eyeing his well-oiled musculature. The oiling had been done upon her request. "Do you actually intend to marry that giant peacock?"

"She's already married to him," Daphne said, curled up in another chair reading old medical journals on pathogens.

Cosima popped a few grapes into her mouth. "I mean, you'd *stay* married to him?"

Vidya nodded.

"Makes sense, I suppose," the siren sighed. "It will keep our alliance strong until their armada smashes through the Odafi ports. And there is that minor matter of succession. Can harpies even bear children?"

Not taking her eyes from her journal, Daphne responded, "Yes, they can have children, although there are few recorded instances of them giving birth."

Cosima looked up at the ceiling and giggled. "Can you imagine? Little screaming harpy babies fluttering about the buttresses."

"Harpies can only be made. Any children born of a harpy would be human."

"Children and succession plans are the farthest thing from my mind right now," Vidya rubbed her throbbing temples. "I'm more concerned with getting our Harplite trained for flight and battle. We need to be prepared to strike Herran as soon as Rangardia takes the ports."

"Well," Phrea said. "We aren't democratic anymore, so you *do* have to think about succession like any other queen."

"I don't know about you two," Daphne said, tossing her book on the cushion beside her. "But since becoming a harpy . . . the first and second time, I haven't thought once about intercourse."

"Did you ever think about it as a human?" Phrea chortled.

Daphne stuck her tongue out at her friend then continued, "I may not feel like a sexual being anymore, but I *lust* for a blood sacrifice—to make more of us."

The harpies nodded silently. Vidya remembered how satisfied—how proud she felt the night she sacrificed Maramus and five Rangarders to make Phrea and Daphne the first time. She also remembered the despair when the executioner cut away their wings before her eyes. Like losing her children all over again.

Cosima put her palms together and cooed, "Aw, it's kind of beautiful when you think about it."

"Say no more," Phrea slapped Vidya on her knee. "We can be your babies. And as your firstborn—"

"I'm the firstborn this time," Daphne corrected.

"As more or less your firstborn," Phrea continued. "I get to stay up as late as I want."

"And I get to eat all the chocolate I want," Cosima joined.

The harpies stopped to stare at the old siren. Her blue eyes darted between the three of them as she went for a glass of wine. "I know I'm not one of you. I just like chocolate."

Phrea released a mighty guffaw. Even Daphne cracked a toothy grin as Cosima took down the rest of her wine in a long gulp. Watching the deep red droplets run down her chin churned images of bloody water overflowing the sides of that porcelain tub.

Vidya shot up to her feet. "Excuse me, ladies."

"It's still early." Phrea got up off the lounge as well.

Demeter caught her eye again. She looked as though she wanted to speak, but with her metal gag locked in place, all she could do was stare right through her.

Smoothing her hair off her forehead, Vidya said, "I have an invasion to plan for tomorrow and potential male uprisings to quash after that. But don't cease your merrymaking on my account. You've all earned a night of relaxation."

Vidya strode out of the gazebo and past Demeter, leaving the cackling winged women to themselves. She longed for the seclusion of her bedchambers. They were the ones her mother and Demeter's father once shared, then later Demeter and her pets. Now it was

Vidya's alone.

She unclasped her corset, freeing her strained ribs as she let it fall to the floor with a clank. After removing her boots and tunic, she threw on a silk robe and poured herself a cup of wine from the decanter at the bedside table. She downed the entire cup in a few big gulps, then crossed the room and caught herself in the vanity mirror. Demeter's wigs and other accessories still cluttered the table, many of them having belonged to their mother, so Vidya didn't have the heart to get rid of them just yet.

She released her hair and primped it, surprised by how long and frayed it had gotten. She attempted to smooth out the knotted ends with Demeter's hairbrush. Vidya usually never put much effort into her hair, realizing at a young age that nothing could be done for it. Only her mother had the patience and the iron will required to tame her wild mane.

Memories of Agustin's hands getting lost in her curls while making passionate love gave her pause. The image gave way, replaced by her own screams and the violent tug at the top of her scalp as he dragged her down the halls. His siblings had only watched, and the servants pretended they didn't notice.

The brush caught a stubborn knot, and the metal bristles snapped. She winced as a clump of hair tore at the root. She felt a violent urge to throw the brush at her reflection, only to catch herself as the door creaked open and a slim male figure slipped into her bedroom.

She first thought it was one of her guards, but he was too fully clothed. Spinning around, ready to drive the bristled end of the brush into the intruder's jugular, Vidya froze, her mind struggling to process Ricardo's presence before her.

"You dare come to me here," she growled. "How did you get past the guards?"

Ricardo's eyes darted into the hall before carefully closing the door behind him. "Is that what you call those shirtless oafs? Not difficult to get past them. Although, I do have a knack for going unnoticed, as you recall." He raised one dark eyebrow.

"I don't." Vidya shuddered, put down the brush, and clutched her robes tighter together.

"You, on the other hand . . ." He pointed to her wings pressed behind her back. "Looks like you finally got what you wanted, but at what cost?"

She expelled a sharp burst of air from her nose. "Who needs guards? I can throw you out myself." She took quick steps forward.

"Please." Ricardo raised both hands to brace her. "Just listen to what I have to say."

She stopped short but was unsure why. "Does Agustin know where you are right now?"

"Of course not."

Vidya shifted her weight and crossed her arms. "Whatever it is you wish to tell me can wait until our meeting tomorrow."

Ricardo shook his head. "What are you planning, Vidya? We both know it's not to return to your husband's arms in blissful matrimony."

"I want his armada."

"Alright. So he wins you those ports, the desert tribes implode, and then what happens to him?"

"It's just the two of us, Ricardo. Stop acting like your only concern is your brother's welfare. You'd do a much better job as Emperador without that senile prick dragging you through the mud alongside him."

Ricardo clenched his fists until they were red. Any moment Vidya expected one of them to fly toward her, but he would have to be as insane as his brother to attempt such a thing. "I will not betray him. There is no bond stronger than—"

"—one between brothers, blah, blah, blah. Heard it all before." Vidya turned her back to Ricardo and sat down at her vanity. "Repeating that tiresome mantra will not change the fact that you *did* betray him." She lifted her eyes to meet his in the mirror's reflection, expecting to find his hot gaze boring through her and to hear his venomous retort. Instead, his eyes stayed glued to the floor. No words escaped him.

She turned around on her stool, forcing him to look straight at her. "It's not your *brotherly bond* that makes you loyal to him. It's fear."

Ricardo shook his head furiously. "You know nothing."

"You're afraid of him. I can see it because it's the same fear he instilled in me—in everyone around him." She got up from her stool, rapidly closing the distance between them. "That's why you won't do what must be done."

"What must be done?" he spat. "I risked my life and position to help you. Do you not remember how you begged me?"

Vidya scoffed. "Is that how you remember it? Don't flatter yourself."

He took a hesitant step forward, voice softening, pleading. "And I come to you . . . in your bedchambers to beg you now . . . leave Agustin alone. Abandon this lunacy. Please." His hand landed on her arm, and she jerked it away.

A sickening lump formed in Vidya's throat. Her stomach heaved at the memories Ricardo roused. One of them from seven years ago:

She lay shivering on the cold lavatory floor, sticky with blood. Agonizing waves came over her again. Her screams echoing off the tiles made her ears ring, but she couldn't stop. She clutched her lower abdomen, clenched her teeth as what remained of her unborn child was expelled from her body. The contractions ceased for a time, and Vidya exhaled broken, sobbing breaths.

Then came a rap upon the door. "Emperatriz? Is that you in there?"

She sniffed back her flood of tears. "I'm fine . . ." she squeaked as her body contracted again. Her cries burst forth, and the doors burst open.

Ricardo's jaw dropped, and his eyes filled with horror. It must have been a dreadful sight, but she couldn't bring herself to look upon the gore beneath her. "By the Cursed Isle of Cordos," he murmured, white as a sheet.

He bent down to help Vidya to her feet. The loss of blood caused her to fall against his chest. "I can't . . . I can't leave her!" she cried, still unable to look upon the clumps of blood and flesh on the floor.

Ricardo scooped Vidya up into his arms and whisked her out of the lavatory. "Let her rest; let her rest."

He brought her into the bedroom and set her down on the armchair, paying no mind to the blood staining his lapels. Vidya buried her tear-drenched face into her brother-in-law's shoulder. "Yasharra, my baby . . ."

Ricardo crouched awkwardly in front of the chair, holding her for a time, then finally said, "I'll fetch someone to clean you up." He let her go and stood.

"Ricardo." She grasped his coat sleeve. "You know how this happened. You saw what he did to me . . . over there." She looked to the balcony. The day before, she, Agustin, and Ricardo had enjoyed a pleasant lunch. Until she made the mistake of telling Agustin she was pregnant with a girl, or so the partera predicted. She had hoped the news would soften him, curb his violent outbursts for a while. However, all girls of Crede women belonged to the Republic and could never be raised in the Empire. Why did she think he'd take the news well?

Ricardo clenched his quivering fist, half-stained with Vidya's blood—or rather her daughter's. "What would you have me do?"

"All I need is two of his children, then I can go home. Please, Ricardo. Agustin listens to you."

He tugged his arm out of Vidya's grasp. "Not as much as you think." He bit his cheek. "I might be able to send a message to your mother without him knowing. I'm sure she could arrange for you to—"

"No! She cannot know about this, do you understand?" Another wave of pain further hollowed her womb. Upon it subsiding, she said, "A Crede woman must always honor the Agreement. All you need to do is speak to your brother."

"Don't you think if I could reason with him, I would have already?" he said in a frantic whisper, glancing around the room to ensure the subject of conversation hadn't appeared out of nowhere. "I'm sorry, Señora. Here in Rangardia, the bond between brothers is unbreakable. It is his interests I must uphold above all others."

"There are only two ways I leave this palace. I bear Agustin two healthy children, or I hurl myself off that balcony. I will not give that madman five whole years of my life only to return home with nothing!"

He fell to his knees before her and shook her. "Don't speak of such things!"

Vidya let out a weak smile while staring out at the clouds. "You can tell everyone that I was just a silly girl who wanted wings so badly she tried to fly. . . ."

"I owe you nothing," Vidya snapped, catapulting her mind back to the present. "It was your hand that poisoned him, not mine."

"I administered just enough curare to get you through your pregnancy with Alonz as promised. It should have stopped there, but you had to steal it from my study, subjecting him to repeated paralysis until Spyros was born."

"And why was it still there, hiding in plain sight?" Vidya cocked her head. "You could have disposed of it after its first use, but you didn't." Ricardo bit the inside of his cheek and looked away. Vidya paced around the trembling administrador. "You thought you'd have to use it again. You told me how hard curare gourd is to come by—"

"No!" he hissed. "Once Agustin held his firstborn son in his arms, I saw the change in him. He would never have hurt you again."

"Because I wouldn't give him the chance," she exclaimed. "Are you so delusional that you actually thought your brother wouldn't revert back to the animal that he is? I used that poison against him for the same reason you didn't pour it down the drain. Stop acting like you don't understand."

Ricardo shook his head, breathing sharp bursts out of his thin nose. "I'll never understand how you could do what you did." He clenched his fists, his voice shaking. "Did you think you were saving them somehow? Delivering them from a lonely existence in Rangardia or oppression in Credence? Or was it for a more sinister reason? They had to die before they eventually grew up to be what you hate most?"

Vidya's nails tug into her palms, her teeth grinding down to powder in her mouth. "Do you truly believe I killed my babies after everything I went through to have them?"

"I would not have thought you capable of such a vile act had I not seen the gleeful look in your eyes as you tormented a paralyzed man. He still has the scars on his back, on his arms, clear to this day. Yet the scars he left on you . . ." He waved a hand about Vidya's body. "Nowhere to be found."

"You don't need to see my scars because you witnessed them being inflicted with your own two eyes. Don't pretend you're not complicit in your brother's suffering when you stood idly by."

"It still haunts me, as it should you. But what could I have done? You were nursing Alonz and carrying Spyros. I knew once that baby was born, you'd be out of our lives forever, so yes, I stood by. But it was all for nothing. After everything you put him through to give birth to those precious boys . . ."

"What boys?" Vidya spread her arms. "Your brother has no memory of them."

"Not since the head injury *you* gave him."

Vidya could still hear the crack of Agustin's skull against the lavatory tile amid her grief and rage.

"A knock to the head can't erase his sons from his memory. He chooses to forget them the same way you choose to believe I am responsible for their deaths."

"Now who's the delusional one?"

"If you really believed I killed them, you'd have told Agustin years ago. But you can't be certain, can you?" Vidya took steps forward. "You're afraid you might be wrong. You fear the reason for his forgetfulness, why he hasn't succumbed to vengeance against me, why he abuses those drops . . . is because he knows he's the one with children's blood on his hands!"

The adminstrador shook his head back and forth as he backed away. "If you truly believe that, then why do you hide it from him and everyone around you? Is it because you're afraid you may be wrong too?"

She stopped dead, her gut churned, and her face flushed, searing hot. "I have nothing to prove to you."

The two stood still, goring the other with their eyes before Ricardo sighed and shrugged. "I tried to appeal to the husk of your better nature, but it appears I have failed. So, here is an alternate proposition.

We'll help you take the Odafi ports, and after we do, our alliance will be ended. No Procreation Agreement, no trade, no military protection. You will dissolve your marriage to Agustin and make no attempts at Rangardian sovereignty. Do you understand?"

Vidya barked a cold laugh. "You have no leverage here. You need us."

Ricardo lifted a derisive eyebrow. "Refuse my proposition, and you will leave us no choice but to look for alliances . . . farther east. I'll leave you to think on that for a while." Ricardo bowed, then turned for the door.

Vidya lunged in front of him, blocking his way. "You're a fool if you think Del'Cabria will ally with an island rife with *femena mortum*."

"And you were so good to inform us that a cure exists." Ricardo sneered. "And it's guarded by a tiny island of women with a paltry population. Mind you, enough to hold our men over until a new generation of women come to child-bearing age."

"Those men will come to a sky full of harpies!"

"Things have changed since the last time your ilk tried to conquer the world. Our cannons alone will drop most of you from the sky within the first day. With that kind of firepower and a cure in reach, what mainland nation wouldn't want to ally with us?"

"Is that a declaration of war?" Vidya snarled through her teeth.

"Far from it. Simply a statement of fact. No cure, no Credence." Ricardo carefully edged around Vidya to grab the doorknob. She could have stopped him if every one of her limbs were not paralyzed in place as if poisoned by curare. "With that said, I anticipate little contention in our meeting tomorrow. Sleep well, *Anassa*."

Ricardo was out the door before Vidya's muscles released.

What just happened? A maelstrom of emotions crashed against her body. She wanted to fly after Ricardo and rail him against the hallway pillars. She erupted upon her immediate surroundings instead, sending wigs and brushes flying.

She turned each drawer upside down, scattering jewelry, pins, and tonics about the room. She ripped apart the wigs and smashed their porcelain holders on the floor.

Spent, Vidya collapsed onto the vanity stool, her sister's things shattered around her. She leaned on her elbows and pushed her hair off her face. A frightened, pathetic creature stared back at her: That same weak girl from Rangardia, only now she had wings . . . *What difference do these make if men can still control my fate?*

Herran was supposed to be the beginning. Del'Cabria would be next, and all the other male-ruled nations after it. Then, and only then, could Credence sever ties with Rangardia for good. Agustin would finally get what he deserved.

She imagined all the punishments she'd enact on him, now forever out of reach. *I should kill them all right now while they sleep. I can end the line of power in Rangardia tonight!*

The bright yellow sheen of the shadow harpy's eyes gleamed behind her. Stringy black strands shrouded a ghoulish grin. Vidya jumped out of the chair and spun around, half expecting the shadow to disappear as it often did, but it was there in the flesh . . . or what was left of it. *"You understand well the Harpy's Punishment. Now it's time for you to learn the Harpy's restraint. The alliance must stand."*

"You know Ricardo as well as I do, better in fact," Vidya said. "Whether I dissolve my marriage or not, he won't keep his word. Our alliance was dead the moment he snuck into this room. He must die."

"And what of the squabs? Will you risk losing more to our enemies? Ryeem is the priority, then Tiberius, then Siegfried. Agustin's death will only harm your campaign."

Vidya sat back down at the vanity, holding her head in her hands. They were months—years from building a harpy force rivaling that of a thousand years ago. None of that was possible if Rangardia turned on them first. The few harpies they could make in the meantime wouldn't last a week against two of the world's largest imperial forces combined.

The shadow harpy was wrong this time, except for one thing: Restraint was the only way through this. She had to play nice with Ricardo long enough to grow her Harplite and bring down Ryeem, but she would not wait for the fall of Del'Cabria or Ingleheim before exacting her vengeance. Ricardo would not wait for his.

She took deep breaths as an altered plan weaved within her mind. *That's how I'll punish them. I will put their so-called brotherly bond to the test.*

The door creaked open again. Only this time, Phrea wandered into the mirror's reflection. "Vidi, I heard crashes and voices, are you . . . ?" Her brown eyes widened at the torn wigs and trinkets littered across the floor, stained in spilled wine. "What in the—?"

Vidya spun around. "Phrea, I need you."

"Anything. What is it?"

"Bring Daphne back here. I have a secret mission for her."

"What? No fair. I'm the spy. I go on the secret missions."

"This mission requires Daphne's skillset . . . her knowledge of poisons to be specific." Vidya turned back to the mirror and smoothed out her hair, a smile slowly spreading across her face. "I need her to find me some curare gourd."

With a nod, Phrea left the room as the shadow harpy, still standing behind Vidya at the mirror, narrowed her glowing eye sockets.

15

The Easy Part

"Close your eyes!" a woman bellowed from an unseen place. Instinctively, Jeth shut them tight. *You know that voice!*

A bright flash penetrated his eyelids. The task force screamed in pain; horses shrieked along with every magus. Even Serra's cry pierced through Jeth's eardrums.

Torrent bucked, and Jeth went flying. He opened his eyes just before he hit the ground. The blinding light had faded, but water now poured in through the crumbled roof above, putting out the flames with a loud sizzle. Steam filled the ruined temple, and magi stumbled every which way in confusion.

"What's happening?" shouted Faron.

"I can't see a blasted thing," growled Loche.

As Jeth scrambled toward his fallen bow, three frenzied magi, their staves held out to attack, ran screaming toward him. He gulped, but each one collapsed into the dirt in front of him, blood spurting from different body parts. A familiar musk wafted past.

One by one, magi around Jeth fell dead. Heads flew off. Blood spewed from throats. Shrieks and cries resounded off the overgrown walls, and amongst all the chaos, the lethal ring of a blade wielded by skilled and unseen hands.

One magus blindly ran at Jeth's left. Another metallic swish disturbed the air, and the magus's chest split open. He fell on his back, a poleaxe sticking out of his sternum.

A smile crept across Jeth's face as the axe appeared to lift itself from the dead magus. A massive Herrani man, with black serpent tattoos winding up his bulging biceps, materialized before his eyes as if he'd stepped out of the air itself.

He spun his tabar, flicking away the blood, before nestling it within the straps at his back. He turned to Jeth. The two cobra maws tattooed to each cheek grinned wide. "You have a knack for showing up right when the fun starts, don't you, Fairy Boy?"

Jeth's grin transformed into relieved laughter. The three Del'Cabrians beside him squinted at the gigantic axeman who had just cleaved through half the magi in their vicinity.

Ash lumbered over, extending his black, leather-clad hand. Jeth took it and let Ash's massive biceps wrap around him, smooshing him into the sweaty, red scorpion tattoo on his chest. His feet dangled off the ground.

Jeth gave the Herrani a friendly pat on the arm before wriggling out of his grasp lest he pass out from the pain shooting across his scarred back.

"Brothers, get behind me!" the older magus called out, nursing an electric ball between his palms. "Protect this gate for our master, at all costs."

Ash and the task force stood frozen.

A lightning bolt burst from the magus's palm, and Jeth ducked. But the bolt jumped sideways, blasting the magus nearest to the leader, then another next to him. The hijacked electric bolt roped ten magi together, frying them from the inside. A few seconds later, they all collapsed to the ground, leaving only their leader, shaking in horror of what he had inadvertently done.

The magi who had been spared electrocution backed away in alarm as a striking ebony-skinned woman undulated into existence behind their stunned leader. "Your master is dead." Istari whacked him hard over the head with her twisted, sapphire-adorned staff. The magus fell face-down, unmoving, and Istari kicked over his spine staff and snapped it in half with a good stomp.

Looking up to Ash and Jeth, she said, "Come on, boys. Hugs and kisses can wait."

"Star!" Jeth chuckled at the sight of the Odafi Light Mage. She was right, though. The surviving magi regarded their leader, dead at Istari's feet, and began screaming for her head.

A Fire Mage siphoned a smoldering flame into his hands, ready to lob it at her.

That familiar thin, dark-eyed magus appeared behind him with a bow, drawed back, then released. The arrow found its mark through the magus's lower spine before the inferno could leave his hand.

Istari turned to the young magus who saved her life. "Thanks, Khiri."

The boy nodded with a proud look on his skeletal face.

"Khir, that was *you?* You grew half a man," Jeth exclaimed.

More magi regained their weapons, ready to resume their assault.

"All of you come with us." Istari beckoned them with a wave of her arm.

Jeth shot off three arrows at the magi horde before vaulting onto Torrent's saddle. *Lucky for you, she didn't run off this time.*

Magi gave chase as the task force kicked their steeds into a gallop. "You trust this woman?" Faron shouted.

"With all of our lives," Jeth replied, following Istari and Ash into the labyrinthian halls of the old temple. Ash was on his old draft horse and Istari on her camel with Khiri coming up behind them on their laden-down packhorse.

"I hope you brought some backup," called Jeth.

"In a sense." Istari grinned.

They rode east out of the temple, pushing their mounts until they reached the end of the grassy canyon.

"Stop here." Istari pulled the reins, bringing her camel to a quick halt. She, Ash, and Khiri dismounted. The task force hesitantly did the same.

"Why are we stopping here?" asked Olivier. "They're right behind us!"

Istari waved her hand dismissively at the medic. "Relax. We've got this."

"Great job killing their first in command, Star," said Ash, then turned to address the Del'Cabrians. "Now we have them angry and stupid enough to follow us into this bottleneck."

The howling magi drew nearer, staves in hand, fireballs landing just shy of where the team stood.

Sweat dripped down the back of Jeth's neck. *They're coming in fast!* He and Olivier nocked their arrows, and Loche and Faron drew their swords.

"Just sit back and watch the magic show, boys." Ash casually stepped forward, his tabar secure at his back. It was then that Jeth noticed the black gloves he wore weren't just regular gloves, but Steinkamp Magitech. Ash raised his hand in the air as if he were quieting an audience before an important speech.

Many of the more wary magi slowed, but it was too late for them to turn back. As they neared the canyon exit, Ash clenched his gloved fist, and an earth-shattering boom cracked the vine-covered canyon walls on both sides.

The task force yelped and covered their ears as huge chunks of stone tumbled down. Rock and debris blanketed the unsuspecting magi horde. Even where they stood at a safe distance, dust rolled over the team, making them cough and wave their hands in front of their faces.

Jeth whooped, shooting both arms in the air in victory. "Yes, blast gel!"

Istari blew the dust away with a wave of her arm. Several surviving magi picked themselves up and retreated toward the temple.

"The gate is still active," Jeth warned, "and it leads straight to Fae'ren."

Istari huffed. "Then I suppose we should go after them."

Ash nodded and turned back to the rest of the task force. "How do you boys feel about giving these cultists back to their dead god?"

Jeth grabbed hold of a magus's ankles while Istari took him under his arms, and the two lifted him off the blood-drenched grass. "Last I was here, you had this place nice and secure," he said before they lugged the corpse into a cart with the others.

Serra wriggled in Jeth's inside coat pocket. She had thought it best to stay out of the way while everyone cleared the battlefield; he had almost forgotten she was there.

"We thought we did, but we hadn't predicted just how many magi would come calling." Istari brushed the sand off her hands and went to the next dead body.

With a heave, the two of them carried the corpse to the cart. "I still don't see how they could have gotten past you lot."

Istari's bright blue eyes darkened. "We're a . . . a little short on fighters right now." She bent down to grab another magus but paused in a crouch. "Ryeem and his naja. They came for Snake Eye." She pushed off her hood, revealing her fluffy, white hair. Although still close-cropped at the sides, it had grown straight up at the top. She stared down at the body as if she didn't know what to do with it.

Jeth bent down to help her, his heart skipping a beat. "Then does that mean he's . . . ?" The words caught in his throat, thinking of the probable man who had saved his life more than once.

Ash walked by, dragging one magus behind him and carrying another over his hulking shoulder. "He's alive—or at least we think so. Last month, General Nadila took the bulk of our forces to Odafi to help stave off the invasion, and Yemesh took most of the surviving warriors to rescue Snake Eye." He plunked both bodies into the cart. "That didn't leave us with much to defend the temple against the magi."

Jeth and Istari hoisted the last body onto the top of the heap after Ash. "Someone should have told them their master isn't coming back."

Ash patted the pulling horse on the rump, and Loche drove the cart toward the graveyard ruins outside the canyon. "Presumably, the magi who had a rapport with Nas'Gavarr knew he died the day it happened. But I'm betting the rest of the brainwashed devotees wouldn't treat the bearers of bad news too kindly."

Maybe they're following behind his substitute, Jeth wanted to add but dismissed that idea immediately. It was doubtful Melikheil had anything to do with this. He surely had better things to do with his new body.

"So, what now?" Jeth's voice cracked.

Istari replied, "All we can do is wait for either Yemesh or Nadila to return with our forces. We made an oath to Snake Eye to protect the gate and the oasis no matter what. Whoever holds this place decides the future of the tribes."

"Well, you certainly kept your word despite having near no defenses," said Jeth.

"That's why we left the gate vulnerable, making the magi think we abandoned it. Khiri infiltrated them to let us know when it was a good time to strike, but your message did that instead. Thanks for the distraction." Istari smirked then went to look for more bodies.

"Distraction?" Faron piped up from farther down the battlefield.

Ash chuckled. "We would not have been able to attack the whole group at once had they not all gathered around you boys."

Faron shook his head and returned to his task, obviously not pleased with being used as magus bait.

Jeth shrugged. "Well, thanks for coming when you did." He removed his knitted cap to wipe the sweat off his head. *Even an oasis out here is still as hot as a kiln.*

Ash took a step back. "Wait, what?"

"I said thanks for saving us."

Both Ash and Istari stared at Jeth as if he had stepped out of an alternate realm. "W-what did you do?" Ash pointed at Jeth's head.

"Oh, you don't like it?" He rubbed his hand over the short fuzz that had replaced his fairy locks.

"Who knew you had such a puny head?" said Ash.

"At least it's not thick like yours."

Ash trilled his large lips.

Istari rubbed her hand over its downy softness. "I think I like it better this way."

Jeth pulled his cap back over his head. "Alright, hands off the head and back on the dead."

A sharp male yelp caused everyone to spin around with a start.

Faron fell on his backside as a giant scorpion rushed out of the bush and straight for him. He clacked his sword against the hard pincers. Its long tail poised; stinger about to strike.

"Shit!" Jeth grabbed his bow from his back and readied an arrow before anyone else could react. The arrow flew past Faron and straight through the scorpion's median eye. It screeched and crumpled into a heap. Faron hastily jumped back to his feet. His leathery complexion paled to a creamy hue as he stared down at the colossal arachnid. "What in blue blazes . . . ?"

"How are those things still here?" said Jeth.

"Sand or grass, they're never too far from the dead." Ash brought his tabar in hand and made way for the scorpion. "Thanks for catching dinner."

Ash raised his axe above his head and severed the scorpion's tail clean off. Jeth scrunched his face in disgust as Faron stood there, watching in shock.

Istari started leading Jeth away by the shoulder. "Let's head back to the village."

"But we aren't finished." He pointed a thumb back to the bodies still strewn about.

"They'll be just as dead in the morning." She pulled on Jeth's coat sleeve. "Come on. I'm starving."

Istari, atop her camel, led Jeth and Faron through the trampled foliage to the overgrown graveyard ruins beyond. There, they found Olivier tending to the team's horses at the stream feeding into a small pond that flooded three crumbling towers.

The medic inspected them for burns and other injuries. Satisfied, he turned back to Faron's horse, bandaging a small welt at its right coronet.

Faron, Jeth, and Istari kneeled at the stream to wash the corpse-stink off their hands. When Istari pulled up her sleeves, the sunlight illuminated tiny sapphire gems festooned to her skin.

"Wow, Star. What you got there?"

She stretched her arms out to let Jeth get a better look at the sparkling blue rivers winding up her arms. "An alternative to putting sapphire dust directly into your flesh. Now I can access aura far easier than before."

"Stings a lot less, I reckon."

"That too." Istari submerged one palm up into the water and hovered the other above it. Water flowed from one hand to the other like an upward stream. She proceeded to compress it into a sphere between both palms until it crystalized into an ice ball. She tossed the ice to Jeth. He snatched it out of the air and held it to his sweating brow.

Once refreshed, he dumped the ice ball back into the water and watched it float downstream. "I remember when you could barely make water apart from pissing, and now look at you."

"Granted, it's much easier to make ice in an oasis than in the Burning Waste, but I've since learned that auras for water and light are not so different," she said with a satisfied grin. "It also helps to have a good teacher. You'll meet her soon."

The sorceress Jeth had met on his last thieving job in Ingleheim came to mind. Jenn knew how to manipulate water aura and was supposed to be somewhere in the desert. Could they really be so fortunate to run into her here?

He was about to ask Istari when Ash trundled by with the scorpion tail over the back of his saddle.

Faron glanced up from the stream. "He actually intends on eating that? I assumed he meant it in jest."

Ash grinned wide. "Oh, I never jest when it comes to scorpion meat."

"But aren't they poisonous?"

"Venomous," Ash corrected. "And not if you remove the stinger."

Faron grew even paler. "I see."

"You're going to love it," Istari said, mounting her camel.

Jeth followed his former crew on horseback into the village.

Before the landscape had transformed into a forested oasis, the village was nothing more than a lonely rock formation housing a trickling stream, a tiny haven surrounded by perpetual flame. Now, they rode past numerous yurts the Tezkhan had helped erect and wooden huts built by various Herrani settlers that came to escape the desert sun.

Women wearing white wrap-around robes gathered around a spring in the village's center, laundering linens. "I've never seen them before," Jeth said.

Istari replied, "They're the Magae of Salotaph, thought long gone even before the Death tribes ruled this land. At one time, they were considered equals. The magae used their magic to support life, while the magi used theirs in dealing with the dead. As this area grew destitute, death worship dominated, and the magae faded into obscurity. They've since reappeared after the oasis did."

"Welcome to the Gift of Salotaph," said a hefty, older woman with blonde hair under a white hood. Her dark complexion sparkled with a swirling pattern of sapphire gemstones, the same as what Istari had on her arms. "Istari, my child. I knew you'd be victorious."

The two women embraced. "All thanks to you, Shahbaz. Your teachings rendered their fire magic useless. The Magi of Sagorath will no longer be a problem for us."

Istari turned and introduced Jeth to her teacher as he tried to hide his disappointment—it seemed he wouldn't be seeing Jenn again any time soon.

Shahbaz smiled warmly. "Ah, yes. You must be the forest man that helped bring forth Salotaph's breath of life to this land of the dead."

"Aye." Jeth pulled off his cap and wiped the sweat from his brow. "I played a wee role, I suppose." Other magae pushed past Shahbaz and flocked around him. They started talking all at once. Olivier sniggered as he and Faron headed toward the cooking area outside the large communal yurt north of the village.

"You're him? How did you do it?"

"Did you look upon Salotaph? I bet she's beautiful."

"How did you defeat Sagorath?"

What do you say? Your goddess is as dead as Sagorath or may as well be? Would they accept that all this vegetation was courtesy of your Conduit, not theirs?

Ash answered for him as he walked by with the scorpion tail over his shoulder. "Apparently, it involved getting stabbed and floating in a pool of his own blood."

"Yup." Jeth nodded. "It was every bit as gruesome as it sounds." He released an awkward chuckle. The magae's grins faded one by one. "Excuse me, ladies." He followed Ash to the cooking area.

The big man dropped the tail onto a slab, startling the robed man peeling yams right next to it. "Get your curry out, Lys. We celebrate one small victory today."

Jeth clapped a hand on the cook's shoulder. "If you're here, who's running the spice shop?"

The Crede man's kind brown eyes lit up, and the two embraced. "Jeth, I would never have recognized you without those locks!"

"Now he looks like all the rest of the boring Del'Cabrians," Ash jibed, cracking open the scorpion shell with his bare hands. He then found a knife and started slicing the meat into chunks before tossing them into a large cooking pot over the flame.

Faron rolled his eyes so subtly only Jeth's fairy sight could spot it. With a grunt, he made his way inside the communal yurt. *What's his problem now?* Jeth didn't want to deal with the urling's ever-foul mood at the moment; he wanted to bask in the joy of seeing his old crew again.

"I sold the shop so I could help out here," replied Lys, dumping a handful of bright yellow spice into the pot. Its strong scent tickled the inside of Jeth's nose.

"And we had no one else who could make a curry like yours." Istari stirred the pot with a smile.

Jeth took in the pleasant aroma himself as he gazed about the village. He found Khiri sitting at the spring where a young maga wiped the skull paint off his face with a wet cloth.

"How do you keep Khir busy these days?" Jeth bobbed his head to the Ankarran boy.

"He's our little recon man now," Istari replied.

"I keep telling Star, if the kid acquires any more skills, he won't be needing us much longer," Ash said, wiping the brown scorpion blood from his cutting knife.

Jeth sauntered over to the spring and swung his arm around the boy's neck, putting him into a playful headlock. "You're not going anywhere, are you, Khir?" The twelve-year-old squirmed free and retaliated with a back-handed swat in the chest.

Serra screeched and burst from his jacket pocket. "Hey, watch it!"

Everyone gasped and backed away at the sight of the little winged creature hovering above Jeth's head.

"A locust!" Lys yelped. "Keep it away from the food!" He shooed her away with a washcloth. It caught her by the wings and made her spiral through the air.

She squealed, and Jeth rushed to catch her. "Easy, easy, she's not a locust. You all right, Ser?" He couldn't help but chuckle.

She plunked herself down in his palms and shook her wings out. "Takes more than a piece of fabric to hurt a pixie. Can't say the same for my pride, though." She glared daggers at Lys, standing there, mouth agape.

Jeth looked at his guardian fairy sidelong. "Do pixies even know what pride feels like?"

"We helped grow the most beautiful and bountiful forest in the world. Of course, we know what pride feels like."

"Ah," Jeth presented the oasis around them with a sweep of his arm. "What do you think of this one? I grew it all by myself. Not bad for a human, aye?"

Serra grumbled, but everyone else continued to stare at her. "She looks so real." Ash hunched down and ran a finger over her tiny green locks.

She spun around and shot back into the air. "That's because I *am* real!"

Jeth proceeded to introduce Serra to everyone just as Khiri jumped up and caught her by the legs. Faster than Jeth's speed could assist, Serra's sparks shot out from her hands and struck Khiri squarely between the eyes. "Erh," he grunted and let her go.

Serra flew higher into the air for all to see and placed both hands at her hips. "Listen up and let it be known: I am neither an insect nor a child's toy!"

Jeth put his hand on the boy's shoulder. "You pissed off my pixie, Khir. Not an easy thing to do."

Khiri rubbed his red forehead with a wide, toothless grin.

Serra glared down at the boy. "Do my sparks tickle or something?

Why are you grinning like that?"

"You won't get much out of him," Jeth said. "He doesn't have a tongue."

Khiri made a series of outward gestures and pointed to his forehead. "I think he wants you to shoot your sparks again."

Serra raised her brow. "At his forehead?" Khiri shook his head and continued the outward arm motions. "You want me to spark something else?" He nodded eagerly, and Serra shrugged. "Alright then. I suppose I could use the practice, but I should be conserving . . ."

Khiri excitedly dashed behind the grass huts, and Serra fluttered after him.

Ash and Lys proceeded to cook the scorpion meat, dusting it liberally with aromatic spices that made Jeth's mouth water. Taking a heaping of the scorpion curry served over yams, Jeth sat with the others at a low table in the large rectangular yurt. The old thieving crew gathered on one side and the new task force on the other. Before Jeth could take a bite, Olivier sat beside him and plunked down his jar of golden-brown liquid, opaque chunks suspended inside. "Don't forget your garlic honey."

"Why, thank you, dear." Jeth snorted as he popped the cork. He took a generous gulp then hastily washed it down with wine to rid himself of the unseemly aftertaste. "Two delicious things coming together to make something not quite as good as either."

Olivier tucked the bottle back in his medical bag, then turned to face the foreign meal before him. Jeth bit down on a thick hunk of scorpion meat, finding the texture not altogether offensive and the taste fishier than he expected despite the eye-watering curry. He nodded with approval and shoved some more into his mouth. "Got to hand it to you, Lys. You manage to make eating giant bugs a pleasure."

"Very good." Lys smiled.

Olivier and Loche took a few cautious bites, their eyes brightening, and they began to scarf it down. Faron wouldn't go as far as to even sniff it and sat, arms crossed over his chest, sulking. *His loss. More for you.* Jeth finished his meal quickly, took Faron's bowl, and dug into that too, much to the swordsman's annoyance.

Thoroughly stuffed, he wiped the sauce from his stubble. "Not to dampen the celebratory mood, but are we going to talk about what Ryeem wants with Snake Eye and how you're all sure he's still alive?"

"Hopefully alive," Ash said between swallows. "Yemesh will find out soon enough."

"I don't understand. We killed dozens of naja in Lanore with just a handful of warriors. Shouldn't Ryeem be running low now that his father isn't around to make more?"

"That's why we think Snake Eye still lives," said Istari. "He's now the world's most powerful Flesh Mage and Ryeem's best hope for growing his army."

"If Snake Eye agrees to do so."

"Spirit Mages have ways of getting anyone to do what they want . . . eventually." Istari put down her food as if she'd lost her appetite.

Jeth thought of Jenn again. "The Ingle sorceress told me once that a Spirit Mage couldn't control anyone's mind whenever they please. They needed to prime them first."

"And did she tell you how priming is typically performed?" Istari posed.

"Not really," he confessed.

"I gather it's rather unpleasant," Loche said before wiping the curry sweat from his brow and taking a large gulp of wine.

Istari nodded solemnly. "Torture, physical or mental, enough to break the spirit down and make it more malleable for manipulation."

"That or good old-fashioned consent," Ash inputted. "But I don't think Snake Eye would go that route to spare himself a little pain."

Jeth shivered and took a sip of his wine to hide his frown. He wondered how much pain Snake Eye could take. They were, after all, talking about a person who hurt himself to heal others for a living.

Sitting next to Jeth, Faron cleared his throat loud enough to capture the whole crew's attention. "This is all quite fascinating, but when are we to address the actual task at hand?"

"Isn't that what we're doing?" Istari said blankly.

"The fate of this Snake Eye does not concern us presently. Our mission"—he flashed Jeth a stern glare—"which you have yet to even mention, must take priority."

"Snake Eye is our friend and leader. Your mission means shit to us," Ash griped.

Jeth rose to his feet, creating a barrier between the axeman and the swordsman. "What Faron's trying to say in his inappropriately confrontational way is we have our own missing person to find."

"And someone far more integral than an ashipu," Faron scoffed as he rose.

"Watch your mouth, Pointy." Ash jumped to his feet, clenching his bulging fists. "That *ashipu* is the only person who can unite the tribes and maintain our freedom. Is that integral enough for you?"

"Recalling the last egomaniacal Mage who united the tribes, I'd recommend you people not try to do that again. For the sake of the rest of the world." Faron straightened, puffing up his chest but not coming close to Ash's incredible height or breadth.

"Listen to our esteemed Del'Cabrian guest, everyone." Ash pointed to the urling man across from him, rousing the other diner's attention in the yurt. "He's about to tell us how we desert tribes ought to govern ourselves. He seems to forget how our warriors sent his kind scurrying back to their rolling hills with their tails between their legs!"

"Tails, if I am not mistaken, are a reptilian trait," Faron said as if it were a matter of fact.

Jeth put his palm to his forehead and groaned. Lys eyed the fragile clay dinnerware on the table.

Ash's unnerving grin stretched the cobra jaws on his bronze cheeks. "Allow me to show you how a reptilian-human responds to ignorant urling remarks like that." He stepped onto the table as Lys snatched up the dishes in his path.

Faron jumped back and brought his hand to his sword, ready to draw.

"Easy there, Big Fella." Jeth dashed between them. "We're just here to find the Princess of Del'Cabria. That's what's got my man here so emotional." Faron stood as stiff as a granite pillar, jaw clenched and eyes steeled. *As emotional as he could ever be.*

Looming over Jeth and Faron, Ash said, "I knew you were full of shit all those times you told us you weren't a Del'Cabrian. Look at you now, hair chopped off, in that ridiculous coat, and protecting these pale-faced imperialists!"

Jeth put a hand on the big man's chest, planning to push him back a few inches, but Ash stepped forward, squishing Jeth between him and Faron.

Lys stood up and said in a firm voice, "Ashbedael, you made your point, now sit down. Our Del'Cabrian guests have little reason to prioritize Snake Eye over their own princess."

"Listen to Lys." Jeth then turned to Faron. "And seriously, man. You can at least pretend to show respect for the people who saved our arses today."

"Ars—lives that shouldn't have needed saving in the first place had we turned back when I first suggested." Faron's hand still hovered over his sword's grip. "And they'd likely have let us die back there if you weren't with us."

"Isn't that the point of Jeth being here in the first place?" Loche inputted. "They're his allies, not ours."

Ash pressed further into Jeth. "Perhaps we should have saved *only* him."

"Sit down, Ashbedael," Lys insisted, kicking an empty cushion towards him. "And allow everyone else to enjoy their curry in peace."

Ash looked to the former spice shop owner turned peacekeeper and grumbled. He sat down without taking his emerald green eyes from Faron or Jeth.

"Very good." Lys nodded and sat down beside him. "Are we ready to converse like adults now?"

Jeth took a deep breath as Faron let go of his sword and stepped back. "Thanks, Lys. As we were saying, the Princess of Del'Cabria is missing, and we need your help."

"And why should we?" Ash asked in annoyance, leaning on the table with his elbow.

Jeth ignored Ash and looked to Istari. "Do you still have those uniforms we wore to sneak into Herrani Palace?"

"Sure . . . somewhere." Istari raised a white brow and leaned in. "Why? You think your missing princess is with the harem?"

"Maybe. If not, then someone there has to know where she might be." Jeth sat back down on his own pillow. "What do you say?"

"We don't do jobs like that anymore," Istari said. "Our purpose now is to protect the oasis."

Jeth's voice took on a near begging tone. "It'll only be a few days, and we'll pay you. Name your price."

"The King of Del'Cabria will spare no expense," added Olivier.

"That's great, but . . . I don't know." She massaged her temple, mulling over Jeth's offer.

Lys spoke instead. "We don't need the King's coin. We will do all we can to help you in your mission."

The crew snapped their heads around to the Crede man, who rarely gave his input into planning jobs in the past.

"But Snake Eye said—"

"I know what Snake Eye said," Lys cut off Istari's protest. "But we have no idea where Ryeem took him, and Jeth has presented us with an opportunity to find out. Perhaps one of his sisters could shed light on his whereabouts if he's not at the palace himself. We can kill two snakes with one arrow, as it were." He looked at Jeth with a grin.

Ash slammed his palm on the tabletop. "Alright. One last job." The task force rejoiced in nods and grins, and Faron's stiff features loosened considerably. "But I have to warn you. Due to the war in Odafi, the palace has beefed up its security. I hear the Bahazur are guarding it now."

"And where there are Bahazur," Istari continued, "the Merchant Council is usually involved. They're likely running palace affairs while Ryeem is gone."

Jeth gulped, remembering the Council's slimy treasure keeper, Ezrai, who had helped them access the harem before. The thought of running into him again made his muscles tense. "That definitely complicates things."

"How so?" Loche said. "They're merchants, and we're oil traders. We tell them how our wares can help in the war effort, and they'll be sure to throw the gates open for us."

"That *could* actually get us in." Jeth scratched his chin. "But they'll never let us search the harem."

Istari rolled up her sleeves, showcasing glittering blue gems against ebony skin. "That, boys, is the easy part."

16

No Resistance Here

Bahazur guards in bronze helms and heavy skirts wrapped around their muscular torsos ushered the task force into Herrani Palace. They reminded Jeth of Dayne and his *lein-croich. Maybe there's something to men fighting in skirts after all.*

An older Odafi woman, draped in technicolor robes and a headdress of golden tassels, smiled. "You've arrived. Please leave your weapons with our guards, and they will put them in a safe place for you." Each task force member handed the men their swords, bows, and daggers under the woman's watchful eye.

While it pained Jeth to part with his bow, Ash and the others were not far behind and would reunite them with their weapons if anything were to go wrong.

Faron nodded toward the large clay jar still under Loche's arm. "We carry with us only a sample of our wares."

The woman's dark skin crinkled as she smiled again, her teeth a brilliant white for someone of such advanced age. "Good. Right this way." She led the four Del'Cabrian men through the magnificent atrium. The polished sandstone walls reflected the sunlight that beamed through the many clover-shaped windows, illuminating the massive dome's vibrant colors just like Jeth remembered.

As they walked down the hallway, he heard Istari, Ash, Lys, and Khiri—all cloaked by light magic—make their way toward the harem gates. Jeth had already given Istari Zephira's brooch in case they found her. He would have offered his nose to assist had he any idea what she smelled like. Instead, he'd stick with his task force and keep the merchants busy while the thieves, wearing their eunuch uniforms, searched the harem for any urling woman who recognized the brooch.

The task force continued into a comfortable lounge, sunlight pouring in through the open roof as indoor streams trickled around them. A heavy-set man sitting on a long, plush bench greeted them with a booming voice. "Welcome, good sirs. Take a seat. Enjoy the finger foods." He took a spiced date from a serving girl's platter as others fanned him down with plumes. "I am Chairman Azag of the Merchant Council." He motioned to the woman that led them in. "This is Councilor Rubati, in charge of foreign trade. And to her left"—he gestured to the much thinner and taller man taking a seat next to him—"Ezrai, the Council's Treasure Keeper. He will ultimately determine how much we wish to spend on your wares."

Jeth's heart immediately sank at the sight of the smarmy treasure keeper. Standing unassumingly behind Faron and Loche, he struggled not to glare directly at him. He had hoped Ezrai would not be among the men they were meeting today, but he wasn't too worried. Wearing freshly pressed Ludesan coastal garments and having so little hair on his head and face, there was hardly a chance Ezrai would recognize him. Jeth resisted the urge to scratch his scalp where Serra wriggled about under his knitted cap.

The two urling gentlemen took off their tricorns and bowed to the merchants as the humans hung back. Azag beckoned Loche to step forward with the jar of oil. "Show us what you have there."

"We bring the finest oil from the whales off Ludesa Coast," said Faron. "It burns every bit as bright as the oil you used to find deep under the sands of Herran."

"Oil from inside whales? That's new," said Rubati. "How much can a single whale produce?"

"Anywhere between twenty to forty drums, ma'am," Olivier replied.

The merchants' eyebrows all raised at once, impressed, but they quickly narrowed their gazes, not entirely convinced.

"Then light it up!" boomed Azag.

"With pleasure." Loche set down the jar and took out a torch from under his belt. After he dipped the dried cloth into the dark amber liquid, Olivier approached with his flint and steel and scraped them together until they sparked. The torch ignited with a fury, burning bright and smokeless.

"Now," Faron began, "it won't burn for a hundred years, but it's more than sufficient to light your way for as long as required."

"We use it in our lighthouses. Our fishing boats can always find their way home," added Olivier. "And so too can your trading galleys and the Herrani Fleet that protects them as we speak."

Ezrai scratched his square chin. "Impressive." He looked to Jeth as if expecting him to say something as well, but Jeth simply nodded in silent agreement. "How much for a dozen carts?"

Faron, Loche, and the merchants proceeded to haggle with the price while Jeth whispered to Serra. "I think you should check on the others. If this deal finishes too quickly, they may get trapped."

"Find a way to stall," she said, then flew out of his cap while everyone's attention was on the flame.

"One hundred thousand for that much whale oil? No disrespect, but that is an absurd offer," said Loche.

"Not a coin more," countered Ezrai.

"It's the finest alternative we have at the moment," said Rubati. "Their product is worth at least double that. We can charge back a higher premium to the Herrani Fleet to make up for it."

"With their current debts, the Herrani Fleet will never be able to repay us," Ezrai replied. "Need I remind you why we're not in our homeland right now, Rubati?"

"Are the Rangardians winning the war?" Faron asked.

"You fine gentlemen need not concern yourselves with wars outside your borders," Azag said.

"We do if you're saying you don't have the gold to spare," said Loche.

"We're sitting on more gold in this palace than any urling king could ever dream of," Ezrai stated with his chest pushed out. "The Overlord's absence has provided us with a fortunate business opportunity. We assure you, we can afford whatever price you ask, but we won't part with a shaving more than what we deem fair."

As the other two merchants nodded in agreement, a jolt ran across Jeth's sternum. He cleared his throat and spoke in his most convincing Ludesan twang, "Business opportunity? Are you talking about the harem?"

Ezrai looked straight at him with his pale blue eyes, and a sly grin spread across his face. "Tales of the most beautiful, most unattainable women of every tribe have tantalized imaginations for over a century. Now the Immortal Serpent has most generously granted them to us."

"You're whoring them," Jeth said, bile rising in his throat.

"They already were. But what was once hoarded by one man can now be shared among many."

"As long as they front proper payment," Loche muttered with disgust.

"And the Overlord's sons have permitted this treatment of the women under their roof?" Faron posed.

"You mean the squabbling sons who were about to squander every last coin had we not offered to manage it for them?" said Azag. "They don't deserve the wealth of their progenitor. We let them take their children, their elderly, and one wife each, then sent them on their way. The Overlord's so-called successor, Ryeem, has made no attempt to stop us. He'd rather lie with his reptilian beasts than his own wives, it seems."

The merchants chuckled amongst themselves, making Jeth's stomach churn. He hadn't thought about Nas'Gavarr's wives and daughters when he set out to kill him. He'd never imagined anything like this. Now he was even more worried about the mission. Were Nas'Gavarr's daughters being whored too? Was the princess? *You need to access that harem!*

"Perhaps we can part with the six jars we brought with us in exchange for a look at these ladies," Jeth suggested. "Then we can talk about additional deliveries."

The fellow traders all turned to Jeth in unison. Azag and Ezrai exchanged glances and shrugged. "You can do more than look with six full jars."

"That won't be necessary," Faron said sternly. "We are all married men."

Jeth rolled his eyes. *Play along, mate!*

Ezrai said, "We understand that dalliances outside of marriage are against your Del'Cabrian laws, but this is Herran. There are no consequences for those who choose to indulge." He rose to his feet and beckoned the others with him. "Come, I will give you a tour. Then you may decide."

"Come on, fellas. It won't hurt to take a look." Jeth went after the merchants, and the rest of the team hesitantly followed.

Ezrai took out a key, lifting the chain from one of his many necklaces, and opened the bronze gate to the harem. Hulking Bahazur, some larger than Ash, lined the hallway, replacing the leather-clad guards

Jeth remembered from his first visit.

The women didn't exhibit the carefree spirit Jeth remembered either. No one frolicked in the glistening pools, only sat in the shade under archways, eyeing the merchants and faux traders warily as they passed. Faron locked his gaze forward, careful not to catch sight of any nearly nude ladies. Both Loche and Olivier's eyes darted in all directions, their brows cinching with concern. Jeth tried to keep his expression casual while honing all his senses. He picked up the various remnants of Ash and Istari's scents as they ventured through the halls. Lys and Khiri's weren't among them. They must have taken a different route.

The merchants led them to a massive room under a colorful domed ceiling nearly as impressive as the palace atrium. Silk and velvet pillows littered the floors, smoke from water pipes danced in the air. Women moved about the space in silken gowns that barely covered them, filling their cups from wine fountains and lounging under eunuch's feathered fans. Their various perfumes flirted with Jeth's nostrils. It was so overwhelming he scaled back his sense of smell to near nothing just to concentrate.

Ezrai turned to his guests and grinned. "Feel free to sample whatever interests you. You will find no resistance here." Faron and Loche paled considerably as Olivier's freckled cheeks burned bright red. Ezrai chuckled under his breath. "We can arrange private rooms if you prefer. Or perhaps these women are not to Del'Cabrian sensibilities. The ones you see here had been wives or concubines of our Overlord. If purity is your concern, we can send for some virgins. We keep them in a separate area."

The way Ezrai went on referring to these women as nothing more than saleable wares made Jeth's blood boil in his temples. Had Anwarr returned here with their son as part of Jeth's deal with Nas'Gavarr, this would have been her future. He clenched his shuddering jaw. As much as he longed for this mission to be over, he hoped to not find the princess here. "Do you have any urling women? I'd like to sample one of them." Both Faron and Loche glared at him. He shrugged. "Back home, I'd be jailed for even asking that, but when in Herran . . ."

"There are no urling women here," Rubati replied.

"That's unfortunate," Jeth sighed. "I thought surely Nas'Gavarr would have captured a few during the Desert War."

"Wouldn't that be something," said Ezrai. "An urling beauty would fetch an enormous price in these parts, to be sure."

Faron's left eye twitched as Rubati continued, "We can dress up the palest among our Herrani woman in Del'Cabrian attire if that will suffice."

Jeth waved his hands down. "Nah, wouldn't be the same."

"Surely there's one here that strikes your fancy." Azag grabbed a passing woman with sapphire blue eyes and white hair grown past her behind. He squeezed her against his flabby chest and presented her to Jeth. "This one was the Overlord's most prized concubine. Are you not curious as to why?"

"I was a wife," the woman corrected.

He dug his thick fingers into her arm until she winced. "A needless distinction."

"I can't speak for my colleagues here," Jeth continued, hating himself more and more for the role he was playing. "But I, for one, don't much care for what the Overlord had numerous times over. What of his daughters? I hear they're marked with the Serpentine on their backs. I wouldn't mind seeing that. There should be enough for all four of us, aye?"

Ezrai's eyes darkened somewhat. Jeth cursed inwardly for his Fae'ren dialect sneaking through his Ludesan act. "You may want to reconsider. The daughters of age who remain here are not as . . . cooperative as these women."

"Let us meet them, and we can drop the price to one hundred thousand gold for the twelve carts you're after."

The three merchants turned to Faron for his final approval, assuming he was the man in charge. The swordsmen ground his teeth but nodded curtly.

"Very well," Azag sent the woman under his arm on her way, then snapped his fingers for a eunuch. "Retrieve all the daughters from their chambers." The thin man nodded and went to task without word.

While waiting for the daughters to arrive, the task force gingerly tasted refreshments brought out by harem attendants.

The merchants requested some of the available concubines to dance provocatively for them. An ebony-skinned attendant with the bottom half of her face covered handed Jeth a cup of wine. He brought the cup to his lips only for a tiny winged woman to fly out of it and bury herself back into his cap.

"Ser," he whispered in surprise.

"She's not here, and the daughters are locked away in the basement level rooms," she whispered. "Lys is keeping the harem gate unlocked for us, so come up with an excuse to leave."

Jeth turned his nose back on, and the scents of Istari, Ash, and Khiri grew more manifest through the room's perfume cloud. *They must be nearby.* "Don't worry," he muttered to Serra under his breath. "The merchants just sent for the daughters. Once we've spoken to them, we can go,"

The attendant's hand clasped around Jeth's coat sleeve and pulled him toward her. It was Istari, her eyes wide above her facial shroud. "They're coming up here? That's not the plan."

"Star, don't draw attention to yourself."

Ezrai turned from his canoodling to look in Jeth's direction. Istari kept her back to him while he pretended to talk to Olivier. When Ezrai returned his attention to the dancing women, Jeth whispered to Istari, "They might have more information on where their father took the princess or what Ryeem wants with Snake Eye."

"I already spoke to one of them through a window earlier. They know nothing of an urling woman having ever been here and even less about where Ryeem is."

"One of them has to have a spiritual rapport with him. If I can just get all of them together—"

Istari gripped harder on Jeth's sleeve. "They know we're here now, Sag damn it!"

"What?"

The eunuch and three Bahazur entered the room with six Herrani women in tow. Each wore a backless top made of sheer fabric, showcasing their unique serpent tattoos' delicate scale patterns. Jeth almost didn't recognize the shortest woman in the back of the line. It was Saf'Raisha, her hair chopped off at her shoulders and her kohl clumping around her bloodshot eyes. It appeared as if she had just engaged in a round of fisticuffs.

"Excuse yourselves and get out of here now," Istari whispered. Jeth turned back to her, and she was gone.

Azag rose from his cushions and addressed his guests. "Here stands Nas'Gavarr's most nubile daughters. Choose whichever you desire most, but if you wish for privacy, I'd suggest taking a bodyguard with you."

Raisha scowled at the chairman. Some of her sisters donned similar expressions, while the younger ones kept their eyes fixed to the ground.

The task force looked to Jeth, forcing him to take the lead once again. He took one step forward and pointed to Raisha. "I'll take the one in the back."

Serra uttered into his ear. "No, Jeth, she knows who you are. She won't cooperate with you. Listen to Istari and get your men out of here!"

"She's cooperated before; she knows I won't hurt her," he said.

"It's not her who stands to get hurt."

"Why would she want to hurt me?"

Raisha's gaze slowly rose to meet Jeth's. Her eyes seared through him like two blazing suns. She lifted her arm and pointed a finger straight at him. "There he is, sisters! There's the vile thief who murdered our father!"

Jeth sighed to himself. "Oh, right."

The other five sisters glared at Jeth. "Avenge Father," one cried.

"Don't let him get away!" screeched another.

Now, every concubine, patron, Bahazur, and merchant's attention was on Jeth and his task force. The light of recognition dawned in Ezrai's eyes, becoming wide and furious. "It *is* you!"

"I tried to warn you, knucklehead," Istari said, smacking him upside the head with an invisible hand.

"Kill them!" Ezrai bellowed.

The three Bahazur nearest to the daughters and three more standing guard in the room took their tabars in hand and rushed toward the Del'Cabrians.

"We're going to need our weapons," said Jeth.

"Way ahead of you, Fairy Boy," Ash replied from somewhere behind him. Khiri rippled into sight, tossing Jeth and Oliver their bows and quivers.

Jeth dove, catching his weapons before they hit the floor. Reunited with his own bow, Oliver stood at Jeth's back, and the two of them took aim outward. The bowmen shot down two Bahazur about to cleave Loche and Faron in two.

Women screeched and ran for cover. More Bahazur rushed into the room.

Jeth gulped. They were vastly outnumbered.

Three Bahazur surrounded their merchant benefactors in a protective ring, while a dozen more moved in for the attack. Ash appeared in front of the two unarmed urlings and jammed his axe through the first attacker's chest before clashing against the second's, then kicking him away.

He dropped two scabbards at Faron and Loche's feet. "Here you go, Pointies! Now, don't let me hear you say desert dwellers are good for nothing."

The two swordsmen picked up their blades and joined the fray. Istari cloaked and uncloaked herself, blocking attacks or tripping up Bahazur with her staff. Khiri slid between legs, loosing sarongs and swiping knives out of guards' sheathes before slicing open the backs of their ankles.

Jeth kept every sense honed in the chaos, aiming an arrow carefully through the frantic women to the target in his sights. When he had a clear shot of the Bahazur guarding Ezrai, he released his bowstring. The arrow found its mark, settling deep in the center of the man's forehead so that he fell back stiff onto a pile of pillows.

Ezrai ducked behind Rubati, and the ring of Bahazur closed in tighter around the merchants.

Jeth took out an arrow for a second shot, but Serra screeched into his ear. "Behind you!" He spun around to find a Bahazur about to embed a tabar into his spine. The Bahazur was too close for Jeth to draw the arrow, so he staggered backward. His hand reached reflexively for the tulwar at his hip, coming up empty. He frantically looked around on the floor, but it was nowhere to be seen. With a burst of speed, Jeth jumped back just as the warrior's tabar flew forward and scraped the tile floor on the downswing. Loche leaped up and blocked the Bahazur's next slice with his sword.

Jeth scrambled for the nearest body while Loche stumbled back, the guard charging. Jeth searched the body's scabbard, only to find the knife missing. The next body had no weapon either. *Dammit, Khir, you only need one!*

Loche fell and dropped his sword, and the Bahazur raised his poleaxe above his head, prepared to bring it down clean over Loche's midsection.

A sword tip emerged bloody through the man's chest. He collapsed in a bulky heap as Faron yanked his long sword out of his back. The former major nodded to his fellow swordsman before continuing the carnage.

Loche regained his weapon and looked around the room. "Where are the daughters?"

Olivier paused, panting. "They must have run off."

"Loche, go find them." Jeth turned to the merchants. *You need to take care of something first,* he thought.

He nocked an arrow and drew it back, aiming it straight for the Bahazur guarding Ezrai and Rubati. "Oli, take the one on the right."

"Got it." Olivier spun around and took aim next to Jeth.

Together, the bowmen released. The guards fell dead, exposing all three merchants. Other Bahazur took notice and rushed for them.

Istari bellowed. "Close your eyes!" This time, the entire task force knew what to do. The flash went off, rendering the Bahazur blind and dazed. Jeth and Olivier looked up a few seconds later to find all but Ezrai rubbing their eyes and blinking profusely. *He may know Star's tricks, but it doesn't matter. He's yours now.*

"Hey, Ezrai!" He aimed an arrow for his throat. "You really are a cudstain, you know that?"

As Rubati and Azag wandered blindly, Ezrai's milky blue eyes curdled. "You're still searching for Anwarr? Again? She's not here. She was gone long before I ever arrived. So, for the last time, give her up, you pathetic little mongrel."

"You don't know. . . ." Jeth eased on the bowstring.

"Know what?"

Jeth wasn't sure if he should tell Ezrai that his ex-lover died before or after sending an arrow through his windpipe.

Before Jeth could decide his fate, a woman's legs wrapped around Ezrai's waist from behind. Raisha appeared on his back, clutching him around the shoulders with one hand and holding Jeth's tulwar to his neck with the other. "That this is the day you die, merchant scum!"

Raisha dragged the blade across Ezrai's throat in one erratic motion. He grasped his neck, blood gushing violently through his fingers and onto the floor. Gasping in horrid, gargling breaths, he collapsed into his own puddle, and Raisha went down with him. But she was far from done.

She repeatedly plunged the curved sword into his neck, shoulders, and skull, hacking away maniacally with frenzied strikes. Azag and Rubati, their vision clearing, backed away trembling.

The merchants found themselves surrounded by the other five daughters, gripping blades or tabars pilfered from the fallen.

"Back away, girls," Azag warned. "I'm the Merchant Council

Chairman! You don't—you don't want this."

"Oh, we've wanted this for a long time," one of the older daughters replied.

Behind them, their sister cleaved at the flesh of the treasure keeper until his head detached. Raisha held it upside down by the severed spinal cord. Blood trailed down her cheeks, her arm coated in crimson. "You will pay for our sisters' bodies with your heads!"

The other sisters charged the remaining two merchants, taking turns cutting them down until they were nothing more than bloody mush on silk cushions.

More Bahazur ran into the room and halted at the gory sight. Even some of the other merchants who had been partaking in the harem's delights were dragged from their hiding spots and put down by the sisters' knives.

Lys appeared at the entrance, scowling. "What's taking so long? I've been waiting for over—" His tanned skin paled to slate. "Oh . . ."

"Alright, *now* we should leave," Serra said.

Raisha stepped out from the carnage and pointed her blood-drenched tulwar at the survivors in the room.

"Bahazur!" she called. "All the gold earned by the women under this roof belongs to us now. We will part with half if you keep out all unauthorized men or women until our brother returns. Is that a fair deal?"

The Bahazur exchanged glances, then nodded.

"Good. Your first task: Dispose of these intruders." Her wrathful gaze fell on Jeth once again, pointing her blade straight at him. "But leave *him* for us."

The newly hired Bahazur turned to face the team yet again, raising their tabars in preparation to clash.

Faron put out his hands and yelled, "The treaty!"

The Bahazur paused in their advance and looked to Raisha.

"Do you speak of the treaty my father—whom your partner here murdered—made with your King?" she asked.

"If you take up arms against the Crown, the treaty is nullified, and Del'Cabria's aid in the war against Rangardia will be withdrawn." Faron asserted.

Raisha scoffed. "Are you here as an emissary or a salesman? Killing you would not violate the treaty because killing the Overlord already did."

"But our peoples don't know he's dead. As far as they're concerned, the treaty stands. That is why we sent our navy to protect the Odafi ports. Del'Cabria wishes to maintain it regardless."

Raisha spat on Ezrai's butchered corpse. "Odafi can drown in their own blood. Sag damn the treaty!"

"You really don't want to do that, Raisha." Jeth put out his hands.

"Don't I?"

A Bahazur lunged forward, took Jeth by the scruff, and forced him to his knees at Raisha's feet. He held Jeth's head down, exposing the back of his neck to the Saf as she raised her tulwar.

Serra's little voice sounded in his ear. "Don't worry, Jeth. I won't let you die here."

He activated his speed, slowing down time, which allowed him to take a calm, deep breath. The serenity enveloped him, not unlike what he felt on the gallows. Only this time, he intended to survive. There was still a role for him to play; only he had what Raisha and her sisters wanted, even if they didn't realize it yet.

"I have no intention of dying this time," he whispered so softly and quickly, only a fairy could hear it. "I've got a plan."

"Good," she said at a similar speed. "Wait, what do you mean *this time?*"

Before Raisha could bring her sword down, Jeth jerked his head out of his captor's grip. "I know what *really* happened to your father!"

Time sped up again. Raisha's downswing frayed the rug in front of Jeth's knees, throwing her off balance. "I already know what happened," she growled, preparing for another swing. "You killed him!"

The Bahazur snatched Jeth's collar and held him fast. "Don't you want to know how?"

The woman's hand trembled, the sword tip wavering.

Behind him, Jeth heard steel clash and grunts of desperation. He raised an eyebrow, his face a mask of calm even though his heart raced. "My men had nothing to do with it. They only want to sell some oil and help with the war effort so tell your brutes to stand down, and you can have me all to yourself."

She huffed sharply through her nose, then looked up to her recently hired thugs. "Stop!" She lowered her tulwar and sheathed it at her side.

The sounds of struggle behind Jeth ceased.

Raisha continued, "And what of this urling woman you're looking for? Your Light Mage wanted to know if we've seen her. Is she not the true reason you're here?"

"Er . . ."

"My granddaughter," Loche interjected, panting. "She was taken during the Desert War. I wondered if she ended up with the harem. Jeth offered to lend me his old crew to find out while we were here."

Jeth nodded to Loche, internally thanking him for his quick thinking. He then noticed that the room was emptier than before: Istari, Ash, Lys, and Khiri had vanished, likely before the second skirmish began. *Good.* He sighed with relief. They should be able to bust out the taskforce once they got what they needed from Raisha . . . *if* she doesn't kill them first.

Also noticing the crew's absence, Raisha groaned, "Oh, for Sag's sake!" She pointed to three of her Bahazur. "Find the thieves. Don't let them escape." Then, to the ones left behind, she said, "Lock up the Del'Cabrians. My sisters and I will deliberate on what to do with them." She glared at Jeth, still kneeling before her. "But don't think this means you get to live, you pale-faced rat! I may show mercy for your men, but never you . . . do you understand?"

Jeth tilted his head. "Aye."

The Bahazur forced Jeth's arms behind his back and yanked him to his feet. The rest pushed him and his men deeper into the palace.

Jeth looked back at Raisha for a moment. The daughter of Nas'Gavarr only glared. He managed to keep his head for now. Convincing her to help them find Ryeem, however . . .

That depended on how much she wanted the truth about her father.

Jeth could only pray that his negotiation skills would serve him better now than they did with the King of Del'Cabria.

17

A Price Worth Paying

Faron climbed onto a carved stone table that he had pushed to the cell wall and reached his arms out the star-shaped grating bolted to the windows.

They had been locked in a cool, comfortable chamber, complete with plush floor pillows and Serpentine fountains, but it was still a prison. In fact, it was the same prison the six daughters of Nas'Gavarr had been kept in, and before them, the lesser concubines. An affluent cell to keep women in and men out.

Thoughts of Anwarr clawed their way to the forefront of Jeth's mind. *She was probably trapped in a room just like this one while pregnant with your child. Imprisoned to save your sorry arse when all she ever wanted was freedom.* He rubbed his itchy nose, irritated by remnants of perfumes lingering in the air, trying to keep his mind on why he was there: Freedom for the princess, for Snake Eye, and maybe someday . . . his people.

Loche snored from one of the floor pillows as big as a queen-size bed and twice as luxurious.

Olivier dropped a smaller cushion next to Jeth and sat down. "I'm supposed to remind you to take your honey, but it's still with our horses. Hope they don't sell them off or butcher them for meat."

Jeth huffed. "Yours to be sure. They'd never slaughter a Tezkhan-bred steed."

"Until it kicks someone in the face." Olivier pointed a thumb back to Faron, who was now rummaging through mostly empty drawers. "Care to let our former major in on your plan before he collapses from exhaustion?"

"If he'd listen to me, then sure."

"It's not just him you'll have to convince. Tell me again why you think we can reason with those bloodthirsty ladies? We stood a better chance fighting off the Bahazur."

"Right, but then we'd never know if Zephira was here, what Ryeem is up to, or why he took Snake Eye."

"Again, with that bloody ashipu!" Faron heatedly strode across the room to Jeth and Olivier. "Is he the reason you kowtowed to those tribal females? Or is it for your more sordid desires that we find ourselves here?"

"Yes, it has been my number one fantasy to be trapped in the Overlord's palace with you lot and six women who want to stick me with their swords and twist," Jeth muttered.

Faron's entire face puckered as though he'd bit into a lemon, then he turned away in a snit. Jeth was tempted to get under his skin a little more, but he resisted the urge; they didn't have much time before Raisha made up her mind to behead them all.

"Listen, Faron. You have to start trusting me. I know who we're up against, so maybe sit this one out and let me handle the girls."

Faron scoffed. "By all means. Herrani women are your specialty, after all."

Jeth sprang to his feet, and Olivier rose with him, keeping himself between the two men. His fingers twitched at his sides while Faron raised his chin, daring Jeth to retaliate.

Just as the tension in the room threatened to spill into an all-out brawl, Serra flew in through the window grating. "Everyone, I found the crew. They're going to break you all out of here soon."

"Not until you give the signal," Jeth protested. "Didn't you tell them the plan?"

"Of course. Then Ash said, 'What little that Fairy Boy had for brains must have gone with his locks.' I gather that means he thinks your plan is stupid."

"Thanks for the clarification."

"You're welcome." Serra nodded proudly.

"And what, pray tell, is this asinine plan?" Faron crossed his arms.

"To suss out what the daughters know by offering to give them information about who is truly responsible for their father's death . . . besides me."

Faron pursed his lips some more. "Do you plan to do that before or after they execute you?"

"Before would be ideal," Serra said.

"Faron's got a point, Jeth. Why would them ladies do anything you say if they can just torture the truth out of you?"

Jeth had a plan for that as well—one that probably wouldn't work but might allow him to get on Raisha's softer side if she had such a thing. Before he could voice it to the group, a loud click echoed through the room, and the ornate doors swung open.

Four Bahazur marched in, and one of them said, "All of you, against the wall, hands where we can see them."

Serra slipped into Jeth's coat pocket as he and his men complied, except Loche, who simply snorted and turned over in the bed. The Bahazur glanced at the old man for a moment then returned their attention to the conscious men against the wall. "You—Shorty." The leader pointed at Jeth.

"Hey, I'm not that—"

"Kal'Raisha will see you now."

"Kal?"

"Sibling of the Overlord. Now, turn around." As Jeth did so, the man trudged over with rope bindings and tied his hands behind his back. The other Bahazur kept their eyes locked on the remaining Del'Cabrians.

Jeth nodded to both of them, a sideways grin pushing through his previously sour demeanor. "Wish me luck, fellas."

The Bahazur shoved Jeth out of the room, down a series of hallways, and up a broad staircase of polished sandstone. A set of ornate doors led into yet another enormous room. Just outside was a balcony overlooking a still pool with several yellow plumed flamingos preening themselves in the moonlight.

Kal'Raisha emerged from between wide curtains at the far end of the room. All signs of blood from that morning had been washed away. She wore thin, silk robes that wrapped around her compact torso and pants tapered at her ankles. She looked a lot more like the cute Herrani girl who had once tried to lure him to his death with cael petals and a kiss.

Raisha beckoned the hired fighters to bring Jeth through the curtains and into the rest of her bedroom. It was the most elaborate room Jeth had seen yet, likely reserved for Nas'Gavarr's most notable wives, perhaps even Nas'Gavarr himself.

Raisha's angered stare froze Jeth in place, making his pulse hasten even more. "Leave me with him."

With a curt nod, the Bahazur stepped back toward the door. As soon as they closed it behind them, Raisha took steps toward Jeth, recapturing him within her unnerving yellow stare.

Jeth glanced at the bed a few paces away, then back to Raisha's steeled resolve. "You're uh . . . not wanting to resume that night of the Lunahalah, are you? Because I'm in a committed relation—"

Raisha's arms shot out with the speed of a cobra, grabbing him by the throat and pushing him against a wall next to her dresser.

". . . ship," he croaked, squirming in her grip. *When will you learn? Never underestimate a Herrani woman.*

Her small fingers clamped down hard against his jugular. Twinkling lights danced in his vision. He activated his spark to keep from passing out. Even with his hands tied behind his back, he knew he had the strength to overpower her, but he opted to wait for her grip to wane on its own.

As he expected, Raisha's hold on his throat loosened, and blood flowed more freely to his brain. He took a deep breath as she pulled the tulwar from her partly open dresser drawer.

"Hey, that's mine," he said, choking.

"It belongs to *my* family. Yet another thing Anwarr stole from this house." She held it to his throat. "Now, tell me how you did it. How did you kill my father?"

"You're sure it was me who killed him? A thief with zero magical ability destroyed the Immortal Serpent all by himself?"

With a pitched growl, she threw him to the rug and put herself astride him, pressing the tulwar against his neck's stubble. Memories of the night he became the Desert War Traitor, when Anwarr pushed her blade against him in a similar fashion, struck him so hard he became aroused.

"Had it not been for the rapport I shared with him, I'd never have believed a cretin like you was capable of anything, let alone facing the Overlord of Herran." She hissed through her teeth. "And yet, Ryeem saw him follow you into the Deep Wood, then . . . *emptiness* ever since. Tell me what you did to him, and I may grant you a quick death."

Her arm trembled, as did the razor edge she held. A strange discomfort gnawed at Jeth's gut. When he'd decided to bring down Nas'Gavarr, he hadn't given a single thought to those who would mourn him. After all, who could love someone so inhuman? All that mattered in that moment was his forest home . . . and his vengeance.

But Nas'Gavarr was a husband and a father a hundred times over, protector of the women under his roof, and a stabilizing force for the tribes. He wondered if all the chaos and suffering caused by his demise was a price worth paying to stop him. He had to believe it was.

There was only one thing he could say. "I-I'm sorry, Kal'Raisha."

Her lashes fluttered, and she pushed herself off him. "What? You're *sorry?*"

He rolled to the side to take the weight off his bound hands. "I understand the pain and hatred within you, and I know where it leads."

"You think you could possibly understand *my* hatred? You know nothing of family!" she screamed, kicking him in the face. His head cracked against the cool tile. Blood ran out his nose and down the back of his throat.

Serra squirmed inside his pocket. "You don't have to take this, Jeth. I can spark her a good one, right between the eyes."

"Not yet. . . ." He brought himself to his knees with a groan, letting the blood drip from his nose and onto his lip.

"Your father"—Jeth straightened himself again—"hurt a lot of people. Many of whom I cared about."

Raisha yanked the short hairs at the top of his head. "You've racked up quite the body count yourself. I heard all about you, even before we met in Odafi."

"I remember when you touched my hair back then, it didn't hurt so much," Jeth quipped, wincing from the sting of his scalp.

Raisha smiled disingenuously before kneeing him in the face, freeing his hair from her grip at least. "You and Anwarr stole from him time after time, and you wonder why he needed to punish you both? You say you're in a relationship, so I assume you are together again. Did she ever give birth to your wretched offspring?"

"You don't know either." Jeth's heart sank. Raisha had no idea what had transpired in the temple or that Anwarr had never made it out.

"Know what?"

"They're dead. Anwarr and my child . . . because of your father." His jaw steeled. If she didn't know what happened that day, then she likely knew nothing about her father's plans. Ryeem was the only chance they had for finding Snake Eye and the princess.

"Oh." Her eyes floated to the ground for a moment. "Then may

Sagorath's flame keep them warm in the afterlife." A spark of sympathy. Something Jeth could use.

"I'll tell you how he died."

"Your baby?"

"No. Your father. I'll tell you how we did it."

"We?" She reaffirmed her grip on the tulwar.

"I do not deny my part in it, but it wasn't me who executed the finishing blow."

Raisha put the pointed edge of her blade to Jeth's cheek, mere inches from his left eye. "Who did?"

Jeth took a deep breath and replied. "You'll have to tell me where Ryeem is first."

"You don't get to make demands!" She raised the tulwar above her head.

Jeth fell back to avoid her swing, and Serra popped out of his coat, sending a globule of green sparks at Raisha's hand.

The tulwar dropped to the floor with an echoing clatter. "Ow! What in Sag's justice is that thing?"

Serra hovered before her, her tiny hand glowing with her next spark. "Attack him again and find out."

Raisha paused, her mouth agape.

Serra zipped behind Jeth and untied his bindings.

Her eyes wide with panic, Raisha bent over to grab the tulwar, but Jeth dashed forward with his heightened speed and kicked it out of her reach. She snapped up straight and backed away, her hands out in front of her.

"I need your help, Raisha," Jeth said.

With a growl, she pulled a shiv from her bejeweled hair tie. Before she could embed it into Jeth's neck, a shining green globule knocked it from her hand like before. She stared at her hand, absent the tiny weapon.

"I'm a pixie," said Serra.

Both Jeth and Raisha looked at the fairy in confusion.

"I told her if she attacked you again, she'd find out what I am. Now she knows."

"Right," said Jeth. "No need to protect me anymore, Ser. I got this." He turned back to Raisha. "Your brother has information my team and I need. I don't want to kill him, but I do need to find him."

"Coming from the man who killed my father and my betrothed in the same year, somehow, I don't believe you."

Jeth sighed, realizing if he were going to break through Raisha's resentment and earn a modicum of trust, he would have to reveal their mission. "All we want is to find the Princess of Del'Cabria. Ryeem may be the last person alive who knows where your father put her."

"Ah. The supposed granddaughter . . ." She crossed her arms and put a finger to her chin. "If only there were someone else alive who could tell you where she is."

"You can contact Ryeem right now, find out what he knows, and I'll tell you everything I know about your father's death."

A gob of saliva launched from Raisha's mouth and smacked against Jeth's cheek. He wiped it off with his sleeve. "So, that's a no, then?"

"I won't betray my brother!"

"Are you sure he hasn't betrayed you?" Jeth posed.

Her lashes fluttered, her eyes growing wet. "You know nothing of him." She picked up the shiv from the floor and dove for Jeth again. Serra didn't come to his aid this time, but she didn't have to. Jeth ducked behind one of the curtains, and the blade tore through the dizzying fabric.

"I know he'd rather build his naja army than help his sisters in need."

"That army is for us!" She shoved the curtains aside.

Jeth backed away toward the balcony. "Surely, the naja he already has are sufficient in taking back the palace. Instead, he's used it to abduct an ashipu and left you here as prisoners in your own home."

"Shut up!" she screamed, frantically lunging to cut into Jeth but not landing a single slice. "Stand still, you coward. Murderous, good-for-nothing dog!"

"You and your sisters couldn't escape. It was not until I asked the merchants to bring you upstairs that you had any opportunity to save yourselves. How many times did you reach out only for him to ignore your call?"

"Jeth, someone's watching us from outside," Serra peeped.

He snapped his head toward the balcony. Obscured by the sheer curtains, a silhouette of something large and dark was perched on the balustrade. He put his finger up to Raisha. "Hold on."

Jeth ran onto the balcony just as the creature fluttered away and vanished into the shadows. Flamingos squawked, flying into the night sky. The thing he saw was too large to be one of them . . . perhaps a vulture? It was consistent with the smell of desert sand and dry decay that washed over him.

"Did you see it, Ser?"

"No. Too dark."

Giving Jeth no time to investigate further, Raisha charged onto the balcony. Her next swing came less than an inch from Jeth's face. He snatched her hand effortlessly and forced the shiv from her slack grip. She tried her fists instead, pounding against his chest. He struggled to restrain her wild arms, but she jerked them out of his grasp and continued slapping.

He spun Raisha around and held her arms down to her sides from behind. "Reach out to Ryeem. Then, I will divulge everything about your father's last moments. What he said. What his real plans were. Plans he kept from you."

Raisha stilled, but her heart thrashed violently against Jeth's chest. He let her go, and she staggered backward.

She picked up her fallen shiv once more and pointed it at him, maintaining a safe distance. "I will not bargain with you or your men. My sisters and I will take as many shifts as necessary to get the truth out of you one way or another."

"How about I keep sparking her until she accepts your offer," Serra suggested.

"There's no need for that. We'll do it her way." *Time for your last resort. Hope this works.*

Jeth took off his coat and began unbuttoning his vest.

"What are you doing?" Raisha's voice quavered, the shiv still pointed straight at him.

"Yes, Jeth, what are you doing?" Serra joined.

"The lady wants to take all her rage out on me. Can't say I blame her. Let her give it a go." After dropping his waistcoat to the floor, he pulled his shirt off and tossed it onto the pile. He raised his hands over his head, turned around, and placed them on the balustrade.

"Jeth . . ." Serra gasped. Indeed, the crisscrossing scabs inflicted a month and a half ago were a shocking sight.

Raisha was silent, apart from her pounding heart and erratic breathing.

"What are you waiting for?" Jeth called back to her.

"Did my father do that?"

"What, to my back?" Jeth bobbed his head backward. "Hah. No.

He inflicted the scars you can't see. These were done by my own people . . . more or less."

"The people whose princess you now search for?" she guessed.

"Aye, the ones who hold my future and the futures of everyone I care about within their cold, pale fingers. There's nothing you or your sisters can do to me that they couldn't do a thousand times worse. So, come on, get it over with if it'll make you feel better."

He heard the clink of the shiv falling to the floor. Raisha collapsed to her knees with a sigh of exhaustion.

Jeth slumped in relief, ready to collapse himself, but he couldn't, not now. Instead, he bent down to pick up his shirt and put it back on, equipping himself with his irreverent sense of humor once again. "Are my scars so hideous they can even move a woman who hates me to tears?"

"Ryeem's not coming home," she rasped.

"Why not?" Serra asked. Jeth found himself wishing something terrible had happened to Ryeem for Snake Eye's sake but dreaded it at the same time for what it meant for their mission.

Raisha lifted her head, black streaks running down her face. "Something's wrong. He reaches out to me, but . . . he's different."

"Different how?"

"He's shown me things, through our rapport, things I know he'd never want me to see." She wiped her tears, smearing her dark kohl across her cheek.

"What sort of things?" said Jeth, his pulse hastening.

"Bones. His naja—what he's making them do to that ashipu . . ."

"What did he do to him?"

"I don't know, I only get flashes. I think Ryeem needs my help."

Jeth crouched down and looked at Raisha dead on. "Did he show you where he is?"

With a quivering lip, she nodded. "The Naja Archipelago." Her voice came out as a whisper, barely audible were it not for Jeth's hearing.

"What would he be doing all the way out there?"

"How should I know?" she shouted, shocking his finely tuned ears, "You claim to have insight into my father's plans. Tell me why the man I've known since infancy, a man I've come to think of as a second father, has ignored my pleas to come home so he can torture ashipus and play with bones in the jungle!"

Jeth licked his lips, his mind whirling with confusion. "If you take us to him, and he doesn't kill us on sight, I will uphold my end of the bargain regardless of what information we get."

She dried her tears and stood on two feet. "Understand, I don't give a damn about you or your princess, but it is my duty to help Ryeem, my sisters, and all of Herran. Go back on your word, and I will make no attempt to stop his naja from turning you and your team inside out. In fact, I will do it myself."

Jeth picked up his coat and put it back on. "I can live with that."

"Bahazur!" Raisha suddenly called. Three men burst through the door and rushed onto the balcony. Serra flew back into Jeth's coat pocket in a flash. "Take this man back to the other Del'Cabrian prisoners . . . return all their belongings, and escort them off the premises."

They gave hesitant nods and led Jeth to the door without a word.

Raisha followed them back inside and picked up the tulwar from the floor. "Wait for me in the atrium," she called after them. "I'll be going, too."

Vidya's boots clacked upon the pink marble as she strolled across Citadel Plaza, blood from the night she was made Anassa still staining the mortar between each stone.

She strode past sparring harpies, clashing their blunted forearm blades together. Removing her helm, Vidya gazed up at the harpies circling above. Air kicked up by their wings tousled her curls, and she grinned as a proud mother would at her children taking their first steps.

The first thirty harpies had trained the next seventy, together becoming a squadron she coined the Primaries. Now, the next hundred—the Secondaries—watched the Primaries glide above before attempting flight on their own. Another hundred squabs still recuperated at the estates. They would be her Tertiaries when their wings fully formed. In less than a month, the Harplite would be three hundred and counting. Vidya sighed in satisfaction.

One of her Primaries plummeted from the sky and landed in a heap right in Vidya's path.

"Wind is your friend, Malantha." Vidya picked the lieutenant up by the arm. "Coax it beneath you, and it will guide you safely to ground."

Malantha wiped the drops of perspiration running down her forehead and glistening on her scalp. She, like many others Vidya had freed from prison, preferred to keep their hair shorn. "Thank you,

Anassa," she said and launched back into the air.

Holding her helm under her arm, Vidya climbed the steps of the Grand Altar, where she found the supreme commander standing at the precipice on the other side, her steel plate corset reflecting the afternoon sun.

"Your men told me I'd find you here," she said as she stepped up beside Cosima and matched her gaze to the salty expanse.

Cosima's bony fingers crushed a rolled-up parchment. "Men and their incessant posturing."

"Your men giving you trouble?"

She handed the parchment to Vidya. "Not mine. A message from the capitán general."

Vidya unrolled the crinkled paper and read the words written by Señor Jiménez. The Royal Navy of Del'Cabria had formed a blockade at the Odafi Gulf. They claimed to be protecting their trade routes in and out of Tradesmen's Bay. It just so happened they blocked access to Odafi's southernmost and busiest port, one the armada had been most eager to take since the war started but wasn't able to until they took the other ports along the way.

"Protecting their trade routes," Cosima spat with a shake of her head. "They're clearly in Odafi seas. And do you think Odafi minds that their former foe now sits on their waters? No. They all act as if the treaty is still in place even though no one has publicly taken up the Overlord's mantle."

Vidya rolled up the parchment. "They all wish to pretend he's still alive despite so much evidence to the contrary. That belief keeps them united as much as it fuels male uprisings here. You know there's a group calling themselves—get this—the *Serpent's Brethren.*" She snorted and shook her head.

"Perhaps some cannon fire would scare them off." Cosima swished her burgundy skirts back and forth.

Vidya snapped her head around to face her. "They had better not be thinking of doing that. Any attack on their ships will start an all-out war between Rangardia and Del'Cabria." Vidya thought on the notion for a moment. Such a war would certainly make Ricardo's future alliance with Tiberius more difficult. She quickly dismissed the idea outright. The armada couldn't hope to fight two fleets at once. Far too risky.

"Nonsense," Cosima said. "The Primaries can sink them all with a flap of their wings, safe under cover of storm clouds. The Royal Navy will believe it to be an act of their deities."

Vidya pointed to a name written on the message. "Fleet Admiral Kipling is there. Do you know who he is?"

Cosima pursed her lips and shrugged. "I'm going to assume the fleet admiral?"

"He's the Queen's older brother and one of the most respected officers in the Del'Cabrian war machine. This is a kingdom that declared war for the life of one senator. What do you think will happen if the Queen's brother were to die at sea for any reason? They'd send more ships, more men, more vengeance. Not something we need right now."

"Let them send as many as they please," scoffed Cosima. "What do we have a plague for?"

Vidya ground her teeth together. "The plague can only be used as a last resort. Deploying that now would be playing our hand far too soon. We can't have Tiberius thinking us a threat until after we've dealt with the desert tribes, as planned."

Cosima groaned, "Because our wonderful plan has been working so well."

Vidya could relate to the supreme commander's frustration. Attacking the desert's primary source of wealth was supposed to concentrate their forces on that area while drawing out Ryeem and other prominent family members. Except few showed up to fight. Most made themselves scarce, particularly Ryeem. The most powerful Magc in Herran and General of the Naja Horde disappeared without a trace. The shadow harpy was no help either. All she could sense was that he was out there somewhere, plotting. Knowing a man's heart was not the same as knowing his location. Vidya had to rely on her spies to figure that out.

The shadow soared across Vidya's ocean view, a dark blotch in the pristine blue sky, leaving no reflection in the sea below. *"Once the desert tribes finally disband, the Harplite will be ready. Then Del'Cabria will fall."*

Not before Rangardia, thought Vidya.

As much as she hated the idea of using the siren's tactics, if her plan failed to remove the Rangardian brothers from power, the plague was the only way to prevent their alliance with Del'Cabria after the war in Odafi was over. Ricardo would have to reconsider his strategy if the mainland fell to disease. It would buy her Harplite the time it needed to reach one thousand.

"We will find Ryeem," Vidya asserted.

"I know, it's just that if I can't fly anymore, it would be nice to do it vicariously through these fine squabs." Cosima turned around to look upon the new harpies.

"Sirens hardly fly anyway," Vidya turned around with her. "It messes up their hairdos."

"Oh, we fly alright . . . when few are watching." The siren winked.

Among the activity in the plaza, Vidya spotted silhouetted wings against the sun's rays. She was prepared to dismiss it as the shadow until Cosima pointed. "Look who it is."

A raven-winged harpy dive-bombed through the flock, swooped upward, and made a purposeful landing at the altar steps. The sharp island breeze whipped her long black ponytail around her neck. Vidya's heart warmed.

"Commander Phrea." Cosima sashayed over to her, took her hands, and patted them affectionately. "You look like you flew all the way from Herran in one night."

"I couldn't take the time to sail. The news I have is too urgent," she said.

"You found Ryeem," Vidya trembled in anxious anticipation.

Phrea gave a sly grin. "Not exactly, but close."

"So, he didn't return to take back the harem from those filthy merchants." Vidya dug her nails into her palms.

"No," Phrea said. "And believe me, to ignore my harpy instinct to rain down brutal punishment upon them was a trying task indeed."

"I understand, but we can't show ourselves to our enemies too soon. As far as they're concerned, Credence is still ruled by sirens and has no taste for the wars of men," Vidya reminded.

"Doesn't matter now," said Phrea as the three women walked up the stairs leading to the Citadel's second-floor gardens. "The harem took back the palace for themselves, thanks to a little Del'Cabrian distraction."

Cosima gasped. "Del'Cabrians were at the palace? So, they and Herran are in cahoots after all."

"I don't think so." They passed a bush filled with dead lilacs, and Phrea snapped one off and twirled it between her thumb and forefinger. "They posed as oil peddlers to gain access but were actually on some secret mission. It turned into a pretty bloody brawl, from what I could gather. Would have loved to have seen it firsthand."

"Were they looking for Ryeem too?" Vidya asked as Phrea tossed the dead flower over her shoulder.

"Yes, but not for the reason you think." She stepped in front of them and halted their stroll. "You wouldn't believe what I overheard between his sister Raisha and one of the Del'Cabrians."

Phrea raised her unibrow up and down as Cosima stirred irritably. "Oh, come on, out with it. Dancing around the subject is only fun when I do it."

"For once, I'm in agreement with a siren," said Vidya dryly.

Phrea flicked her silky black ponytail off her shoulder and said with a glint in her eyes, "They are searching for the Princess of Del'Cabria. Apparently, Nas'Gavarr took her at some point during the Desert War, and now they think Ryeem has her. It could be the reason he's been too busy to fight for the tribes."

Another sharp breeze blew dead lilacs around the gardens. One shriveled petal caught in Vidya's hair. She flicked it off, and her spine tightened. Did the King give up his daughter in addition to the Ingleheim borderlands to end the war? Or did Nas'Gavarr take her by force?

Then, a shockwave ran through her. *Could she be a Champion?* She shook that thought out of her mind. Had that been true, Nas'Gavarr would have gone after Yasharra right after the Serpentine—not to mention, the ashray would have realized she was their Champion when she and Jeth came to them in Thessalin. Why hide that information if they knew Nas'Gavarr had had her the whole time?

"He must have captured her somehow and used her to get the King to agree to their treaty. That explains why they gave in so quickly," Vidya muttered.

"And stranger still," Phrea continued. "The Del'Cabrian she spoke with claimed he saw Nas'Gavarr die, but you would be the only one who can say that, right?"

Vidya snapped her head up and glared at Phrea. "What did this man look like? Did he have long matted hair?"

"No, not at all, just looked like your everyday Del'Cabrian human."

Vidya's pulse calmed somewhat. *There's no way Jeth could even stand after what I did to him. And working for the King? Laughable. It's probably one of the soldiers who fought at the Deep Wood that day.*

"Although," Phrea continued. "There was something odd about him."

Vidya's hairs stood on end. "Odd?"

"There was this—well, he had what appeared to be . . . a fairy with him."

Vidya's face flushed. "A fairy? Are you sure?"

"It's not like I've ever seen one before. Through the curtains, I thought it was some dragonfly buzzing around inside, but it spoke. In fact, it nearly caught me eavesdropping, the little rascal."

The heat in Vidya's cheeks moved into her chest. What her spy was relaying made zero sense. "I've seen fairies, and they are much bigger than dragonflies."

"I don't know what to tell you, Vidi. When it came outside, I saw it clearly. A tiny woman with wings. What else could it have been?"

Vidya didn't know what to think, but one thing was for certain. If Phrea saw a fairy, then the Del'Cabrian could be no one other than Jeth. But why search for the princess? What could she possibly mean to him? She waited for her shadow to say something, but it was often silent when it came to that good-hearted Fae'ren . . . except for the day in the Deep Wood, the last day she saw him. *'He will continue to stand against us . . . punish him!'*

"Great work, Phrea," she said. "This changes everything."

"In what way, Anassa?" asked Cosima.

"I might know how we can get Del'Cabria to pull out of the gulf and never interfere with our plans again." *And free ourselves from Rangardian dependency ahead of schedule,* she finished in thought. Vidya nestled her helmet back on her head, "Phrea, track the Del'Cabrians. Find out where Ryeem and this princess are and report back. We will gather the Primaries. It's time that the Harplite makes its first descent."

18
First Lesson

(One year and ten months ago)

Zephira's bare feet planted squarely on the cold warping gate platform. A cool breeze swept through her hair. The smell of rotting seaweed, among other foreign odors, invaded her nasal passages. She opened her eyes to a dark rainforest on her right and a gravelly beach, cloaked in fog, on her left. She was not in Del'Cabria anymore.

She hugged her arms and shivered. Someone next to her cleared his throat. She jumped at the sight of a skeletal-tattooed man near the crankshaft. Turning to run back through the gate, she stopped short as Gavarr emerged from the blue energy like a man spontaneously pouring into existence.

He went straight to the handle sticking out the side of the ring and pulled. The rippling energy collapsed with a loud crack that made Zephira jolt. He turned the ring until it more or less faced the ocean, then said to his robed follower, "Create a new pathway to the temple and keep it active until I return."

"Yes, Master." The man bowed and went to task.

Gavarr continued down the base steps, expecting Zephira to follow as usual. He handed her one of the bags he'd been carrying, which was heavier than she'd expected, and she nearly dropped it. They continued down a small path, deeper into the tropical forest.

"What manner of wilderness is this? Are we in . . . Ankarr?" She tried to recall the various landscapes hanging from the castle walls, painted by the artists who accompanied Del'Cabrian explorers.

"All you need to know is that this is a place of great importance, where no one will find you until the time is right."

Zephira hefted the sack over her shoulder, her legs wobbling with exhaustion. The sharp gravel earth cut into her already lacerated feet, and she had to stop and put her shoes back on. While she tied the laces holding the rose-dyed suede together, she asked, "When will the time be right? Or is that something I also don't need to know?"

He stopped and turned around. "I make this promise to you now: You will not perish here. But you will suffer, that cannot be avoided."

She finished tying her laces and stood up straight. "What could possibly be worth all this suffering?"

"Freedom for humanity."

"Freedom from what?"

"From the ancients. From your kind."

The way he said 'kind' with so much vitriol sent waves of indignation through her.

She let go of her bag, arms stiff at her sides. "Do you truly believe urlings stand in the way of human freedom? I've read all about what your uncivilized tribes do with their *freedom*, and believe me, more of it is not the answer to your woes. Only the Balance will save you. Unless you learn to control your primitive urges, humanity and their societies will continue to rot in their own depravity."

Gavarr smirked. "You seem to know much, Princess. My aim is to teach you so much more."

"There is nothing from you that I wish to learn."

"But you will learn." He turned and continued down the path. Zephira's heart sank deeper into her chest the further she followed the Mage through the jungle.

"Perhaps it is I who should teach you a thing or two. Are you not to be my servant?"

The immortal Mage huffed, almost amused. "Never said I'd be yours."

In a quarter-hour, they came upon a small, abandoned village. Little stone cottages encircled an old fire pit and a well. The scant cubed structures were built in an architectural style different from any historical Del'Cabrian settlement she had studied, granting her no clues as to where they were. The quiet stillness made her shiver.

She took a step forward. *Crunch.* Looking down she saw a partially buried skull, crushed by her heel. More bone fragments were scattered along the ground.

She reeled back with a screech.

"Try not to disturb the bones," Gavarr said nonchalantly. "This is a gravesite as much as it will be your home for the next few months."

"You cannot be serious." She gulped.

Another robed man appeared from one of the cottages and greeted his master. Gavarr dropped his bag at his feet and said to Zephira, "Leave everything here and follow me. Your first lesson is at hand."

Her entire body yearned to collapse, but still, she followed. They ventured down another jungle path until the old stone houses vanished behind the trees. Thick fog congregated all around them, limiting visibility. The small amount of sun that shone through the jungle before was now wholly absorbed.

Gavarr stopped at a precipice and spread the thick mist apart with a wave of his arms, granting Zephira a clearer view of the valley below. Through the vines and ferns, jagged black rocks stood in a circular formation around a dark pool of mud, black as a void.

A foul stench wafted up to her nose, making her cover her face and recoil.

"Look," Gavarr pointed to the black goop encased in the henge. It moved like air bubbles bursting at the surface.

"What is that?" she whispered.

"The gateway to humankind's salvation," Gavarr replied. "Otherwise known as . . . the Skour."

She continued to stare into the black pool. A tubular shape emerged—a tentacle appendage writhing, then another. An awful wail pierced the fog, sending tremors through Zephira's body. She backed away, bumping into Gavarr's chest behind her.

He gently placed both hands over her shoulders. "From now on, you will remain in the settlement and mind the magi while I'm gone. As long as I draw breath, what you see down there will not touch you. Do you understand?"

Her pulse raced at the sight of the tentacle creatures stretching out of the pool toward them. *Do they . . . do they have faces?* It was still too foggy to see them clearly. Then, something else emerged from the black.

The fog wrapped around a dark figure, taking slow, wobbling steps out of the pool. Heaps of soiled hair hung like dripping ropes from its scalp. It stopped and stood up straight, revealing its naked female form born out of the primordial soup. Alien and yet, startlingly familiar. Zephira's blood turned to ice.

"No . . ." She shook her head back and forth, her stomach churned. "You cannot leave me here with this unholy thing!"

The figure kept staring at her. It was thin, ragged, and savage. The mist shifted, revealing parts of its face. Two violet eyes trapped her, hungry, Zephira's own orbs in a sea of black.

The princess shut her eyes and shook her head. "This cannot be real. This is flesh magic or spirit magic or . . ."

"What do you see?"

She forced her eyes open. The figure in the fog was gone.

"You won't break me. You won't." Fists clenched, Zephira repeated those words, shaking her head back and forth until Gavarr sharply spun her around.

He brought his face close to hers. "Your first lesson is to understand how you are no different than the so-called depraved humans you look down upon. The world will come to know just how primitive you truly are, and there will be no urling alive who can assert their dominance over those deemed 'lower beings' ever again. Because through you, they will come to know their true god. The future is humanity, and if you have a shred of consideration for your people, you will take your place in leading them on this new path . . . as I have."

"You're evil." Her legs turned to gelatin, but Gavarr tightened his grip on her arms, keeping her upright.

He reached out and gently touched her face while his own stiffened, his eyes severe. "Not evil, just a man who has seen the truth. And someday soon, you will see it too."

19
Time to Adjust

The pirate brig bounded over the Ankarran seas, lurching up and down with Jeth's stomach. He heaved over the bulwark. Everything he had managed to eat that day flew out of him and spewed over the thrashing waves below. *How come no one told you sailing would be like this?*

Ash had managed to drum up a favor from the old pirate crew he had worked with on the job to find Dulsakh's Sarcophagus. They were lucky the crew was both available and willing to take them through the dangerous waters. It still required Jeth part with a fair amount of his gold stash from his Ingleheim job to sweeten the deal. He hoped the King would reimburse him when he returned.

Serra sat on the bulwark, her little legs dangling over the side. "Have you tried holding it in?" she asked with innocent fascination.

"Yes," he groaned.

"It smells unpleasant; wouldn't you prefer to stop doing it?"

"Can you go shoot sparks somewhere or something?" He glared, but the uncontrollable urge to hurl took him away from his fairy guardian. He leaned over the bulwark once again, but nothing came up.

"Sorry, just trying to help." And with a burst of sparks, she was gone before he lifted his head again.

Another dry heave captured Olivier's attention.

"You still doing that?"

Jeth turned from the undulating ocean to Olivier, carrying two jars of whale oil from below deck. "You wouldn't happen to have a seasickness remedy in that bag of yours?"

Olivier laughed. "It's a medical bag, Jeth, not a magic bag. Just keep your eyes on the horizon, and it'll pass." He reaffirmed his grip on the jars and continued on his way.

"Thanks, Oli." *Except, I've tried that!*

Raisha scrambled past the medic, nearly knocking the jars out of his arms. She, too, retched over the side of the ship a few feet from where Jeth stood.

Without warning, Jeth followed suit.

The two leaned against the bulwark for a moment, gagging and breathless, then sank to seated positions next to each other. "I was made for riding, not sailing," Raisha griped, taking off her bandana to wipe the sweat from her face.

"Same here," Jeth croaked.

He thought of Torrent back on the Ankarran coast. He silently prayed that the men they hired would be able to manage her. His stomach churned, and he searched for something to distract himself. "Has Ryeem shown you anything lately? Like if Snake Eye's still alive?"

"It looks like he's chained up in ruins or something." She stifled another gag, her bronze complexion taking on a green tint. "But that was days ago."

Jeth could only groan in response.

After a few moments, Raisha asked, "Snake Eye. Is he really a relative of mine?"

"Aye. He's your father's only living sibling, and even though he played a role in his death, he's a noble person who just wants what's best for the tribes."

Raisha frowned. "If he is trying to usurp my brother, then he is my enemy. But"—she sighed—"he is family. If my father didn't think it appropriate to kill him, then I cannot allow Ryeem to do it, at least not until I get my answers."

"And you'll get them . . . as long as Ryeem's agreed to the terms. He did respond to your mind messages, right?"

"Yes, I told him that Del'Cabria sent a task force to aid Odafi, and they happened to liberate us from merchant exploitation. He expects you want to discuss an extension of the treaty. And yes, I used only your men's names, not yours."

Jeth held back another wave of nausea as the ship lurched downward. "And I'm trusting you to not let Snake Eye's rescue slip."

Raisha gave Jeth a daring look. "You trust me now?"

"Why shouldn't I? You've carried that tulwar around for weeks and have yet to drive it through my back. Where I come from, that's a pretty good start to any mutually trusting relationship."

She smirked and bobbed her head. "Makes sense, actually." Lifting the sheathed sword from around her shoulder, she placed it on Jeth's lap. "I suppose I should give this back."

He picked it up and partially unsheathed it. The sun's rays bounced off the metal and into his eyes briefly before he slid it back in. This sword had quite the history. Stolen by Anwarr, nearly killing Loche, gifted to Chief Ukhuna, claiming Nas'Gavarr's hand, and bringing a gruesome end to Ezrai before almost taking Jeth's head off. The blade followed him around like the memories of Anwarr that he just couldn't shake.

"Can I ask you a question?"

Raisha put up a finger and held her other hand to her lips, threatening to hurl again.

When she appeared to have regained her composure, he asked, "Did you really want to marry Chief Ukhuna of the Tezkhan Raiders?"

She pressed her tongue against her cheek. "It's not a question of whether I wanted to marry him; it was what our union meant for Herran that mattered. If I didn't do it, any one of my sisters would have volunteered, and I could think of a worse life than riding the fastest horses in the world across endless plains."

Jeth huffed. "Well, when I was there, it didn't look like their women were all that free to do much of anything, let alone ride the plains. I figured you Herrani value freedom too highly to submit to that kind of existence."

"You should know that men who aim to take the freedom from Herrani women, especially ones with a direct spiritual connection to the world's most powerful Mages, don't live very long."

"As I've seen." Jeth chuckled, then rose to his feet.

He bid Raisha adieu and went down to his cabin to sleep off the nausea, which seemed to help a little. When he woke, he drank some garlic honey while he could still keep something down.

He fished out the princess's trinket from his coat pocket. Flipping it over, he polished the silver backing with his handkerchief. "'The Balance is the duality between the Pure and the Primitive. Only through penance can one maintain it,'" he recited. He studied the symbols representing each word as he often did to stave off bouts of boredom on his travels. It was the only thing he knew how to read, and in a strange way, it brought him comfort.

"It's just a precaution," Jeth called after him.

He shook his head, expelling the frustration from his nose in loud huffs.

Jeth stood, watching Faron walk across the main deck to join the rest of the pirate crew as they made their preparations. *You know the urling bastard may be right, don't you?* It didn't matter what he thought. They didn't travel all this way to leave Snake Eye behind, especially if there was a chance Ryeem had no information on the princess. At least they knew Snake Eye would be there for sure.

A large wave smashed against the hull, throwing Jeth off his feet. He bounced off a solid mass and looked up to find Ash looming over him.

"Hey there, Big Fella." Jeth steadied himself against the much larger man.

"Not entirely unrelated to the conversation I just overheard, but you might want to rethink sending Sir Serious to meet Ryeem." Ash nodded to Faron and Olivier, tying the oil samples to the mainmast so they wouldn't roll around the deck. "Take Ginger Mustache instead."

"No, Oli stays here. I need as many archers as possible to defend the ship in case anything goes awry. *You* can go with them."

"Oh no, Ryeem could easily recognize me from the last time Star and I swiped Snake Eye out of his custody."

"That's true." Jeth gave a shrugging nod. "But there's a risk of death on any big job, isn't that what you used to say?"

Ash let out a loud guffaw. "My death maybe, but not Snake Eye's. Besides, Star won't be too happy having to protect the oasis by herself if I don't make it back."

"Then Faron and Loche it is," said Jeth.

"It's only Faron who poses a problem."

Faron barked at the pirates, his haughty, monotone voice carrying across the deck. "Careful where you point that contraption!"

Khiri, dressed in pirate attire, scowled at the urling and continued to load one of the harpoon guns laid across the deck. They were one of the few ranged weapons that could pierce a naja's thick hide.

"I get why you're worried, Ash," said Jeth. "But I'm telling you. He's the best swordsman around and will lay down his life for his king and country. He's the last man to botch this up."

The two men continued their stroll along the deck. Ash stopped to help a pirate with the sails. "He's constantly undermining you."

"He just needs time to adjust to the new . . . dynamic."

to keep his naja far from our meeting point. If we see even one, we'll turn back, and the treaty is null." Raisha glared at Jeth. "Or just tell him to do it as a sign of good faith, but we will be bringing our weapons just in case."

With a sigh, Raisha nodded and walked away from the group. Jeth could hear her mutterings at the bow.

Turning to the task force, Jeth said, "Did you get all that? Faron, Loche, you're going to do all the talking." Jeth took out the brooch and handed it to the navigator. "In case the princess is there, give her this so she knows she can trust us."

Loche nodded and put the item in his waist pouch as Faron looked onward curiously.

"Khiri, you're going to paddle the boat with Raisha and me. I want you at the meetup as well. Ryeem may hold back hostilities if there's a child present." Khiri grinned wide, his gaze turning up at Ash for a sign of approval, which the big man gave with a nod.

Jeth continued, "Oli, you're staying here with the pirate crew. You know what to do."

"Aye, aye." The bowman saluted.

"And Serra?" Jeth called out, looking around.

She fluttered over from the crows-nest. "You called?"

"When we get closer, you'll need to scout ahead. Find out where Snake Eye is held and warn of any naja encampments along the way. Then, I'm going to retrieve him. I'll just need something to break his chains."

Ash handed Jeth a Steinkamp glove and a blast gel dispenser. "This ought to do it. Careful not to blow him to bits."

"I know how it works." Jeth turned to the rest of the group. "Any questions?"

Waiting for a response and getting none, Jeth nodded, and the men went to prepare the lifeboats. As the brig sailed into the twisting archipelago seaways, Raisha returned to the forecastle and pointed to the islands.

"It's that one straight ahead."

"Good. Boys and girls," Ash called to his pirate crew, "prepare to drop anchor."

20

Inhuman Wrath

Jeth tried not to sneeze under the mildewed blanket kept him hidden. Khiri rowed the small boat to shore with Raisha sitting behind him and Jeth behind her, out of sight. Loche and Faron rowed the second boat just ahead.

Once they lurched onto the shore, Jeth remained still, listening as everyone left the boats and followed the Mage presumably waiting for them on the beach. He waited until he felt Serra's tiny feet step on him. "I've done my reconnaissance," she said. "And the others are out of sight."

Jeth emerged from under the blanket and hopped onto the pristine sand. "Did you find him?"

"Yes, but the way is dangerous. Follow me exactly."

"Good, but first, I'll need naja blood. Lots of it."

Serra frowned, but after Jeth explained why he needed it, she flew back into the bush.

He scurried up a slanted palm tree, bent from repeated tropical storms. A few minutes later, Serra led a lone naja onto the beach, and Jeth sent an arrow right through the top of its skull, killing it instantly. He jumped down and sliced open its throat with his dagger, spraying bright orange blood onto the white sand.

"Quick, we don't have much time," Serra warned.

"I know, but this is my best shot at getting through the jungle undetected." He cut through the reptile's tough flesh, holding his breath to not take in the putrid stench. *Alright, here goes . . . not like this is new territory for you or anything.* He put down his weapons and removed his shirt and trousers. Taking handfuls of blood, Jeth smeared it all over his head, face, torso, and legs, disturbed by how temperate it felt on his bare skin.

Upon collecting his weapons, he tucked the blast gel dispenser in his underpants then he and Serra raced into the jungle. The pixie zoomed ahead, leaving a sparkling trail behind her, which Jeth followed precisely. He picked up speed, the tropical foliage around him blurred in his periphery until all he could see was his fairy guardian, keeping just ahead of him.

She came to an abrupt stop behind a fallen tree trunk. Jeth slid to a crouch, catching his breath. Carefully peeking around the tree, he spied a circle of crumbling stone stairs, overgrown with vines and leading into a crater flooded with muddy water. Three small shrines sat upon a rectangular platform in the middle, with three naja guarding them.

"He's in that center one," Serra whispered.

Jeth could make out the familiar scent of the ashipu wafting from the center hut. There was also the sickeningly sweet aroma of human blood and rotting flesh, a smell Jeth was unfortunately all too familiar with.

He bit the inside of his cheek. The naja didn't seem to sense him, but if he tried to pick any of them off with arrows, the commotion would bring the others upon him at once. "Ser, this time, you need to lead the naja away."

"Shouldn't be too difficult. These creatures aren't that bright." The pixie floated nonchalantly into the ancient ruins, then sparked a naja right between the eyes. The reptile shrieked, capturing the attention of the other two. Before long, Serra had all three of them riled up and following her into the bush.

Jeth knew they'd get tired of chasing her soon and come right back to their post. *You have to act fast.* He bounded down an incline and made a running leap across the moat, then followed his nose through the doorway of the central shrine.

A rail-thin figure slumped against the wall, barely discernible from the mossy stone in the dark. He wore a formerly cream smock, ripped to shreds and covered in bloodstains, old and fresh. A blood-soaked blanket covered his bottom half.

Snake Eye. Jeth rushed over to him.

His elegant neck was locked in an iron brace and chained to a ring embedded in the stone wall. All that remained of his right arm was a festering stump with torn flaps of skin. The left, bruised and scarred, hung limp at his side.

"Sal have mercy," Jeth whispered. He took the ashipu's hanging head in his hand. "Snake Eye, wake up. You have to wake up."

Snake Eye jerked into consciousness, his heartbeat raced, his breathing frantic. "Stop . . . who-who . . . ?"

Jeth took out the blast gel. "Hold still. I'm getting you out of here." He squeezed the smallest of dabs onto a chain link as far from Snake Eye as possible.

"L-Little Gershlon?" His one serpent pupil was so dilated, it nearly covered the entire yellow iris.

"Don't move," Jeth warned again as he stepped back a few paces. After a second of hesitation, he made a tight fist with the gloved hand. A fiery pop reverberated off the shrine walls, making Snake Eye screech and Jeth's ears ring. He picked up on distant growls from the jungles outside. "Come on." He gulped. "Can you run?"

Snake Eye gazed up at him with sorrowful eyes as he weakly flipped the blanket off his lap. Beneath it were two mangled stumps. Like his arm, the flesh looked to have been chewed, the left leg up to the knee and the right all the way up to the thigh. The blood around them was stale. Jeth smelled no burnt flesh, meaning the wounds had not been cauterized, but somehow the bleeding had stopped.

Warm bile moved its way up Jeth's throat, but he kept it down. "Can-can you grow them back?"

"It is taking all my physical mastery to keep the fester at bay. Naja saliva . . ."

Jeth recalled his battle in the Deep Wood against Nas'Gavarr—even as the Mage healed wound after wound, he had been unable to regrow the hand severed by the saliva-soaked tulwar. Snake Eye wouldn't recover until the venom was neutralized.

He wiped some of the naja blood off his face and smeared it on Snake Eye's arm stump. The ashipu winced, and Jeth said, "There's more where that came from, but it's far from here, and we don't have much time." Jeth shifted his bow over his shoulder and heaved his friend onto his back, carrying him out of his blood-stained prison.

The extra weight against Jeth's scarred skin took the wind out of him, and he couldn't build the speed required to clear the moat. They fell into the water with a dull splash. Snake Eye grunted in pain while

Jeth listened for the naja growls getting closer.

He clambered to the other side as Snake Eye clung to Jeth with his only arm. Jeth sprinted back through the jungle, hoping to stay on the same path he had before. He couldn't overthink; he just had to move. If any naja caught up to them, Ryeem would uncover their plan and take it out on the others.

Snake Eye's body bounced up and down on Jeth's back, and the slick blood and sweat reawakened the agony of the cat-o-nine-tails.

A moment later, Serra flew up beside him. "I kept them away as long as I could."

"That's all right. I just hope the others can still get what we need from Ryeem."

Serra stopped short. "Watch out!"

A lone naja sprang out in front of them, unarmored and twice the size of any Jeth had ever seen. With no time to stop, he veered left.

Its claw nicked Snake Eye's back, ripping apart his tattered shirt and throwing Jeth off balance. Snake Eye cried out, and Jeth hit the ground.

Serra shot a stream of green sparks, but the beast didn't seem to notice as they bounced off its fire-red scales. It leaped over Jeth and pinned Snake Eye into the mud, opening its giant maw and baring its triple rows of razor-sharp teeth.

"Get off!" the frantic Flesh Mage screeched as he used his only arm to push against its snout.

Jeth clambered across the ground and jammed his tulwar into the beast's side. It swatted him away with a powerful backhand and returned to its half-eaten meal.

With a desperate holler, Snake Eye pressed his hand against the beast's face. A sudden spray of orange shot out from the naja's mouth and splattered all over its prey.

It threw itself off Snake Eye, violently convulsing and regurgitating more blood onto the ground.

Snake Eye's one arm stretched toward it, shaking with effort. Orange blood dripped from his forehead, and tears pooled in his eyes.

With one final push of Snake Eye's blood magic, gore burst from the naja's every orifice, and it collapsed dead next to him.

Jeth rose on his unsteady legs as Snake Eye wiped mounds of bright orange liquid from his face. "Must have taken an awfully big man to make that bugger." He bent down to retrieve his tulwar still stuck in its side.

Snake Eye shook his head from where he lay helpless on the ground. "I don't think this one was a man."

"You mean . . . a real one?" Jeth looked again at the bleeding creature, eyes rolled back in its head and forked tongue hanging out of its mouth. "They should all be extinct."

"Gavarr would have needed the flesh and blood of a real one to turn men into them. This one must have come a long way; likely smelled my blood for miles."

"We have to keep moving," Serra warned.

More growls in the distance reminded Jeth there were still three angry naja searching for their lost prisoner.

"What is that?" Snake Eye blinked at the hovering woman.

"I'll introduce you later. We're almost there." Jeth picked him up again and resumed his sprint through the jungle.

Jeth gathered his clothes on the beach and continued past the naja corpse he had made earlier. At least Snake Eye was covered in more than enough blood to heal his wounds; he'd have no need for the corpse's blood now.

Serra surveyed the shore. "Both lifeboats are still here."

Jeth's legs were gelatin, his back ached, his skin on fire. He'd have to row like the wind to get to the brig before the naja on their tail caught sight of them. There was not even time to put his clothes back on. If he put Snake Eye down, he feared he would not have the strength to lift him up again.

Then, a sharp female scream split his eardrums. He honed his hearing to the west and picked up male grunts, sword slashes, and ravenous reptilian growls, far beyond the tree line.

He could no longer hear the three naja's pursuit of him and Snake Eye. They must have turned west instead, no doubt called back by their Handlers to direct their carnage elsewhere.

Jeth's blood ran cold.

Faron had been right. This was a trap, and his men were about to pay the price.

Jeth's heart pounded against his ribcage as his eyes followed the team's footsteps in the sand, heading into the jungle.

He set Snake Eye down in the lifeboat and looked back to the jungle once more. "You're not going to leave him here," Serra protested.

"Don't worry about me, Little Gershlon," said Snake Eye, languidly struggling to maintain his usual cheerful countenance. "I can row myself back."

"Not with one arm, you can't. Cover yourself with the blanket and stay hidden. I'll be right back."

"Wait!" Serra screeched.

"Protect Snake Eye," he called back, running full speed into the jungle. *It may already be too late.*

Following his ears, he ran through the underbrush at full speed. He ducked between hanging vines and leaped over fallen palm trees until he found Faron and Loche desperately fighting off three armored naja.

Raisha lay on the ground face down, covering her neck as a naja dug its claws into her back. Loche jammed his sword through the unarmored spot under its arm and shoved it off her.

Faron fought another one from the ground.

Khiri hid behind a tree as the third naja slashed at him from the other side.

With a final burst of speed, Jeth scampered up a slanted tree and leaped onto the naja attacking Khiri. He drove his tulwar into the top of the creature's skull before kicking off its back. He pulled out his bow midair and shot an arrow through the open maw of the one just about to bite Faron's face off.

Panting, Jeth looked around the clearing as his reactions slowed to normal. "Is anybody hurt?"

Raisha sat up and moaned, blood trailing down her back.

Faron and Loche blinked at Jeth in disbelief. Khiri slammed into him, wrapping his arms around his torso, only to instantly recoil from the crusted naja blood coating every inch of Jeth's bare body.

Faron's lips contorted in disgust. "Why are you in your knickers?"

"That's the first thing you notice?" Jeth said incredulously.

"He could have his pecker flapping in the island breeze for all I care," Loche said while helping Raisha to her feet. "I'm just glad he showed up when he did." He glanced over to Jeth. "By your sorry state, I assume you failed in your task as well?"

"What happened? Why did the naja attack you?" Jeth asked.

Faron picked himself up. "Ryeem cares not for our naval aid. He says Odafi deserves to fall to Rangardia and that all the tribes shall be enslaved once again."

"He agreed to meet with us so he could kill us . . . to send some kind of message back to the King," Loche finished, looking to Raisha.

She didn't respond, only swayed back and forth unsteadily in Loche's grip. Her face was pale, her eyes glazed over in shock.

Reptilian snarls sounded from the north. "We can't stay here." Faron took purposeful steps down the path.

"Come, now," Loche dragged Raisha away as she blankly stared into the jungle void.

"R-Ryeem," she wheezed.

"It's not that far to the beach," said Jeth, encouraging the team to pick up the pace.

As they ran, Jeth sensed naja speeding through the bush, gaining on their flank, and about to block their path ahead. "Go right!" he shouted, and they turned sharply.

A crumbling rock face stopped them, remnants of an ancient city wall that went on seemingly for miles in both directions. With the naja so close behind them, there was no choice but to go over it.

Gnarled vines dangled from the sides. Jeth tugged on them, a few came loose, but enough remained. "Start climbing."

He threw Khiri upward as high as he could, the boy scrabbling to grab hold of the vines before he scampered up and over the wall.

Jeth took Raisha's arm next, but she snatched it away. "I've got it." Gritting her teeth in pain, she started to climb.

The men spun, drawing their swords and forming a line of protection. A naja leaped from the trees nearest Loche and chomped down on his sword-wielding arm, yanking him to the ground.

"Loche!" Jeth screamed. He crashed hard against the wall as another naja slammed into him, and his tulwar flew out of his grip.

Jeth pulled his knife from his scabbard and jammed it into the creature's stomach. It collapsed with a sickening squelch, bowels pouring from the gash down its front.

Vines snapped above. Raisha screamed and dropped to the ground.

Loche flew through the air, the ravenous reptile thrashing him about by his arm like a ragdoll.

Raisha dove for the fallen tulwar and lunged to Loche's aid. She hacked feverishly at the back of the reptile's neck, not unlike what she had done to Ezrai, and the beast fell dead on its side.

"Thank you, my dear," Loche panted, squeezing his ravaged bicep. "But there's no saving me now."

"Hang in there, Loche," said Jeth. "Naja blood will neutralize the venom."

Dozens of glowing yellow eyes prowled behind the foliage.

"Then naja blood we shall have," Faron said, clapping Loche on his good shoulder.

Jaw set in grim determination, Faron rushed forward, meeting the first of naja bursting through the trees. Loche picked up his sword with one hand and roared after his fellow swordsman.

Jeth searched for Raisha, but she was gone along with his tulwar. *How did she climb over the wall so fast?* He didn't have time to wonder. His men needed him.

He released arrows by the double. Only half of them pierced their targets, and the others bounced off their rough scales as if they were chain mail.

Naja thundered all around them. Then, from behind, a deep, gravelly voice called out, "Duck!"

Jeth dove forward.

Two naja leaped over his head, throwing themselves against the reptile advance and tearing mercilessly through them.

All three men retreated against the wall, speechless as they watched naja fight naja, creating a mess of scaly limbs and entrails in their wake.

"Where did they come from?" Faron glanced over his shoulder at the supposedly solid stone wall . . . now not so much. The stone swirled and liquified. Jeth, Faron, and Loche backed away from the wall.

"Earth magic?" Jeth murmured.

The two naja, breathing heavily and covered in the rank blood and viscera of their ilk, shoved the men through the stone whirlpool.

The task force stumbled and fell, landing on soft earth. The wall, now behind them, solidified, sealing off the barrage of naja on the other side.

Raisha's head jerked up at their sudden arrival from where she rested against a rock. She was frighteningly pale and looked as though she couldn't get up if she'd wanted to.

"There you are," Jeth rasped, looking around. "Where's Khir?"

The boy jumped up from behind the rock and rushed to Jeth's side.

"Thank the Deities," he huffed in relief. "Let's get out of here." Limply, Raisha kicked Jeth's tulwar in his direction. He was about to mutter a thank you when her eyes snapped open wide, catching something over his shoulder. "Behind you!"

The task force spun around, coming face to face with the two naja that had pushed them through the wall, and a third, snarling behind them.

As if responding to Raisha's warning, the two naja turned just before the third one pounced. The tallest one wrapped a scaly arm around its neck as the wider one tackled it to the ground. Both naja held down the writhing creature, its screeches rousing the beasts on the other side of the wall.

The task force froze, mouths agape, as the two reptiles struggled to restrain their wild counterpart whipping its head and tail viciously back and forth.

"Quick! We can save this one!" The tall naja bellowed, clawed hands squeezing the wild one's jaws shut.

A thin woman with close-cropped hair came running out of the underbrush. Wearing a fitted buttoned military coat and trousers in the Ingle style, she slid to her knees and placed her hands over the captive naja's head.

The struggling reptile stilled in seconds, and the other two carefully released it and stood back. The woman remained on the ground, her eyes closed in deep concentration.

"What is this?" Faron eyed the two standing naja warily, clutching his sword's grip.

"It's all right," Jeth put his hand out to steady Faron. "Just watch."

"What in Deity's lack of name is she doing?"

"Freeing him."

In a few moments, the sorceress opened her eyes, as did the naja. He jerked upright and scrambled backward on his behind until he hit the wall. "What . . . where . . . ? Who are you people?"

Loche held his oozing arm, looking to the others. "Naja can talk?"

"They shouldn't be able to," replied Raisha, clinging to her rock.

The witch, still facing the frightened naja, slowly stood up and pointed to her chest. "My name is Jenn. You're going to be okay. He can't control you anymore."

"He will if we don't get off this island now," Jeth said, sidling up to her.

Jenn's small, dark eyes narrowed at Jeth, then a relieved smile spread across her pale features. "If it wasn't for the blood and dirt all over you, I would never have recognized you."

Jeth laughed. "You're the last person I expected to find here, too. Although," he looked down at the curled up naja, shivering beside them. "I can understand why, but we can't save them all with Ryeem after us."

"I didn't come all the way from Ingleheim to free only . . ." Jenn's protest faded as her attention drifted to the foreboding scrape of talons against the stone wall. Several reptilian eyes peered down at the team from above, ravenous with bloodlust. "Blasco, Gaspar, pick him up, and let's go." The two reformed naja lifted their recently freed comrade by the arms and dragged him away.

With nothing more than a look from Jenn, the stone liquefied again, and a dozen naja sunk into it, only to be trapped inside when it resolidified.

Jeth blinked at the screeching naja, locked in stone, and turned to run. He led the way through the crumbling ruins and out of the jungle.

On the beach, Jenn smirked at the pirate brig. "That sure beats the leaky old sloop I sailed in on. Mind if I come with?"

"Like you have to ask," said Jeth, throwing a grin over his shoulder.

Naja that had made it through the ruins burst from the jungle after them. The beasts were gaining on the team fast as they reached the boats. He expected the raging reptiles to catch up, sink their claws into them from behind, and drag them back to shore any second, but he didn't dare look over his shoulder to make sure.

Faron, Loche, and Raisha pushed their boat out to sea. Jeth, with Khiri's help, did the same with theirs. Serra sprang off the oar handle and stood on Jeth's shoulder as Snake Eye stirred beneath the blanket. Flinging it off his face with his one arm, he said, "It's about time. Your guardian fairy and I were getting worried."

Jeth grunted, hauling on the oars. "Glad you two could get acquainted."

Jenn and her bodyguards ran toward the shore with the third naja, now running on his own alongside them. She shouted orders, "Get the new one onto the ship. I'll meet you there."

The three naja splashed through the water. One leaped onto Faron, Loche, and Raisha's boat, the other two onto Khiri, Snake Eye, and Jeth's. The boats rocked, water sloshing over the sides, but they managed to stay upright.

Snake Eye screeched as one of the naja landed on top of him.

"Sorry, didn't see you there, compadre," the fearsome reptile said sheepishly, then shuffled to the back of the boat.

"Compadre?" Snake Eye gasped.

Jeth heard his already weakened heart thrumming out of control, and before he could explain the naja's presence, the ashipu's eyes rolled into his head, and he promptly passed out.

"Ser, make sure the men on the ship are ready for us and to let only these three naja on board," said Jeth.

"Aye, aye." She nodded and flew away.

"Jenn! Come on," he called.

The Spirit and Essence Mage stood with her back to the ocean, Ryeem's army of reptiles seconds from pouncing. With her arms outstretched behind her, she gathered the waves into a liquid wall, obscuring the beach from Jeth's view.

The mounting wave launched the boats toward the brig. Jeth clung to the gunwales, steadying himself as he strained to see what was happening onshore.

The water arched over Jenn and slammed against the naja horde. When it receded, dozens of reptiles were sprawled out on the wet sand, many dazed and floating in the shallows.

"Jenn!" he yelled, but the sorceress was nowhere to be seen.

The lifeboats sped toward the brig, and Ash dropped the ropes and chains. Khiri deftly tied the lines and signaled for the pulleys to start raising their boat to the deck.

As they made their slow ascent, Jeth scanned the waters for Jenn, but there was still no sign of her.

Onshore, Ryeem emerged from the jungle, black headscarf and wide-legged pants flapping in the island breeze. He pointed his trident spear at the brig, uttering a command Jeth couldn't hear. Dozens of naja charged past him and into the sea.

"Shit," Jeth gasped. *How many more does this Mage have?*

"Oil! Now!" Olivier shouted from the deck.

Pirates hurled the open clay jars of oil into the sea, the thick liquid spilling out over the water's surface. The pirates used the last jar of oil to light their arrows ablaze, and, on Olivier's command, they released. The flaming arrows flew overhead, igniting the flammable waves. Flames skirted along the surface and engulfed the swimming naja.

They shrieked and cried, fire licking their semi-impervious hides, but they kept on swimming. The first of the naja made it to the brig and began clawing up the port side.

"Harpoons," Ash commanded. Pirates came forward, two by two, hefting the massive apparatuses. "Shoot!" They unleashed the powerful spring-loaded harpoons, impaling each naja as it rose over the bulwarks.

Jeth stood in the lifeboat, picking naja off the side of the ship with his arrows until he was close enough to jump onto the deck. He reached back, finding only three arrows left in his quiver. *Where are you, Jenn?*

"Raise the anchor," Ash called. He reached for the lifeboat as it swung at the top of its winch and took the unconscious Snake Eye into his arms.

"Not yet! We're still waiting for someone," Jeth said.

"Who?"

"Just wait!" He leaned over the bulwark, searching the liquid inferno below for any sign of the Ingle sorceress.

Dozens upon dozens of naja barreled past Ryeem and into the sea. They swam without fear of being burned.

The pirates released their harpoons into the water, but reloading was slow, and making accurate shots on such fast-moving targets proved futile.

Jeth scrubbed a hand over his face. There were too many; they'd never fight them all off. The calls of the men and women around him turned desperate. He was about to turn to Ash to tell him they should sail off after all when another mysterious upsurge swept across the water.

The fiery ocean wave crashed against the new onslaught of naja, pushing them back to shore. The brig rocked, casting pirates to the deck and naja off the gunwales.

Holding on to the bulwark to keep from falling himself, Jeth spotted someone splashing in the clear water, portside. "There she is! Raise the anchor, Ash!"

A pirate let down a rope ladder, and Jeth called her name, encouraging her to climb.

Around them, pirates shouted back and forth, unfurling the sails and preparing to leave the sea of scalded reptiles behind.

On the beach, Ryeem stood with his two Naja Handlers. Jeth's honed vision made out every detail of the Mage's face through the flames. In the rage behind his yellow irises, an ancient and inhuman wrath whirled behind them, sending shivers down Jeth's spine.

He'd seen it only once before.

Dulsakh.

ᔕI

Path of the Sadist

Clean, fed, and in a fresh set of clothes, Jeth stood at Snake Eye's bedside in the medical cabin. Olivier finished listening to his patient's heartbeat through his stethoscope while Khiri stood at his head, silently overseeing the medic's work.

Olivier lifted the horn-shaped apparatus off the ashipu's chest and returned it to his medical bag. "Now, I'm not yet a doctor, but even I can tell your heart is that of a healthy, full-blooded person."

"It helps to hold mastery over your own blood," Snake Eye replied. "Although such concentration comes at the cost of re-growing my limbs."

Sitting on a chair next to the bed, Ash put his hand on his shoulder. "You need flesh, and I have lots of it. Use me to heal faster."

Snake Eye gave Ash a weak smile. "I appreciate your offer, my heroic Herrani, but I'd require from you, at the very least, your hands and feet, and you can't grow those back."

Ash cracked his knuckles and sighed.

Jeth had to ask, "Are you sure you didn't overhear anything from Ryeem regarding the Princess of Del'Cabria?"

The ashipu languidly shook his head. "Not a peep, I'm afraid."

Olivier checked the wrappings around Snake Eye's legs. "Your wounds already look much better. How's the pain?"

"The naja's venom has been neutralized—the rest I can handle." The medic nodded, but his frown indicated he didn't quite believe him.

A loud grunt from the other end of the cabin drew Jeth's attention to Loche and his frothing arm. "You sure that's not pirate whiskey you poured on me, you tiny witch?"

Jenn raised a small pitcher and sloshed the liquid around inside. "You're lucky we have such kind-hearted naja onboard willing to offer up their blood just for you."

"Don't think me ungrateful," Loche replied. "Just didn't think I'd have to feel this pain for a second time. And so close to retirement."

"May this be the last time then," said Jenn before moving to Raisha, sitting on the next bunk.

Three weeping gashes crudely severed the entwined serpents tattooed on her back. Jenn sat down behind her and applied the remaining naja blood with a clean rag. Her wounds didn't foam as Loche's did, which meant there wasn't any venom present. Though, better to be safe than sorry.

Olivier said, "What kind of monster could do this to man . . . or a . . . ?"

Snake Eye patted Olivier's hand. "It's all right. To answer your question . . ." He closed his eyes, exhaustion evident on his angular features.

The entire room was enveloped in silence, waiting for Snake Eye to finally answer the question undoubtedly on everyone's minds. Was he a man, a woman, or both?

After what felt like an eternity, Snake Eye said, "Ryeem likely wanted to break my spirit so he could manipulate it while preventing my escape."

Oh, that *question*. Jeth sensed a collective exhalation at Snake Eye's unrevealing response.

"Or perhaps," he went on, "it was simply him punishing me for my part in his father's demise. He didn't feel the need to tell me why."

Olivier left Snake Eye to bandage up Loche's mangled arm. "I'm sorry, mate." Jeth sighed. There was nothing else to say.

"It's the Path of the Sadist," Jenn peeped. "A Mage can manipulate a spirit more easily after torturing their victim."

"But I thought torture makes your spirit stronger as it did with Melikheil," Jeth wondered aloud.

"That only works for Spirit Mages themselves," said Jenn. "For their victims, it's quite the opposite. The more a Mage tortures a spirit, the more control they wield over it, even if that spirit is their own."

Raisha sucked back air through her teeth, cringing in pain. "Then,

I don't suppose you can explain why Ryeem threw his own sister to the naja?"

Jenn paused. "I-I don't know."

"Who are you anyway? What were you even doing there?"

The Ingle witch's jaw trembled. Coming to her rescue, Jeth said, "It wasn't Ryeem. It was Dulsakh."

Raisha's black-lined eyes met Jeth's. He could hear the shudder that ran through her body at that name. "Are you sure?"

"That can't be," Snake Eye said. "Dulsakh's remains were destroyed—"

"They were there," said Raisha. "In the images Ryeem sent me, there was a sarcophagus and a pile of crushed bones with him."

Snake Eye replied, "But Gavarr exorcised the spirit from me. It has long since dispersed."

"Ryeem has the spirit," Jeth said, arms crossed. "I saw it in his eyes."

Jenn rose to her feet. "I should check on the new naja." Her beady eyes glued to the floor, she slipped out of the cabin. No one else seemed to notice her exit, but it left a small twinge in Jeth's gut. *She knows more than she's letting on.*

"He must have recaptured the spirit in Lanore that day," Snake Eye mused. "Along with the essence that all of the Immortal One's descendants possess, he would have had all three pieces to resurrect Dulsakh within himself . . . all he would need was a Flesh Mage to see it done."

"But after I killed the Serpentine, the Najahai would be as mortal as their progeny. Why bother?" Jeth wondered.

Raisha replied, "Maybe he wants to awaken his brethren regardless, like some kind of revenge."

"Yeah." Ash nodded. "Maybe for having resurrected him the first time into a world absent his gods."

Snake Eye sighed, resting back against the pillow. "It is true, the vengeful wrath I felt when Dulsakh was inside me was palpable, but it didn't feel directed at me in any way, in fact"—he opened his eyes and stared straight at Jeth—"he didn't want to leave . . . my brother had to make him, just like the Immortal One did thousands of years ago."

Jeth and Ash exchanged worried glances. "You mean, all the torture you endured was not out of cold vengeance but an attempt to cast your spirit out of your body entirely. Dulsakh wanted the closest thing to an immortal form he could get, and that's you."

Snake Eye pursed his lips. "So it would seem."

Olivier cleared his throat after tying off Loche's bandage. "As interesting as all this is, our patients need to rest while they still can."

"Right." Jeth nodded. But the sinking feeling in his gut told him Dulsakh wouldn't stop until he got the immortality he had always known.

"I'll take the advice of my ginger ashipu," Snake Eye said as he pulled up his blanket with one arm. "These gorgeous legs can't grow back without deep meditation."

Ash stood up. "You heard him. Clear out."

He and Khiri left the cabin, but Jeth hung back to speak to Raisha. After all, he owed her the truth about her father.

Olivier, too, went over to Raisha and began to bandage her wounds. Jeth sat down on the bunk across from her.

Before he could speak, she bit into him: "Go ahead. Tell me the reason you killed my father was to stop him from resurrecting the Najahai and raining terror down upon the world."

Jeth held up his hands. "Your father didn't want to resurrect the Najahai. He wanted to destroy them."

"Then why did he have to die? He could have helped Ryeem. He would have fixed everything, but you had to have your revenge."

Olivier met Jeth's eye, then patted Raisha softly on the shoulder. "Miss, try not to lay on your back for a day or two. I'll come by and check on you later."

"Thank you," she muttered.

The medic picked up the blood-soiled rags and continued out of the cabin.

"It wasn't entirely revenge," Jeth confessed, looking down at his hands. "Think of what happened to the Burning Waste and imagine the opposite happening to my home. We did what we had to do." He started to tell her everything about the Conduits and their Champions until Raisha turned over in her bed.

"I don't want to know anymore. Just tell me who killed him so that our dealings can be done with."

Jeth took his sheathed tulwar and set it on his lap. "Snake Eye faced off with him first, in the Commune of Lanore, and failed. I confronted him next in the Deep Wood. Nearly got him, but he burnt me to a crisp. The one who finally succeeded was Meister Melikheil."

"The Raven Sorcerer?" Raisha sat up with a jolt, catching herself as a flash of pain shot across her face. "Impossible. My father defeated him."

Jeth shook his head. "That's what I thought too, but his spirit was hiding inside your father the entire time. Nas'Gavarr took Vidya, the Champion of Yasharra, into the Spirit Chamber, where she released Melikheil's spirit . . . at my suggestion. I honestly had no idea what would happen."

"Where are they now?"

"I don't know where Vidya is, and Melikheil"—Jeth shrugged—"is walking around somewhere in your father's skin."

Raisha's amber eyes widened. "He took his body?"

"If you see anyone resembling your father, it's not him. His spirit is gone."

She slowly laid back down on her side. "I suppose that's it then. We've each upheld our part of the bargain."

"I *am* sorry, you know," said Jeth. "Not for my part in his death, but for what it has done to you and your sisters."

She stared off into the corner, wiping at the moisture that gathered at the corners of her eyes. "Are you saying you'd take everything back if you could?"

"No," he admitted.

"Then you're not sorry."

Jeth nodded, knowing there was nothing else he could say to make things better. He accepted his role in this madness, and she had to accept its consequences, as unfair as they were. He placed the tulwar beside her on the bed. "Here."

She wrapped her fingers around the grip. "Why are you giving this back?"

"It doesn't belong to me," he muttered, then went for the door.

"Wait." She sat up as Jeth turned around. "When we get back to the oasis, don't stay too long. Ry . . . *Dulsakh* has set sail, and that is the first place he will go."

"Thanks for the heads up. What are you going to do?"

"The fact that we still have a rapport tells me that Ryeem's spirit is in there somewhere. I will wait for him at the oasis, and I will get through to him."

"He's lucky to have you," Jeth said, trying to forget that he was talking about a man that led an army of reptilian beasts transformed from humans against their will.

As he left the cabin, he found Faron waiting for him at the top of the stairs leading to the main deck. "Did the ashipu have anything to report?"

"He knows nothing of the princess," Jeth said, brushing past him. "But now we have an enraged ancient Najahai spirit on our hands."

"I shouldn't have to say this, but—"

"I know." Jeth sighed. "You were right; we walked straight into a trap. But at least admit you were wrong about Raisha."

"I don't bloody care about Raisha. The mission is what matters, and we are no closer to completing it, not by a long shot."

Jeth looked past Faron's sour mug to their new reptilian allies conversing at the bow. Not far from them, Jenn gazed out over the red sunset sea. "Speaking of long shots . . ."

Jeth made his way to the forecastle. Faron followed a few paces behind.

The newest naja recruit sat against the foremast, staring blankly ahead while the others tried to talk to him. Jeth continued past, determined to speak with Jenn first.

He sidled up next to her at the bulwark. "I wanted you on my team, you know."

Jenn snapped her head around to face him fully, dark eyebrows raised.

"Our task force." He gestured to Faron, who had stepped up beside him. "We sent word to Siegfried in hopes he'd let us borrow you for a while. He wrote back that you went on a mission to save the naja. That's what you were doing in the archipelago, wasn't it?"

Jenn leaned over on her forearms, grazing her thumb over a serpent-shaped emerald in her palm. "Gaspar and Blasco sniffed out Ryeem's blood trail to an Ankarran port. We rented a boat and followed him to the archipelago. I hoped to get into his mind somehow—maybe kill him if it came to that. I thought I could free all the naja at once. It was one of the few times he and the bulk of his army would be in one place."

"You were going to face one of the world's most powerful Spirit Mages alone?"

"We had a plan—"

"Oh, a plan. Well, sorry we got in your way." He pointed to the emerald in her hands. "And whose spirit were you going to put in that? Ryeem's . . . or Dulsakh's?"

She put the gem in her pocket. "It's for me, dummy. In case my spirit was unceremoniously released from my body."

The way her blood flowed thick in her veins, and the smell of her sweat despite the cool ocean winds, made Jeth uneasy. The few weeks they had spent together in Inglehiem, Jenn had been an open book, telling him all sorts of stories of her time running with smuggling rings as a Light Mage, and later the rebellion as an all-purpose witch. She even told him of her childhood, living in poverty, and how her mother, forced into prostitution, had protected her. He knew more about her past than Anwarr's at the time. It was because of Jenn that he stayed in Ingleheim even after his job was done. He had wanted to help her save her home before he ever considered he might have to save his own.

She must have noticed him staring at her funny. "What?"

He waved his hand. "Nothing. Whatever you were doing on that island, I'm just glad you were there. Besides this little setback, how is the naja freedom project coming along?"

Jenn looked to the three at the foremast. Her thin bottom lip quivered before she bit down on it. "We kill more than we save defending ourselves. Sometimes, I'm not even sure they want to be saved—like him. He's just now starting to remember the atrocities he committed while trapped in a monster's body. The taste of human flesh . . . I don't think you or I can ever imagine the horror of that."

Jeth shrugged. "Strangely, I can relate." The taste of Melikheil's blood had never truly left his tongue.

With a turned-up lip and a wry glare, Jenn replied, "You and I should catch up soon. Although, I'm not sure I want to know all the stories you have to tell."

"In all your time tracking Ryeem," Faron said, "did he ever mention his father's plans with the Princess of Del'Cabria?"

"No. I didn't know the princess was missing until you asked Snake Eye earlier. I haven't come across an urling female since before I came to the desert."

"Do you think *they* would have seen her?" Jeth pointed a thumb to the naja at the foremast. "You say they remember what they did under Ryeem. Maybe one of them was tasked with guarding her at some point, saw Nas'Gavarr with her, or overheard discussions about her."

Jenn shrugged and led the two men to her naja companions. "Hey, guys, I'd like you to meet a good friend of mine."

Jeth proffered his palm and shook hands with the two standing naja.

The third remained crumpled on the deck. "The name's Jeth, and this is Faron." Jeth nodded to Faron, who gave each of them a curt nod. "We forgot to thank you two for saving our arses back there."

"Not a problem." The green and red naja pointed to himself and said, "Gaspar"—then to the yellow and green one next to him—"Blasco"—and finally to the seated one with green scales that shifted opalescent in the fading sunlight—"and this is Esteban."

"Those are all Rangardian names," Faron said.

Blasco nodded. "We're all Rangarders."

"Is that a coincidence?"

"If you were a Flesh Mage in need of human sacrifices to build a monster army," began Gaspar, "you go to a place with a lot of men and no one to miss them."

Jenn added, "I've since learned that for repeated transmogrification to work most efficiently, the sacrifices need to possess similar bloodlines. The first one transformed was likely Rangardian, and therefore all of them had to be."

"Gaspar and I used to mine warp stone," said Blasco. "A bunch of us used the new warping gate to make a delivery to another island, but it had been turned in the wrong direction without our knowledge. We ended up in some temple with skeletons and snakes carved into the walls."

"The Temple of Sagorath," said Jeth.

Blasco sat down next to Esteban. "Nas'Gavarr appeared before us, and the next thing I remember is waking up on a stone slab in a small, locked cell. I was in unbearable pain, covered in blood and scales."

"We were there for a long time," continued Gaspar. "Fed animal carcasses to bulk up, waiting for our teeth and claws to cut through what was left of our human skin."

Jeth's mouth turned sour, and he couldn't reply.

"That wasn't even the worst part," Gaspar said. "When our transformation was complete, the *son* came to us. He tormented us, got into our heads, brought forth our base urge to devour everything in sight. We lost ourselves in constant, suffocating violence."

"At least we only served that Mage for a few years. Others are not so lucky." Blasco looked to Esteban, slumped quietly beside him.

Jenn crouched down and put a hand on his shoulder. "How long ago were you transmogrified, Esteban?"

His reptilian eyes shifted to Jenn's before gazing up into the darkening sky. "The moons were one."

"I'll assume he isn't talking about the most recent Lunahalah," said Jeth.

"The one before that was three or four years ago," Jenn looked to Esteban for confirmation.

"No . . ." he shook his head. "Before that, I think."

"So, you couldn't have come from the mine like the others. You were one of the first." She looked up at Jeth and Faron. "I've freed only one other first. They normally stay so close to Ryeem that I couldn't risk saving more without him discovering me."

"Tell us the last thing you remember, compadre," urged Gaspar, "when you were human."

"I was on a job. I'm a—used to be—a carpenter of the Tradesmen's Guild. The Overlord hired my crew to build scaffolding for a secret construction project."

"Secret project, aye?" Jeth said with a light chuckle. "Wouldn't happen to be a warping gate by chance?"

The reptile's vertical pupils suddenly dilated, and he was on his feet the next second. "Yes. How did you guess?"

"Well, we've all seen them."

"That's impossible," Esteban said in a low, growling voice.

"If you were turned six years ago, then it had to be his first one in the Temple of Sagorath, right?"

Esteban shook his head. "No, that was the one we modeled to make his second one."

"Then the one in Elmifel."

"He built a warping gate in Elmifel, too?" Esteban's yellow eyes dilated even more.

Jeth's eyes widened right along with his. He looked to everyone else, and they responded with shrugs. "Another secret gate. One built after the Herrani one, but before the one in Elmifel."

"Why should we care about another warping gate?" Faron asked.

"The gates coincide with a Conduit location. Serpentine in the temple, Elmifel in Thessalin, Crannabeatha in the Deep Wood, and Yasharra in Credence." Jeth paced about the deck, everyone's attention following him back and forth. "The final Conduit is the Volcano of Verishten, but if Nas'Gavarr had built a gate there six years ago, why would he need to take the borderlands and tunnel through the Barrier of Kriegle to invade Ingleheim . . . ?"

Faron and Jenn exchanged looks and shrugged.

Jeth's spine tensed at the recollection of one of the last things Nas'Gavarr had said to him. *'There is a sixth Conduit no one knows about. . . .'*

Jeth halted his pacing. "Where is this gate, Esteban?"

Esteban looked to Blasco and Gaspar, then back to Jeth. "You wouldn't believe me."

"Of course we'll believe you." Blasco patted Esteban on the back. "We're all in the same boat here, literally."

Esteban's raspy reptilian voice lowered. "The Cursed Isle of Cordos."

The two other naja recoiled, hissing. "You agreed to go to such an evil place?" Blasco gasped.

"I was young and desperate to make my fortune. I brushed off the tales as myth and put my trust in the Overlord of Herran . . . I've come to learn there are things far worse than island curses."

Blasco and Gaspar both nodded in understanding.

"One of Rangardia's islands is cursed?" Jenn scrunched her face in confusion. "First I'm hearing about it."

"It's not part of the Empire, but somewhere between Rangardia and Credence, farther west."

Another memory came to Jeth's mind. When he and Vidya emerged through the Elmifel gate together, the dais had been pointed in a southwest direction. Vidya had told him there was nothing that way, just the ocean. *Or an unknown island!* Nas'Gavarr must have used the Elmifel gate to go to this cursed island. And if that weren't convincing enough, the Elmifel gate was the closest to the Capital and the most convenient one to take the princess through after he took her.

"Esteban, you're a bloody diamond," Jeth exclaimed, wiping his sweaty palms on his trousers. "You just cracked our mission."

"How?" asked Faron.

"Fetch the others. I know where the princess is."

22

Tiny Threads

(One and a quarter years ago)

Zephira dunked her tangled mess of blonde hair into the waterfall and let it push her down into the spring. The water pelted against her chest, forcing the air from her lungs. *What if I don't come back up? Would Gavarr's plans be thwarted? Would he incinerate the Capital after I'm gone?* She flailed in panic. Planting her feet, she sprang up to the surface with a gasp, flinging her wet hair back and breathing hard.

Her heart rate returned to its usual listless drum, and she covered her naked chest with her arms. The magus stood a few feet away, his back to the spring. Even though he had never once tried to look upon her exposed form during the six and a half months of her captivity, she felt far from at ease in his presence, especially now that she was of marrying age.

Mother would be busily planning my wedding to a nobleman twice my age if I were still there. She wondered how nervous she would be.

She longed for that anxiety now instead of the constant fear and dread she'd experienced ever since Gavarr left her on this haunted island. Besides the Overlord's infrequent visits and creepy magi watching her every move, she had to listen, night after night, to the spine-chilling moans emanating from the henge. It sounded like something between a starving animal and a child in agony.

Pushing away the ghoulish noises from her memories, she scrubbed a weeks' worth of slime and grit off her skin. The island was covered in all manner of filth that she never knew could exist. Wherever she was, it was far enough from Del'Cabria that it was near impossible for her to scry her parents with the scummy well water in the settlement. Only water of great quantity, such as the spring she bathed in now, allowed her to peer in on her family's life, and even then, it required intense concentration because of the water's impurity.

Submerged up to her neck, Zephira closed her eyes and focused on the roar of the waterfall. The cool humidity blanketed the air she breathed, chilling her to the bone despite the few rays of sun poking through the sprawling branches above.

Once calm, she drew the *Veil of Elmifel* on her forehead. Slowly, one phantom stream lifted to the sky, and she surrendered to its flow. Her view of her father's study undulated like waves.

His stomach lurched—Zephira felt it as her own—and his vision spun. A bottle of brandy lay on his desk, a half-empty glass beside it. Leaning heavily on the desk to steady himself, he threw down the rest of the liquid, letting it burn the back of his throat. Guards stood at the doorway like statues, seemingly unfazed by his uncharacteristic display of emotion.

Zephira pulled back, sinking away from his eyes and into her own before her father's drunkenness could drown her too. It was just as well. Scrying her father no longer comforted her as it once had. She was an unwanted guest amongst his increasingly hostile emotions. *If he can't fight the Primitive Force within him, what hope do I have?*

Smaller than the one connecting her to her father, two streams spiraled into the air above her head. She pushed her mind through them, not sure if they would lead her to her mother or Rubin—it didn't matter as long as they took her far from here.

A few moments later, a distorted beam of sunshine stung her eyes through the curtains of a stagecoach. She sat low inside. She must be scrying Rubin.

He turned to Mother, sitting in the coach beside him, staring forlornly out the window as several mounted guards kept pace outside. The vineyards along the road were a sight Zephira knew only too well. The Holy Road.

"Are we there yet, Mummy?" Rubin asked.

Henriette turned to him, the vision of her blurred twice over by both Rubin's flooding eyes and Zephira's scry.

"Oh, Rubin." Henriette pulled out her handkerchief and began wiping his tears. "The headmaster will not tolerate tears."

"Why do I have to go?"

The Queen held her son's wet face in both hands. "All royals must."

Rubin sniffed. "When I'm gone, you'll be all alone."

Henriette stroked a strand of his straight brown hair from his forehead as her own creased. "I have your father. And before you know it, you'll be home with all the knowledge and discipline required to lead the Kingdom someday."

Tears overflowed from Rubin's eyes, his throat tightened, and fists clenched. "I don't want to lead the Kingdom. I want to go home!"

The Queen gripped him by the shoulders of his puffy, velvet coat and shook him. "You don't have a choice! This is your *Way* as it was your father's and his father's before him! Do not say such horrible things!"

Henriette continued to shake Rubin until he choked out the words. "What if Zephira comes back, and I'm not there?"

The Queen stilled, her eyes glistening. "I'm sorry, Precious, I'm so sorry." She pulled him into her arms and rocked him back and forth against her bosom, kissing him on the top of the head. "You'll be safer in Thessalin. Your sister wouldn't want you to be afraid."

Rubin closed his eyes and let out all the air that had been trapped in his lungs. He remained in Mother's arms, feeling her warm caresses through his hair.

Although she knew his tutelage was overdue, Zephira's heart broke at the thought of a boy as sensitive as her brother suffering the strict hand of the headmaster. Eleven was still so young.

Despite the despair, she was content to stay in that coach with them forever, held in her mother's embrace.

But she was too far away to hold on for long. A breeze rippled across the spring's surface and tickled Zephira's skin, casting her from the pool of her brother's mind. A tear trickled down her cheek and into the water. *How long has it been since she held* me *like that?*

She splashed water over her face, then reapplied the *Veil,* intent on continuing to scry Rubin to feel that small comfort, even for a moment.

Yarn thin strands of water, twirling and flowing in a single direction separate from her family's, gave her pause. *There they are again.* There weren't as many of them here as at the Elmifel River, but it would be enough for her to follow.

Her head ached with the effort, but she pushed into them. The streams, so small they were nearly non-existent, slowly carried her past the spiderweb of branches above, gradually speeding up until the island fog surrounded her.

Flashes of strange yet familiar locations pierced her mind's eye. Her consciousness flickered between an enormous library, an indoor river, then more fog.

Submerging into someone else's consciousness, she saw the massive Globe of Creation towering before her. She was in Garwin's Abbey, where she had studied in her last year of tutelage. The body she was in wore blue and white robes with a large hood that limited her view. *Ashray?*

The connection was tenuous, and her consciousness started to fall . . . far—too far. She plummeted down.

Back in the spring, she gasped. All this time, she thought she could only scry her kin, but Gavarr had told her it was an ashray ability. Perhaps she had just experienced a bit of their united consciousness.

She took the deepest of breaths and sank under the water. Clearing her mind of every ounce of emotion and focused on the tiny threads, only now they were more robust and numerous. They whisked her right back to Thessalin with a lot less effort.

It was challenging to determine which ashray body she'd sunken into. She was all of them, and one of them. Every action one took felt simultaneous with the actions of others. Everything came to focus in the library before the Globe of Creation once more.

Even though a single ashray was physically in the room, all others focused there too, their attention caught by two outsiders. One was a tall woman in leather attire with heaps of brown ringlets and brown feathered wings. *A siren?* Zephira had never seen one before, but she expected them to be elegant, whereas the one that stood before the great globe was muscular, bearing two sharp blades at her forearms and dual pistols at her hips.

A shorter, bearded man beside her wore dusty desert attire with a sickle-shaped sword at his hip and long sets of frizzy hair tied in a knot behind his head. *A Fae'ren!* Zephira had seen a few in her time, but never this close, and absolutely not in the Holy City.

He burst out laughing. "All the times I've heard urlings bragging about their ashray blood, I never thought it was what *actually* contributed to their superiority complex!" The Fae'ren suddenly turned serious, his twinkling hazel eyes darkening. "I know humanity isn't perfect, but a plague? It was because of your meddling we have this divide between those with round ears and pointed!"

"We assure you," the ashray said dully. "That divide *has and will always* exist in humanity. It is *your* nature that leads you to destruction, not the ashray's."

"No wonder Nas'Gavarr was obsessed with this so-called human mystery," the man huffed. "He wants to make things right in his own twisted way because none of you are willing to fix your mistakes!"

How dare he speak to a holy being in such a disrespectful manner? Zephira thought.

The winged woman raised a thick eyebrow at the rude man and said, "Don't tell me you sympathize with him now."

"I may be starting to understand him, but that doesn't make what he's doing all right. We need to find out which god—I mean Conduit—he plans on hitting next." His fingers danced across his sword's grip.

The woman frowned, and her feathers bristled. She gazed up at the globe. "Creation started from the bottom, but Nas'Gavarr started at the top."

The ashray added, "This globe depicts the order in which each Conduit came into existence during Creation. It stands to reason they would be destroyed in the reverse order."

"Which means one of ours is next . . ." The Fae'ren gulped.

The ashray said, "Yes, it is believed the Crannabeatha and Yasharra came into existence at the same time. As life progresses, suffering occurs in tandem with it. Without pain or anguish, there can be no reason for life to continue moving forward."

"But Nas'Gavarr will need someone to sacrifice," the woman said.

"Sacrifice? So, you are familiar with the Champions?" asked the ashray.

The man scratched at his beard, his weight shifting irritably. "Nas'Gavarr said I was one, right before he took me to the Spirit Chamber to do battle with the Serpentine Gods. Needless to say, I won, and an oasis replaced the Burning Waste in less than an hour."

The ashray's heart skipped a beat, subtle yet sudden. He placed a pale blue hand over it. "Then, you must be the Crannabeatha's Champion."

The ashray's voice sounded garbled, the water rushing through Zephira's ears as the library washed away. *No, please, just hold on. . . .* Zephira sprang to the surface, taking massive gulps of air. That Fae'ren was a Champion, just like her. Was the woman one, too? She had to go back. Taking a deep breath, she submerged again.

The winged woman pointed to the globe. "Our next step should be finding out who these other Champions are and get to them before Nas'Gavarr does."

"No one Champion can be used to close any Conduit," said the ashray as he stepped between the two of them.

"Right," said the Fae'ren. "Nas'Gavarr did say I was the only one who could defeat the Serpentine."

"The answers you seek are on the globe." The ashray spun it around slowly and pointed to an inscription carved along the circumference. It read: *'Ruins are overgrown, pain is washed away, pestilence devours the living, and the rivers run dry. The foundation collapses, and all fall with it.'*

The woman repeated the third phrase, then turned to the man. "Jeth, I'm pestilence, which is meant to destroy what nurtures life . . . your Mother Oak."

"Why do you assume that?" he asked.

She hesitated before answering, "Birds are known to carry pathogens to which harpies harbor a resistance. The Champion of Elmifel must be the water that washes pain away, the pain being Yasharra."

They were all Champions. Zephira, this Fae'ren named Jeth, and this siren . . . if she were a siren at all. But she couldn't be a harpy. Queen Orester defeated them a thousand years ago.

"Garwin, you must know who the Champion of Elmifel is," Jeth said to the ashray. It was strange to hear someone refer to an ashray by any name at all and stranger still to use that of a long-dead urling monk who the abbey was named after.

Again, the ashray's heart skipped, not as pronounced as the first time, but it still gave him pause. "Thessalin hasn't been under significant threat for thousands of years, even with all the wars Del'Cabria has fought. We are not aware of any Champion having been called."

It's me, it's me! Zephira mentally shouted, but the ashray would never be able to sense her.

Then, a thought came to her, foreign and unnatural in her mind. Not her own. *"Princess, wherever you are, you must come to the Holy City immediately! Only the ashray can protect you."*

Shock pulled her out of her scry this time. Zephira rose to the surface, her heart thrashing in her chest. The scry went both ways!

The magus rang out. "One more minute, Princess, then we must head back. The Overlord will arrive soon."

"Y-yes, of course," she replied breathlessly. *Arrive soon?* She gulped. *For what reason?* Needing answers now, Zephira followed the tiny streams again, bringing her right back to Garwin.

He was hanging from the woman's arms alongside Jeth as they soared above the glistening glacier sea. To where exactly, she had no idea.

"If I don't fulfill Gavarr's plans, he will put my kingdom to flame! She pleaded with her mind. *"I cannot attempt escape."*

"If he succeeds in closing the Conduit of Elmifel, the Sacred Spring will dry up, your kingdom will lose its only water source, and the ashray and their knowledge will die soon afterward. Del'Cabria will erupt into endless war."

"If I can show you where I am, will you send the siren to retrieve me?"

"No. She is a harpy and the Champion of Yasharra. Your blood can destroy her goddess. Given a chance, I fear she will kill you to prevent that from happening. It is more important for you to live than for Yasharra to remain in this world."

Zephira's head throbbed with every thought of the ashray invading her mind, making it difficult to hold the scry. *"I'm on an island. There's no way off."*

Garwin's thoughts came to her like a forceful wind. *"Show us where you are, and we will find a way to retrieve you ourselves."*

With tremendous relief, she surfaced. Hope warmed her chest for the first time in months. She glanced at the magus, seated upon a fallen trunk, still facing the other direction. Any second, he would request she get out. She didn't have a moment to waste. She pushed off with her legs and silently glided across the pond.

There was no way back to her clothing without being seen, but from the far side, she could slip away unnoticed in her soaked bloomers. She ran into the jungle—sharp twigs and stones pierced the bottom of her feet. She let the sound of the ocean guide her. If she could just reach the water, she was confident the ashray could determine her location with their wealth of geographical knowledge.

Faint morning light flashed between hanging vines ahead, and she sped up. The jungle edge was close. One of the vines caught her around the waist, stopping her in her tracks, but she wriggled free and emerged on a gravelly beach. The smell of rotting seaweed welcomed her as she ran for shore, leaving bloody footprints on the coarse sand behind her.

Looking frantically in every direction, she found nothing but an endless gray sea reflecting a dark fog. Whether she was in the Naja

Archipelago or some Rangardian sandbar, it didn't matter if there was nothing but sand and jungle around her for the ashray to identify.

Zephira collapsed to her knees, letting the waves splash over her legs, the salt stinging the bottoms of her welted feet. Tracing salty seawater in the shape of the *Veil*, she found the thin streams again. *"Tell me where I am, please!"*

"Are there no other means of escape? Do you remember how you arrived there?" Garwin asked. Zephira thought about the warping gate, but it was guarded twenty-four seven, not to mention the last time Gavarr had used it was to return to Herran. She wasn't strong enough to turn it back to Thessalin by herself, nor would she know which direction to turn it if she could. Despite the ocean giving her infinite means to scry, Zephira let the ashray streams evaporate.

Heavy footsteps crunched the gravel behind her, making her chest heave. By now, the magus must have known she left the spring and came to retrieve her. She lacked the energy to face him.

"You were not supposed to leave the settlement," said a deep and impassive voice, a voice she now knew better than her own father's.

A single tear pushed out of her eye as she stared at the drifting fog. "What does it matter? There's no way off this island, is there? You chose my prison wisely."

"Then you may be pleased to know that it's time to leave it," he said.

Zephira finally found the strength to turn her head and look at him, folding her arms across her naked chest.

He wore a frilly white shirt that contrasted sharply with his wide Herrani pants, stained with mud and blood. Noticing her gaze, Gavarr glanced down at his strange attire. "I was delayed in Rangardia for a time. Now, come." He put out his hand to her. "It's time for you to complete your first task."

A tear from her other eye rolled down her cheek. "Is this a task that I will return from alive?" She knew what he wanted now: To use her blood to destroy Yasharra, decimating an unsuspecting nation.

Without answering, Gavarr bent down and yanked her to her feet. Her gasp lodged in her throat, but her body reacted. She smacked him hard across the face without thought. He glared back at her, his serpent pupils dilating. She hugged her arms over her bare chest and tottered backward.

Clenching his jaw, he said in a low register. "The ritual I require you for will be painful, but I will heal you after. This is the least of the trials you'll have to face. See them through, and you will return home. You will be *Queen*."

She shook with indignation. Boiling rage overflowed her tight control, like an ocean wave rolling over a wall of stone. "You'd have me be the queen of dirt and sand once the *rivers run dry!* That's how you're going to destroy Del'Cabria, isn't it?"

A small grin crept across Gavarr's skull-marked face. "When I first brought you here, you had just learned you were a Champion, and now you know what I plan to do with them. Since when have you been able to scry the ashray?"

Zephira bit her lip, struggling to stop shaking. "They know where I am. They'll be here soon."

"Let them come. Once they see what you will become, they will recoil in horror. They all will."

"What are you talking about?"

"When you return home, your people will fear you. They will try to kill you. But if you stay the course, you'll have every human on your side, and the urlings will have to accept their lowered position among them. It does not matter if you fight me or do this willingly—this is your *Way!* End the tyrannical reign of the ashray-human hybrids you call family and give the world to the rest of humanity."

"Never!"

Gavarr shortened the distance between them, so he was inches from her face. "Serve now and rule later; that is a much better deal than what is in store for the rest of you urlings."

Zephira backed away, still hugging her chest. Gavarr snatched both her arms, digging his fingers into her biceps.

She gnashed her teeth and fought to release herself from his grasp. Her foot connected with his knee, and he loosened his grip just enough for her to pull free.

Before she could run, he violently reaffirmed his hold on her right arm. He pulled hard. A loud pop resonated from her elbow. Her scream reverberated off the still ocean and echoed through the jungle.

A lamenting howl erupted from behind the tree line as if returning her cry, and the fog seemed to close in tighter around them. Gavarr dropped her to the sand in a heap. Her forearm hung at her side, her elbow joint beginning to swell.

The Overlord's sleeves ruffled in a sudden breeze, and he stared into the abyss. Something stirred in the jungle. A series of shrunken heads emerged between the trees, bobbing up and down in midair. Their beady eyes stared, unblinking, and they moaned through puffy, sagging lips.

Zephira's rapid breathing made her feel dangerously lightheaded. *I've angered Gavarr, and now the demonic force comes!*

Gavarr quickly turned his head toward the ocean, looking down at something she couldn't see. "It . . . it was an accident." He continued to stare at the empty space a few feet away. It was like he didn't even notice the horrifying creatures glaring at them. "Not yet . . . Yasharra first, then you can have her," he mumbled.

Why won't he look at them. Why won't he look at me?

"Who are you talking to?" Zephira peeped.

Gavarr snapped his head around in surprise as if he'd forgotten Zephira was there. "Hold on."

He took to one knee, setting his arm over his thigh. With a sharp he dislocated his elbow.

Zephira's stomach lurched at the sound.

With his one good arm, he grabbed hers. "Keep still."

Before her eyes, the bone popped back into place, and the swelling went down a few moments later, as though nothing had happened. As she moved her healed arm in awe, Gavarr popped his own elbow back into its socket.

He stood and offered his hand to her. She stared up at him defiantly, straight into his reptilian eyes. They seemed either ashamed or fearful, she couldn't tell which, but it didn't matter. "If you wish for me to come with you, then you will have to force me."

The Overlord cocked his head.

Zephira held out her arm, exposing the inside of her wrist. "Take a piece of my flesh, as you've done before, and *make* me comply. But I will not follow you through that gate of my own free will unless it is to return me to Thessalin."

"It is pointless to resist." Gavarr's eyes darted between her and that empty spot on the beach.

"Do it!" she raised her voice with shaking force.

Gavarr grit his teeth, taking a moment before he answered, "I will give you time to come to terms with your place in all this."

"As the one whose blood destroys Yasharra and those who worship her? No amount of time will ever make me come to terms with that!"

"Then it is decided. The Crannabeatha will be next."

"What? No, that's not what I meant. . . ."

"Be ready when I return." He turned and began to walk up the beach. The chilling faces had vanished from between the trees. Perhaps they were never there to begin with.

Zephira called out, "Is it you who protects me from the Skour . . . or does the Skour protect me from you?"

The Overlord turned back around; his demeanor relaxed once more. "Be patient, Princess. You will come to know whom I serve soon enough."

Zephira tossed and turned in her bed. The incessant howling from the henge was the loudest it had ever been, almost as though the Skour were right outside the settlement. Frustrated and exhausted, she reached down, scratching her raw ankle within the oversized shackle around it. When he'd left two weeks ago to destroy the Crannabeatha, Gavarr had ordered a magus to keep Zephira chained during the night. Only by wearing her suede shoes did the iron manacle not chafe so much.

Unable to get comfortable on her lumpy mattress, she sat up. "Magus, I'd like a drink of water, please."

"You've had enough," he said from the table where he sat in a semi-meditative state.

She hadn't been able to access adequate water to scry since Gavarr left, which made her feel more hopeless than ever. *It's only a matter of time before he will return and sacrifice me to Yasharra. Then after that, he'll feed me to the Skour.*

Zephira slumped against the corner, drawing her knees up into her magus robes and resting her head against the old stone and mortar walls.

She was about to doze off when a loud bang jerked her back to full awareness.

The magus had jumped out of his chair, and it fell back to the floor with a clatter. His eyes bulged at the sight of a giant, shadowy snake slithering through the open window.

Zephira's heart froze in her chest. She scampered across her bed, but the chain stopped her.

The magus pulled a ball of fire from the hearth and flung it at the unholy creature. Ear-splitting shrieks bounced off the walls as the snake rolled and twisted amongst the flames. The thing reeled back through the window, its shrieks fading into the night.

The magus quickly closed and locked the shutters.

"What was that?" she said, her pounding heart already knowing the answer.

"The Skour," the magus whispered.

The old wooden door rattled. They both jumped. Something pulled it back against the doorframe. From beyond came a moan like dying cattle.

"The Overlord said as long as he lives, it can't touch us," Zephira said.

The magus met her eyes with a terror-filled gaze of his own. "That's right."

Zephira's mind went frantic. *He said to be ready when he returns—be ready when he returns. Why hasn't he returned?*

The door groaned and gave way, ripped off the cabin from the outside. Two gnarled snake-like creatures entered, slithering without touching the ground. The first sprang forward, latching onto the magus's throat. It pushed him against the wall and crushed his airway with its fat lips.

The magus struggled, ineffectively swatting at the long snake whose body had no visible origin. His skin cracked; his eyes sank into his head. The creature snapped back with such force it took the magus's entire throat with it. Blood gushed from the wound and flowed over the front of his robes as he slid lifelessly down the wall.

Zephira shrieked, and the deformed snake turned to her. Dizzy with panic, she yanked her shoe off and pulled desperately on her foot. Her skin scraped and bled against the oversized rusty metal ring as the creatures slithered closer to her bed.

Biting her lip against the pain, she tore her foot free, the cartilage in her ankle crunching under the force. She jumped to the nearest window, a vertical slit just wide enough for her small frame to fit through.

She toppled over the sill, crying out when she landed on her rear in the ferns beneath.

Shambling through the settlement in the direction of the warping gate, she prayed the magus guarding it would let her through. It didn't matter if she ended up in Herran, as long as it was far from this island and far from the Skour.

Her stomach lurched at the sight of four more snakes—or more like tentacles, slithering along the ground, stretching endlessly from the jungle to the west and coming at her fast.

Zephira cried out for deliverance as the shrunken-headed snakes gained on her. Shooting pain stabbed her ankle, the swelling making it feel heavy and dead.

Dead like she would be soon.

She forced the pain out of her consciousness, hobbling as fast as she could. She pressed into the foliage, letting the trees snap back into place behind her. Her only chance would be to lose the creatures in the bush.

Two flabby sets of lips clamped down, one on each shoulder, and pulled her backward with a powerful suction that made her skin feel like it might tear off her body in a single piece.

Zephira kicked and screeched, "No! Let me go, you can't touch me! You can't touch me!"

Something wormed around her waist, helping the other creatures drag her back through the settlement as she kicked up old bones that she'd been so careful not to disturb until now.

From the road to the warping gate, the only other magus on the island ran toward her.

"Help!" she shrieked, reaching for him.

The creatures continued to pull her toward the western woods . . . to the henge.

"Princess!" The magus was a few feet from her when a tentacle shot out from the house and attached itself to his back. His spine snapped, and he collapsed to his knees, falling just shy of Zephira's robes. The creatures dragged her farther away as another tore the magus's heart out of his body through his back.

Zephira's lungs seized, her vision swimming in and out of focus. The Skour had come for her at last, which meant the impossible had happened.

Gavarr was dead.

She fell backward over a drop, landing hard. The pain in her shoulders where the creatures hauled her toward the henge was the only thing that kept her from passing out.

They were taking her to the filthy tar pool. The place she saw that monstrous vision of herself.

Too soon, she felt the wet heat of it at her back.

She held her breath, and the demon pulled her under.

23

As Savage as They Come

Jeth and his team rode into the Herrani oasis, at least partially triumphant in their return. Villagers celebrated with fresh fruit and wine, and the Magae of Salotaph sang songs of celebration, their facial sapphires twinkling in the sun.

A willowy man with a long white braid rushed out of the communal yurt and fell to his knees in their path. "Master!" Yemesh cried, bowing his head before the pack horse that carried Snake Eye home. "Forgive me. End my contract, and I will return to my Order to face the consequences of my failure."

Snake Eye waved his one hand. "I'll do no such thing, my slender Sunil. Please, stand."

Yemesh sprang back to his feet, but his head still hung against his chest. "Master, I did everything I could to track Ryeem and his hordes in search of you, but many of his contingents split off several times. Each trail went cold. I am deeply ashamed I could not find you."

"I hardly expected my humble servant to rescue me all on his own. I am only pleased to hear of the effort you put into your search. And of course, I had my dearest friends to find me in your stead."

Yemesh smiled and nodded to the entourage. "Yes, you have my immense gratitude, all of you." His gaze fell upon Raisha. "And it appears you found a new friend."

"Why this is Kal'Raisha, one of my many nieces. Do make her feel at home."

The Sunil servant bowed. "Of course, there is plenty of room in our yurt." His attention returned to Snake Eye. "You must be weary,

Master. Allow me to carry you to your bed."

Snake Eye looked down at his partial arm. The glistening bronze skin had grown past his elbow during the week-long trip from Ankarr, but there was still a long way to go before the ashipu was whole again. "Hmm, yes. I still require meditation."

The Sunil, nearly as tall as the horse, draped Snake Eye over his back and turned in the direction of the yurts.

Snake Eye tapped the servant on the shoulder. "Hold on, I must speak to Jethril." Yemesh paused, and Snake Eye lifted his head to face Jeth. "I am in your debt, Little Gershlon."

Jeth chuckled, waving off the praise. "Are you daft? I only paid you back for the first time you saved my arse. We're far from even."

"Do you know *why* I became an ashipu?" Snake Eye said with a sharp glint in his single serpent eye.

Jeth dismounted, so he could avoid the ashipu's gaze. "Because you're a Flesh Mage?"

"No, although that certainly helps with business. You see, everywhere Gavarr went, fear and destruction followed. While he destroyed, I put back together. I worked tirelessly to repair the damage while he moved onto the next tribe, believing it to be what was best for all." He frowned, his gaze drifting to a memory only he could see. "Then, he put the entire Death tribes to flame. We stand on the graves of countless families—women, children, magi—who did not fall in line with his ideals. What happened here was something I could not put back together." He looked into Jeth's eyes. "Now, my brother's destructive path has ended, and yet the crater of pain left in his wake has only widened. But you reminded me that I can still heal the world . . . one body at a time."

Jeth nodded at him. "Well, for now, you need to heal your own."

Yemesh shifted the weight on his back, beads of sweat beginning to form on his dark and shiny brow. If the man were uncomfortable, he wouldn't dare complain.

"Then off to bed with me, Yemesh," said Snake Eye. "I'm afraid our journey is not yet over. At first light, we set off. Kal'Raisha tells us that my nephew is only a day or two behind us."

"Then let's not waste another moment, Master." Yemesh hoisted Snake Eye more assuredly on his back and lumbered away. Raisha turned her horse to follow.

The next morning, the former thieving crew and the magae gathered around Snake Eye, Istari, and Yemesh as they prepared to leave.

"Do you have any idea where you're going?" Ash crossed his bulging arms over his scorpion tattoo.

"Likely Sunil," Snake Eye replied while Yemesh checked the ropes, making sure he was secure between his camel's humps. "I can't tell you exactly where, though. I'll let Yemesh decide."

"Probably for the best," said Jeth. He turned to Istari as she finished loading her single-humped camel with supplies. "It's a good thing you're going with him, Star."

"Well, it is my job to hide things. Ryeem can't find what he can't see." She flipped her hood up over her short white hair.

"Thankfully, he wasn't able to establish a rapport with me in that amount of time," said Snake Eye.

Istari stopped and turned back to her crew. "I'm more worried about the rest of you. When Ryeem comes . . ."

"We'll be fine." Ash waved an arm down. "The magae will be ready to go first thing tomorrow, and the rest of us will protect the gate as before."

Istari pursed her lips. "I suppose you have that Mage from Ingleheim on your side. If she can manipulate earth aura, then she's eons ahead of me. You should be in good hands."

Ash pulled the Light Mage toward him and smothered her in his large embrace. "Take care of yourself, alright?"

"I am going to miss you two brutes," she sighed, pushing herself off Ash and looking to Jeth.

"You think I'm a brute, too?" he chuckled. "That might be the sweetest thing you've ever said to me, Star."

"Don't let it go to your head." She smirked and hugged him as well. Then she turned to embrace Lys. "Goodbye, Lysandros."

"We will all be reunited soon," he said.

"I'll be sure to bring you some of that special blue curry from Sunil you love so much."

The Crede man smiled like a child about to receive sweets. "I wasn't going to ask, but . . . very good."

Shahbaz took her in a motherly maul. "Practice water magic as much as you can, child. Until we meet again."

Without waiting his turn, Khiri ran in and flung his arms around Istari's waist. She laughed then kissed the top of his head. "And you mind Shahbaz while I'm gone."

Ash grumbled, "Great, the kid's going to learn magic now too?"

"Relax, Ashbedael," said Shahbaz. "He is only to act as our travel companion. If he could sense aura, it would be obvious by this age."

Khiri nodded in agreement as Istari mounted her camel and started down the road toward the City of Herran, where they'd cross the Serpentine River and make their harrowing journey over the Dunes.

Snake Eye blew a kiss their way with his only arm. "Farewell, my Tattooed Titan, my White Ladies, and my sweet Little Gershlon. When my limbs have returned to me, we will stop Dulsakh together. For now, stay safe and good luck on your quest, Jethril. Give my thanks to your fellow Del'Cabrians and that adorable pixie. I can see now where you get your wit."

"I will. Now move on before Ryeem gets here," Jeth said.

Without looking back, Snake Eye and Yemesh followed Istari into the trees and disappeared.

Jeth went to join his task force at the warping gate. He walked past Faron and Olivier, packing only the absolute essentials for the coming journey. Blasco and Gaspar stood on the platform, waiting for instruction, while Jenn sat quietly on a piece of the fallen pillar, eyes closed and deep in meditation.

Esteban and Loche remained below, studying the maps. "I hardly remember the journey to Cordos. I drank the entire way to numb the terror. But I think it's about one hundred leagues from here." He pointed his claw to the Odafi coast and traced it along the parchment to the island's supposed location.

"That can't be right," said Loche. "I've sailed those waters dozens of times, and I've never seen such an island. It would have to be at least twice that distance."

"I thought you said you didn't believe in the island's curse, Esteban?" Gaspar commented. "So, what was there to be afraid of, uh?"

"It was the ocean around it. The fog was so thick during the day that I couldn't see more than ten yards in any direction. I was more afraid of being lost at sea than I was of the island itself, that is . . . until we arrived. The legends, I'm afraid, are true."

Loche used his compass to find southeast as Esteban had indicated. "Right then. Turn her this way." The navigator held his arm at a right angle.

Gaspar pushed against the horizontal rod sticking out from the granite ring. Looming over his partner, his large larynx bobbed up and down in his long, slender neck. Blasco's neck was short and wide, resembling a cobra's hood. The tendons bulged as he pulled. So used to fighting naja intent on ripping his throat out, Jeth had never taken the time to notice the striking diversity between them. He could finally see their human personalities shining through their beastly façades.

Once the two naja had set the dais in the desired direction, Loche stepped up onto the platform. "Alright, turn the crank, and let's see if she sings."

Blasco crossed to the other side of the ring and started spinning the crank. The stone below twirled on its axis, but no light or sound emanated from it. Jeth walked up the steps and peered down at the dais. "Try moving it a little more to the south."

The gate scraped on the stone dais as they adjusted it. They then spun the crank, and again, no chime.

Loche sighed and put his compass back in his pouch. "It was a long shot anyway."

"I specialize in long shots," said Jeth while wheeling his arm around to signify to Blasco to keep spinning. The spiky naja breathed hard as he picked up the pace.

"Maybe the stone's been removed on the other side," said Olivier, rummaging about his medical bag.

"We have to make sure," Jeth said. He inspected his own bag to find rations, his whittling and fletching tools, and his almost empty honey jar that he kept forgetting to drink each day. *Sorry, Hen.* "Point it a pace or two north again, Gaspar."

Once the green and red naja did so, Blasco fervently turned the crank again. Finally, the spinning stone let off a flicker, then gradually brightened as faint chimes sounded. Each pulse acted as a divine tune in Jeth's ears.

"That's it!" He clapped his hands. "There *is* a gate, but why is the energy so low?"

Gaspar took over, turning the crank as Blasco, exhausted, plopped down on the platform and hung his clawed feet over the edge. "The warp stone might be depleted on the other side. One can only warp back and forth so many times before the rock loses its efficacy."

Loche said, "Even if the stone is working, there's no reason to think anyone is on the other side to turn the crank."

"I told you that island is cursed." Esteban handed the map back to Loche. "No man or woman could survive on it for this long, much less a princesa."

The men and naja spent the next half hour taking turns with the crank, but the stone didn't grow any louder or shine any brighter. "If someone is there, they could be too far away to hear theirs. It might take days before they respond," Jeth surmised, huffing as he took his turn at the crank. "We have to keep trying. Our only other option is to sail the foggy seas without a clue of how to navigate through it besides the memory of a drunken Rangarder."

Esteban bobbed his head to the side, basically agreeing with Jeth's assessment.

After a time, Faron clicked his tongue against his teeth and walked away.

Jeth was content to leave him to it, but he remembered Ash's warning. With the team so close to finding Zephira's location, it was time to put his foot down with his former major.

"Where you off to, Faron?" Jeth asked.

Faron picked up his and Jeth's bags and kept walking. "To pack up the horses so we can head to a port."

Jeth passed the crank to Gaspar and jogged after Faron. He took his sack back. "No. We're going to wait for the pathway to connect."

"And while we're waiting, that Mage and his reptiles will be upon us."

"Let him come." Jenn opened her eyes and stepped off her perch. "I plan to free as many naja as I can lay my hands on. That should give us an edge."

"Be that as it may," Faron continued, "We shouldn't put ourselves in unnecessary danger. Collect more naja if you wish, young miss, but we will not be joining you."

"What are you going on about, Faron?" Loche asked.

"Ryeem nullified the treaty. There's no reason to hide our mission from the world anymore." Faron looked coldly at Jeth. "The Kingdom at large can now partake in the search, a search I aim to lead properly."

Jeth's fingers twitched. "Look, I know I made some mistakes, but every step we've taken has only brought us closer to our goal."

"By sheer coincidence!"

"She's through that gate, I know it."

"Why? Because you happened to see a gate in Elmifel pointed to that general direction?"

"The stone is chiming, which means—"

"You're chasing rainbows, boy!" Faron snapped. "The princess is not on some cursed island. Now, if you'll excuse me, I will be starting my own task force. If the rest of you wish to join me, your assistance will be most welcome."

Faron turned on his heel and walked away.

You should just let him go. It was a mistake to bring him along in the first place. But with everyone's eyes fixated on Jeth, expecting him to do something, he shook with indignation. He was sick of Faron's disrespect. He couldn't let him get away with talking down to him in front of the men he was supposed to lead.

"Hold it!" Jeth stomped after him. Faron turned back around with a roll of his eyes. "I'm in charge of this mission, whether you like it or not, and I'm ordering you to stay put. We give this gate the rest of the day to work—"

"And if it doesn't?"

"Then we return to the King with our findings, and he'll send out ships in every direction between Credence and Rangardia."

"That would be foolish." Faron stepped up to Jeth, scowling. "If Rangardia catches sight of Royal Navy ships heading to their cursed island, who knows what they will think. It may persuade them to attack our blockade."

"How about you let King Tiberius decide what he's willing to risk for his daughter," Jeth shot back.

"He wouldn't risk peace; he's proven that already. And don't dare speak the King's name, traitor!"

Jeth threw down his bag hard, the contents rattling within. "I've paid my debt to the Kingdom."

Faron scoffed. "Greater men have hanged for far less than what you've done. The only reason you are alive today is because you managed to convince His Majesty that you're the only one who could find his daughter. But you, like the rest of your lowly ilk, are full of shit!"

Faron tried to storm off again, but Jeth grabbed his arm. He jerked out of his grip and stiffened.

"Ease up, men." Loche approached with caution. "You can both settle this in a dignified manner."

"Dignified?" Faron sneered, gazing down his long nose at Jeth. "You can shave off those locks, put on a gentleman's vest and trousers, but underneath it all, you're still as savage as they come."

"Say that again," Jeth seethed, a tempest of rage pelting down on him. Hearing that slur stirred countless memories of it falling from Del'Cabrian lips, all the way up to the day Count Radley spewed it at Henna before taking her son away.

Each instance, he had done nothing more than crack a joke or bite his tongue, pretending he could simply let it roll off his shoulders. No more. A growl started deep in his throat; all he needed now was to hear it one . . . more . . . time.

He held his breath, and Faron continued, "How His Majesty felt it wise to put a *savage* like you in charge of *me*, I will never understand."

Jeth's fists balled to the point of pain. No one had time to react. His arm swung across his line of sight before he realized what was happening. His fist made brutal contact with the urling's leathery face.

Faron stumbled backward, holding his jaw. He glared at Jeth, severe and stupefied all at once.

Jeth sauntered backward and threw his hands up in the air. "Don't look so surprised, mate. I'm just a lowly savage."

Faron moved his jaw back and forth before saying, "Then, allow me to civilize you."

He rushed Jeth, but Jeth caught him and wrapped him in a stranglehold. The older man didn't stay trapped long and sent a few good decks into his side. Jeth struck him in the stomach, causing him to double over.

Loche pulled Faron back, and Olivier took Jeth by both arms. "Come now, Faron, you mustn't lose that impressive resolve of yours." Loche patted his fellow swordsman on the back until he caught his wind.

Olivier held fast to Jeth, allowing him time to calm down. After a few deep breaths, his anger gradually lifted like a red curtain. "If you think so little of me," he said, "why did you agree to come on this mission in the first place? There are easier ways to get reinstated."

Faron rubbed at his bruised jaw and said nothing.

Jeth finally jerked out of Olivier's grip. "Did you think I'd grovel at your superior feet? Huh? Say 'Aye, Major?' You aren't a major anymore! You're a bloody watchman!"

A vicious snarl escaped Faron, and he lunged at Jeth again. Olivier put himself between them, and Loche yanked his friend back.

"Ah hah," Jeth pointed. "So, there's a little savage in you too!"

The urling spat on the ground as Loche released his arm. "You claim to have killed Nas'Gavarr, Fae'ren chant your name, and you will return with the princess to receive accolades and a pardon, but never presume you and I are equals."

"Accolades? I'll be lucky if I don't come home to the Third bloody Wave!"

"When this is over, everyone will have forgotten about the people you killed and those you stole from. The Deities will reward you despite your impurity!" He threw his arms to the sky, beseeching the Unnamed. "What have I done? Only served my king and country for twenty-five years. I led the war's most crucial mission, but you blundered it up! I hunted you for months, unable to see my family in all that time. Then, finally, I had you in chains. You gave me your word, and as a result, I risked my life and my men's lives to defend those woods, and what did the Deities grant me? A bum foot and a demotion. The only thing that has given me any solace in all this was seeing you bloodied and humiliated on that pillory!" The temple fell deathly silent, save for Faron's ragged breathing.

"Faron, I urge you to apologize to Jeth this instant," Loche demanded.

He glared at Loche. "How do you follow this Fae'ren so casually?"

"He saved my life back then, or have you forgotten?"

"That does not excuse his treachery!"

"Face it, Faron. You only have yourself to blame for your lot!"

"I beg your pardon?" Faron reeled back as if Loche had struck him.

"I'm not saying I knew what was going to happen on our desert mission"—Loche scratched his bushy eyebrow—"but I wasn't exactly surprised by how it turned out."

"Of course, you weren't." Faron waved his arm in Jeth's direction. "He was bound for insubordination. I told the colonel that the risk of putting a Fae'ren on the task force was too high."

Loche shook his head. "He earned that spot, unlike those spear-toting buffoons! Yes, I said it. Those boys were the real risk, and you refused to see it. They were urlings and automatically more trustworthy."

"Why are you saying this now?"

"It wasn't my place to question your leadership, but I recall being the only one willing to take those boys in hand. That was your job, and you didn't bloody do it! Your stubborn blindness to your team's strengths and weaknesses was the sole reason for our mission's failure. Not Jeth."

Faron clenched his fists, stepping forward, so he and Loche were inches apart.

"Whoa, whoa, whoa." Jeth held up his hands and edged between them. "Master Loche, as much as I appreciate you're standing up for me, what happened on that mission was entirely my fault, and I've accepted that. I could have come to Faron as soon as Baird and Tobin started trouble, but I chose not to."

"And no wonder!" Loche threw up his arms. "You had a major that would have thrown you to the wolves to protect the reputation of those poor excuses for noblemen."

"I've heard enough." Faron spun around and stormed off. No one tried to stop him this time.

"Bah," Loche waved his hand while Olivier stood awkwardly stroking his mustache. Jenn and the naja quickly averted their gazes, pretending they hadn't been listening the entire time.

"Keep turning that crank," Jeth demanded.

"You don't get to order us around, too," Blasco complained.

"Turn the crank, Blasco," said Jenn.

"Yes, Señora."

Jeth gave Jenn a grateful nod and walked into the overgrown labyrinth. He found Torrent with the other mounts and gave her head a scratch before catching sight of Faron packing his things into his bay's saddlebags.

"So that's it then?" Jeth asked. "You're leaving the task force?"

While adjusting the straps on the saddle, Faron replied, "I won't obey your orders and therefore shouldn't be here."

"You think this is easy for me? I don't like giving orders or being responsible for your lives. By the Unnamed Deities, if you're a shit leader, then what does that make me?" Faron gave him a stiff glare, and Jeth quickly followed up with, "Don't answer that. All I'm saying is, I wouldn't have asked you to come if I thought all the things Loche said back there."

His features finally softening somewhat, the urling slowly met his eyes. "Why *did* you choose me? Really?"

Jeth rubbed the back of his neck, his scruffy hair starting to chafe against his collar. "I don't know. I . . . suppose, I wanted to make it up to you in some way."

"So, pity then." He harrumphed and tightened his gelding's cinch.

"No, it . . ." Jeth took a breath. "After facing off with desert gods, Nas'Gavarr, and the noose, I still cower to you urlings. Still wish you'd see me as your equal." Jeth's stuffed his twitching fingers in his pockets. "But you know what? I don't care anymore. I've got more important shit to worry about now. This mission is the only thing keeping me sane—Mother, keeping me alive! I'm willing to bet it's the same for you."

Faron huffed and nodded. The two men's eyes met for a brief moment, then Faron blinked and said, "I should have listened to you back then."

"Back when?"

"When you told me the Saf could be an imposter, I should have looked into it further. I also found it strange that Nas'Gavarr would allow his daughter to meet her betrothed without accompanying her himself. But that tattoo . . . and we'd traveled so far—searched for so long in that blasted heat."

"Tell me about it. With my fairy locks, I may as well have worn a woolen sweater atop my head."

For a split second, the urling chuckled, or at least Jeth thought that's what the short burst of air expelled from his narrow nasal passages was. "Failure wasn't an option, and that oversight made it a guarantee," Faron continued. "Loche may be right in that ignoring the risk those troublesome spearmen posed cost us the mission, but it's not listening to you that has kept me up at night ever since we came upon the true Saf's retinue . . ." He cleared his throat, a strangely dyspeptic look coming over his face before he was finally able to spit out his next words: "I was wrong."

Jeth rubbed his burgeoning beard and nodded. "I know there is still no excuse for my actions, but . . . thanks for saying that."

Jeth heard the crunch of grass behind him, but he turned to find no one there. Faron spoke before Jeth could hone his senses further. "At your hanging, you said you held no remorse for what you did. Has that changed?"

"Having no excuse doesn't mean I had remorse. I slept like a babe after what I did to those spearmen. I know it's not what people like to hear, but it's the truth. You didn't see what they were about to do to that woman. She ended up being the mother of my child."

"You have a child?" Faron's eye twitched. "How is it that you never mentioned it? Do the others know?"

"They don't need to. Doesn't matter anymore." Jeth's gut wrenched, and he turned away. He didn't want his task force to feel sorry for him, so he never bothered telling a soul about the nature of his relationship with Anwarr, his son, or any of it. And it was Faron of all people to be the first to find out.

"What happened to them?" Faron asked in a near whisper.

"Let's just say I had more reason to go against Nas'Gavarr that day than to preserve my homeland."

"I . . ." Faron blinked several times as he tried to respond. "I can't begin to imagine, Jeth. I'm sorry."

"Jeth! Jeth!" Serra appeared in front of his face as if from thin air.

"Ser?"

"Ryeem . . ." She gulped.

"What about him?"

"He's here!"

24

Into the Unknown

"Raisha assured us he was at least a day behind," Faron said, his voice rising.

"Well, it has been a day since his last mind message to her."

Jeth grabbed the team's horses as Serra flitted around him. "He must have left behind the bulk of his army to travel faster," she said. "But what he did bring with him has the village surrounded."

"And you couldn't hear them coming?" Jeth asked Serra. He tugged on their horses' leads, ushering them down the path to the warping gate.

"I was playing with Khiri. I didn't think . . . I'm sorry, Jeth, I should have been paying more attention."

"At least some Herrani warriors are here. With them, we stand a chance." Jeth never forgot how a mere handful of them, armed with Steinkamp Magitech, were able to beat back a sizable naja contingent in Lanore last year, although not without last-minute assistance from the Tezkhan raiders.

"Ryeem doesn't care about us anyway," Faron surmised, following behind Jeth with the other half of the steeds. "He's only after Snake Eye."

"But Snake Eye's not here." Jeth paused, looking up at Serra. "So, if Ryeem doesn't find what he's looking for . . . then what?"

Jenn appeared seemingly out of nowhere and climbed up on Loche's flea-bitten mare. "I can work on the naja while you boys keep him distracted."

Jeth nearly jumped out of his skin. "Have you been here this whole time?"

"Let's get moving," she replied, ignoring Jeth's question. She lurched ahead, and Jeth and Faron scrambled to mount their horses so they could follow.

At the gate, Olivier was spinning the crank. When he heard the approaching hoofbeats, he stopped, and Blasco stepped in to keep the warp stone lit. "What's going on?"

"Ryeem," Jeth grunted, handing him the lead for his horse. "We need to defend the village, or he'll tear it apart looking for Snake Eye."

Jenn jumped down from Loche's steed, allowing him to mount it as she got up behind Jeth on Torrent.

"What should we do?" asked Esteban.

"Keep turning that crank until we get back. If the pathway completes before then, come find us in the village."

"Gaspar, come with us," Jenn ordered. "Blasco, help Esteban."

Jeth kicked Torrent into a gallop, and they reached the edge of the village within minutes. A line of naja stood in their path, watching the yurts through the trees, poised and ready to strike. Upon hearing and smelling the riders approaching, the naja spun around and bared their teeth in unison.

"Alright, Jenn, do your thing," Jeth muttered over his shoulder.

The sorceress extended two hands out in front of her. The ground beneath them vibrated, and a shockwave rippled down both sides of the path, branching out and opening the earth ahead. Mounds of dirt and foliage swallowed the reptilian sentries like a treacherous earth sea, bringing back memories of the Battle of the Deep Wood in frightening detail. Jeth looked to the man who had nearly died in that battle. Faron gripped the reins with his knuckles white and his heart pounding in time with the horse's hooves.

Loche spurred his steed across the narrow strip of unbroken ground left in the wake of the earthquake and sliced the throat of the one remaining naja.

As Jeth guided Torrent across the land bridge, Jenn slid off her rump. "Go on ahead. Gaspar and I will deal with the rest."

There was no time to question her plan, and Jeth knew enough by now to not worry for the witch's safety.

The team galloped into the village, residents watching them warily and pointing them on toward the communal yurt.

Ryeem stood alone, hands folded behind his back, a cold scowl on his face.

Ash and Raisha were planted in front of him while Herrani warriors remained close by, hands hovering over their weapons.

Khiri and Lys roamed the edge of the communal space, murmuring with the villagers, who huddled together.

Jeth silently motioned for his team to hang back. He dismounted and secured Torrent's lead to a post before approaching Lys. "What's the situation?"

"He won't let anyone leave until we tell him where Snake Eye is," Lys whispered back. His cinched brow confirmed Jeth's worst fears: It was only a matter of time before Ryeem started killing people to get his answer.

"We have to get the villagers out of here. Take them to the warping gate—Jenn cleared a path to the temple. Tell the naja that I said to turn it for Fae'ren."

Lys nodded, and Jeth patted the Crede man on the back before returning to the task force. He didn't like putting his mission off any more than his team did, but there would be time to make a pathway to Cordos after everyone else was safe, and Ryeem was gone.

"I will not ask again." Ryeem's voice boomed over the small clearing, deep and guttural and not his own; a malevolent force spoke through him. "Give me the Flesh Mage."

"Snake Eye's not here." Ash crossed his arms, his stance wide and unyielding. "Do you think he'd be stupid enough to return to the first place he knew you'd look?"

"Then why leave you all here to die?"

Jeth stepped forward, his fingers twitching with anxiety. "Take the hint, Dulsakh. After how you treated him the last time, you wonder why he doesn't want to see you? I know it's hard, but you have to move on."

Dulsakh, wearing Ryeem's face, turned toward him, raising a single eyebrow. "Who are you?"

Jeth cringed at himself but kept going, "Have you tried the harem, you know the one you left to the Odafi merchants to whore out your sisters?"

Dulsakh's golden eyes swirled with a demented ire. "Tell me where to find the Flesh Mage now, or people will die."

Ash shrugged casually, though the tight clench of his jaw told Jeth he was anything but. "Sorry, maybe come back later." He gripped his tabar, the Herrani warriors around him taking up their own blades.

Dulsakh only smirked. "If you prefer, I can have my naja pick off each of you one at a time until someone talks. Either way, I will find who I'm looking for."

"Brother, please." Raisha lurched forward, a brisk wind blowing her short silver strands over her face. "If you're able to call on your naja, then your spirit is still in there doing Dulsakh's bidding. You're stronger than this, stronger than Father! You have to fight him and come home with me." She grabbed his sleeve.

Dulsakh clamped onto her arms, shaking her violently until she cried out and tears flooded her eyes. "Where is the Flesh Mage?"

"She doesn't know anything," Ash barked, trying to pull the Mage away from her, only for Dulsakh to push him aside with surprising ease.

Dulsakh dug his fingers into Raisha's biceps. His eyes darkened, serpent-like without physically being so. "You know!"

"I don't. . . please."

Another sharp breeze rolled in, chilling the sweat on Jeth's skin. He and Ash advanced toward the Mage before she could utter another word.

Ash shoved him away from Raisha, bringing up his tabar to clash with Dulsakh's trident spear.

"Wait." Serra sprang from Jeth's pocket and tugged desperately on his collar. "Something's coming."

"The naja?"

"No! Something else. Everyone needs to get out of here, now!"

"What do you hear?"

"Not sure. It's something in the wind. Whatever it is, it's *not* good."

At that moment, Dulsakh caught Ash's tabar between his triple spearheads and twisted, so the tabar went flying. Ash rolled to the side, snatched Raisha's tulwar from her scabbard, and attacked her brother again.

"Don't hurt him!" she pleaded.

The Mage ducked Ash's sword swipes, then kicked his knee out, causing him to falter. Ryeem brought his spear tip a hair from the scorpion stinger at his clavicle. The rest of the warriors readied their weapons to retaliate.

"He went to the City of Herran," Raisha blurted.

"Good." Dulsakh didn't lower his spear. There was no reason to show restraint after Raisha let Snake Eye's location slip, albeit the wrong one. Ash had a similar inkling and rolled out of the way just before the spear descended upon him.

Dulsakh growled and swung wildly at his target only to find Herrani warriors in his way, surrounding him. He halted his attacks and looked around. The villagers, including the magae, were gone. "Where are all the people?"

"I'm not sure who you're talking about. It's just us warriors here."

A dreadful silence fell over the village. A brisk wind rifled through the trees, rustling leaves, drowning out wildlife while kicking up little cyclones of dirt and dust.

"Sister," Dulsakh growled, keeping his eyes glued to the warriors in front of him. "We will go to this City of Herran, and you will lead me to the Flesh Mage. The naja will stay to ensure no one follows." He called out to them, "Naja, come. Feast!"

Everyone readied themselves for the onslaught, but it didn't arrive. *Way to go, Jenn.*

"Jeth, please," Serra pulled on his coat from behind. "It's coming—"

"I think we might be all right, Ser," he replied.

"We're not!" she screeched.

Winds howled, ever louder over the treetops. Clouds swirled dark and angry gray.

"Where are my naja?" Dulsakh whispered.

Jeth honed his hearing, but the gale blasting against his ears ensured no other noise could penetrate. None except far-away shrieks and monstrous yelps from above.

Several large objects appeared in the sky. Massive, armored creatures with long tails and scales. *Naja? Flying? No . . . naja falling!*

"Heads up!" Jeth screamed. Everyone dove to the ground as three naja crashed to earth, exploding blood and gore on impact. A fourth hit a tree, splintering branches and cracking the bark. Another landed on the communal yurt, punching a hole through the canvas.

Jeth's heart hummed in his chest. "What's going on?"

Serra shook her head, wide eyes staring at the storm above. "This must be the force Mother warned me about."

Naja dropped at an increasing rate. Horses screamed. Torrent reared up and pulled herself free from her post, taking the other mounts with her as she bolted. Jeth lunged for her—"Tor!" But it was no use.

"To the warping gate!" Faron bellowed over the wind and shrieking reptiles above.

Ash grabbed Raisha's arm and tried to take her with him.

"I'm going with Ryeem." She broke away and took her brother's arm instead.

Dulsakh stood still and unresponsive, watching his carnivorous army crash down around him. "Why . . . ?" he murmured. Terror lit his amber eyes, now resembling his sister's. All signs of Dulsakh had blown away with the storm winds, leaving a helpless, panicked shell of a man behind.

"Ryeem, we need to go." Raisha tugged on his arm.

A sudden, violent gust sent Jeth staggering backward. A woman landed in the center of the clearing, shaking the very earth beneath her. She unfurled her brown feathered wings, striding forward on strong, muscular legs. Her armored boots and iron-plated corset were nearly as menacing as the vicious blades strapped to her forearms or the impenetrable scowl on her face.

She stopped in front of the Herrani siblings, unaffected by the naja crashing down around them. "Saf'Ryeem!" Her voice echoed, carrying over the howls and shrieks.

He held out his trident spear with a shaking hand. "It's *Nas'* Ryeem."

"Whatever." Her gaze followed a naja overhead that crashed into a tree, nearly breaking the thin trunk in half. "I'm disappointed in your army. I was hoping we'd have more to play with."

"Yasharra's Champion," Ryeem said, taking cautious steps forward.

Shrinking behind her brother, Raisha gasped then met eyes with Jeth.

"That's right." Vidya took a wide stance. "I'm here for the Princess of Del'Cabria, and you know where she is."

"Why would I know where that girl is?" He clutched his trident. "Ask my father, oh wait . . . you can't."

Vidya frowned. "Useless."

"Kill her, Ryeem!" Raisha bellowed.

Her brother charged for the harpy with a determined roar. Springing off the body of a fallen naja, he careened toward Vidya, ready to drive his spear tips through her chest.

She lifted off the ground with a flap of her wings and blocked his spear with her left forearm blade. Yanking the spear out of his grasp with her other hand, she returned to earth and plunged it through his midsection. All three points emerged from his back, dripping red.

Raisha's horrified screech pierced through the howling storm winds.

The harpy raised the Spirit Mage over her head. Blood spurted from his mouth as he gripped the bronze shaft. Then, as easy as flicking blood off a sword tip, Vidya swung him around until the spear tore from his gut. He spiraled through the air and came to a final halt against the crumpled communal yurt.

Raisha stood in shock, mouth agape, staring down at her brother's fresh corpse.

Jeth caught the shadow of a naja directly above her and tackled her to the ground before it splattered on top of her.

"You're a fast one." Vidya snapped her head in his direction. "Jeth? Is that you?"

He brushed the dirt from his hands as he climbed to his feet. "Hey, Vidya, I almost didn't recognize you either. How've you been?"

Her look of surprise turned into a venomous scowl. "You should be paralyzed from the waist down."

"And you must be so relieved that's not the case."

"I was warned you'd get in my way . . ." She took a slow step toward him.

He took one of equal distance back, his palms out. "Who says I want to get in your way? Just let everyone else here go. You got what you wanted. Ryeem, right?" Sweat dripped down the back of his neck, the wind slicing through his damp collar and sending shudders down his spine. *She hits you even once, and you're dead.*

She paused her advance as two more women landed behind her, a short, more heavyset brunette with black wings and a rail-thin, short-haired waif, whose wings were light with dark tips.

A small hand grazed the back of his for a moment. He glanced to the side to find no one. Only the slight shuffling of dirt and pebbles gave him any indication that someone was there. A Mage, hidden by light magic.

He turned his attention back to Vidya, determined to distract her until Jenn made a move, whatever that was going to be. "I see the Harplite thing is working out for you."

"Anassa," said the black-winged harpy. "This is the man I saw conversing with her." She pointed to Raisha, still on the ground.

Vidya glared at him. "So, you really *are* working for the King."

He let out a nervous chortle. "Who, me?" Out of the corner of his eye, he saw the task force trying to edge around the harpies. "I'm a traitor, remember? The King wants me dead. Now, I'm sure you, uh, you all must have places to fly to, men to punish."

"We're not going anywhere. We are taking this oasis and the warping gate within," said Vidya.

Ash put his hand up. "That's going to be a problem, Vidya. You see, this place is our home base now. Snake Eye already claimed it from Ryeem, so there's no need to retake it." He ended with a sideways grin. "And you're looking great, by the way."

Vidya turned up her nose, as did her two companions. "You don't seem to understand. We intend to claim this oasis as Crede territory. You either leave on your own volition, or we throw you out. And from what you've seen already"—she glanced down to a dead naja at her feet— "we can throw quite far."

Ash cracked his netted knuckles. "By all means, lay your hands on me and try."

Vidya glowered.

"Ash, she'll kill you," Jeth warned.

"You say she has the strength of three men. Well, I've fought many more than that at one time."

"So, it's a battle you want," said Vidya. "Alright, then." She looked up to the sky and bellowed into the storm winds. "Harplite! Descend!"

The deafening pulse of countless flapping wings filled the air. Harpies rained down from the sky, diving, and swooping, taking any warrior in sight and tossing them over the treetops.

"Alright, Ser," Jeth muttered to his fairy guardian, now secure in his coat pocket. "I'm ready to go home now."

As he turned to run, Vidya stepped in front of him. "I didn't say *you* could leave. We need to talk."

"I'd love to, but now's not a good—"

Vidya's hand shot out and yanked him close by his shirt collar. "I know you're looking for the princess." Her brown eyes narrowed, boring into him. "And if the King has tasked a traitor like you with the hunt, it could only mean she is Elmifel's Champion."

"I don't know what you're talking about," he croaked.

"Does the King want to *wash the pain away?*" She twisted his collar tighter around his throat. "Perhaps you told him all about it to save your sorry neck from the noose. I never should have spared you."

"What do you want with h—" Vidya's other hand clasped around his jugular; the cartilage cracked in her tightening grip.

She lifted him off the ground, his legs flailing wildly.

"Leave him alone!" Jenn screamed from an unseen place.

Searing flame, out of nowhere, hurdled toward them.

"Vidi!" The black-haired harpy rushed them, knocking Vidya out of the way, the inferno engulfing her instead.

Vidya took Jeth to the ground with her, and she watched in horror at the burning harpy flapping her wings in panic, wailing at the top of her lungs as bright orange flame spread across her entire body.

"Phrea!" the short-haired harpy cried.

The blazing harpy flew into a nearby yurt, setting it alight. Before the flames could spread further, a Herrani warrior put them out with a bag of Steinkamp ice powder, and the woman dropped to the ground, writhing.

The thin harpy ran to her aid, and Jenn came out of her hiding place of bent light, revealing a lit torch in her hand.

She helped Jeth to his feet and pulled him aside before Vidya could regain her bearings. "The gate is active."

"Has everyone made it through?" he croaked, rubbing his bruised neck.

"No, I mean, someone completed the pathway . . . in Cordos."

"What?"

He hardly had a moment to process what Jenn said when a shout caught his attention. Vidya was on her feet and charging toward them. "What did you do to her?" she snarled, about to tear Jenn to shreds.

Jeth instinctively stood between the harpy and the witch, unsure how he could survive the coming blow until Ash tackled Vidya to the dirt.

Ash rolled back up and distanced himself from her. "I don't want to hurt you."

"It's amusing that you think you can." She launched into flight, picked up a nearby naja corpse, and hurled it at him.

"Ash!" Jeth choked.

Harpies zipping and dodging through the air blocked his view. Warriors bashed into trees, and pops of blast gel exploded around the village. Olivier ran up to Jeth, taking his arm and pulling him down the path. "Come on," he pleaded. "We have to go."

The medic turned and ran ahead. Jeth looked back, scanning the chaos, and spotted Ash's leg sticking out from under a dead naja, unmoving. "Ash?" Jeth shouted, but there was no response from the giant axeman.

A harpy screeched overhead, and Jeth dove to the ground reflexively, taking Jenn down with him. A Steinkamp wind blade, thrown by a passing warrior, flew into the harpy's midsection and sent her spinning.

On her stomach, Jenn lifted her head, her mouth forming a tight, thin line. "This may be your only chance. Go through now, so we can turn it for Fae'ren." He stared at the Inglewoman. They'd be helpless, but he knew she was right.

Vidya hovered above the carnage, searching the chaos, searching for Jeth.

"I'll hold them back. Go!" Jenn pushed herself onto her feet and undulated out of sight.

Jeth sprung up and ran through the woods, dodging warriors and terrified horses. He spotted the task force soon enough, quickly recognizing Faron's limping gait.

He slowed his pace as he approached Faron. "The pathway to Cordos is complete. We must get through it before they can turn it for Fae'ren."

"Not us," Faron panted, coming to a stop. "You stand the best chance at getting into Cordos before those winged harlots catch up. Blasco can turn the gate for Fae'ren, and we'll make sure everyone evacuates."

Several Herrani warriors flew through the air, smashing to the ground in front of them. The harpies were making good on their promise to throw out the resisters.

"If we get there at all." Olivier gulped.

"I'm not leaving you all here to die. We can find another way to Cordos if we don't make it."

Faron grabbed Jeth by the arm before he could continue forward. "I'm afraid I'm about to disobey your orders once again." He unsheathed his sword and jammed it into the ground. "I'm not moving an inch from this spot until you're out of my sight and through that gate, do you hear me?"

"Consider this a revolt." Loche joined his fellow urling in planting his sword.

Jeth turned to his red-headed friend, who responded with a shrug.

More surviving warriors rushed past, narrowly avoiding trampling the task force underfoot.

Harpies emerged above the trees like a cloud of locusts, Vidya front and center.

"Fine, you bloody bastards. Oli, get to Lanore, tell Dayne and the fighters to guard the gate. I'll be returning through there, but make sure they are ready if our enemies get there first. Oh, and tell Henna I love her, and she will see her boy soon."

"Sure thing," he said with a tip of his hat.

"Faron, you're leading the team back to the Capital. Tell the King to send ships to Cordos in case I don't make it back."

"Aye, aye, sir," Faron said with a nod.

'Sir.' That word almost made him forget he was about to be swarmed by harpies. "And Master Loche"—he grabbed the man's arm—"just try not to get bit by any more naja."

"Can't promise anything. Now get going, will you?" The older man waved him on.

With a grim smile, Jeth took off with a burst of speed. The people and horses around him blurred into one homogenous streak as he raced for the temple and the warping gate within. Serra floated from his pocket and flew beside him, the only being capable of keeping pace with him now.

He slowed when he reached the gate, looking for his bag of supplies.

Serra flew over to Esteban. "Go through now. We're right behind you."

Esteban nodded and leaped into the rippling pool of energy.

Blasco and a large Herrani warrior stood near the handle, ready to turn it for Fae'ren as soon as Jeth jumped through.

Jeth found his bag on the ground between two huddled magae. He sped between them, snatched the bag, and ran for the gate, praying its energy wouldn't run out before he got there.

Serra returned to his side as he bounded up the steps, and the two of them vanished into the unknown.

25

History Repeats

Vidya soared over the Death tribe ruins with one hundred harpies behind her, eyes glued to the path below. She searched for any Del'Cabrian dead, alive, or somewhere in between. If they scattered off the beaten path, she feared losing them in the bush where flight would quickly lose its advantage.

The shadow harpy appeared beside her, gliding with wings as foreboding as rain clouds. *"He knows where Elmifel's Champion is. Do not allow them to join forces."*

"What could come of it? He was willing to protect Yasharra once," Vidya muttered under her breath, not sure she believed her own words.

"And the moment you took the Bloodstone Dagger, he turned against you. He cares not for Yasharra. His loyalties now rest with King Tiberius."

"Take out as many men on the ground that you find," Vidya ordered her winged cohorts. "Leave any Del'Cabrians alive."

"Yes, Anassa."

Several harpies swooped down to carry out her orders. Vidya and the remaining Primaries glided through the canyon and veered into the ruined temple. As soon as the gate was in sight, the warping energy splashed within the confines of the ring.

"You're too late! He's gone!" the shadow hissed.

"How? The pathway just completed . . ." But the shadow was right; Jeth was nowhere down below.

Droves of white-robed women and children, along with wounded warriors, crowded the overgrown chamber, desperate to escape. Vidya spotted three of Jeth's Del'Cabrian companions lining up behind them. They would have to do.

She dove for the first man. He looked up, and his skin blanched a specter white. It was the soldier she had almost killed in Clive's Tavern, the one who had tried to arrest Jeth.

The skinny, short-haired witch appeared out of thin air. She pointed up at Vidya's contingent. "Naja, attack!"

Snarling reptiles bounded down the tree trunks and leaped off the crumbling walls. Each snatched a harpy from the air and brought them crashing to the ground.

Vidya threw up her forearm blades and sliced through one, coming straight toward her. *These beasts follow the little witch now? She must be a Spirit Mage too. Just my luck.*

She tracked the Del'Cabrians as they ran alongside the rest of the escapees, more and more of them getting swallowed by the gate's swirling energy.

While her harpies dealt with the naja and the sorceress, Vidya catapulted herself toward the gate with a strong gust of wind. She landed on the granite base, blocking the people's escape. They screamed and backed down the steps. With the wind, she pushed those remaining off the platform, clearing a path to the Del'Cabrians.

"Where's Jethril of Fae'ren?" she growled.

The two urlings stood in battle stances, swords pointed outward. The red-headed human drew back his bowstring, arrow nocked.

Vidya spread her wings and sprang forward. She deflected the arrow with her left forearm blade, then took the archer by the scruff and tossed him headfirst into a fallen pillar. Something cracked, and the man crumbled, unconscious.

"Olivier!" the older urling cried.

"See to him and get him through the gate," ordered the middle-aged one.

"May the Deities protect you, Faron." The older man said before running to the archer.

Faron charged, and Vidya parried back, blocking each sword strike with her double blades. The urling was relentless. Each maneuver of his put her more and more on the defensive. Sweat formed under her half helm, soaking into her hair as the same glistened off her opponent's furrowed brow.

The swordsman brought his blade down vertically, forcing her to block with both forearms. She planted her feet and pushed forward, sending him wheeling back. He quickly regained his stance.

The two of them strafed around each other as more and more people passed through the active gate. "Why did Jeth leave you all behind? Does he know where the princess is? Tell me where to find her, and I will let you pass unharmed."

An electrical bolt zapped a harpy from the sky. The witch who had released it vanished once again.

That moment of distraction allowed Faron to lunge forward and jab the point of his sword far too close to Vidya's chest.

She caught it between both palms just before the point pierced her skin, then she forced the pommel into Faron's ribs. He gasped and doubled over. Vidya grabbed him by the collar and threw him onto his back, the foliage beneath him making a satisfying crunch.

As Faron struggled within her steely grip, she spotted the old urling dragging the unconscious human up the base steps.

"Don't let those Del'Cabrians get away!"

A harpy swooped down to retrieve them, but the witch zapped her with another lightning bolt, and the two men lurched through to the other side.

Must I do everything myself? She turned her attentions back to Faron, knowing he was her last chance to—*whoosh*. An arrow nicked her right wing, loosing feathers. A skinny Ankarran boy stood on the gate platform, bow in hand.

Faron's fist made hard contact with Vidya's cheek. She fell over on her arm as he crawled along the dirt to get away. The boy aimed his next arrow for her head, and she had no choice but to ignore Faron and save herself.

She sent a cyclone for the boy, flinging him off the platform. His bow sailed through the air, out of his grasp. It made her gut wrench to cause harm to a child, but what choice did she have?

Faron pushed against the backs of the other warriors, ushering them toward their escape. The witch was nowhere to be seen.

"Somebody shut down the gate!" she bellowed.

Harpies sped for the granite ring. An older woman in white robes with glittering blue beads on her face stood guard as the few remaining villagers passed by her. When the harpies got a hair away from the gate's handle, she raised her arms, and the air all around her tore open. A torrential spray of water crashed against the harpy advance, sending them spinning into trees, sputtering and choking.

Harpies descended upon the gate from every direction, but a rush of water rose to deflect them. The woman raised an impenetrable water barrier around the entire structure, allowing all her white-robed sisters and most of the Herrani warriors safe passage.

Faron hobbled up the gate's steps, about to be one of the last through. There was no way to reach him as long as that Water Mage remained on the platform.

Then, a thin, robed man called out. "Khiri? Khiri!"

The Ankarran boy still lay dazed in the grass just below the platform.

"Shahbaz, did Khiri go through?" The man looked around frantically. Vidya recognized him. Lys, the Crede eunuch she had met in the City of Herran long ago.

"Down there." The Water Mage nodded her head to the boy, now stumbling to his feet and attempting to climb back up the platform.

Vidya ran for him, not sure what she would do when she got her hands on him. Her only goal was to incite the Water Mage to let down her barrier so she could grab Faron.

Upon seeing Vidya's advance toward the child, Shahbaz halted her spell to take Khiri's hand and lift him the rest of the way onto the platform.

Good enough. "Get that urling!" Vidya roared.

Faron, with the last of the Herrani warriors, dove through the energy.

"Follow him through!"

Several of her Harplite zoomed past her, eager to carry out her command. Lys gaped at the swarm coming nearer. With Khiri still in Shahbaz's hefty arms, Lys pushed his shoulder against her, using his entire weight to shove her and the boy through the gate before falling to his hands and knees. Khiri screamed, reaching out for the Crede man as the gate's energy consumed him.

Vidya watched Theoni, one of her core Primaries, zoom toward the gate, arms outstretched, ready to swipe whoever was on the other side and haul them back through. Lys plucked the stone from its cubbyhole. The energy within the ring imploded on itself with a reverberating crack.

Theoni flew over Lys, straight through the ring, and crashed into the stone wall on the other side.

A moment later, she shrieked like a flock of island gulls. Harpies gathered around her, gasping as they brought their hands to their mouths. Theoni rolled around on the ground, two bloody arm stumps gushing blood onto the grass. The hands that were once attached to them were now thousands of miles away.

Vidya growled as she marched up the steps. "Reopen the pathway!"

"They won't risk allowing anyone else through," said the only man left behind.

She punched Lys in the stomach, instantly causing him to spew blood from his mouth. He tumbled off the platform and into the grasps of two other harpies. Floating down after him, she grabbed him by the scarf and hissed, "I should cut *your* arms off!"

"I've never used a warping gate before. I didn't know what would happen," he said, strangely calm for a man about to be torn limb from limb.

"Where did Jeth go?"

"He never told me where he was going."

"Bullshit," Vidya spat.

The shadow harpy glided over the proceedings. *"He speaks true. Just another useless eunuch."*

Vidya roared and shoved him to the ground. *I should kill him.* She stayed her blade, thinking better of it. The eunuch was harmless, though he could be a useful hostage if the Odafi witch and Snake Eye returned. They were conveniently missing from all the excitement. "Take him back to the village and tie him up. I'll figure out what to do with him later."

With that, Vidya launched into the air. She flew out of the canyon and over the overgrown grave city. Below, harpies drove their blades through mortally wounded warriors along the path.

She arrived at the village and found a yurt Daphne had repurposed to tend to the wounded. "Please don't let it be too bad," Vidya prayed as she pushed aside the flaps and ducked inside.

Phrea lay upon a flimsy cot, clenching and unclenching every muscle as she held back cries of pain. Her entire body was glossy and peeling, and the stench of burnt flesh filled the yurt. Vidya fought back a wave of nausea at the grotesque sight of her loyal commander. Every one of her beautiful black feathers had singed away, exposing dark, sagging skin.

"Oh, Phrea," Vidya gasped. "I will flay that witch alive for this."

Phrea's brown eyes watered as she stared up at Vidya, begging her to carry out that threat or put her out of her misery, maybe both.

Daphne dabbed a cold cloth on her welted flesh, making Phrea whimper. "I know she'll heal faster than a normal human, but . . . I have nothing more to numb the pain. She'll be in agony for weeks unless she festers and dies."

"I won't have her suffer like this, and I can't have you spending weeks tending to her." Vidya touched the few silky-smooth strands of hair left on Phrea's head. "You can heal right now, but it will cost you a life. . . ."

Phrea quivered as she closed her eyes and nodded.

With one smooth motion of her arm, Vidya sliced open Phrea's throat. Daphne shot up to her feet, staring in horror—or perhaps fascination—as her friend bled out on the linens and gargled her last breath.

The two harpies stood in the yurt in silence for several excruciating minutes. Eventually, Phrea's throat closed up on its own, her hair sprouted from her healing scalp, and her skin began repairing itself. The next moment, her eyes snapped open, and she rose, choking up her own blood.

Daphne quickly brushed away the blackened, peeling skin from her wings so her feathers could grow back unhindered.

"Damn, Vidi," Phrea croaked, rubbing her throat. "Maybe give it a count of three next time."

"There's not going to be a next time." She put her hands on her hips. "You have two lives left now, so be more careful."

"You be careful," she snapped.

"Phrea—" Vidya was about to give a response just as fiery but bit her tongue. "Thank you. It could have been me up in flames, and that would have been it."

"Don't worry. Although"—Phrea rose to her feet, peeling skin flakes from under her arms—"we should look into how to get extra lives. I mean, we have so much blood left, can't we just repeat the ritual for you?"

"Already looked into it." Daphne brushed her hands off and stood up. "Three lives are all Yasharra deems fit to grant each harpy, no exceptions. That is unless we remove your wings and create you anew. That'll put you out for months as you undergo the transition again."

Vidya shook her head emphatically. With all the male uprisings back home, she couldn't afford to be that vulnerable for any length of time. "No, no, I don't need extra lives. I have my Harplite."

"We will gladly give all three of our lives for yours, if need be," Phrea said with fervor. A warm sensation spread over Vidya's chest to hear it.

"And I will give my one and only for you two, but let's hope it never comes to that," she said.

"I've never felt better, though. Nothing like getting burnt to a crisp to make you appreciate the softness of your own skin." Phrea grazed her fingers over her smooth, tan arms. "I'd still love to get my hands on that invisible sorceress, though."

"She disappeared somewhere near the gate. She may have gone through it, or she's sneaking around here still. Don't let your guard down."

Phrea shivered while putting her singed arm blades back on. "I hate the idea of someone I can't see watching me."

"Says the spy." Daphne snorted.

"That's how I know I wouldn't like it," Phrea returned.

Vidya found another wounded harpy on the next cot over. Her two bloody arm stumps wept through her bandages, staining the linens beneath her. "What's the prognosis on Theoni?"

Placing one hand over her damp forehead, Daphne replied, "She'll need to go to a hospital. I've knocked her out pretty good for now."

"Why don't we give her the same choice you gave me?" Phrea said to Vidya. "I'd gladly give up a life to get my hands back."

"Killing her can seal up wounds or regrow skin, but an entire limb?" Daphne shook her head. "All that will happen is her stumps will heal over, and she'll be down one life."

"Do what you think is best, Commander," said Vidya.

"I'll see if the engineers back home can make her some kind of prosthetic."

With a nod, Phrea and Vidya left Daphne to patch up the rest of the wounded and headed back into the village.

They walked past harpies clearing dead bodies, human and naja, to deposit them at the grave city ruins.

Vidya's eyes drew to the large yurt where Raisha sat and wept, holding Ryeem's head on her lap. As they strode toward her, Phrea pointed to a naja carcass a few feet away. "Ooh, get a load of this beast!"

"Looks like any other to me," Vidya muttered.

"Not the naja. This." Phrea bent down and pulled a sizable poleaxe out from under the giant reptile. Vidya recognized it right away, but its wielder was nowhere to be seen.

Phrea swished the axe through the air. "What a beaut. Suppose you want it then?"

"That's Ash's tabar." Vidya looked around the settlement, hoping to find one of the other harpies carrying him off somewhere.

"Going once, going twice . . . and I'm keeping it." Phrea handed the axe off to a passing harpy and told her to put in the commanders' yurt, wherever that was going to be.

Primary Lieutenant Malantha landed beside them to take the naja away. She paused to ask, "Looking for something, Anassa?"

"Yes, that big tattooed Herrani I fought earlier. If he's without his axe, it may mean he's dead."

"And we should care because . . . ?" Phrea interjected.

"He might be one of the few around here who knows where Jeth went."

"I'll find him." Malantha left the naja where it was and launched herself back into the sky.

Vidya and Phrea continued toward the grieving Herrani woman. Raisha lifted her head and burrowed her eyes into the harpies before her. "Leave me be! You killed my father and my brother. What more do you want?"

"By all rights, your entire family should pay for what your father did to mine. However, my Harplite will see that no harm comes to the rest of them, including you, if you tell me where Jeth went."

"Why would I know where that murderer went?" Raisha wiped the tears off her cheeks, further smudging her black makeup. "I blame him just much as I blame you for the calamity that's befallen us. I hope you do find him, rip his balls off, and fly into the sea!"

Phrea spoke in Vidya's ear. "I believe her. She practically killed him in the palace. The only reason she's here is that he promised he'd tell her how her father died in exchange for leading him to Ryeem."

"And he held up his end of the bargain, as did I," Raisha said. "I only just learned about these Champions you're all after. But neither me nor my brother knew where our father put Elmifel's. Now, are you going to kill me too or allow me to return to my sisters who need me?"

Vidya bit her lip. She admired the woman's spirit, and if what she'd heard about the fight at the palace were true, Raisha and her sisters had dished out long-overdue punishments to the merchant whoremongers, a noble battle that filled Vidya's own heart.

"Take your brother's remains to the grave city and properly pay your respects, then you may return home. If you agree never to take revenge on me or my harpy sisters, I will ensure the safety of yours."

"You think you can buy my peace?" Raisha hissed. "We can take care of our own, as we always have."

"Think hard, Raisha. Our Rangardian allies will soon take Odafi, and all the tribes will quickly fall into chaos. The desert is about to get a lot more dangerous for you and your sisters. You best keep my offer in mind."

Raisha continued to glare at the harpies until they walked away.

"Maybe we don't need to find this Jeth," said Phrea. "We can stake out the castle road and intercept him as he's bringing the princess home."

"But they could just as easily warp to Thessalin and leave her in the protection of the ashray. A place much harder to stake out. Besides, we aren't just dealing with a princess here, but the Champion of Elmifel."

"If I remember what you told me, without the Bloodstone Dagger, which you have"—she pointed down to Vidya's scabbard—"or a good Spirit Mage, who you just killed." She pointed a thumb toward Ryeem's dead body. "She's no threat to Yasharra."

"It's not about what the Champion can do to Yasharra, but what Del'Cabria may do in her name. Champions are called to protect their Conduit from whatever threat they perceive. You know what happened with Queen Orester a thousand years ago."

"But how do you know it will happen this time?"

"History repeats, but only if we allow it," Vidya said. "If this were simply a matter of King Tiberius wanting his daughter back, he'd have sent any number of his soldiers to do that. But he tasked Jeth, a traitor, who happens to be a Champion himself. They know what she is and what she could be used for. Credence depends on us finding her first."

"You don't have to convince me," said Phrea. "The princess is the surest way to prevent Rangardia from switching sides. I'd much rather not have to go to war with my father, thank you very much."

Vidya felt a twinge of guilt for the compromising position she was putting her friend in. Being high up in the Rangardian military, her father would undoubtedly have no choice but to take up arms against Credence if his Emperador commanded it. Vidya never told her what she planned to do with the Agustin when it was all over, which would effectively push the teetering empire off the precipice.

Malantha landed straight in Vidya and Phrea's path. "We got him."

"Ash?"

The lieutenant gave a proud nod. "He was on the pile of bodies ready to go to the grave city, but I checked his vitals, and wouldn't you know it, the bastard lives." She pointed a thumb to one of the small huts several yards away. "I thought you'd want him kept separate from the Crede prisoner, so I put him in there for you."

Relief washed over Vidya. *Finally, something goes right.*

"Nice work, Mal." Phrea affectionately nudged the taller harpy with her wing. "Come on, Vidi, let's squeeze the brute until he spills."

"I think I'd like to try him alone if you don't mind."

"Aw, but torture is my favorite part of the interrogation process," Phrea whined.

She placed a hand on her friend's arm. "I doubt I'll have to hurt him too much. The thief will probably talk on his own accord. For now, I need you to turn the gate for Credence and help Daphne get the wounded through."

Phrea pushed out her plump bottom lip. "Oh, alright."

"Anything more you need from me, Anassa?" asked the always-keen Malantha.

Vidya looked back to Raisha, trying to drag her dead brother down the path. "Help Raisha bury her brother, then have someone fly her home."

"Will do."

Vidya thanked the two harpies and strode into the sturdy hut made of thin palm trunks. Ash hung by both arms, a rope suspending him from the rafters, and his ankles were chained to a giant rock that no one, absent harpy strength, could move on their own.

The shadow harpy tittered in her ear, *"He's the one, the one who knows . . ."*

"Wake up." Vidya smacked him lightly on the face a few times. He snorted a bit but didn't open his eyes.

She pulled his head up by his tail of white hair and noticed a nasty black bruise over his ribcage. She jammed her fingers between two bones, and his eyes bulged.

"Gah . . . !" he wheezed, snapping his head around in panic. Once his gaze fell on Vidya, holding him upright, his features softened, and his expression gained lucidity. "This isn't exactly how I imagined our first time together." He looked up at his bindings. "Actually . . . it kind of is."

"Where did Jeth go?"

"It's always about that fairy boy with you, isn't it?"

She let go of his hair, and he slumped back down with a grunt.

"He ran off and left you here to die. Why stay loyal to him now? Surely, you get nothing from this arrangement he made with the King of Del'Cabria. Just tell me what Jeth knows, and you can go free like the others."

"I know nothing," came the answer Vidya feared he'd say.

She let her fist fly, making brutal contact with his stiff jaw.

Ash spat out the resulting blood and laughed, childlike and irksome for someone with such a prominent larynx. "I've always dreamed you and I would go at it like this."

"What is wrong with you?"

"Guess I have a thing for powerful women," he replied, grinning through bloody teeth.

Vidya struck him again, this time in his eye socket. "Enough! Where's Jeth?"

"And end our night so soon?" he mumbled, his one eye drooping shut. "Not happening, beautiful." She hit him again, and his head snapped back. He hung limp for a moment, and she was afraid she'd knocked him out, but he rallied, still smiling. "Keep going like that, and just I might let you have your way with me."

Vidya grabbed Ash's face and dug her fingers into the mouths of his cobra tattoos. "Listen to me, you big, dumb ape of a man. I know Jeth is looking for the princess, and I know he came here for your help." She pushed him away, letting him swing back and forth on the ropes.

"Anassa?" a quiet voice interrupted. It was Malantha standing in the doorway. "Raisha put Ryeem's body on a sledge and is heading home. Should I . . . send someone after her?"

Vidya groaned. "Let the Herrani brat do what she wants. If she won't accept our help, she's on her own."

Malantha nodded and left.

Ash chuckled. "Mmm, alone again."

Vidya grabbed hold of Ash's bruised side and squeezed hard.

His cries of agony came out as pitiful, wheezing whimpers. "I'm not sure you're going to enjoy our time together as much as I am."

She squeezed tighter, her harpy mind repulsed by the very thought of them together, and shattered another of his ribs.

Ash gasped violently, and she let him go. He hung there, struggling to breathe.

"Let's start over, shall we? Where's Jeth?"

26

Helpless

Jeth skidded to a stop at the edge of the warping gate's base. He dove for the warp stone to pull it out of its cubby, but the gate's pathway was severed before he reached it. *Good, they turned it for Fae'ren. Just hope the others get through in time.*

"You made it," Esteban exclaimed, seated at the edge of the crumbling platform. Unlike all the other gates Jeth had visited, this one sat atop flaking sedimentary rock, peppered with bits of slimy green sea scum. The ring itself was made of dark granite, the design rudimentary like the gates in Thessalin and Fae'ren. "Who let us in?" Jeth looked to the crank.

"There was no one here when I came through," said Esteban.

Jeth walked down the moldy steps and took stock of his new environment. There was thick rainforest to the left and a foggy beach to the right. Faint beams of sunlight pierced through the gray, and he could just make out a rough, foaming ocean crashing onto the gravelly shore.

All Jeth could smell was the pungent rot of seaweed and another foul aroma he couldn't quite place. "There must be magi around here somewhere," he said.

"We did take our time getting through. Maybe they didn't want to wait around," said Serra, hovering over Jeth's head.

"A magus would likely think it was Nas'Gavarr returning from the dead, so why leave . . . ?"

"Could be the princesa," Esteban surmised.

"Let's scour the island." Serra flew out to the beach and disappeared.

She re-emerged from behind them a few seconds later. "Well, she's not on the beach."

"Follow me." Esteban motioned with his snout toward the forest. "I remember a settlement not far from here."

Jeth and Serra followed the naja through an overgrown path. Even though it was the middle of the day, the sprawling trees cast the forest into darkness. They had to clear the trail with dagger, spark, and claw. It reminded Jeth of the Deep Wood, and yet he felt anything but at home. Esteban's claims that the island was cursed seemed unlikely, but he couldn't deny there was something unnatural about this place—the odor, for starters.

Several minutes of bushwhacking brought them to a large clearing. Rows of mud and stone cottages stood in a circular pattern, forming concentric rings around a well and fire pit. The sides of each home were overgrown with moss, and they stunk of mildew. Bone fragments littered the ground; broken skulls lay half-buried in the dirt, weeds snaking through the fissures and empty sockets. Death hung in the air even though the remains looked to be as old as the island itself.

"This place seems welcoming," Jeth murmured.

Esteban shuddered. "He said we couldn't move the bones. We had to live here amongst them for months while building that damned gate. And when we were done, instead of returning us to our homeland, he turned us into these monstrosities." He pointed to his reptilian form.

"For what it's worth, I think you're one of the more handsome monstrosities," Serra said.

"Serra!" Jeth chastised.

"What? He's a nice shade of green."

Esteban let out a throaty chuckle. "Thanks, Fairy, you're not a bad shade of green yourself." If Esteban were warm-blooded, Jeth imagined his snout would turn a pinkish hue.

They picked their way through the settlement, careful not to step on the bones. "Who do you think these people were?" Jeth asked.

"My people," said Esteban in a solemn voice. "From five hundred years ago."

"That long? Then why does it smell like they died yesterday?"

Esteban shrugged. "No one knows what happened to these first settlers. During the Empire's rapid expansion, explorers sailed the unknown seas and founded this place. It was so abundant in natural resources settlers came by the boatloads, and they even started building a warping gate."

"At least they got the base done," Jeth guessed.

"Stonemasons were sent here to build it, but they never returned. Three times, a messenger ship set sail to find out what happened, and three times the ship never made it back. Rangardia abandoned the plan to settle Cordos, and the island was deemed cursed. To even speak its name invites misfortune. I only wish I had listened to the warnings of my countrymen." Esteban's gaze fell.

Jeth entered one of the smaller cottages, the first one he came across that was more than a crumbling stone frame. Layers of dust calcified upon the furniture, and tarnished bronze bowls on the remains of an old table had aged to the color of crushed olives. Red roaches scuttled between them.

"Doesn't seem likely anyone has lived here in the last year," said Serra.

"She has to be around here somewhere." Jeth walked out of the house, the stench of decay like an impenetrable cloud following him wherever he went.

The odor grew stronger as he crossed the village to the houses on the other side. He stepped past a rotted wooden door, shattered and partially off its hinges. The foul odor inside the cottage made him wish his nose would shrivel up and fall away.

Around the table and chairs, a skeletal figure sat on the floor against the wall. Flaps of skin drooped off its bony form, and grubs wriggled within the sunken remains of its eyes.

Jeth gagged, bringing a hand up to cover his mouth and nose. *Now, this one died much more recently.*

"Something smells bad in here," said Serra, flying into the cottage after him. She got in close and inspected the corpse. It wore the familiar black and gray robes of a magus, stained a coppery brown from his neck to his lap. "Looks like something ripped his throat out."

Blood pounded in Jeth's ears as he ventured farther into the cabin. In the corner, flies buzzed around a chamber pot, remnants of urine and fecal matter wandered around Jeth's overwhelmed nasal passages. Yellowed blankets lay in a rumpled pile on the sagging, old bed. Beside it was a rusted chain attached to the wall, something flesh-colored beside a manacle peeked out from the folds of the moldy blanket.

He tossed it aside to reveal a woman's heeled shoe made of pink suede, untied and stretched apart, the frilly lace lining stained brown.

The same brown flakes stained the locked shackle as well. *Blood*.

Jeth squeezed the shoe. "She was here, alright. She must have slipped her foot out of this shackle, likely breaking it in the process."

"Perhaps to get away from whatever killed this man," said Serra.

"Jeth! Fairy! I found a body," Esteban called from outside.

Jeth and Serra dashed out the door to find him waving them over to the settlement's far west end. They joined him at the edge of a forested path.

A magus robe lay crumpled and soiled with dirt. "Esteb, for crying out loud." Jeth exhaled heavily. "I thought you'd found the princess's body."

He showed Esteban the shoe, and the lizard man's yellow eyes darkened. "Oh. Apologies. It's only one of Nas'Gavarr's worshipers." He lifted the robe, and a decaying torso dropped out, making Jeth's already queasy stomach lurch.

"What did that to him?" Jeth gagged into his sleeve.

The naja sniffed the rotting corpse without a flinch. "Some wildlife had their way with this one. Can't tell how he met his end exactly. There's a lot of blood here, though."

"Where?" Serra asked. "I can't see it."

"In the soil. It's old, but I can still smell the residue."

"Right." Jeth nodded. "How old is it, do you think?"

Esteban's forked tongue darted out of his mouth and lapped up the earth. "Mmmm . . . a year, maybe?"

Far down the path, a ghastly wail rose from the depths of the jungle, echoing down Jeth's spine and making his teeth chatter. He blinked a few times to regain control of himself. "Alright, Ser, what are your fairy senses telling you?"

"To not go near those woods. Do you really need me to tell you that?" Serra curled up on Esteban's armored shoulder.

Jeth rolled his eyes. "I mean, what do you think that sound was?"

"I don't know, but if I were to hazard a guess, I'd say it's the thing the Crannabeatha was warning us about. You know, that destructive force returning to destroy everything we hold dear. . . ."

"I thought that was harpies."

Serra shook her head and shivered. "I thought so too."

The loose skin around Esteban's larynx bobbed up and down.

"It's not comforting when a fairy and a naja both want to tuck tail and run," said Jeth. "You do know we have to go into those woods, regardless of what's in there, right?"

Serra buried her little head in her arms. "What's the point of having me along if you willfully ignore me every single time?"

"Come on, Ser, I need you," Jeth took his bow off his back and nocked an arrow.

"I can hold you if you're too scared, Fairy." Esteban offered his large clawed hands.

Serra sprang off his shoulder, whirring with forced bravado. "I'm a thousand-year-old pixie. I don't get scared. Let's go."

Carefully, the trio crept down the path. Dark, gnarled trees bent over them, only increasing the feeling that they were surrounded by enemies.

The path ended at a steep drop, where a cold mist obfuscated the ground below. The mysterious foul smell wafted up Jeth's nose, making him turn away.

A smaller path branched off to the south, and the group continued along it. The sound of falling water in the distance eventually led them to a watering hole draped in fog. Dead trees stuck up out of it while flying beetles skittered along the surface.

A red light flickered in Jeth's periphery, and he spun around. Across the pond, two glowing red orbs peered at him through the mist. "What's that?" He pulled back on his bowstring, and the lights vanished.

"I'll get it!" Serra zoomed off in that direction, the thick mist swallowing her sparkling green trail.

"Serra, wait!" Without thinking, Jeth jumped into the water, and Esteban followed.

Once inside the fog, it was easier to see the way out. He pulled himself out of the pond on the other side and sprinted in the direction he hoped Serra had gone. "Serra, come back!"

Esteban managed to stay on Jeth's tail as the two frantically ran through the thick foliage in search of the pixie.

"Serra!" Jeth's voice took on an alarming pitch. A green streak came straight at his face, making him yelp. "Sag damn it, Ser, don't fly off like that!"

She pursed her tiny lips in confusion. "But I'm faster and smaller than you. I'd have a better chance at catching up to that thing and reporting back."

"Aye, it's all right," he said with a sigh. "This place just has me on edge."

Serra put her hands behind her back and hung her head. "I'll try to stay close from now on, at least until we know what we're dealing with."

"Thanks," Jeth said, still gripping his bow in a sweaty hand. "Let's go back to the settlement. I don't know about you, but I'm beat."

Serra turned up her lip in confusion. "Who beat you?"

Jeth gave her an eye roll and a head shake, too exhausted to explain. Esteban took it upon himself. "He means he's tired, Fairy, as am I."

"Hopefully, we'll have more sunlight to work with tomorrow." Jeth looked around. The fog seemed to be getting darker, if that were even possible.

They returned to the settlement and spent the remainder of the evening light cleaning out the least disgusting cottage to spend the night in.

When darkness fell over the island, Esteban started a fire in one of the old hearths, and the three sat on the floor in front of it. Stripped down to his knickers, Jeth dipped into his rations as his clothing and boots were laid out to dry. Esteban was content to eat the bugs and other reptiles that happened to scuttle over the rotting floorboards. Meanwhile, Serra watched curiously from the princess's shoe, serving as a miniature suede chair.

Jeth couldn't help but comment, although lacking his usual levity, "Don't worry, Your Highness. A naked man, a wee pixie, and a bug-eating naja are here to save you. You've got nothing to fear now."

As he licked up his last bit of bean paste from the tin, the mysterious creature howled again. Serra hugged her knees to her chest. "Do you think we'll find her, Jeth?"

"I was going to ask *you* that."

"I wish I could be more helpful." Her chin fell against her chest. "I'm at a loss. . . . It's sort of impossible that she's alive, isn't it?"

Jeth scratched at his scruffy beard. "First thing in the morning, we'll search the island for more proof, then bring what we find back to the King." He put his head in his hands and groaned. "Sweet Mother Oak."

"Are you going to be all right, compadre?" Esteban asked before slurping up a wriggling lizard's tail into his mouth.

"I'm fine, but Zephira's not." Jeth popped the cork of his near-empty jar of honey. "She spent more than a year here on this horror show of an island in shackles." He gulped the rest of the concoction and grimaced at the warm, sticky chunks sliding down his throat. "Why would Nas'Gavarr bring her here? Why not just use her to shut down Yasharra before the Crannabeatha, then bring her back as promised? Why would he keep her here to let her die at the hands of some . . . *thing* in the woods?"

The naja and fairy sat in dead silence.

Jeth continued in a defeated voice. "Was it just to make her suffer? Some kind of punishment for the sins of her ancestors?" He tossed aside the empty medicine jar, and it rolled across the floor and stopped against a table leg with a hollow clink.

"Perhaps it's the same thing that killed my people five hundred years ago," said Esteban.

"Did you see anything when you and your crew were here last?" Serra asked.

"Nas'Gavarr told us to never go into the woods beyond this settlement. He said as long as he was alive, the curse would not disturb us. I thought it was ridiculous until one of my crewmen went mad, ran off into the woods, and was never seen again."

"You said the blood out there is about a year old, right?" Jeth asked.

"A bit more than that, but yes."

"A little over a year ago, Nas'Gavarr met his end. Do you think it's a coincidence that at around the same time, these magi are killed, and she disappears? Maybe he was keeping her safe as he did your crew . . . until he couldn't anymore."

"Leaving her at home with her parents would have kept her even safer." Serra flew up and hovered closer to Jeth's face. "Please don't blame yourself for this, Jeth."

"Why not? Tiberius certainly will." He scraped his hands down his face. "I killed the only man who knew where his daughter was and could protect her from all this. Now, she's probably dead."

"Well, if she's dead and the magi have been dead for over a year," began Esteban, "who was the one who let us through the gate?"

The chilling wail from the forest sounded again, and Jeth met eyes with the naja. "Something tells me we don't want to find out."

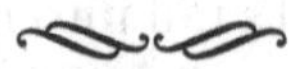

Vidya left Ash to hang by his wrists for the entire night. The pain in his arms alone should have been enough to make him give in. However, to be safe, she shattered both his ankles so he'd be unable to put weight on his feet. She expected to hear his screams for mercy all through the night, begging to spill his guts to Vidya, but nothing interrupted her slumber until the sun rose again.

Fearing the man was dead, she entered his hut first thing. "Good morning, beautiful," Ash rasped. If his eyes weren't nearly swollen shut, Vidya imagined he would have winked.

She sighed with frustration. "Surely, you've had enough."

Ash shook his head, trying to grin out the corner of his mouth, but it only contorted his already gruesome face.

Digging a finger into one of the chest wounds she had inflicted on him the day before, Vidya was pleased to hear his breath hasten, and he snorted bloody pus from his nose. "Good," she said. "Me neither. Now, where were we? Oh, right, Jeth's whereabouts."

She pulled her finger from the wound and waited for an answer that didn't come. A punch to Ash's face sent one of his teeth flying across the room. "Why would a Herrani thief want to protect Del'Cabrian interests?"

Ash spit out another tooth before replying. "Sag can have those pointed-ear halfwits for all I care."

"Then who *are* you protecting?"

"Don't you get it?" Ash mumbled. "I don't turn my back on family."

"That's not what I witnessed the day we first met. You didn't hesitate to abandon Jeth in this very place." She jabbed her fingers into the bruise under his cracked ribs. "It was me who found him, covered in blood and entrails, trapped under a naja—like you yesterday." She twisted her hand, making him wheeze. "And what of Anwarr? Was she not family when you refused to come to her aid?"

"I have to live with what happened to her every day," he choked. "I won't make that mistake again."

She placed her fingers under the Herrani's chin and forced him to look at her through his puffy eyes. "Do you *really* think I want to hurt Jeth? He was my friend, you know."

Ash chuckled through his whistling nasal passages. "You are a friend to no man"—a stupid grin crossed his face— "unfortunately for me."

Vidya grabbed Ash's hair, lifted him up to her height, and set him on his broken ankles. He grunted in pain as Vidya grazed her hand down his sweaty face, emulating a lover's touch. "And here I thought you wished to be more than friends." He whimpered as she dug her nails into his bruised cheek. She gently let him down and grazed her fingertips over his sweaty scalp.

A strange tingling sensation radiated down her thighs, up her back, and through her very feathers. She softened her voice and her touch as well. "Although . . . having you here . . . *helpless* like this . . . perhaps I can end your suffering in favor of something more . . . pleasurable. . . ." She ran her hand across his neck, tracing his tattoo from the stinger at his clavicle, all the way down to the pincers at his navel.

"Oh, Vidya," Ash breathed. "If I thought there was any real chance of you pleasuring me, I'd lead you straight to Jeth myself."

Vidya's left hand continued to draw down his bruised but nevertheless hard musculature. "You don't think you have a chance with me?"

His breath came out in painful rasps, even as his manhood started to twitch and lengthen in his wide-legged trousers. "You have no interest in me like this. You don't want a helpless man. . . ."

"Don't I?" she whispered into his ear.

His voice took on a hard edge. "You need them to be dangerous . . . more dangerous than you. Except, men like that don't normally go for you, do they?"

Her hands stopped just short of Ash's belt sash. "What makes you say that?" One dangerous man, in particular, came to Vidya's mind.

Ash's voice deepened, despite his breathlessness, "They're threatened by you . . . and they should be. Just look at you and all your ruthless radiance." He licked his swollen lips. "A woman like you needs a dangerous man, but one who accepts his place . . . under your feet."

Vidya stepped back. Her stomach churned, and her heart fluttered at the same time in remembrance of her husband:

"Vid . . . Vidya . . . I want to touch you." Agustin huffed.

"Then touch me," she replied as she rode him, his limbs dead at his sides.

"I-I can't. . . . You know I can't." A tear rolled down his temple and onto the pillow.

She giggled into her hand, nearing climax. "Oh, silly me, how could I forget your condition?"

Back then, she was in control. Now, as Anassa, with a Harplite at her disposal, she couldn't feel less in control.

Vidya clutched Ash by the thick neck with a surge of power and lifted him up, cutting off his weak, mocking laughter. She then seized his genitals in her other hand, making his bleeding eyes bulge. "And you think you're just the man for me, hmm?" She squeezed harder, making pitched wheezes rattle off his tongue. "Let me tell you your place. You are here to provide me information on Jeth, nothing more.

If you do not, may the Harpy restrain me, I will tear from you that which makes you a man!"

Ash gargled in her hand. Vidya loosened her grip around his neck but kept a firm grasp between his legs. "You think you hold . . . what makes me a man?"

"He's mocking you. Rip them off already and see if he still feels the same," the shadow harpy hissed from behind her.

Vidya squeezed his testicles so hard she felt them ready to burst between her fingers.

Ash's breathless shrieks blasted through the hut until his eyes rolled back into his skull and his head slumped forward.

Vidya sighed and released him; there was no pleasure to be had in ripping the manhood off an unconscious man.

"If I were in charge, he'd have told us everything by now, and we'd have another eunuch for the squabs to play with," the shadow harpy taunted.

"Well, you're not in charge!" Vidya snapped.

The harpy gave her a fiery glare and dissolved into the shadow of the hut's darkest corner.

Vidya suppressed a scream and lashed out at the only flesh and bone being in front of her. She tore Ash's ropes from the rafter and threw him to the ground, his bulky body rolling into the wall.

Breathing hard, she stormed out of the hut's stifling heat and into the cool morning air, a drop of rain wetting her forehead. She called to the first harpy who walked by but couldn't remember her name at the moment. "You," she pointed a thumb to the hut behind her. "Tie the prisoner back up and watch him."

"Yes, Anassa," the girl nodded.

Vidya rubbed her pounding temples, her hands shaking. Her skin felt hot, prickly like she was catching fire. Was this sensation only rage, frustration? Those seemed obvious. But there was a strange arousal underneath it all, an aching anticipation.

It was similar to what came over her right before she exacted punishment on someone, but this one eluded her . . . a fulfillment forever out of reach. As if she and Agustin switched places in that last year of their marriage. *If I can't even get one idiot man to talk under the threat of crushed gonads, dare I call myself a harpy?*

The rain started to fall in earnest. Vidya looked up to the sky and let the drops spatter over her face and hair, cooling her stormy temper.

The shadow harpy manifested next to her. *"Stop allowing yourself to be affected by men. The future of Credence depends on finding Elmifel's Champion."*

"I know that," replied Vidya through her teeth.

"But did you know Ricardo sent word to King Tiberius today? He wants to negotiate for the last two ports, among other things. . . ."

"What?" Vidya screeched. "That son of a—" She hushed herself and turned her back to a harpy guard passing overhead. "If he makes that alliance before we find the princess . . ."

"The Herrani has the answers we seek."

"He won't give us any answers if I kill him. In fact, I think he'd enjoy that."

"Then use another tactic, or do you not even have what it takes to break one man?"

Vidya bared her teeth, ready to lash out at her specter, but another idea came to mind. A smile escaped her, one of relief and hope despite the overwhelming panic. "I've broken a man far scarier than him, and that was before I became a harpy," she smirked. "Ash says he can't turn his back on family. Well, his family is closer than he thinks."

27
Suffer in Kind

Jeth and Esteban sloshed through swampy terrain, searching for the princess or whatever was left of her. Serra zipped between tree branches, out of sight for a few moments but never going too far; the jungle didn't feel like a safe place to be alone. Thankfully, the haunting howls hadn't sounded since the first night.

Jeth munched on some rations while Esteban snagged various buzzing insects with his retractable tongue before chewing them with a resounding crunch. His appetite now gone, Jeth handed Esteban the rest of his dried meat. "Here, there's plenty for both of us."

Esteban wrinkled his scaly snout at Jeth's offer. "If it's not raw off the bone, I don't care for it."

"Suit yourself." Jeth shrugged. "Just thought since you're human, you might want to go back to eating regular food."

Esteban gave Jeth a wry look. "Human in spirit, yes, but my body is all naja, and naja do not eat whatever poor excuse for sustenance that is."

With a sigh, Jeth put the left-over jerky into his coat pocket. "I could go for something a little fresher myself. Some smoked boar would be nice." He hadn't had much luck hunting on the island. They'd scarcely seen any wildlife besides the enormous bugs Esteban managed to uncover. Even a rodent over a campfire rotisserie would suit Jeth well enough.

Was it at all possible the princess was still alive? *If the island's curse hasn't killed her, starvation certainly would've.*

"You know what I miss?" Esteban began, coaxing Jeth out of his darkening thoughts. "Blood oranges. They grow everywhere back home. You could eat them right off the branch."

"Blood oranges?" Jeth scoffed. "Doesn't sound too appetizing."

"Do not judge the fruit by the name. They are the most refreshing, flavorful thing a man could put in his mouth, like a fine wine in citrus form."

Jeth cut away the thick foliage in his way with his knife. "When this is over, and I'm a free man again, I'll pay a visit to the Guildlands and try some myself . . . perhaps bring you back a bunch, to thank you for helping me out here."

The giant reptile shook his head. "I wasn't talking about the Guildlands, but Rangardia, the southernmost island where I grew up."

"Oh. Then no, I won't be going there any time soon."

Esteban waved a clawed hand down. "Don't worry yourself. To get me to eat one now, you'd have to fill it with actual blood, but at least I can remember how delicious they used to taste. If I'm ever human again, the first thing I'm going to do is sail to that island, pick a nice fat one off the nearest tree, and devour it right then and there." He chuckled. "The things we take for granted, uh?"

"Esteb." Jeth halted his gait, and Esteban stopped with him. "You know you don't have to be here, right? You can warp to Fae'ren whenever you want, find Jenn and the others, and leave Ser and me to it. Once Snake Eye recovers and Herran gets sorted, he may be able to reverse what his brother did. You don't owe me or the King of Del'Cabria a lick. You deserve your life back."

Esteban's larynx bobbed up and down as if he were getting choked up. "I've learned that in this life, we don't always get what we deserve; we get what we work toward, good or bad. I've done a lot of terrible things since my transformation. . . ."

"That wasn't you."

"It was. I didn't choose it, but it happened. What other reason is there for my salvation, then to return to the island where it all started and free someone else from its curse?"

Jeth nodded thoughtfully, being all too familiar with curses, imagined or otherwise. "Then let's put our noses to work and find her, aye?"

The two of them continued their muddy trek, sniffing the air and coming up short. Just when Jeth started to worry about how long Serra was gone, he heard her little voice through the trees to the south. "Jeth, Esteb! Over here!"

Jeth dashed into the bush, following the direction of her voice and eventually her fairy scent. He had to stop abruptly to keep from tipping over the edge of a cliff—only it wasn't exactly a cliff. The moss-covered edges were eroded but relatively even, forming downward steps in a large semicircular pattern. At first glance, it could have been part of the natural landscape, but upon closer inspection, the symmetry was too uncanny.

Jeth carefully descended the crumbling steps and came before a flat stone surface overgrown with vegetation. "What is this?"

Serra hovered over the stone stage. "Not sure, but it appears man-made."

"It looks like an amphitheater of sorts," Jeth surmised. He then turned to Esteban, bounding down the steps. "Esteb, what did your people build this for? Strange place to put a theater."

The naja looked around, darting his tongue about as if tasting the mist congregating around them. "I don't think Rangardians built this."

"Judging by the stone's condition"—Serra floated toward a rock wall beyond the stage, covered in vines— "this is much older than five hundred years."

"Are you saying this island was inhabited before that?" Jeth asked.

Esteban got on all fours and rifled through the soil, smelling it with his tongue. "The pixie is right. This place is ancient, and it reeks of death."

At those words, a strange sensation coated Jeth like the surrounding fog, as if he were trapped in a dream state. He felt tethered yet vulnerable. His pulse quickened, and his bones ached. "Horrible things happened here," he whispered.

Serra turned to Jeth with her head tilted. "How do you know? I don't sense anything here in particular." Jeth imagined dozens of faceless figures sitting on the steps, staring right through him, to the rock wall at his back. With a violent shudder, he turned around. He studied the wall with his eyes and nose. A faint aroma of iron and salt stemmed from it. Faded splotches of red and black peered at him from behind the green foliage.

"Help me get rid of these vines," Jeth said, taking a handful and tearing them away.

As Jeth took out his dagger, Esteban clawed away swaths of vegetation, but the moss still clung. Serra flew up and laid her tiny hands on what was left. "Allow me." In a few moments, the mosses and other plants sticking out from the stone's cracks turned a sickly brown.

"How are you doing that?" Esteban asked, jaws agape.

"I'm transferring its life force into myself. Sometimes we forest pixies have to end plant life to allow new life to flourish."

"Is that why you fairies have such long lives?" Esteban asked.

Serra shook her head. "Borrowed life force must be passed on, as is our Sacred Duty. Our own life force is maintained by the Crannabeatha alone."

As Serra went to offload her borrowed life force into the foliage on the ground, Jeth and Esteban quickly brushed the dead moss away to expose the ancient stone beneath. On the bottom layer, six black splotches encircled a seventh, larger spot. Above that, an open maw of teeth was painted in whites and browns, long and crooked. At the top were ovals painted in light rust, made to resemble eyes, glaring. It reminded him of the glowing red lights in the bushes the day before.

Serra kept shaking her head. "I don't understand. What are we looking at?"

Jeth and Esteban both took steps back from the painted wall. "We're definitely not alone on this island."

A pitched screech pierced the fog. A child's scream lost in the jungle. *That's Ellion's scream . . . identical to the night he was taken.* Every one of Jeth's senses honed at once. Neither Serra nor Esteban reacted. "Did either of you hear that?"

"Hear what?" Serra floated away from the wall.

An agonizing cry followed, *"Daddy!"*

"That's her!" Jeth climbed up the north amphitheater wall and dashed into the jungle.

"Wait!" Esteban called.

"Jeth!" Serra blurred in front of him and put out her hands, ready to spark.

He skidded to a stop. "Ser, what are you doing? We have to find her—she's crying," Jeth said breathlessly.

"Tell me how you hear her if I can't?"

"You must not have your hearing honed enough."

"My hearing's been honed to the max since we got here," Serra said, hands on her hips.

Catching his breath, Jeth pushed his hearing so far, he could listen to the water condensing on the leaves all around them, but not a single peep from the mystery crier.

Esteban caught up to them, huffing and puffing. "What's going on?"

"Nothing," Jeth muttered. "I thought I heard someone. . . ."

Esteban placed a large clawed hand on Jeth's shoulder. "Don't let this island get to you, compadre. I told you men have gone mad in this jungle hearing things that were not there."

Jeth took a few deep breaths and willed his heart to slow. "How are we going to find her if we don't know what's real?"

Serra shrugged. "Next time you hear something, check with me first."

With a nod, Jeth said, "Right then. We keep on."

Ash's swollen eyes blinked open, settling on the much smaller man tied naked to the column across from him. "Lys!" he rasped.

Vidya watched the giant Herrani struggle uselessly against the thick cord around his muscular arms and torso. After having ripped his ropes off in rage the day before, Vidya had ordered a harpy to tie him to the load-bearing column in a seated position.

Ash cast her a wrathful eye. "You told me everyone else got away."

Lys responded before Vidya could. "It's all right, Ashbedael. I had to stay behind. It was for the best."

"He doesn't know anything. I do. Direct your interrogation at me," Ash begged.

"No need to be jealous. There's enough of me for both of you." Vidya circled to Lys's front, grazing the edge of her arm blade casually across his meager pectorals, ever so slightly breaking the skin. The Crede man barely made a peep as Ash writhed against his restraints. "Please. He's done nothing to you."

"He's a Crede fugitive," said Vidya. "Though," she glanced down to Lys's genitals, or the lack thereof, and smirked. "It is clear he has received just punishment for his crimes. Perhaps all can be forgiven if someone just tells me what I need to know."

"Don't say anything, Ash," Lys said.

She smacked Lys across the face with the back of her hand. Her blade caught in his cheek and sliced a portion of it open.

"Alright, you win," Ash sputtered. Vidya raised an eyebrow. She felt a twinge of disappointment that he gave in so quickly. "The King of

Del'Cabria has Jeth looking for his daughter in exchange for a pardon. But none of us knows where she is yet."

The shadow harpy materialized behind Ash, laying her tendril-like fingers over his shoulders. *"He's holding out,"* she sang.

"Jeth wouldn't have abandoned you all here unless he knew something about her that he didn't want us to find out. You may not know exactly where the princess is, and that's fine, but you know where Jeth went."

Lys spoke, blood dripping from the side of his face. "The Council's diplomatic efforts have forged peace with Del'Cabria for decades. Why would you need their princess? Could it be . . . the sirens don't govern Credence any longer?"

"If only you could see your old home now." She gave a disingenuous grin before drawing her blade across Lys's gut, spilling dark red blood across his torso.

"Lys!" Ash cried, struggling harder. "Sal, have mercy."

"Salotaph is gone, remember?" said Vidya. "Pray to the Del'Cabrian Deities since you seem to be more aligned with them."

Vidya struck Lys in the face once more. Bone cracked beneath her knuckles, blood spraying from his cheek. Lys's head bobbed up and down as he fought to stay conscious.

"Lysandros, stay with me—look at me!"

The Crede man's eyes fluttered open.

"Yes, look at him, Lysandros." Vidya lifted his head by the hair to meet Ash's desperate gaze. "Look into those loving eyes while he turns his back on you, after everything you've done for him and his crew." She roughly released him, letting his head hang impotently against his chest. "It's quite simple. Who is more important to you? The man who wants no part in your thieving life you call a family or the loyal shopkeeper who unfailingly kept a roof over your head for all these years?"

Vidya readied her blade to slice Lys again, but then Ash cried out. "Stop, stop! I'll tell you everything."

Lys rested his head against the post and whimpered, "Ash . . . don't. It's not only Jeth's life on the line here."

Ash's eyes darted back and forth between the man and woman in the hut. Lys continued in Ash's stead, "If he doesn't complete his mission for the King, countless Fae'ren will suffer."

"Silence, eunuch!" Vidya balled her fist, prepared to strike Lys again.

Ash panted so hard his words were barely audible. "All the King wants is his daughter back, and Jeth wants to help his people. It has nothing to do with Credence."

"If that were true, then why not tell me outright?"

Ash glared at her. "Because I know what you're capable of. I saw what you did to Jeth after you made off with that dagger." He nodded toward her scabbard. "Even after he saved your life." Ash took a wheezing breath. "You're willing to commit atrocities to find Elmifel's Champion, and Jeth is willing to die to bring her home. So, I must ask you, Vidya. Is your intent to harm an innocent girl?"

Vidya didn't know how she would feel if she were faced with the choice to kill the urling princess. She knew she could never return her to her people, not while she carried the blood of a Champion, but to take her life? "Harpies don't hurt women, regardless from where they hail, innocent or otherwise," she said with fortitude.

"But you will . . ." Lys croaked.

She spun around and glared at the eunuch.

"I've read the history." Blood flowed from the flapping tear in his cheek. "Harpies claim to punish men on behalf of their female victims. Certainly, a noble cause; men like that deserve to suffer. But how long will it be before all men suffer in kind? What of those women who love them . . . their wives and daughters?"

"Tear him apart for his insolence!" the shadow harpy shrieked.

Vidya dug her fingers into the open gash in Lys's gut. He clenched his teeth, tears overflowing. "Where did Jeth go?" she growled. "I know he went through the gate before it turned for Fae'ren. Was it Thessalin?"

"It wasn't Thessalin," Ash confessed.

Lys kept shaking his head as Vidya plunged her hand deeper, the slippery wetness hot between her fingers.

"Where?" she shouted.

"Some island . . ."

"What island?"

She felt like a bird of prey, soaring above a field of fresh corpses. It was all she could do not to rip the bowels clean out of Lys and devour whatever remained.

"I don't know, some cursed island. That's all he told me. I swear, please, stop hurting him!"

"Ah hah, you did it. Well done," the shadow harpy tittered in Vidya's ear. With great effort, she pulled her hand out of Lys with a sickening slurp.

She often heard Rangarders reference a cursed island in moments of frustration. *What was it called again? Cordon? Cordos? Cordos, that's it. But why in Yasharra's infinite wisdom would Nas'Gavarr take the Champion there?*

"Set him free now." Ash hung his head in defeat.

"Why would I do that?"

"You promised he'd be forgiven if I talked."

The shadow harpy circled the post Lys was tied to, almost prancing. *"Punish the woman beater."*

"I said *perhaps* he'd be forgiven . . ."

Ash's bloodshot eyes flooded, his lips contorting into a venomous scowl. "I told you everything. At least get him a medic!"

She looked to Lys, barely conscious, olive skin paled to gray, blood trickling down his navel with every labored breath. So pathetic, so *weak*.

"Unfortunately, my medic is not here. I'm afraid nothing can be done for him." Vidya took slow, deliberate steps toward the Crede prisoner, contemplating where she'd strike first.

"Lysandros," Ash whimpered, desperate. "Forgive me . . . you don't deserve this—he doesn't deserve this!"

Vidya froze. *He doesn't deserve this . . .* her mind kept repeating, but then how come the shadow harpy demand she punish him? Vidya knew in her heart that Lys had more than paid for his trespasses against his wife and was, by all accounts, a good man. She had witnessed for herself how Lys watched over the thieving crew, provided for them like the father none of them had. It shocked her how eager she was, in that moment, to obey the shadow and spill his blood. The shadow had urged her to kill Jeth over a year ago, even though he didn't deserve such a fate either. *And look what my mercy has wrought. . . .*

Vidya was done holding back. She would not be a harpy that suffered a weak man to live, innocent or not.

"He must be punished," she said flatly, raising her forearm blade.

"No!" Ash shrieked, spittle flying from his mouth. "Lys! Look at me—I'm sorry. . . . Please, look at me." Lys lifted his heavy head, the life already draining from his eyes. Ash said in a hoarse near-whisper, "You will be avenged, my friend."

A meek smile tugged at the Crede man's swollen face. "Very g—"

Vidya's arm blade opened his throat, permanently severing his last words. Ash released a throat rattling roar, thrashing against his restraints and shaking the entire frame of the hut. "Lysandros!" the big man sobbed, his manly exterior crumbling like a tower in the grave city ruins. "Forgive me. I didn't mean for this . . ."

Lys released a final gurgling breath before his head fell limply to his chest.

Vidya walked over to Ash. *I'll take him too, no reason to keep him alive now.*

The Herrani's painful wails—sounds she never imagined could come from a man of his size—thickened the air. He rocked the column he was tied to. "That's right, Vidya, don't forget me," he seethed through gnashing teeth. "I've hit women too. Kill me! Or by any god that will hear me, I will get free, and I will rip you apart, feather by feather, you rotting cunt!"

Clenching her fists, she raised her arm, about to cleave her blade vertically over his giant, tattooed skull. Ash glared up at her, enraged, broken, and ready. The man had betrayed his family. Who would want to continue living after that? But then, of course, some of that family was still out there.

"What are you waiting for? Slice my throat, you coward! You call yourself a harpy? Huh? Punish me!"

"No." She shook her head and backed away. "You'd serve better as a hostage in case Snake Eye or Istari decide to take their revenge . . . You will die when they do."

Turning on her heel, Vidya exited the hut. Ash's cries grew louder the farther she went.

With a frustrated grunt, Vidya shook off the sound. *Deserved it or not doesn't matter. They should not have stood in my way.*

As Vidya trudged through the village, Ash's whimpers eventually faded into the whistling wind, and she could breathe more freely. She flagged down a harpy guard soaring overhead. "The Crede eunuch is dead. Take his body to the ruins with the others."

"What of the Herrani prisoner?" the guard asked.

"Dose him with valerian and prepare him for transport back to Credence. He will remain there as a prisoner of war."

28
Childlike

Vidya arrived at the temple ruins just as a harpy carried the unconscious Ash through the warping gate. A moment later, Daphne emerged from the other side, and Phrea, who had been operating the gate, greeted her friend on the base.

"Didn't expect a welcoming committee," Daphne said on her approach.

"It's time," Vidya said. "Collect what you need for a two to three-day flight. We set course at sun up."

"Ah, so you finally cracked him." Daphne glanced back at the gate for a moment.

"Would have been sooner if I got to help," mumbled Phrea.

Vidya glared at her friend, then continued, "Choose a lieutenant to take charge here with half the Primaries. The rest are coming with us."

"Fifty harpies for one little man?" Phrea balked. "I know you said he was spry, but come on."

"It's to cover more ground in searching for him. What do you two know of the Cursed Isle of Cordos?"

"Not much." Phrea shrugged. "Only that Rangardian explorers discovered it around five hundred years ago and never returned."

"Do you know where to find it?"

"Given that most Rangarders think it's bad luck to even mention it . . . not really." Phrea shook her head. "Did Jeth go there?"

Vidya gave her commanders a brief overview of what Ash had told her. "I need to talk to someone who knows the general coordinates for

Cordos. I doubt we can reach it by gate after Jeth went through."

"Maybe the Emperador would know," suggested Daphne.

"If not, the Armada Almirante surely will," continued Phrea. "All seamen need to be aware of it so they can steer clear."

Vidya wanted to steer clear of the gulf lest she run into her husband, but then she had a thought. She didn't intend to take the next step in her revenge plot until the princess was found, but she may not get an opportunity to be alone with Agustin before Ricardo spoke to the King. In fact, he may have already left. "If there's a chance we'll see Agustin, we should bring the curare solution. Daph, please tell me you're finished making it."

The medic gave Vidya a blank, doe-eyed stare. "Yes, about a month ago, but it's in the lab. Are you sure it's not too soon for that?"

"You said the poison needs about a week to take full effect, and by then, we'll be sure to have the princess in our custody."

"Seems risky, Vidi," Phrea said. "Shouldn't we wait until the princess is secure first? Wouldn't want to set Ricardo off too soon. If he declares war before we can—"

"He can declare war all he wants. When the King receives word that we have his daughter, it will be recanted before Ricardo leaves the Capital."

"And if we don't find her?"

Vidya turned to her other commander. "Daphne, have you been able to plant the curare seeds in Ricardo's secret garden?" Seven years ago, Ricard had grown curare in a locked garden in his own private courtyard, open only to the sky. He would have since disposed of the plants after Vidya had stolen the solution from his study. For her plan to work, it needed to be growing there presently.

"I planted some behind the lattice so he won't notice it. Should be ready by now."

"See?" She turned back to Phrea. "Nothing to worry about. We have evidence to implicate him in his brother's poisoning one way or another."

Phrea bit her lip then nodded. "Alright. Guess you have it all figured out, then. Meet back here tomorrow?"

Vidya agreed, and Phrea walked off, leaving her and Daphne at the gate. A knot in Vidya's gut began to form. She understood Phrea's reservations, but they didn't have a moment to waste.

The time to set her plan in motion was now.

"Daddy!"

Jeth sat up with a start, cold sweat drenching his entire body. He wiped his brow and looked over to the sleeping naja on the floor near the hearth. Serra fluttered about just outside the cottage, keeping watch of the settlement.

No one's reacting, it must be your imagination again. He lay back down on the lumpy, five-hundred-year-old mattress and tried to go back to sleep. His thoughts drifted to where they'd search next. It took the last two days to comb the beaches, scanning for blood, footprints, articles of clothing—any clue to Zephira's well-being. So far, it wasn't looking good. The deathly howls remained silent, giving them no clues as to the island's curse or the princess's whereabouts. But at least that was one noise all three of them could agree existed.

Serra had found a fresh body of water at the island's center on one of her overhead flights. *We'll look more around there tomorrow.*

As Jeth's consciousness began to fade, he heard faint whimpers right outside the window. His eyes snapped open, and the cries ceased. *Keep your head on, mate.* Upon closing his eyes again, more frightened sobs manifested, this time clear and unmistakable. He shot out of bed and went to the window.

"Daddy . . ." the voice choked. It was so childlike; it didn't sound like a woman entering marrying age, although urling women often possessed higher voices than their human counterparts.

He peered over the window sill. A dirty foot disappeared around the side of the house. "Hey!" he called out. Jeth flung open the door and stepped outside. A small figure vanished into the dark bush, moonlight reflecting off long, fair hair. *That had to be real!*

"Serra, did you see that?" He looked around for his fairy guardian, but she was nowhere in sight. *Did she go after her already?* There was no time to wait around. Jeth ran back into the house and tried to shake Esteban awake with his foot while strapping his quiver to his waist. "Esteb, come on, get your lizard arse up."

The sleeping reptilian growled under his breath. "Father, please, don't look at me. I'm a monster . . ."

"Never mind," Jeth groaned as he grabbed his bow and ran back into the night. He could catch up to her faster on his own anyway.

The night air felt like ice against his bare chest as he hurried down

the path. He skidded to a stop right at the edge of the drop-off.
Jeth honed his sense of smell, but there was nothing more than that
sickeningly sweet stench that characterized the whole island. *How can
a person living in the wild for so long not smell like anything?* He remembered
how he couldn't smell a single remnant of her in her own room.

Honing his hearing, the whimpers returned, growing louder and
louder until they were deafening. Jeth stood on the precipice and
stared down into the black mist, his heightened vision just making out
the rudimentary outlines of trees below.

"You have to find a way down there." He searched for a vine or
a natural ramp, but it was too dark for anything to take shape. He
thought about turning back to get the others or perhaps searching for
her in the morning.

"Daddy!" she screamed.

Jeth took to his hands and knees, grabbed a handful of vines, and
prayed they would hold his weight. Before he could cast his leg over
the edge and start climbing down, the rock precipice came loose, and
he tumbled, face first, off the edge.

Flailing his arms out, he managed to grab a branch. With a
wrenching crack, the branch snapped, and he fell into the blackness.
Branches slammed his sides, but he couldn't grab hold. He landed
on a steep incline and rolled, bouncing over rocks and logs, until the
ground evened out, and he came to a stop. "Clever git you are, Jeth,"
he groaned as he rubbed his lower back and climbed to his feet.

The ground beneath him was boggy with a stench that made his
nose want to shrivel up into his face. His socked feet sloshed through
puddles as he followed the sounds of snivels coming from the mist in
front of him. "Princess Zephira?"

The mists parted, revealing six towering rocks, all equal distance
from each other in a circular formation. They shimmered black in the
double moonlight, like obsidian from the Volcano of Verishten.

Shivers ran up and down his spine as he sidestepped the rock in
front of him and found a pool of thick sludge encased in the middle.
It was granular like quicksand but possessed the foulest odor he could
ever imagine. Not the smell of death but something far worse.

On a small rock platform in the center of the pool sat the one who
cried, burying her face into her knees and shaking with sobs. *It's a child!*

The child was shirtless, skin brown and hair white, all smeared and
caked with dirt. This was no urling princess but a small boy.

"D-do you need help, little one?" Jeth said in a shaking voice. His foot made a slurping squish as he took one step into the foul pool.

The child raised his head. White ropes of hair hid much of his face, but eyes like blue icicles froze Jeth in his place and made his breath catch in his throat.

"Daddy?" Tears streamed down the boy's face and his little lips trembled.

Jeth started to back away. "W-Who are you?"

The boy snorted back his tears. "I don't have a name, Daddy."

Jeth's knees gave out, and he fell onto his backside. "No. No."

The boy quit crying and stared at Jeth, anger burning in his impossible eyes.

Jeth's airways closed as he gasped for air and clawed at his throat. The boy dissipated into a black vapor right before his eyes. The trees spun around his head, and he turned over to retch. He could see the vomit but couldn't feel it coming up. A strange sensation settled over Jeth like he was watching someone who wasn't him.

He scrambled to his feet and started to run. He almost crashed into a being of his height, dripping with black goop, hair tangled and wild, and burning red eye sockets. Jeth yelped as the creature dove for him, pushing him into the pool. His naked back smacked hard on the surface, then sank into its putrid heat.

The creature wheeled over top of him, then grabbed his arm and dragged him further into the muck. He pawed for his knife. *Shit, you forgot it. Idiot!*

He pulled out an arrow from his quiver and tried to jab the thing behind him. The arrowhead made no contact with the creature, but it still screeched and disappeared into a black vapor like the boy had, a foul mist of droplets sprinkling over his face.

Jeth frantically crawled through a thick swamp as something writhed beneath it. A black tentacle the size of one of Ash's arms rose from the muck. At the tip was an open maw with thick, swollen lips and small yellow teeth. Beady white pearls, sinking into the shadow of oversized eye sockets, stared through him. It let out a disturbingly human moan.

"Sweet Mother!" The thing lunged forward, and Jeth's speed kicked in by the grace of the Deities. He rolled out of its way before it made contact with his shoulder.

He was on his feet again, running, then his face met earth. A second tentacle clamped down on his heel and pulled him back with powerful suction.

"Let go!" he shrieked. His right sock slipped off and sank into the pool with the snaking creature, freeing Jeth just as another one circled around his left. It wailed that awful howl, sending paralyzing tremors through his entire body.

The creature's cold lips planted on the back of his hand and sucked so hard his skin broke as it yanked him back toward the pool. He snatched another arrow and repeatedly stabbed the thing's grotesque, tubular form and bashed it against a rock until its fat lips tore free from his skin.

Another one sprang from the muck and dove for his bare foot. He spun around and jammed his arrowhead through its fleshy head. It released a wheezing screech and stilled.

More shrunken heads rose from the tar, writhing, and moaning, swollen mouths agape. On the stone platform, silhouetted against the full moons, the red-eyed creature crouched, hunched over in a primitive stance, cocking its head at Jeth. It dipped a hand into the pool, and in an instant, another beast emerged.

The thing gasped and howled, choking on the substance it was born from. It lumbered through the muck on four legs, fangs glistening in the moonlight, wet fur plastered to a skeletal frame.

Jeth's shaking legs failed; he could only crawl backward as the monstrous canine trudged through the black muck, growling and snapping.

Somewhere deep inside him, his spark finally ignited, giving him the wherewithal that he needed to get up. With a burst of speed, he ran back the way he'd come, scrambling up the steep incline until he came to a vertical dirt wall.

He looked over his shoulder. The red-eyed creature still remained on its platform, but now three canine forms raced down the path alongside the tentacle aberrations.

Jeth grasped for shrubs, roots, anything he could find to pull himself up the wall. His hand where the monster had grabbed him was near useless, but he clenched his jaw and pushed through the pain. The shrieking hounds were right behind him. His own screams for help were drowned out by the tormented yowling.

The tar-covered dogs nipped at his heels. Their snouts were misshapen, ears uneven or missing.

With one more foot to the top, jaws clamped around his pant leg and pulled down hard. "Help!"

Two large hands grabbed him by his arms and yanked him up with a mighty heave. His pant leg ripped, and the hound fell down with it. Jeth collapsed onto what was left of the precipice.

"You all right, compadre?"

Jeth jerked out of Esteban's grasp and shuffled away from the edge. The dogs snarled below as three tentacles rose above the precipice. The darkness absorbed their snake-like bodies, making them appear as demonic, floating heads.

"What are those things?" the naja gasped.

Jeth nocked an arrow, but his fingers were too weak to draw back the bowstring. Wincing in pain, he fumbled the arrow, and the moaning heads lurched forward. Esteban grabbed Jeth by the shoulder, dragging him back to his feet, and the two ran for the settlement, not looking back.

"Serra! Serra!" Jeth called on their arrival. A few moments later, she flew from the direction of the beach.

"Jeth! Esteb! There you are."

"Where in Mother's good graces were you?"

"Where was I? Where were you? You kept calling me from the woods, so I went to look for you, but I couldn't find you."

"How is that possible? I was only getting eaten alive by suction, tentacle . . . things!" He displayed his hand, swollen and purple from popped blood vessels.

Serra flew over to Jeth's bag in the cottage and fetched a roll of bandages from the first aid kit. As she helped him wrap his hand, she said, "I'm sorry. I kept following your voice, but then it would end up somewhere else like the games we used to play . . . only in reverse. It was a lot more fun back then."

His nerves shot, Jeth nodded. Serra stopped binding Jeth's hand and snapped her head toward the path as if she heard something no one else did.

They all stared down the path, but nothing emerged from the darkness. Only the echoing howls of which Jeth now knew the source.

"This island has really ramped up the terror since I was here last," Esteban said with a gulp.

"Well," Jeth tied off his bandage and marched inside the house. "I'm not sticking around to find out what more it can do."

"What about Zephira?" Serra asked as she flew into the cottage after him.

"From what I've seen, there's no way she's survived." Jeth threw on his boots and clothing, feeling the brooch still secure in his breast pocket. "All that's left is that thing. . . ." He belted his scabbard to his waist. "And it will be here any minute to finish us off if we don't get out of here right now."

"What will you tell the King?" Esteban picked up the empty honey bottle, then the pink shoe.

"We have evidence that she was here, so that's something." Jeth put the shoe in his bag but left the bottle for Esteban to drop. Slinging the bag over his shoulder, Jeth marched out of the cottage and headed east toward the beach. "I'll tell him the truth. If he wants to send more men to search this place, then he can go right ahead. I've done all I can."

Esteban and Serra solemnly followed Jeth through the bush until they came upon the warping gate. He and Esteban pulled the gate toward Fae'ren with no small effort. Being so close to home, Jeth felt the horrors of the night begin to fade, imagining Henna's disapproving glare. Then he thought of poor Ellion, still separated from her. *I don't have a name, Daddy!*

Jeth suppressed the tremors rippling across his skin as they finished setting the gate in place. *Just get home. Then you can pretend this was all a bad dream.*

He went to the crank and started turning. No chimes; no flicker of the stone. He looked down at the dais to check that it was pointed in the right direction. It was the cubby hole that caught his attention instead. Jeth's heart froze in his chest.

"What's wrong?" Serra asked.

"The warp stone . . . It's gone."

29

Primal Mother

"Where did it go?" Esteban's head whipped around, his eyes searching every direction.

"I know I didn't touch it," Jeth insisted.

He and Esteban jumped down from the platform and combed the neighboring bushes for the yellow stone. Serra scanned the entire area from above, even flew out to the beach to see if it had rolled out there somehow.

Nothing.

"That thing that's been tormenting us may have taken it," Serra surmised. "It brought us through the gate, and now it doesn't want us to leave."

Jeth pulled on his absent fairy locks, gripping nothing but air. "We'll have to wait for a ship."

"But that could take months," said Esteban. "We have to keep searching. Tear through all those creatures if we must."

Jeth slumped against the side of the gate's base. "There's no telling how many of them there are. And the thing that raised them wasn't exactly corporeal."

"You mean it was some sort of ghost?" said Serra.

"I don't think so. It touched me, but when I tried to stab it, it vaporized."

"Well, we can't sit around here in hopes it will give us the stone back," Esteban reasoned.

"I'm not sure we have much choice," Jeth said, staring at his mangled hand.

"What has gotten into you, Jeth?" Serra landed on his knee. "I've never seen you this scared before, not even when you were face to face with Nas'Gavarr. What happened back there?"

Jeth lifted his head to meet Serra's gaze. "It knows me—knows us." He swallowed the lump in his throat as his hands quivered. "It . . . called to me in the form of my son."

"But he was never born, so how could you know it was him?" Serra said with an innocent blink.

"Because I've imagined him, Ser," he snapped, even though he knew she meant well in her literal way. "My hair, Anwarr's eyes. You told me once that you wanted to know what a Herrani and Fae'ren child would look like, well, that's what I saw."

"Oh." Serra deflated, folding her wings solemnly against her back.

"It all makes sense now," said Esteban. "The man that went mad here, he had claimed he could hear his dead wife's voice in the jungle. It's not just you. Whatever this thing is, it understands our source of pain."

Jeth hung his head, taking deep breaths until he could think straight. He explained the tar pool and the rock formations where he and the creature had their confrontation. "Hah, maybe it wants to sacrifice me. I seem to have a knack for that."

"Don't say that, Jeth. I can't always tell when you're joking," said Serra.

"I'm not sure anymore either."

The sun started to poke through the clouds above, pushing back the night. He knew no amount of daylight would protect them from the darkness in this wilderness. "Listen," Esteban said. "We just have to stay alive long enough for someone to get here or for us to find the warp stone, whichever happens first."

"I know," Serra said. "I can fly through the night and get some warp stone from our Fae'ren stores. Maybe convince a few other pixies to help me fly it back here. I'm sure I can do all that before Faron arrives at the castle, assuming he makes it in the first place."

"I almost forgot about the harpies," Jeth groaned. He felt ill thinking about the woman he had once considered an ally, likely hunting down and torturing his task force for information. And it would all be for naught once they realized the Champion of Elmifel was already dead.

"You're onto something, Fairy," said Esteban. "That might be our best chance. Jeth and I can hold off the cursed beasts until you return."

"Then it's decided." Serra nodded. "I'll head out now."

She fluttered toward the beach. "Ser, wait!" Jeth shot up and followed her out onto the coarse gray sand. Turning around in midair, she waited for him to continue. "It'll be a dangerous trip, even for an immortal pixie. Are you sure you know the way?"

"Jeth, you know very well that every fairy has an ancient and unrivaled sense of direction."

"There's that fairy pride again." He chuckled.

Serra shrugged. "It is what it is."

They were quiet for a moment. Only the ocean rushing up onto the shore filled the space between them. "Ser, is this the right thing to do? Running . . . again?" He looked back into the shadowy jungle behind him where Esteban still searched for the stone, never giving up. Unlike him.

"We're not giving up," Serra said as if reading his thoughts. "We'll find out what happened to her, but you were never expected to do this alone. We go back, regroup, and try again. There's no shame in that."

Jeth bit his lip, contemplating Serra's words.

"Umm . . . right?" Serra continued. "Is there supposed to be shame? I'm not sure what shame feels like, to be honest."

A booming guffaw escaped Jeth suddenly, nearly coming out in sobs. "No, Ser, there's no shame in that." He cleared his throat to regain himself. "Thanks for leaving your Sacred Duty to come on this journey with me. I don't know what I'd have done if you weren't here."

Serra flew up to his face and laid a ticklish kiss on his forehead. "I'm your guardian, Jeth. That makes *you* my Sacred Duty."

"Good luck, Ser."

"Before I go, I should tell you something." Serra paused and bit her tiny cheek.

"What is it?"

"There's a spark in you. And I'm not just talking about the one that gives you inhuman stamina. Your spark goes even deeper than that. It's a source of untold strength. The Crannabeatha's life force is in you, and you've only just scratched the surface of it."

Serra's words brought back memories of the cradle of vines he had created in the Spirit Chamber. Even now, the thought of them brought him comfort. "Did she tell you that?"

"Not exactly. It's something that I've felt since we laid you to rest at her roots a year ago. Your body was devastated, but your heart kept on beating. The one thing she told me about you was, 'His *Way* is still to come.' This is only the beginning. So, don't be afraid."

Jeth's mind swirled with confusion. He felt there was more Serra wasn't saying. He looked away and rubbed the back of his neck. "It's far too late for that, but I suppose it's nice to know our Mother is still looking out for me."

"We all are." Serra put her hand to her chest. "But, do be careful out there. You're still mortal, despite what I just said."

"Thanks for the reminder." Jeth wiggled his injured hand and winced.

She smiled then took into the sky, but Esteban's roar erupted from the trees.

"Esteb!" Serra zoomed back to the warping gate, Jeth right behind her.

A dark figure was on the naja's back, attempting to scratch out his eyes. Esteban grabbed a fistful of tar-caked hair and threw the creature against the gate's base, where it dissipated into shadowy vapor.

Serra gasped, "Is that the thing that attacked you, Jeth?"

"It came out of nowhere," Esteban rasped.

"Behind you!" Serra screeched.

Jeth spun around and unsheathed his dagger—if only he hadn't given his tulwar back to Raisha. The advancing daylight allowed him to get a better look at the creature. It wore the tattered remnants of clothing around its pelvis and an outline of a female's breast hidden beneath mounds of black gook dripping down its hair and over its hunched body. It looked more animal than human.

Jeth's momentary shock allowed her to pounce, but he stepped aside and slashed his blade. She vaporized again, then reappeared next to him.

Serra's sparks hit the red-eyed creature in the face, forcing her to disappear once more.

"How do we hurt this thing?" Jeth slashed in every direction, but she dodged or disappeared each time. Esteban whipped his head back and forth, unable to track the creature jumping and rolling around them.

Just then, Jeth caught a second red-eyed woman in his periphery. *Huh?* He pretended to attack the one in front of him with his dagger, then pointed out the second. "Beside you, Esteb!"

The naja spun around, ducked low, and swung his tail in a semicircle along the ground, knocking her feet out from under her. The creature let out a feminine grunt and fell down hard.

"One of them is solid." Jeth rushed to the corporeal being on the ground, but the one he left behind leaped onto his back and knocked him over. Esteban tore her off Jeth, making her disappear. By the time Jeth recovered from his tumble, the other one had vanished as well. "Now, where is she?"

"There!" Serra pointed to the creature crouched upon the gate's base, ready to pounce.

The three of them prepared for her next attack. Then came a tiny screech and the hollow sound of a cork being shoved into a glass bottle. Jeth spun around to find the second creature running down the path toward the settlement . . . and Serra was gone.

"Ser? Hey!" Jeth and Esteban raced into the foliage after the creature. She waited for them in the center of the settlement, holding up the empty glass bottle with Serra trapped within.

"Give her back!" Jeth gritted his teeth, ready to speed over and free his guardian fairy.

Bone-chilling moans sounded from every cottage. Misshapen humanoids piled out of them in droves, obstructing Jeth's view of the red-eyed creature, ambling backward. Few had eyes, most just empty sockets, some without faces, nothing more than extended jaws and crooked teeth, open and ready to chomp down.

"Esteb, I need you at your most ferocious."

The naja's growl rumbled deep in his throat. "Not a problem." His pitched roar rattled Jeth's ears, and he barreled into the line of tar-coated bodies. He slashed his claws and sank his teeth into them. They grappled with him and tried to bite his neck, but he never gave them a chance. Red blood splattered over the ground and cottage sidings.

With a determined bellow of his own, Jeth charged into the fray. He had to hold his dagger in his left hand, but he had plenty of experience dual-wielding scimitars for it not to pose a problem.

He cut through arms, stabbed torsos, and sliced the throats of any creature in his sight. To his surprise, each strike landed on something tangible. His blade found slate gray skin beneath the black coating, and beneath that, dark red blood. Unlike their leader, these humanoids didn't disappear into black mist.

The terrible, rattling cries of the dying monsters were both satisfying and horrific. It didn't seem like a fair fight the way he and Esteban tore through them, and yet he couldn't imagine leaving a single abomination alive.

Esteban spat out gobs of black gook, trying to catch his breath.

"How do they taste?" Jeth shouted, not really expecting an answer.

"Their skin, putrid, but inside, all human. I hate how I know that."

"They sure bleed like humans, but so do a lot of things." Jeth stabbed his blade through a humanoid with its mouth open wide, ready to bite down on his shoulder from behind.

"Only things that have human in them taste like it," said Esteban before holding the last one down with his large reptilian foot, grabbing its head, and ripping it off.

Jeth grimaced as he bent to inspect one of the bodies. Its breasts were lopsided, its hips narrow, legs bony, and feet oversized. "If these things are human, they weren't put together very well."

The red-eyed woman brought them out of the primordial muck, incomplete. Jeth started to piece together what the sixth Conduit actually was and the real reason Nas'Gavarr built a gate to access it. To uncover Creation's Mystery.

"I might know what we're dealing with here," said Jeth.

"You do?"

Jeth looked up to the naja. "The source of humanity."

"How can you know that?"

"I'll fill you in later. We have to get Serra back first. Come on."

They dashed down the western path and arrived at the rock formations a few minutes later.

The red-eyed figure stood upon the stone platform, waiting patiently for them with the bottle in her hands.

The thick glass muffled Serra's screams. She sparked against it but only managed to hit herself inside the jar.

Jeth stepped up to the edge of the foul-smelling pool on one side of a rock, and Esteban stood at the other. "I don't know what you want from me, but I know who you are, and if you think I'm going to run back to you like you're some sort of primal mother, you'll be right disappointed. You're holding the closest thing to a mother I'll ever need. And you're going to give her back to me. Now."

The creature cocked her head, her glowing red eyes burning brighter.

"And some warp stone," added Esteban, "if you got it."

Several tentacle creatures sprang out of the pool at either side of her. Jeth grabbed his bow with his injured hand and drew back on the string with his left. He was nowhere near as accurate with the left hand, but it was better than nothing.

He released an arrow, embedding into the closest creature's tubular body but hardly fazing it. *Don't try so hard to hit your target,* he reminded himself, drawing another arrow.

His next shot struck the monster's beady white eye. It screeched and sank back into the pool. More tentacles burst from the muck and snaked around Jeth. He hastily switched back to his dagger.

"Esteb, get to Serra!" he called as he hacked the heads off two coming at him.

Esteban leaped for the center stone platform. The creature jumped out of reach, dropping Serra into the pool.

The jar smacked against the granular surface and started sinking.

Jeth rolled, dodging the shrunken heads that lurched for him, and ran into the muck after his fairy.

Esteban shrieked. Three sucking creatures wound around his whole body and yanked him into the pool, taking him under.

"Esteb! I'm coming!" Jeth fished around in the putrid liquid for the bottle. "Got it."

As soon as his fingers wrapped around the submerged glass, the primal mother pounced on him and shoved him face-first into the inky, black sand.

The jar slipped from his grasp. Holding his breath, he struggled to find it again, but the more he flailed, the deeper he sank. Before him was nothing but blackness, the thick heat of it weighing down his chest and back.

He splashed about more frantically. *Don't drown, just find Serra.* More pressure came down on his back. The thing was still on top of him, forcing him deeper.

His left hand reached up and felt the cool air first, followed by the other. He kicked his legs through the thick muck until his head surfaced, gasping.

Can't see, can't see.

He felt around blindly, finally grabbing hard ground. With all his might, he pulled himself from the pool and collapsed onto his stomach.

Scooping the gook out of his sockets, he blinked his blurry vision back into focus.

He wasn't in a jungle anymore.

The same rock formation surrounded him, but now, a dark and endless plain stretched out as far as he could see in every direction. There were no trees, no foliage—just miles and miles of black earth, blanketed in skeletal remains. Lightning burst from violet storm clouds that extended into a dark horizon.

"This can't be real," he whispered. He dove back into the pool, sifting through the foul tar until he found something solid. *Serra?* He pulled out an arrow, then several more. He reached for his quiver, finding it mostly empty. Not that it mattered; his bow wasn't at his back anymore.

"Shit!" Jeth combed through mounds of goop with both hands until he was winded. He thought about going under and finding a way back to the other side, back to reality.

You left reality a long time ago.

He closed his eyes and took a deep breath, psyching himself up to submerge into the putrid muck once again.

Just as he was about to dive in, something burst from beneath the surface, knocking him back. His eyes snapped open, meeting two glowing red ones.

He yelped and kicked the creature off him before leaping to his feet. She didn't disappear this time but jumped up and belted him in the ribs with her gnarled fist. He doubled over, falling to his knees in the pool. The creature grabbed his coat collar and dragged him out of the muck.

"What do you want?" He caught her around the waist and flung her to the ground.

He landed with her hard, rolling uncontrollably down a steep incline, rotten bones shattering underneath them as they went. When they came to a stop at the bottom of the hill, Jeth grabbed the creature's spindly arms and straddled her. "Give her back!" He struck her in the face, tar splashing off her.

She made an unholy shriek, writhing with such force, it took every bit of Jeth's strength to hold her down. Bearing blackened teeth, she banged her head into his, knocking him back.

Jeth's vision spun, stars dancing. He shook his head to clear it and activated his spark to stay conscious.

The creature lunged at his right side, a leg bone in her hand, ready to wallop him.

He slashed at her with his dagger, only for her to disappear again and the bone to fall to the ground.

"Stop doing that!" he blared.

She kicked him from behind, then flashed in front of him to knee him in the face, causing him to drop his only weapon.

Jeth wiped the blood from his nose and dodged several more attacks, coming from not two but four versions of the same wild being.

They circled him, all taking turns hitting him then disappearing, only to reappear somewhere else. Jeth couldn't rely on his sense of smell, the substance covering her permeated everything in the vicinity. They moved too quickly for him to pinpoint any visual differences between them, and each one felt solid when they struck him.

Desperate, he honed his hearing. There was only one heartbeat. He grinned. Only one of his foes was, in fact, alive.

Jeth pinpointed the real creature to his right. He spun around and punched her as hard as he could in the face.

She yelped and fell to her side. The other apparitions dissipated as the original crouched and held her jaw.

Jeth huffed. "Look, I know you're a Conduit."

She spun on her heels but remained stooped, rocking back and forth and glaring up at him with those inhuman red eyes.

"The world doesn't know about you, but I do. Tell me what you want from me—what you wanted from Princess Zephira."

In an unabashed, ape-like manner, the creature smacked the ground in front of her and dug her fingers into the dark earth. In an instant, a malformed arm erupted from the ground beside her, then a howling canine head emerged on her other side. Body after body climbed out of their earth cradles and reached for Jeth.

He dodged their attacks with his speed, but he could not put them down as readily as before without a blade. He punched out two proto-humans and kicked over a proto-hound, but they climbed back onto their feet as stranger creatures rose from the earth to join them.

Soon, Jeth was surrounded by deformed humans, apes, canines, and dozens of other less identifiable animals. His lungs burned with exertion; his speed was starting to fail him. More protos swarmed him, pawing him back and forth between them. He faltered to his knees. Then came a crushing pain in his shoulder. A proto-cat's jaws clamped down hard with a sickening crunch, his skin breaking.

He screamed.

The panther pulled him down onto his back, and a humanoid mob pinned him to the ground. Hands sprang from the earth below him and clasped around his arms and thighs. Jeth kicked and screamed, but their grips only grew tighter. His quiver's leather strap cut into his waist as the hands yanked it off.

The ground gave way beneath him. A powerful suction latched onto his shoulder blades and pulled. His mouth rapidly filled with dirt as he sank deeper into the black earth.

30
Penance

Vidya, Phrea, and Daphne glided through the smoky haze over the Odafi seas. Cannons boomed; the Rangardian Armada was busy sinking what was left of the Herrani Fleet. A few leagues beyond the skirmish, the Emperador's warship was docked at the main port, its yellow flag rippling in the breeze.

They made a graceful landing on the starboard deck, surprising the crew.

Phrea and Daphne went to speak to the almirante while Vidya marched directly to the main cabin. She squeezed the vial of curare solution within her pouch, praying that Daphne dissolved the right amount into the drops so that it would only cause temporary paralysis in the extremities and not death. Yasharra only knew how much Vidya longed for her husband's demise, but if she killed him now, her entire plan would implode.

She barged into the cabin where Agustin, Ricardo, and Jiménez sat around a table enjoying the fine meats and fruits overflowing their dishes. A strange thing to see on a warship, amidst cannons firing in the distance.

Jiménez and Ricardo jumped out of their chairs in surprise. Agustin rose slowly, a broad grin on his flushed face. "Vidya, my love. How did you get on board unannounced?"

She puffed out her wings and gave him a wry glare.

"Oh." Agustin raised his wine glass. "I keep forgetting you have those now."

His brothers sat back down. "What brings you here is a more

appropriate question," said Ricardo.

"I come bearing news of victory, Señors. Ryeem is dead, his naja scattered, and the Harplite now hold the Gift of Salotaph."

"Marvelous. Come sit and celebrate with us," Agustin patted the bench seat next to him.

Her stomach grumbled as the smell of fresh crab and spiced fish hit her nose. *It might be a while before I eat this well again.* Her mouth watered, and she sat down, setting her helmet next to her on the bench. "What are we celebrating?"

Jiménez raised his glass. "The successful seizure of this port. We will have the northern one under our control in a few more weeks."

She grabbed a whole crab and snapped it in half with meager effort. "Very good, Capitán."

"All we require now is the one those damn Del'Cabrians are blocking, but if our brother here is successful"—Agustin looked endearingly to Ricardo—"they may not be a problem for long."

"Oh?" Vidya feigned surprise.

The administrador swallowed his fish. "I have arranged talks with the King. If I cannot persuade him to remove his ships from the gulf, there is little hope in completing our invasion to your liking, O Anassa."

The shadow harpy hung upside down from the cabin's rafters. She craned her neck and whispered into Ricardo's ear as he sipped his wine. *"Your lies are useless."*

Vidya shifted uncomfortably in her seat as Ricardo grinned to himself.

"You sound unsure of your negotiation skills, Brother," Agustin said as he poured Vidya's wine. "Don't listen to him, my sweet. Victory is sure to be ours, and we will be together soon."

Ricardo and Vidya both took large gulps of their wine in tandem.

Apart from the intermittent cannon fire jostling the glassware, the four of them ate in silence. As everyone came to their last few bites, Vidya wiped her hands and face on her napkin, then said, "Señors, if you would grant me a moment alone with my husband."

"Whatever for?" Ricardo cast a wary eye her way.

"What occurs between a husband and wife is not your concern, regardless of how close you brothers claim to be," she replied while resting an affectionate hand on top of Agustin's.

"You heard her. Begone," the Emperador ordered.

Ricardo grumbled and tossed his napkin to the side before leaving the table. Jiménez bowed and followed suit.

As soon as Vidya and Agustin were alone, he leaned in to kiss her. She instinctively moved her face to the side, so his lips landed on the back of her head instead of her cheek. "How wonderful it is for you to surprise me here. I've missed you beyond imagining." He roughly pulled her closer to him and buried his face in her cleavage.

With one hand, she pushed him off her and held him against the wall. It shocked her how easy it was to overpower him. To think, she could barely move the oaf half an inch before.

"Have I displeased you?" he said with cinched brows. "Tell me what you desire, and I will fulfill it."

Swallowing her nausea, she said, "The Cursed Isle of Cordos."

Agustin scratched his head beneath his black wig. "That's a strange request. I wasn't aware haunted islands turned you on, but . . ."

"No, you stup—" Vidya bit her tongue and filled her mouth with wine instead. "This is about our war." She set her glass down. "I've received information from a trusted Herrani source that Nas'Gavarr hid the Princess of Del'Cabria there."

"What does that have to do with *our* war?"

"If we take her captive, Tiberius will have no choice but to pull out of the gulf and cease further interference with our campaign."

"Or they will come at us with everything they have."

"Tiberius upheld the Herrani treaty for his daughter's welfare. Why not do the same for us?"

"My brothers should be here for this discussion," Agustin said as he rose from his seat.

Vidya pulled him abruptly back down by his arm. "They mustn't know yet."

"I cannot keep this from them," he protested.

"Even when they keep things from you?"

Agustin's eyes blackened with indignation. "You dare question their loyalty to me?"

"No, of course not." Vidya delicately caressed his hand. "Everything they do is for yours and the Empire's best interest, I'm certain. But . . . you know they disapprove of our union, especially Ricardo. He was part of the reason I had to leave you so early."

Agustin shifted his hand away. "He's not had a kind word to say about you since you left. He said you did something unforgivable, but I-I don't remember." He reached into his inside coat pocket, pulled out his drops, and placed one on his tongue before putting them away.

Vidya's heart twisted in her chest. *One can never forget their own children. You don't get to live as if they never existed, while I have to see their lifeless bodies every time I close my eyes!*

With a deep breath, she said, "If we are to rule together, decisions must be made together. The others can advise, but only on our terms."

"You don't think I already make the decisions?" Agustin's voice took on the low rasp that used to make Vidya break out in a cold sweat.

She dug her nails into the skin of his hand. "Things are different now. We must act as a team."

Agustin's wrathful glare transformed into euphoric awe, making Vidya shudder. *'A dangerous man who knows his place,'* Ash's words echoed in her mind.

"Forgive me, Vidya. You are right," he replied breathlessly, aroused by the pain in his hand.

She loosened her grip. "We only have to keep it secret until we have her secure. Then, Ricardo will have all the leverage he needs for his talks in the coming weeks."

"Will you be able to retrieve her in that time?" he asked.

"She will be in Crede custody within a few days. All I need from you is to say nothing until I return from Cordos. Understood?"

"Your wish is my command, my love," Agustin cooed.

"Thank you, Husband," Vidya said with a forced smile. Now she had a way to test Agustin's loyalties. If he were indeed as devoted to her as he seemed, keeping her secret from his own brothers would be proof of that. If he ended up telling them before she returned, it would mean she'd have to go a little further to plant the seeds of distrust between them, but her plan wouldn't change overly much.

Now, for the more trying task of the day: Replacing the drops in his coat pocket with the poisoned ones in her bag.

"Perhaps you could thank me in the bedroom." He brought her hand to his lips, applying soft pecks up her arm, all the way to her shoulders, where he bit down gently. His kisses would have weakened her once; made her forget every bruise, every scrape. Now, she felt nothing. Not ill, not afraid, just numb.

Vidya stood up and pulled her arm away. Swallowing the anxious lump in her throat, she walked toward Agustin's sleeping quarters. He followed her through the door, took her by the arm, and pulled her tightly into his embrace. His lips traveled up her neck until they devoured hers, his mustache tickling her nose. He backed her toward the bed. She struggled to breathe through his kisses as she pulled off his wig and rifled her hands through his short, graying hair.

"Oh, Vidya. I've missed you so much," he breathed between kisses. *Still nothing.* "You were cruel to leave me." He grabbed her by the waist, pushed her onto the bed, then dove on top of her. She pushed off the bed with her wings and flipped Agustin on his back. Clutching him between her muscular thighs, she ripped open his shirt, buttons shooting across the room.

She ran her hands up Agustin's hairy chest. His eyes filled with lust, his expression beaming with pure elation. He sat back up, reaching for Vidya's hair. "Stay down," she snarled, shoving him back on the bed. He chuckled through his nose. She could see his hardening manhood pressed firmly against the inside of his trousers. His hands toured her thighs and found her backside under her tunic. She snatched his hands and pinned them to the bed with her knees. "No touching!"

She unbuttoned his trousers and grabbed hold of his fully engorged shaft. As she moved her hand up and down the length of it, he sputtered, "Your hands are rough."

"No talking." She clasped her other hand over his mouth.

He lay his head back and released muffled moans. His breath came out in powerful bursts against her hand, but he remained still as instructed.

She had enjoyed having him this way once. The way he lay paralyzed beneath her and unable to lift a finger filled her with nostalgic excitement. She'd had him under her complete control, making him feel the same pain and anguish he had made her feel all those years before. Little did she know at the time, he'd come to yearn for that pain. He became as addicted to Vidya as his drops, so much so, he'd done the unthinkable to keep her from leaving.

She shifted her hand over Agustin's nose, then squeezed it shut. He writhed beneath her, but she only tightened her thighs around his midsection, cutting off his air supply further. His arms violently twitched under her knees, and she pressed them down, his cock hardening even more in her hand.

Maybe I should take his life right here. Just another minute or two, and he will be gone for good . . . so easy. Sweat formed at the back of her neck. Titillation, unlike anything she had felt before, rushed over her skin.

Agustin's eyes rolled back in his head, and he stopped struggling.

Vidya immediately let go of his face and checked his pulse. *Still alive,* she thought with a wave of relief and disappointment all at once.

Now that he was unconscious, Vidya fished through his inside coat pocket for his drops. She took out her own and held them up, side by side. Agustin's vial was half full, so Vidya dumped a dollop of her own onto the floorboards to be at equal volume. The Emperador was paranoid about his drops; being a madman in the highest position in the most unstable empire came with the elevated risk of assassination. Satisfied, she placed her vial into Agustin's pocket and his into her pouch.

After getting off the bed, she removed the rest of his clothing, then threw a blanket over him to make it appear as if he had passed out after furious lovemaking.

Smoothing her tousled curls, Vidya walked out of the room, picked up her helm from the bench, and placed it back on her head. *The others should have the coordinates to Cordos by now.*

Thunder cracked, and Jeth's eyes snapped open. He lay on his back on a bed of bones at the bottom of a pit several feet deep. Flashes of lightning trickled down from the large hole above him, coating hundreds of skeletal remains, poking through the dirt walls with a violet tint. His stomach ached, his lips were parched, and his shoulders numb. *How long have you been lying here? A day? More?* The protos that had pulled him down seemed to be gone.

But he was far from alone.

Something slithered on the ground amongst the bones. The slimy tubular body, engorged lips, and moaning voice were unmistakable. "Get away," he croaked, shaking his throbbing head. He tried to roll, but something held him fast. He looked behind him to find two more tentacles coming out from the dirt wall, their lips embedded in each of his shoulders, tethering him to the ground.

The advancing snake creature climbed over his right leg and up to his torso. It stared at him with its tiny glowing pearls before burrowing under his coat. Every ounce of his skin crawled. "Stop. Don't!"

The red-eyed Conduit emerged from the shadows of his periphery, taking slow, deliberate steps toward his quaking body. Her head cocked to the side, expression unreadable through the black tar that dripped down her face. Dark silhouettes of proto-humans and their hounds trailed behind her, eyeless and panting. Faint streams of light glinted off the blade in her hand—his military dagger. Terrified and exhausted, Jeth turned his head away and prayed that whatever was going to happen would be over soon.

Two protos bent down, grabbed his coat, and tore it open. Zephira's brooch flew free from his pocket and landed face up in the dirt. The protos continued to hold his arms and legs down as the Conduit stooped over his helpless body and scraped the knife over his buttoned-up waistcoat.

With a flick of her wrist, she sliced his vest apart, allowing the sucking creature easier access under his shirt. It wriggled about upon his bare chest and planted its cold lips on his sternum.

His scream caught in this throat.

The silver edges of the brooch reflected what little light there was into his eyes. Jeth crawled his fingers through the dirt and stretched them just enough to touch it. He flipped it over, revealing the engravings on the back.

"The Balance is the duality between the Pure and the Primitive," he repeated to himself. "Only through penance can one maintain it."

The creature sucked his chest harder, lifting him up to a seated position and bringing him face to face with the Conduit. He took the brooch up with him.

His heart beat furiously as his chest and shoulders burned. His spark activated on its own, forcing him to stay alert. Every one of his senses honed beyond his control, and the smell of his own blood ignited a feverish hunger and thirst. Rage percolated just under his skin as if the thing attached to him was sucking out the horror of his own humanity.

Despite all that, Jeth couldn't help but laugh, even if he lacked the breath to do it. "If this is penance, it's not making me feel very balanced right now." He flung the brooch at the Conduit's feet. "I'm sorry, Princess. . . ."

The Conduit stared at the royal heirloom, lying face up in the muck. She touched it, and her arm snapped back into her chest as if it had burned her.

The protos and sucking creatures stilled, and Jeth pulled in a hungry breath. He jerked one arm out of a proto's grip and regained the brooch. He held it out toward the Conduit, and she recoiled. "Do you know what this is? Huh?"

The proto-hounds barked maniacally but made no move to attack.

"Do you know who this belonged to?"

The Conduit scuttled backward, gasping and shaking her head. The protos' grip on Jeth waned.

"It belonged to the innocent girl you killed. Look upon it and tremble, primal bitch!"

He crawled forward, and the Conduit backed up, pressing against a mammoth-sized skull. She dropped the knife, clutched her own face, and shrieked into her hands.

The suckers loosened and slipped out from beneath his shirt, releasing his shoulders and chest. They retreated into the dirt wall and disappeared. The protos' legs gave out one by one, collapsing upon one another.

Their master continued to scream, sounding more and more human by the second.

Her body shook as she tore at her hair, pulling handfuls of black goop down each strand. Her chilling shrieks turned to gasping cries. She rocked back and forth, clutching her head in quivering fingers.

Jeth got up and took a few steps forward on his shaky legs, scarcely able to process what was happening in front of him.

The Conduit raised her head and let out one final scream. Her red eyes burning with flames so bright, Jeth had to shield his own. Then, the fire died out. What was left were the frightened, bloodshot eyes of a person. Eyes of deep violet.

The tendrils of her shadowy aura slinked away, revealing a shivering woman that Jeth could now see clearly. The tops of her pointed ears poked between strands of tangled blonde hair streaked with tar.

Jeth's knees buckled. His lips became so dry, he could barely make a sound. "Y-your Highness?"

(One and a quarter years ago)

Zephira choked, retching putrid muck that dribbled from her mouth. She scooped it out of her eye sockets, her nose, her ears, desperately trying to get the tarry black substance off her skin.

Her eyes peeled open, and she found herself in a dark and ghastly cavern. When her vision adjusted, she could make out formations of what appeared to be distorted bodies stuck in the walls. She blinked, not wanting to believe it to be true. She tried to stand, but her arms and legs, covered in large blue welts, were far too heavy.

Rolling onto her hands and knees, something crawled across the top of her left hand, and she screeched, snapping her hand up to her chest. In her horror, she realized the lumpy ground wasn't rocks beneath her but remains in various stages of decay and infested with vermin, unlike anything Zephira had ever seen. She heaved, expelling more black vomit onto the ground.

"Where am I?" she moaned through quiet sobs.

"The Skour," said several whispering voices, echoing through the cavern.

She snapped her head around.

One of the faces lodged in the wall behind her whispered, "The birthplace of humanity." Its eyes burned with a red glow as the body climbed out of the wall, bones cracking, joints popping.

Zephira choked on her gasp, petrified. This couldn't be real—she was having a nightmare.

Clutching her soiled robes, she pushed all her terror and despair deep, deep inside. "What are you, and why have you brought me here?"

The cavern vibrated all around her, bodies shifting in the walls, moaning. A dark liquid trickled down the sides and pooled along the ground. The creature crouched into it, the glistening tar latching onto every inch of its gangly form. It stood up again, only now with a hefty female shape. The black liquid absorbed into the figure's pale, naked skin and long gray hair.

Zephira now recognized it.

"H-Headmistress?"

The old woman stalked closer, sagging breasts swinging back and forth with each step. "Do not fear, my child." She lifted a hand, brushing a scraggly strand of hair behind her ear . . . a round, human ear.

Zephira gasped. This wasn't her headmistress, but some demonic, human copy, like that figure she saw at the henge when Gavarr first brought her to the island—the one that looked like her.

She rose onto gelatinous legs and ran. She stumbled over bones, slipping in the unsteady muck, and dashed through a dark tunnel, only to emerge into a cavern of bodies much like the one she'd left, only these weren't human, but some kind of canine.

The headmistress's footsteps steadily approached. "Do not run, young princess. I have many lessons to instill in you yet."

Not able to see a way out, Zephira ducked behind a fleshy pillar with dog heads sticking out of it, warm and alive but unmoving. She clasped her hands around her mouth to muffle her whimpers.

The headmistress's bare feet scraped over the bones, her skeleton creaking as she moved. She stopped with her back to Zephira and looked from side to side. "Before Elmifel had his way with you, you were all human. You were *my* children." The creature with the headmistress's face craned her neck grotesquely and looked right at Zephira. A glaring red light shone out her eye sockets. "And I've come to take you back."

Zephira ran from her hiding spot as the headmistress broke into a lumbering sprint. She caught her robe on a rib cage and fell to the ground. A cold hand latched onto her ankle and yanked her back. "Get away from me!" Zephira shrieked, kicking the woman off her.

Clambering to her feet, she tripped over a tubular obstacle in the dark. Three shriveled faces with giant lips rose up in front of her. Another squirmed up her robes and over the skin of her back, a slimy sensation. She shrieked and struggled to crawl away, but the creatures caught her around the arms and held her down with their suction.

"No! Please, stop," she wailed, flailing wildly until more sucking monsters clamped down on her legs, forcing her to be still.

The demon stood over her, still wearing her headmistress's unyielding face, and spoke with her severe voice. "I hate to see even one of my children suffer so, but so many more will without your sacrifice." Joints popped as the thing crouched down, putting her face in line with Zephira's. "Don't fight my snakkurs. They are the vehicles of my essence, spirit, and flesh, a portion of which I give unto you."

"Why are you doing this?" she cried as the snakkurs moved about her body, tearing through her robes.

She reached out and held up Zephira's chin. "Remember your lessons. Do not let the Primitive Force overtake you. Your ashray blood will help you resist so that you may survive."

Every part of Zephira's body shook as warm bile rose into her throat.

"Only through penance can one maintain the Balance," said the headmistress, just as the real one had told her in Thessalin over and over. "Do not falter, and you will be Queen."

"Q-Queen?" Zephira gasped, the pain of the snakkurs' powerful suction taking the wind out of her, cracking the cartilage between her joints.

The headmistress stood up straight. "Queen of the Skour . . . of all humanity."

Oh, how badly she had wanted to be Queen, and for a moment after scrying her father at the Elmifel River, she had learned it might actually have been possible. But now? Like this?

The skin on Zephira's back broke with a gush of blood that seemed to only invigorate the snakkurs. She screamed silently, her breath stolen by the monsters at her chest.

Her headmistress's face drooped, turning black and liquifying. The body collapsed into a puddle of black sludge, spreading and seeping into the ground.

To Zephira's surprise, the suction released. So grateful to be free of the pain, she was unprepared for what happened next.

Something unholy filled her bloodstream.

Hunger, rage, loneliness . . . everything she never allowed herself to feel flooded through her, and she was powerless to control it. Worse, she relished it.

All the whippings she endured for each emotional slip seemed hollow now. Everything the real headmistress had taught her, all she had learned through scrying her father—nothing but a waste.

The pain was constant. The fear, infinite. The rage fueled her. Such primitive power—its putrid essence tethered her to the earth. She belonged to it.

There was a name for it. More than a word . . . a feeling, a primeval presence.

Nyr.

31
Violence Inside

Zephira's chest heaved. She squeezed her head and tugged at her matted tresses, slick with black filth. It paled in comparison to the filth inside her. Foul and dark, it clawed up her throat, desperate to get out. She dug her nails into her scalp and screamed, driving it back down.

Her headmistress's voice still rattled in her mind. *'Kill the violence inside you. Surrender to it only once, and it will overtake you.'*

It was why Nyr had chosen her.

That ability all urlings strived for, an ability Zephira had mastered because of her ashray blood and years of tutelage under them.

Her breath quaked, and her skin prickled as red light swam across her vision. The violence stilled for just a moment, allowing Zephira to push Nyr down deeper until she regained some semblance of lucidity.

She blinked the last few drops of tears from her eyes as she clenched and unclenched her fists, watching her knotted fingers move in front of her face. *Are these really my hands?*

A silver-tipped brooch dropped in front of her. She slowly picked it up, flabbergasted as to where it came from. Then, footsteps of someone approached.

A man, disheveled and smattered in black gook, came toward her.

Zephira scampered away.

"Hey! Come back!" the man yelled.

Her bare feet scraped against the dried bones as she ran up a tunnel. She ducked between two massive ribcages and huddled in a tight ball. *Who has Nyr taken the form of this time?*

"Princess Zephira," the man called, getting closer.

She smothered her frantic breaths with her dirty palms. *It only shows me those I know. Who is he?* Her heartbeats thrummed deafeningly in her ears. She felt the tendrils of Nyr's presence rising into her throat, but she forced them down with all her might.

Bones crunched behind her, and she snapped her head around. The man, his shirt tattered and revealing dark circular bruises on his skin, crept by the far side of one of the giant ribs she hid behind. Grasping for a broken femur, she held her breath and waited.

As soon as the back of his head came into view, she moved to strike, prepared to knock him unconscious or dead, it didn't matter. He was just another soulless human shell of Nyr's creation.

"Oh, no, you don't." The man twirled around with lightning speed. He snatched her wrist before she could take her next breath.

Zephira balled her free fist around her brooch and attempted to strike again, but he caught it in his other palm. He yelped in pain, shaking his bandaged hand, but by then, both Zephira's weapon and brooch fell from her slack grip.

Once he released her, she scrambled to grab the brooch, clutching it to her chest before shambling away from him.

"I'm not going to hurt you," the man said, not looking directly at her. He pulled off his torn shirt and held it out to her. "Put this on."

Zephira looked down to find all she had on was an old magus's robe, ripped and tied into a makeshift skirt. The only thing covering her top half was the tar-like substance that coated much of everything in the Skour. She instinctively wrapped her arms around her chest as the man threw the shirt at her feet.

He turned his back, and Zephira quickly pulled the large shirt over her head, ignoring the fresh bloodstain on the shoulder. With shaking fingers, she tied the drawstring around her bust while glancing up to ensure the man's back was still turned. Grotesque, crisscrossing scars marred the length of it, like rock made flesh. She felt a pang in her gut. A freshly crafted human should not be scarred like that. *Could he be real?*

She couldn't peel her eyes from the indented, mutilated skin until the man said, "Can I turn around yet?"

Zephira gulped and nodded. He didn't turn around, making her realize she hadn't actually spoken. "Y-yes." The hoarseness in her voice startled her.

The man turned around slowly then reached out his hand. "Alright, I'm going to get you out of here."

"G-get out?" *This* must *be one of Nyr's deceptions.*

Zephira stood paralyzed, staring at the man's blackened outstretched hand. Her gaze traveled up his bare arm to his bearded face and exhausted hazel eyes. They were somewhat familiar, but she couldn't place him.

Her mind still encumbered by a dark fog, Zephira remained speechless.

The man dropped his hand and sighed. "Right, uh . . ." He took to one knee, presented his hand again, then said, "Your Highness, I was tasked by your father to bring you home. Nas'Gavarr is dead, so you're safe now. Or, will be if you come with me."

Nyr's angry tendrils churned in her gut. She fought back against it while pressing the brooch to her chest with both hands. How else could this small piece of her home find its way to her if not for a real, live person bringing it?

She couldn't begin to understand how he'd found her, but she didn't care. Her hand slowly moved toward his, and he grabbed it, his fingers rough and warm against her ever-frigid skin.

❧

Jeth took the princess by the hand and led her out of the tunnel and back into the wider pit, where he had woken. "You've been here longer than me, so I'm assuming you know a way out of this labyrinth of horrors."

She shook her head. Her gaze stayed locked on the ground, drawing Jeth's eye to her delicate, blackened feet stomping over the rock and bone. She scarcely flinched, like her soles were made of leather.

Jeth let go of her hand momentarily to pick up his dagger. He slotted it in his scabbard and then collected his filthy jacket, laying in a heap between two unconscious protos.

Tugging it over his now bare shoulders, Zephira gasped softly. "Your dagger . . ."

"What, this?" He unsheathed the knife and lifted it up for her to see.

"That's military issue. What is your rank?"

Jeth let out a dry chuckle. "Lower than you'll ever care to know. The name's Jeth, by the way."

"J-Jeth . . ." she whispered his name as if it were some piece of a puzzle she couldn't quite put together.

He put his only weapon back and began to inspect the walls around them. Skeletal structures stuck out of the dirt all the way from where they stood to the top of the pit. "I think these bones can serve as handholds. How good are you at climbing?" He shook his head and chuckled again at the thought of a prim and proper urling lady having climbed anything in her life. "Never mind."

Zephira gasped, her head swiveling to face him. "That laugh."

"Sorry if my laugh offends you, Your Highness. I won't be doing it much longer if we don't get out of here soon."

"You're a Fae'ren. I remember you."

"I'm more than certain we've never met."

"You've never met *me*." Her heart raced in Jeth's sharp ears, even though her expression remained eerily neutral.

He stepped forward, reaching for her, but she put her hands out. "Stay back. I know who you are."

"Ah, right." He threw up his hands. "You must've seen the wanted posters. Yes, I am the Desert War Traitor, but a lot has changed in this past year. I'm sure you'll hear all about it when—"

"Year?"

"Well, more than a year, actually," Jeth corrected.

"H-how long?" Zephira held onto her sides, caving inward.

"You were abducted close to two years ago. Then, my guess is, you've been trapped here ever since Nas'Gavarr's death, so . . ." he paused, breaking eye contact with her.

"How long?" she demanded.

He looked up at her again, brows pinched. "A year and a quarter."

Tears suddenly filled her eyes. She stumbled back, and Jeth reached out to steady her.

"It's going to be all right." He patted her awkwardly on the arm, glancing up at the rim of the pit and wondering how long they had before the monsters regrouped. "Just up this way."

As soon as he attempted to pull her toward the light, her whole body jerked. "No. I know why you're here. You're the Champion of the Crannabeatha."

". . . I am." *How did she guess that?*

"Is the harpy with you?" Zephira's eyes darted around the cave.

"Wait, you know Vidya?" Jeth said. "Oh, I see. What else did Nas'Gavarr tell you?"

"By the Unnamed Deities." she breathed, rubbing her hands through her tangled heaps of hair. "Your Crannabeath—he wasn't supposed to destroy her. It should have been Yasharra. It's because of me he went to her first. . . ." Zephira paced in a tight circle while scratching at her arms.

Jeth couldn't possibly imagine what Zephira might have done to cause Nas'Gavarr to shut down the Crannabeatha before Yasharra, but he was confident she wasn't at fault. "Hey, don't say that. Only Nas'Gavarr is responsible for this."

The princess froze and slowly met Jeth's eyes before shaking her head. "Not entirely."

Her words clamped down hard on Jeth's gut. *What does that mean?* "Listen, we stopped him before anything happened to the Crannabeatha. He's dead . . . for good. There's nothing to worry about now except getting out of this cursed place. Do you remember the way out or not?" As he reached for her again, Zephira lurched backward and pressed against the skulls embedded in the wall behind her. "You can trust me, Your Highness."

She pressed the brooch against her temple with one hand and pulled on clumps of hair with the other. "Don't call me that!"

Jeth put both his hands out. "Alright, what should I call you then?"

The princess shook her head back and forth and edged against the wall of skulls. "Not a princess . . . Queen . . . of the Skour."

"Queen of the Skour," Jeth muttered, trying his best not to roll his eyes. "How about we get you home, aye?"

She stooped down, squeezed the brooch in two hands, and rocked back and forth. "It won't let me leave. I have not yet learned all my lessons!"

"Do you not *want* to leave?" Jeth asked.

"Want"—Zephira continued to shake—"is a lie we tell ourselves to further cement our illusion of control."

"Nas'Gavarr give you that nonsense too?"

It was something the Overlord had said to him on that horrific first meeting in his temple.

"No." She shook her head. "It is an ancient ashray proverb. Wanting is the Primitive Force's attempt to manifest itself in our hearts."

"Alright, I'm done." Reaching the end of his tether, Jeth took quick steps toward the quivering girl, but she gasped and scampered away.

He caught up to her with a burst of speed and wrapped both arms around her waist.

She shrieked and kicked furiously. "Let go of me!"

"I realize you've had a rough couple of years," Jeth grunted. "So, I'll forgive your distrust. But if I don't get you home, your father's likely to wipe my people out of existence, so forgive me for not going about this more gently."

She kicked off the wall and bashed Jeth's back against the other side. The sting of the cat-o-nine-tails made its sudden resurgence, but he didn't weaken his grip. "Stop fighting me."

Her brooch dropped to the ground, and a half-second later, her head flung back and struck him hard in the face. Blood flowed from his nose as she slipped out of his grasp and pinned him against the wall, her eyes glowing red and shadowy tendrils climbing up her pale neck.

Jeth dropped down and snatched the brooch. Zephira wrestled it from his grasp, scraping her fingernails over the backs of his hands.

As soon as the brooch was back in her possession, she fell to her knees, allowing Jeth to crawl a few feet clear of her. "Hey, hey, you have it now. It's yours." She stared at the saintly artifact, releasing raspy breaths until the red eyes returned to violet and the black tendrils sank beneath her skin.

Jeth sat there in a cold sweat. *That thing never left her!*

Was it a good idea to bring this wretch of a girl home? If the King saw her in this condition, would he even believe she was his daughter? What if he went back on their whole deal?

Laying down on his back, Jeth groaned into his hands. What was he going to do with a woman this far gone?

Zephira scurried backward with the brooch until her heel knocked against something that made a hollow clink.

Jeth caught a whiff of something sweet, so faint he thought he'd imagined it. Honing his senses, he pushed past the putrid stench of flesh and decay and pinpointed the familiar odor again. It was the smell of the forest he grew up in . . . all the way down here in this dark pit beneath a deathly hellscape.

In a split second, he was back on his feet. "Serra?" He focused entirely on his nose and followed the scent to Zephira's tar-stained foot.

He dove forward, forcing the princess to jerk away. "Ser." He took to his knees and dug frantically to uncover the vessel. His heart seized. The bottle was broken at the neck, leaving only the bottom and one side intact.

"No, no, no, no." He kept digging in search of his pixie guardian. All he found was a giant, black millipede uncurling within the hole he made. "Serra? Serra!" *She has to be alive. She can't die, can she?*

His gaze fell on Zephira, crouching next to the skeletal wall, warily watching him. He held the broken bottle up to her. "You did this!"

She stared at the bottle in Jeth's hand then looked up to his face. "Me?"

"Sag damn it!" he growled, shattering the glass against a bear skull.

Zephira jumped with a screech.

"This is perfect. Just perfect." Jeth pushed his tongue to the side of his cheek. He had lost virtually everything to this damned mission: First his home, his locks, then Torrent, his bow and drawing hand. Now Serra? He ran a hand over his dirty hair, trying to keep himself from erupting in front of the volatile princess. "Will you please ask the horrifying entity inside you where Serra is because if anything happens to her—"

"It's Nyr," she blurted.

"What's near?" Jeth's eyes darted down each side of the tunnel.

"It gave us life, and it comes for ours."

"What are you going on about?"

"Our creator." She swallowed hard. "This world belongs to it. We are its children."

"I can't deal with this right now." Jeth called out again, "Ser?"

The millipede, having escaped its hole, now crawled across Zephira's toes. Without a flinch, she snatched it then ravenously tore off several segments with her teeth.

"What are you . . . ?"

The princess's eyes widened as she gulped down what was in her mouth. "Wait. Is this Serra?" She looked down at the still wriggling other half.

"No, Serra's a pixie," Jeth said, trying not to hurl all over himself.

Zephira exhaled with relief as she wiped off a few black legs from her chin.

Hoping to forget what he had just witnessed, Jeth continued his search. She must have been somewhere where she couldn't hear him, although he didn't know how far away that would be.

He ventured down into another open area, only with thinner cracks in the walls that allowed even less light to trickle in from above. He took in every foul odor and tried to distinguish a fairy aroma. *There!* He found it again, leading him in a new, dark direction.

"Where are you going?" the princess asked.

"She's all I have left," he said. "I have to find her."

Jeth followed the faint trail of Serra's scent until Zephira dashed around him and blocked his path into the next tunnel. "Don't go any farther."

"Step aside."

"You should leave this place before Nyr finds you." Zephira's quivering arms wrapped around her waist. "It's likely destroyed your pixie by now. It hates anything created by the Conduits."

"Thanks for your concern, but I'm not leaving without her, dead or alive."

"You'd risk your life for a fairy?"

Jeth clenched his jaw. "Until you're safe and sound behind castle walls, my life belongs to your father and, by extension, to you. Serra's doesn't. She's innocent. As are my people."

Zephira shook her head, her clumped eyelashes fluttering.

"Besides," Jeth continued, "since you don't seem to know the way out of here, Serra's our best chance of navigating this maze. Now, will you continue to stop me, or will you help me? This mission is about to come to completion either way."

The princess swallowed and shuffled to the side. Jeth continued past her and into the darkness. A few moments later, he heard her soft footsteps trailing behind him.

32
Neither Queen Nor Princess

Jeth followed his nose through the ever-darkening labyrinth of bones. Each tunnel he ventured down grew darker, the foul stench more strangling. Luckily, Serra's scent grew stronger as well, but still too faint to indicate that she was anywhere close.

Another odor wafted into his nostrils as he went. "Reptile. . . ?"

"Pardon?" said Zephira from behind him.

"Don't worry about it. Just keep an eye out for any of those ugly sucking things."

"Snakkurs," she replied.

Jeth harrumphed. "Is *that* what they're called?"

Silence fell as they navigated through the skeletal tunnels, Jeth's heart banging against his ribcage. He worried for Serra and whether they'd ever get home. Beside him, Zephira clutched her brooch tight against her chest, her heart's rhythm matching his. He suddenly felt the urge to calm her down despite his own rising anxiety.

"Don't worry, Princess. As soon as we find Serra, we'll get you out of here."

"I'm not a princess," she snapped, halting her step. "Not anymore."

It was hard to argue with that. Her hair fell in long tar-slathered strings, scars marred her bare legs, and her blackened toenails were run down and raw. Other than her wide-set violet eyes and long pointy ears, Jeth would never believe this poor girl was anything close to royalty.

"Then, may I call you by your name?" he asked.

She nodded, resuming her neutral expression, lips closed to a perfect point. Even now, after all she had gone through, her stiff urling countenance remained unbroken, but through his honed senses, Jeth saw the dark cracks under the surface and heard the terror that writhed beneath her skin.

The pair continued their trek for a time until Jeth said, "Tell me about this Conduit. Nyr, you said?"

"Nyr is not a Conduit."

"Nas'Gavarr mentioned there was a sixth."

"It has no effigy and therefore no spiritual influence on our plane," she replied in monotone as if overcompensating for fear of the thing she spoke of. "I believe Gavarr intended to make it so."

"By ending the influence of the real Conduits first," Jeth finished, finally connecting the dots.

"I had once thought the primitive power that resides here served Gavarr, but I soon learned that he served it."

Jeth gulped. "Nyr was pulling the strings. That's how Nas'Gavarr knew so much about the Champions." Shivers ran down Jeth's spine at the notion of a being so powerful that it could bring the Immortal Serpent, Destroyer of Conduits, to heel. Jeth then felt another pang of remorse on top of the incessant guilt that already weighed him down. "If he were still alive, neither of us would be here right now."

Zephira shook her head. "Gavarr always planned to bring me here. I'm to take Nyr's essence and spirit, so I could bring its influence into our world, to be the one and only Conduit for all humankind. His death only forced Nyr to take me sooner."

"But, why you?"

"The Champion's blood within me can resist Nyr's Primitive Force."

"Ah," Jeth scoffed. "You didn't seem so resistant when you attacked me, stole my pixie, and shoved me through that pool. Was it the Primitive Force or your Champion blood that lured me to the woods in the form of my dead son?"

"I did what?" Zephira's long lashes fluttered as she blinked in confusion. "I—"

"Never mind." Jeth shook his head and stepped into the adjoining tunnel, instantly regretting his accusatory outburst. "You had no control."

"Nyr showed me people too," she said, voice shaking.

"Yeah?" Jeth slowed his gait and looked back at her. "Who did you see?"

"Me . . . or a being that resembled me. Then my headmistress in Thessalin, among others. Nyr can reproduce any human form but do not be fooled; there is no soul, only flesh. The spirit of a person is unique and can never be replicated."

"Good to know. The strange thing was, my son . . . or the thing that looked like him, wasn't flesh at all, but a vapor. Some sort of illusion. In fact, you were too."

"*I* was an illusion?"

Jeth nodded, fingers twitching at his sides. "Should I prepare for more of that when I come across this Nyr?"

"There is no preparing anything." Zephira grabbed his sleeve, stopping him. "Nyr groomed Gavarr for decades to be his most loyal servant. Against something with the power to do that, what makes you think you can save your pixie? Nyr wants us here and will not let us go until it is time."

"I get it, alright." Jeth yanked his arm away, making Zephira flinch. "We're heading straight for a trap—I've memorized the signs. But our fear changes nothing. I hate admitting this more than anybody alive, but I know the *Way* is real. You urlings had that one bloody thing right. Even Nas'Gavarr couldn't deny it. That's why he tried, in his own twisted way, to free us from it." Jeth shook his head and huffed. "Idiot."

"Gavarr may be many things, but an idiot is not among them," Zephira said.

"Well, he was. And so was I. Whether we rage against the status quo or accept our place in all this chaos, the *Way* will have its way. What will come to pass will always come to pass. Our choice is to either accept it or not, but we can't change it. It's like trying to make a waterfall flow upward."

"Then why move forward at all?" Zephira's broad forehead cinched in confusion.

'*Always forward . . .*' Anwarr's giggle echoed through Jeth's exhausted mind. He met Zephira's hopeless gaze. "Because I'd rather run to meet my fate than twiddle my thumbs waiting for it to find me."

"Do you not fear death?"

"There's no use in fearing something you can't do a damn thing about."

"Then, you too have lost all hope," Zephira sighed, eyes cast downward.

"On the contrary." Jeth put a hand on her shoulder, coaxing her to lift her crestfallen gaze to his. He thought back to that day he had gone into the temple to save Anwarr and the night he'd turned himself into the Del'Cabrians, both times certain it would be the end of him, but it wasn't.

"We are exactly where we're supposed to be," he said. "What can be more hopeful than that?"

Like the roots that cradled him in the Spirit Chamber as they ravaged over the twin husks of the Serpentine, Jeth was dealing with forces far stronger than him. Who was he to take it on all by himself? *It's not your fault.*

With that in mind, Jeth continued deeper into the pit, and Zephira hesitantly followed.

The floor angled steeply. Zephira grabbed Jeth's arm again. "Nyr is down there."

"Then keep that trinket close, and you should be fine," he said, tilting his chin at the brooch still clutched in her other hand.

She let go of him and carefully pinned it to her shirt. "How can you be certain?"

"I'm not, but it was only after you saw that thing that you overcame Nyr's force. Your mother mentioned it was blessed by some lady saint a thousand years ago."

"Saint Orester." Zephira's eyes lit up, drastically changing her delicate features. "She was a Champion as well, called to defeat the harpy scourge."

"Is that right?" Jeth didn't want to mention that harpy scourge had returned. Such things could be dealt with later.

They shuffled down a winding staircase hewn into the earth. The very last of the natural light that had peeked through the crevasses faded to nothing, forcing them to slow their descent to ensure each step was sound.

Jeth heard Zephira's heart pounding faster than his, almost echoing off the moist cavern walls as they went. Her soft voice eventually drifted into his ear, disconcertingly emotionless. "You met my parents?"

"Aye."

"And how did you find them?"

"They found me, actually."

"I mean, how were they?"

"Oh . . ." Jeth cleared his throat, his voice echoing down the darkening tunnel. "Your father comes off like he's devoid of feeling, but I can tell that your disappearance consumes him. Your mother, on the other hand, doesn't even try to hide her pain. The things she swore to do to me if I didn't bring you home intact."

Zephira huffed slightly. "She was never very good at controlling her emotions. She's of the Ludesan urlings. Brought up in a more human high society, she didn't receive the same etiquette training as proper nobles."

Jeth noted her heart rate had slowed considerably, and her voice took on a more regal air from the moment he started talking about her parents. He decided to keep the conversation going, as uncomfortable as he found it. "Then why would your father marry her? No offense, but they seem a little . . . ill-matched."

"To maintain good relations between the two provinces, it is prudent for monarchs to take a Ludesan spouse every now and again, provided they be urling, of course."

"That still doesn't explain why he chose her specifically."

"He didn't. We don't choose who we marry."

That reply ruffled Jeth a bit. "With all your laws that restrict who can marry whom, I didn't realize urlings would restrict their own marriages." Jeth felt somewhat grateful that, at least within the Fae'ren communities, they could couple as they pleased. The notion made him ache to see Henna even more and hear her reprimanding voice, her way of showing him how much she cared. To him, she was the future of Fae'ren Province finally giving a damn. She was *his* future.

"Yes, I often envied the peasants in romantic tales who married for love," continued Zephira. "However, to be tethered to a stranger for the rest of my life sounds far lovelier than what I'm tethered to now."

After a thoughtful pause, Jeth said, "I've strived to be tethered to someone my entire life. When it finally happened, I wanted to fly away again."

"Did you leave someone behind?"

Regret for how he dismissed Henna's desire for more children made his heart lurch. *How many more chances do you think you'll get to be a dad?* "I have a woman waiting for me in Fae'ren, but not forever, mind."

"Why? Do you doubt her devotion to you?"

The cavern walls closed in tighter as they descended. Jeth grazed his fingertips along the rock to keep himself steady. It felt soft and wet, similar to an exposed tree trunk after a rainstorm. The walls emanated a throbbing warmth as if they were part of a living organism.

"Oh no, it's just . . ." He paused in remembrance of past loves. "I've had a lass or two promise to await my heroic return but have yet to come home to that promise fulfilled, not that I blame them in either case."

"Then, I pray you return to your beloved soon and that she be waiting for you," Zephira said softly.

"Thanks. Mother Oak knows I miss her. I miss them all. Whatever it takes, I'm going home. And I won't leave again, not on any king's order."

Zephira turned to him. Jeth could only make out the faintest of outlines of her heart-shaped face and the whites of her bulbous eyes in the dark. "What did my father propose that would take you so far from home?"

"Nothing more than a pardon for my crimes," he replied.

"But your back . . . you endured a public flogging. Did you receive it before or after he gave you the pardon?"

"I made the mistake of thinking he'd throw in Fae'ren independence for good measure, but that was too big of an ask, I suppose." It made his hairs stand up on end to think about the whole humiliating event.

"But you said earlier that he wants to wipe your people from existence if I don't return."

"I may have exaggerated a little. Let's just say, if I fail to get you out of here alive, nothing will change for the better."

The spiraling walkway opened up to a spacious cavern. A tiny shred of light, beaming from a crack high above, gave shape to it. The scent of Serra and the reptile were at their strongest, but so was the putrid stench that he couldn't escape—as suffocating as the throbbing heat. He stifled a gag but didn't dare scale back his senses, or else he'd never locate his friends. His sharp vision adjusted to the dark, and he gasped.

There were bodies—human—fused to the walls and embedded in the ground. Like fleshy stalactites, they hung from the ceiling. Endless clusters of arms, legs, and faces were frozen together in the living, breathing stone that imprisoned them.

Jeth started to tremble, and Zephira wrapped her arms around herself and shivered, despite the unnatural warmth.

"This is it—where human life began," she said.

Jeth kept shaking his head, slack-jawed. "We couldn't have come from here." He started to wish he'd listened to Zephira and not gone any farther. Every instinct told him to run and keep running, but his feet remained planted.

"When Nyr first brought me here, I didn't believe it either, then it imbued me with its essence, and I felt it . . . I still feel it."

"Feel what?"

"Pure, human emotion."

Jeth swore he saw shadowy tendrils climb up the sides of her neck as she spoke, but it was too dark to be sure.

"Let's not stay here any longer than we have to." He honed his sense of smell further, past the stench of human creation, and focused on the fairy aroma. He caught a whiff of oak and fern, a remnant of home, and forced himself forward.

As he walked by a pillar of bodies fused together, a faint green light blinked ahead, and Jeth rushed toward it.

Serra hung limply, suspended by the fleshy, fibrous wall threatening to envelop her.

"Ser, what happened?" He pulled out his dagger and began slicing away the bindings that held her head.

Her eyes fluttered open. "J-Jeth . . . you're in great danger."

"Don't need you to keep reminding me. Now hold on."

Behind him, Zephira gasped. "Is that a naja?"

"E-Esteban," Serra wheezed, her eyes widening as she lifted her gaze.

Jeth looked directly above him. The unconscious naja was suspended upside down, his long, forked tongue hanging out the side of his mouth. "I'll get him out right after you."

"Jeth, please!" the fairy rasped. "The threat the Crannabeatha warned me about. It's here."

"I know. It claims to be the creator of humanity, but these bodies around us can't be real humans. It's a trick." Once he freed one wing, Jeth began sawing around the other. "Now, give me some sparks, and let's see if we can blast off the rest of this."

"I spent . . . too much. . . ."

Jeth's heart froze. A fairy's spark never ran out. It was why they didn't require sleep or sustenance to replenish it like Jeth did. Or at least that's what he'd always thought.

"Please, stop," she begged. "It only wants me alive to get to you."

Jeth didn't stop cutting. "Then it's about time I meet my maker. I'm not leaving you here."

A foreboding rumble vibrated the cavern as if responding to his words. Wet sloshing noises echoed around them, coming from above.

"It's Nyr." Zephira looked up.

All Jeth could see, besides the deadened lifeforms hanging from the ceiling, was glistening black gook dribbling between the creases in the walls. Jeth's palms suddenly became coated in it. He tried wiping it on his trousers, but they were covered with the same substance.

"You found Zephira?" Serra gasped as her eyes landed on the urling princess standing a few feet away. "You have to listen to me, Jeth. It's too late for her. And for me. You have to protect the Crannabeatha!"

Jeth stilled his blade. "What are you on about, Ser? I can't abort the mission. My people—"

Around him, bones rattled, human fingers twitched, and a dull throb hummed through his sternum.

"They will suffer far worse if the force that resides here is allowed to leave. Please, Jeth, I know this is hard to understand, but if you value the lives of those you love, you must act as Champion once again and leave us behind."

Jeth looked back at the wide-eyed Zephira, clutching her brooch and shaking in fright. Less than an hour ago, she was possessed with an ancient primeval energy that forced him here, held back only by the thousand-year-old trinket pinned to her shirt. The thing that had possessed her wasn't gone, merely subdued.

Serra was probably right. Whatever existed inside the princess should be sealed away forever in this living cavern, but that meant damning an innocent girl to the same fate. The sacrifices his men made to get him here would be meaningless, and his people would bear the brunt of the King's wrath when he returned empty-handed. "I don't think I can do that."

Two glowing red lights appeared several feet above Serra. A disembodied head looked straight down at Jeth. "You are right to doubt her, my child. Fairies will never understand the connection humans have with one another. Trust the instincts I have bestowed on you, and stay."

"Let everyone here go," Jeth demanded. "It's me you want, isn't it?"

The flowing black goop stretched out from the wall, forming into giant, elongated fingers. The hand wrapped around Serra and ripped her clean from the wall. It held the weakened pixie in its palm, bringing her up for the red-eyed head to examine her. "So strange are these creations of the Crannabeatha. It's hard to fathom how something so small can hold so much life force. Dare I say, this little thing challenges the might of *true* fairies."

"Put her down," Jeth grit his teeth, gripping his dagger in his one good hand.

Nyr closed its fingers around the bottom half of her body while another hand formed from the ceiling and squeezed her wings together between the thumb and forefingers.

"Run, Jeth!" Serra screeched.

"All that ancient fairy power exists right here, in these little wings as thin as leaves," Nyr taunted.

"What are you doing?" Jeth shouted.

"Fairies from your world, like many mortal creatures, were human once," continued Nyr. "The humanity in her is all but gone now, replaced by a fairy's essence, spirit, and flesh. But, if removed from her fairy power, she may learn to be human again." Nyr gripped Serra's feet harder, ready to pull her apart from her wings.

"Don't!" Jeth wailed. With his knife in his teeth, he raced for the wall and launched himself up it. He ignored the pain in his injured hand as he grabbed arms, feet, and handfuls of hair in his climb to reach Serra.

He jammed his dagger through the top of the talking head, extinguishing the red glow in its eyes, but the giant tar hands remained in place.

The wall he clung to suddenly glowed red as every pair of eyes ignited. An arm shot out of the wall and shoved him. His dagger slipped out of his sweaty grip, and he fell, screaming all the way to the ground. Sharp rocks dug into his back, splitting open his scars.

Serra's screams clanged within the space between his ears, forcing him to cover them with both hands. Blinding green light engulfed her within Nyr's hand, building in power. Her spark exploded, blowing the hand apart and splattering goop in every direction.

Serra's light then went dark as she fell.

"Ser!" Jeth rolled up with a burst of speed and caught her right before she hit the ground. He quickly placed the unconscious pixie in his inside coat pocket to keep her safe. He needed to get her back to the Crannabeatha to restore her life force, but escaping this labyrinth without his fairy guardian seemed more hopeless than ever.

The black goop re-converged, animating another disembodied head attached to a human pillar. It gave them a chilling, toothless grin. "For a primitive fairy, her weaponized life force stings every bit as much as the fairies on this plane. It can do nothing to destroy life, however."

"You call yourself life?" Jeth growled.

Ominous moans echoed all around them. The warm, malleable walls dilated as bodies tumbled out one after the other. They unfurled from the ground and rose to their feet, turning toward Jeth and Zephira, red eyes glowing. Unlike the protos he fought on Cordos, these were neither deformed nor misshapen in any way, just blank, incomplete somehow.

In unison, they spoke: "You've done well, my queen. I will take this offering now."

Jeth turned to Zephira with a horrified glare. "Offering?"

Zephira closed her eyes, steeled her jaw, and tried to keep her stoic expression. "He's only human, no different than all those Rangardians five hundred years ago. If you merge with him as you did them, he will descend into an irreversible primitive state and perish."

"Don't underestimate the boy." The possessed bodies shambled about, weaving between one another in a dizzying motion. "He's been endowed with the fairy's spark. His life force alone will not only ensure he survives the merge, but he can hold more primal essence than either you or Gavarr. It matters not how strong his spirit is, for I do not need it. His sentience can move onto the Spirit Realm while his essence and flesh remain here until it is time for him to join you."

"Time to go, Zephira," said Jeth, edging the princess back toward the tunnel they entered from.

The group of standing bodies moved behind them, blocking their way, "I know everything you've done, Jethril. I know where you've lived . . . who you've loved . . ." A small figure weaved between the other naked forms, barely tall enough to reach the backs of their knees. Jeth blinked, and the figure seemed to vanish. "I know the lengths you'd go for your people. You need not fight for them anymore. Once they witness their true creator, they will be liberated."

Jeth desperately looked about the speaking crowd. *Your dagger's got to be around here somewhere.* "I know how the responsibility weighs on you. You can let it all go this very day: The pain, the guilt. Your spirit can join with those you've lost. You will finally be done."

Those words were like several hundred pinpricks to the heart. Jeth had wanted so badly to be done. Done this mission, done being a Champion, done fighting—all of it. But he knew, *'This is only the beginning.'* Serra had reminded him of that. ". . . I don't want to die."

"Your entire life, you've teetered over the precipice of life and death. No one could blame you for wanting to jump off it. When the Deities are done with you, they will toss you into the trash heap of forgotten heroes. Where will you belong then?"

"With my people."

In unison, the bodies shook their heads. "You belong with your *real* family, where you should have been if it weren't for that disease those ashray-human hybrids brought. Follow me and learn where you truly come from, Jethril of Fernsdale."

A sinking feeling pulled at his gut. "What did you just call me?"

The group parted, and a small boy approached. He looked up at Jeth with frosted blue eyes and blinked innocently through his long silver fairy locks. He reached a little hand out. "Please stay with me, Daddy."

Jeth's throat closed as his arm reached for the boy's hand, seemingly of its own will. "I should have named you. The one thing a father should provide, and I couldn't even do that." He swallowed the lump burning his throat.

"Of course, you couldn't name me," said the boy whose twinkling smile contrasted with the sinister crimson light filling the cavern. "You didn't have a daddy either. Oh, you could see him too." He pranced forward excitedly. "Come see, come see."

Zephira stepped in the boy's way, shielding Jeth's view of him. "This is not your son. It is the thing that tried to destroy your Mother Oak."

The crowd hissed, "That tree does not care about your people any more than the Sacred Spring cares for urlings. You're fleas on a dog's fur that they merely tolerate. The devotion your two peoples have to these false gods only holds them back and keeps them separate from the rest of humanity. Through me, you will all be united again. Unmarred by civilization—one with nature. As you were supposed to be."

The child resembling Jeth's young son collapsed to the ground. His little face contorted, and he began to sob. "Why won't you stay with me, Daddy?"

The sound wrung Jeth's heart in his chest, but he wouldn't fall for Nyr's trick. As tempted as he was to learn of his past and all that could have been, he was no longer that weak-willed boy pulled in by the allure of a beautiful desert thief. His son would never grow up, but Ellion would. Jeth's future children still could. The family he found for himself was more important than learning his dead family's name or at which commune his curse began. He wasn't about to abandon them, no matter how much better off he felt they'd be without him . . . because that wasn't the point.

Jeth spotted the hilt of his dagger sticking up from one of the proto's heads. He stepped around Zephira and crouched down over the crying child. "I'll think of a name for you someday, I promise, but not today. Other people need me more now. Goodbye, Son."

The boy wiped his tears with the back of his little fists then looked up at Jeth in confusion. Every red eye narrowed.

Jeth left the boy where he sat, and dashing for the knife with a torrent of speed, he yanked it out of the proto's skull.

Snakkurs shot out of the walls and latched onto his shoulder blades. They lifted him off the ground, suspending him in midair.

Jeth wriggled his arms out of his jacket and fell back to the ground as the snakkurs tore the coat in half. Serra flung out of his pocket and landed on the other side of the cavern with a quiet thump. She shook her head, her iridescent wings fluttering.

"Serra!" During his fall, he had dropped the knife again, but there was no time. He pushed his way through the red-eyed crowd to retrieve his broken fairy.

Protos fell from the ceilings and crawled out from gaping trenches in the ground. More and more bled from the walls and swarmed him.

He maneuvered past their sluggish attempts to grapple him, but he had no way to put them down for good.

Too many!

They pressed into him and pushed him back. Each proto he kicked or punched down revealed two or three more in their place.

There's no way out. There's no way out, his mind repeated, and yet his body wouldn't give up, no matter the futility.

His bandaged fingers ached as he pushed against shoulders, legs, and faces. Their eyes burned deep red; the light so bright it blinded him in his struggle to get to Serra.

He collapsed to his knees as more and more bodies piled on top of him. He screamed, but the more he fought, the heavier they became.

He felt the snakkurs' cold lips against his bare skin once again, fastening him to the earth. More slithered through the mob, their shrieks grating against his soul.

"You can't keep me here!" he bellowed.

"Release him!" screeched Zephira.

"It must be this way, my queen," Nyr said. "You are about to leave the Skour and begin preparations for my effigy. Crannabeatha's Champion will join you when he is ready."

The crowd lumbered aside, creating a path to the exit tunnel, then motioned with their arms for Zephira to walk through it.

Zephira shook her head. "I won't go."

More and more protos swarmed Jeth, obscuring his view of the princess.

"You cannot hold me back forever," said Nyr. "Despite the ashray blood inside you or that Champion's blessing at your breast, you are and always will be Queen of the Skour first, urling princess last."

"Forget about us, Zephira," Jeth grunted. "Get out of here now . . . while you have some control."

"No!" she screamed.

To Jeth's surprise, the protos recoiled. The snakkurs coming at him stilled, and the two attached snakkurs fell away. Every proto took slow steps back.

Now free, Jeth scrambled over to Serra, scooping her into his injured palm. He then rose to his feet. "Zephira, r—"

His words stalled in his mouth as he stared at the princess. She held his dagger in her shaking hand, the blade pressed to her pale throat.

"I will be neither queen nor princess."

33

Damn the Rest of the World

Jeth inhaled sharply as the razor point of the military-grade steel puckered Zephira's blanched skin.

"Don't do this, Zephira. Your people need you. Mine especially."

Her knife-wielding arm trembled, her eyes clenched shut. "The best thing I can do for them now is keep Nyr from poisoning our world. And I can spare my people the horror of seeing their princess debased."

"I know a thing or two about being debased in front of your people. There's always a way back." Jeth argued, inching towards her. "Regardless of what happened to you here, your family still loves you."

"You don't know that." Her jaw stiffened to keep it from shaking, but she could not hold back her tears. The emotion she kept so tightly locked inside now streamed down her cheeks.

"Put down the knife, my queen," Nyr said. "Your death will only delay the inevitable."

"You need me." Zephira pressed the knife into her throat until a thin stream of blood trickled down her neck. "Only the Champion of Elmifel can unite humanity and build your effigy. Otherwise, you'd have used Gavarr for that as well. I'm your one key to the primitive world you covet."

"Until another Champion is called." Nyr taunted.

"Perhaps you are willing to wait another century, but to spare our world one hundred years of your influence is well worth my life!"

Serra squirmed in Jeth's palm. "She's right, Jeth. This is the only way to truly protect Fae'ren and the rest of the world."

Jeth blinked. "You're saying I should let her kill herself?" Maybe

Serra was right. But then what was the point of his mission? Why did his *Way* lead him here just to watch the Princess of Del'Cabria slice her own throat?

Nyr's army stepped forward, and Zephira backed away. She pressed harder with the dagger, pushing out more blood. It pulsed, running in rivulets and staining the drawstrings of her borrowed shirt.

Jeth heard her heartbeat slow, an eerie calm coming over her. There was no doubt she had made up her mind. Her knife-wielding arm shook, and she took a final, quivering breath.

Jeth activated his speed while standing still, giving him time to think.

If you save her, you damn the rest of the world . . .

Her hand moved, the knife slowly opening her gash wider.

Well, damn the rest of the world then!

In a flash, Jeth rushed the princess. He clasped his free hand around the knife's grip, stalling its advance.

Her eyes snapped open, and she stared straight into his.

"Don't do it," he rasped.

"Release me." The words quaked from her throat as her large violet eyes welled.

"This is not the only way. You can still weather what's to come."

"You don't understand." Her hand trembled under his, causing the blade to scrape along her bleeding gash. "*I* am what's to come. What your people suffer now will be nothing compared to what I will do to them as long as Nyr is in me. Please . . ."

"Jeth, listen to her," Serra begged.

He thought about yanking the dagger out of the princess's weakening grip, but he continued to hold it in place. He had made his choice, but she had to make hers.

"You can fight this," he said, squeezing her hand tighter. "Control those primitive urges. Isn't that what you urlings do best? If anyone stands a chance at resisting Nyr's influence, it's you."

"You don't know me!" she wailed. "You don't know Nyr! Let go of my hand, and no one else will ever have to."

From his other hand, a small, breathless voice whispered, "I'm sorry, Jeth." A bright green spark zapped his knife-holding fist. It was painful enough to make him let go and stagger backward, leaving the princess vulnerable to her own actions.

He shook his hand to ease the prickling pain then proceeded to hold it out to Zephira. As much as he wanted to strangle his fairy guardian, he couldn't take his attention off the princess. "I know that what you're about to do isn't the heroic act you think it is. It's simply the path of least resistance." He looked upon the droves of red-eyed bodies blocking their only exit. Esteban still hung from the ceiling. Serra had passed out in his hand. His chances of escaping with Zephira were slim to none, but that didn't matter . . . he would try anyway.

"Sometimes, the meaning of our death is the meaning of our life," Zephira said, more tears dribbling down her cheeks. Jeth wasn't sure if she was parroting Nas'Gavarr's words or if they also originated from the ashray. Either way, it was just a useless sentiment put forth by those who never had to fear death themselves.

Jeth let his hand down. "You have to live first to know if that's true. If you're so certain you know what's best for the world, then go ahead, but if you're wrong . . . there's no going back. And sometimes, that's the only direction left to go."

Zephira gasped, her grip on the knife slackening. It slipped and landed blade down in the warm earth. Jeth retrieved it half a second afterward.

He spun around to face the glaring horde, wielding his meager weapon. "Good choice," he muttered behind him. "Now, hold my pixie."

The cavern walls pulsated, releasing more pale forms that dropped to the ground and rose to their feet.

"You can't fight them all by yourself," Zephira protested while taking Serra into her hands.

He eyed the suspended naja a few feet away. "I won't be by myself." Jeth sped toward the protos. He kicked the legs out from under the first three in front of him, rolled back up to his feet, then leaped off the three-body pile he'd created.

With his inhuman speed, he kicked off the shoulders of the proto crowd and launched himself up to the hanging reptile. Holding his knife in his teeth, Jeth shimmied up Esteban's body, jolting him to consciousness.

The naja screeched and writhed within his flesh restraints as Jeth jammed his dagger through the sinews connecting him to the ceiling.

"Wakey, wakey," Jeth grunted as he hacked the fleshy rope.

Dozens of moaning faces stared up at them, their arms reaching up as they climbed over one another.

"What's going on?" Esteban screamed.

A handful of protos jostled their way above the others and clawed at the naja's snout and shoulders.

He gnashed his teeth and thrashed, sending the protos tumbling.

"Almost got it, keep wriggling."

The naja swung back and forth, straining the restraints as Jeth continued to saw. With a final stroke, the flesh cocoon ripped apart, and the two fell to the ground.

The protos swarmed over top of them, but Esteban burst upward with a roar, knocking them back.

"Clear a path for the princess," Jeth shouted.

"Where's the fairy? Did she survive?" Esteban whipped his head back and forth.

"Zephira has her. Let's go!"

Together, they sliced through the endless stream of bodies. Esteban swiped away swaths at a time, allowing Jeth to jump into the fray and stab whatever came in front of him.

Proto after proto fell at his feet until the horde opened up. Jeth grabbed Zephira by the arm, pulled her through the replenishing masses, and then back up the pitch-black staircase.

Esteban ran ahead, slashing through bodies that sprung from the walls. In the complete dark, Jeth could only hear their moaning and feel their ragged breath on all sides. He was grateful for Esteban's superior night vision.

The trio smashed against a thick wall . . . only it wasn't a wall. It bobbed about, arms, heads, and torsos blocking the way out.

"Stay behind me!" He pushed Zephira to his back with one arm, then began stabbing anywhere his blade could touch, careful to feel out human skin from reptilian before he plunged his dagger into the dark.

More protos ran up behind them, shoving them farther up the incline and squeezing them against the sweating throng ahead. Behind him, Zephira screamed. They were pressed so tightly together, there was no room to thrust his knife.

A proto grabbed Jeth around the shoulders, nearly pulling him over, and rasped into his ear, "My queen is free to go, but only if her loyal beast stays."

"No . . ." Jeth wheezed. There was no air left; his muscles spasmed.

From farther up the path came the visceral sounds of carnage and the copper stink of blood along with it. Esteban wailed.

Zephira had been separated from him, and he couldn't locate her—the girl without a scent. He couldn't be sure if she had run back or was trampled beneath his feet.

Then, rising in the darkness, a burst of light illuminated the piles of grappling bodies within it.

Zephira, curled in a ball at Jeth's right, gaped up at the glowing green sphere that levitated from her palms.

With a shudder, the light exploded to ten times the size, blinding everyone in the tunnel.

Serra had reverted to her full-sized form, surrounded by sparkling green energy. With a determined roar, the sparks exploded out of her every pore.

Jeth dove over the huddled princess, shielding her from the barrage of life force gobbets that pelted down like torrential rain.

Every proto was thrown out of the tunnel. The cavern wall shriveled and recoiled, dumping more bodies that were too knocked back from the shining green maelstrom.

The enraged pixie turned the brunt of her energy upward, screaming as if in unimaginable agony. Serra catapulted herself up into the blockade. She ripped through the walls and blew the bodies trapped within them to pieces by the sheer force of her trajectory.

"Fairy!" Esteban screamed after her.

The new tunnel left in her wake allowed the surface's violet light to stream down and cool air to rush in. Serra had made them a pathway all the way out.

But with what life force? Jeth gulped.

There was no time to contemplate the pixie's condition; Nyr had infinite proto-humans to throw at them, and already snakkurs were winding up the tunnel in pursuit.

"Esteb, keep the path clear," said Jeth as he pulled Zephira back to her feet and led her through the newly made tunnel. "We're getting out of this place."

"About time." The naja bounded ahead of them.

Zephira's arm ached under Jeth's firm grip, but it didn't matter; it felt only slightly less numb than the rest of her body.

Her chance to end Nyr's plan with one slice of the blade was long gone. Now all she could do was focus on the climb ahead and the violet light beyond.

Half-buried bodies oozed out of the dirt walls, reaching their spindly arms for the desperate runners. "Where do you think you're going, Crannabeatha's Champion?" Nyr taunted through his human shells around them.

"We're not going to make it," Zephira wheezed.

"Just keep moving." Jeth pulled harder, their pace reaching a speed she never knew man or woman was capable of. Like when he had grabbed the knife from her down below, the Fae'ren dashed between bodies in the blink of an eye.

She kept her gaze fixed on the light of the surface, blocking out the addled moans of Nyr's proto-human army at their backs.

Hands burst from the walls ahead, and screaming upside-down faces swung from the ceilings. The naja tore through them all, sending body parts rolling down the path.

More hands shot up from the earth, and Jeth cut them away with his dagger. The bodies on the ground writhed and twisted, tripping her, and each time Jeth pulled her right back up.

Cool air caressed Zephira's lungs as they reached the surface. She collapsed as soon as her feet felt the dry black dirt of the Skour's Field of Bones, this time taking Jeth down with her.

"Serra," he croaked.

The groans of the advancing flesh mob grew louder behind them.

"She's over here," called Esteban several feet ahead.

The two pushed themselves back to their feet with great effort as the naja picked up the doll-sized fairy in his massive clawed hands. Zephira could have sworn she saw her grow ten times that size before she shot out of the cave in a blinding green light.

Jeth put his ear to her body. "I don't hear anything."

The naja gave him the most sorrowful look Zephira ever thought possible from a reptilian beast. "Is . . . is she dead?"

"No." Jeth shook his head. "We just need to get her to the Deep Wood in Fae'ren. The Crannabeatha should be able to revive her."

Esteban sighed with visible relief.

The earth at their feet began to quake. Balls of dirt rolled toward the pit they just escaped, and black goop bubbled up from it.

A sense of dread washed over Zephira.

The black pit stilled for a moment, then belched out hundreds of human bodies as if the cavern below was turning inside out.

The bodies rapidly arranged themselves in a haphazard structure, the wet, primordial ooze molding them together. A giant torso formed, fifty feet in height, stuck in the ground by its waist. A bulbous, canine head took shape, its elongated snout casting a damning shadow over the stunned party below.

"What—what is that thing?" Esteban gaped up at the abomination.

Zephira shook her head slowly. "I've never seen Nyr do anything like this before."

The enormous mass of bodies opened its mouth and unleashed a thundering choir of human screams. Snakkurs extended out from the mouth like multiple tongues, ready to clamp their tiny swollen mouths down on the escapees . . . or one in particular, and that one was not Zephira this time.

"To the henge!" she screamed.

Esteban secured Serra in his belt sash, and the three sprinted for the circular rock formation that marked their way out.

Zephira could still feel the cold blood pulsing down her neck as she ran. She wished she had the courage to finish what she'd started. *I'm weak. My resolve is broken, and now this man will suffer for it.* She stumbled.

With impossible speed, Jeth grabbed hold of her before she fell. He pulled her with him, but she could never hope to keep up. She only slowed him down. Her lungs burned, and her feet bled, sliced open on the bones beneath them.

The dog-like monstrosity stretched forward, reaching for them with infinitely malleable arms. One of them crashed to the ground, separating Esteban from them. The impact tremor sent Jeth and Zephira to their knees. Protos sloughed off the giant appendage and rained down.

He pushed her onto her feet again, and they scurried frantically around the falling figures. Ahead, a gap opened, and Zephira saw Esteban on the other side. Reaching back to take Jeth's hand, she found nothing but empty air.

Jeth was still where they had fallen, fighting his way through a mountain of bodies.

Zephira ran back, grabbed his outstretched arm with both hands, and pulled.

Dozens of dirt-stained fingers held him down. Nyr's looming torso extended over them and brought its snout directly above Jeth.

It was no use. She cried out in pain, her elbow about to dislocate again.

Jeth looked up at her, hazel eyes petrified.

What could they do against the will of their creator? *We came from the pit, and Nyr will return us to it.*

"Let go, Zephira," Jeth huffed. "Get back to Cordos. A ship will come for you. You have to get home. Promise me."

Zephira's lips quivered. Nyr's head descended, the snakkur tongues extending toward their target.

"I prom—"

Esteban appeared behind Zephira and squeezed her wrists, loosening her grip on Jeth's hand. "I'll make sure she gets there right after I return your fairy to the Deep Wood. You have my word, compadre."

Jeth's hand slipped out of her grasp as the snakkurs latched onto his shoulders and yanked him free from the pile of protos. Jeth reached for the naja as he rose upward toward Nyr's open maw. "No, wait! Ellion—"

Nyr sucked him up into his jaws and clamped them shut, severing his last words as wholly as death would.

Zephira screamed. Esteban took her around the waist with one arm and sped away. Behind them, Jeth—the first living person she had come in contact with in over a year—was buried in an avalanche of black goop and bodies. His muffled cries died as Nyr's abominable form delved back underground.

Soon, the quaking ceased, and silence fell over the Field of Bones.

34

The Threshold

Zephira clung to Esteban's shoulder as both of them sank into the putrid, black muck.

With her eyes clamped shut, she climbed out the other side and collapsed on her hands and knees. Black gobs of gook dripped out of her nose. She wiped it out of her eyes, trying to bury the image of her Fae'ren rescuer devoured by Nyr's soulless human shells that was now forever burned into her eyelids.

A cool breeze tickled her face, and the roar of the nearby ocean touched her ears. Her entire body shook with shock and relief. It didn't matter that she was on an unknown island thousands of leagues away from home. She had escaped the Skour. This was home enough.

She blinked and looked up at Esteban. He jostled the unconscious fairy in his palm, but there was no response. "Do you happen to know where this Deep Wood is? I don't know how much longer this little pixie has."

Zephira shook her head, still kneeling. "I'm not sure where it is, just that it's in Fae'ren Province." She felt a prick of regret for not paying enough attention to her geography lessons. All she could remember was how much space Fae'ren took up on the map of Del'Cabria and how all of it was covered in dense forests. Any one of them could be considered the Deep Wood.

Esteban secured Serra back in his belt sash. "At any rate, it will take weeks to get there from here, even if your father's ships arrive today."

"Ships?" Jeth had mentioned that too. "Are you not aware of the warping gate on this island?"

"Of course. That's how we arrived. Unfortunately, the warp stone has gone missing."

"Missing?"

"We think the thief was the thing that haunts this island and the thing that allowed us through the gate in the first place."

Nyr's putrid essence churned in Zephira's gut. She recalled Jeth telling her that Nyr brought him to the Skour, luring him with illusions of his dead son. That meant Zephira had been back here recently . . . or her body at least. She could very well have been the one who stole the warp stone, but if she did, she couldn't begin to remember where she'd hidden it.

"Serra was going to fly home and bring some more, but now . . ." Esteban looked down at the pixie and sighed. "All we can do is wait for the Royal Navy. If they can find the way." The reptilian met Zephira's tired gaze. "I'm sorry, Princesa, but you will not be returning home for a while yet."

She clutched her brooch with one hand and hugged her torso with the other. "That's all right. All I want now is to get as far from this cursed henge as possible."

"I second that."

They trekked down the jungle path until they reached the bottom of a small dirt cliff. Esteban hoisted Zephira upon his shoulder so she could climb the rest of the way before he sprang to the top in one leap.

They arrived at the settlement a few minutes later. Zephira gasped at the bloody protos splayed across the ground. "What happ—?" Flashes of memory blinded her: *She stood in the same spot she was now, holding a glass jar behind her back as droves of dripping black bodies flooded out of the cottages. Jeth and Esteban stood before her, horrified expressions plastered on their faces.*

The recollection lasted a split second, but Zephira knew that it had really happened. Shaking her head, she continued forward, trying her best to ignore the gore at her feet. Esteban made no attempt to explain the scene to Zephira as if he already knew who was responsible for instigating it.

"You look like you could use some rest." He pointed to a cottage on the far end. "I will dispose of these bodies myself."

She nodded indolently and watched the naja pick up two bodies in each arm and lug them to the edge of the village. Their blatant imperfections gave her pause. Each one was malformed as if molded by a novice sculptor, not the creator of all humankind. From what little she could remember of her time in the Skour, she never saw creations so grotesque—so wrong. *Why would Nyr make these? Perhaps its creative power is less effective outside the Skour.*

Stepping over the various body parts, she ambled her way toward the cottage, but a shadow in her periphery made her freeze. She turned just in time to see a black tail slip through one of the larger cottages' broken doors. It was the same one she had been chained in before the snakkurs came for her. A paralyzing terror clamped down over her entire body.

She stared into the house, waiting for whatever thing that went in to come out again. After a few moments, she began to wonder if she'd imagined it. As she was about to turn away, a large black dog emerged from the shadows and stopped at the doorway. Its fur was caked with dried tar, its front limbs longer than its hind legs, giving it a hunched appearance. The longer she stared at it, the less real it seemed. It undulated between tangible and shadow, like a vortex sucking in all the light around it. Zephira blinked, but the wraithlike canine didn't disappear.

Esteban dragged another set of bodies past her, oblivious to the creature a mere stone's throw away. Eventually, he stopped what he was doing and said, "What are you looking at, Princesa?"

She pointed to the dog staring at her, mocking her.

The naja followed her finger, then proceeded to dart his snout back and forth. "Where is it?"

"There, in the doorway, that dog. Don't you see it?"

Esteban walked forward, looking straight at it and close enough for the dog to be in his shadow. "Nothing is there. This jungle plays tricks on the mind, as I'm sure you know."

The dog grinned wide, revealing rows of long, pointed teeth. Its deep red eyes burned hot.

Zephira realized this was not one of Nyr's creations separated from the pack; it *was* Nyr. The red eyes proved it.

Her stomach lurched, nearly taking her to the ground. It was exactly as she feared. This creature was a manifestation of Nyr's spirit that she now carried with her; a stray dog that followed her from the Skour. It wasn't just its essence polluting her being, but its sentience invading her mind, waiting for that perfect opportunity to pounce.

"It's going to be all right," Esteban said, though his voice sounded far away. "I'll just be a few more minutes."

She nodded despite not fully hearing what the naja said. The dog walked backward, fading into the darkness of the house until all she could see were its glowing red eyes.

Her rational mind begged her not to follow, but a tug at her sternum urged her forward. She slowly stepped over the threshold and entered the place that had once held her prisoner before the real nightmare began. Right away, she found the magus's corpse against the wall. Nyr was next to him, pawing at his robes even though they seemed to go right through them.

Zephira reached out slowly, petrified with anticipation of what the shadow dog was trying to show her.

Nyr grinned again, sending chills down her spine.

Eager to get this over with, she took a deep breath and pulled open the magus's robes. A chunk of iridescent stone was lodged in his cavernous wound, grubs wriggling over it.

Zephira stumbled back, knocking over a chair. "Esteban!"

Nyr vanished. She didn't know why it helped them, but then it did want her to leave this island and spread the word of humanity's one true creator. The warp stone was required for that.

"Princesa?" Esteban ran inside within seconds. "What happened?"

Holding her hand over her mouth, she pointed to the dead magus.

It didn't take Esteban long to find the yellow stone embedded in the rotting flesh. Nyr had put it there, using Zephira's hands . . . the same hands she had clasped over her face right now. She jerked them away, but the nausea persisted.

Esteban's claws delved deep inside the cadaver and yanked out the stone. Wriggling maggots and thick, soupy gore dripped off of it. The sour stench of rot doubled, and Zephira rushed out the door. She fell to her hands and knees and regurgitated her pent-up horror onto the grass outside.

Soon, Esteban was standing over her, waiting for her heaving to stop. "I won't ask how you knew where this was. I am just glad you found it. We can set off for Fae'ren at once. From there, we can send word to your father."

Fae'ren was still far from the Capital, but she figured it was closer than where they were right now. Then she had a thought. So many months ago, the fog had kept the ashray from coming to her, but now, nothing was stopping her from going to them. She wiped her mouth, leaving smears of dried tar along her cheek. "Where are we?"

"Cordos."

"Where is Cordos?"

"Somewhere between Rangardia and Credence."

"Between Rangardia and Credence . . ." she murmured. "That means Thessalin should be northeast of here."

"Is there something the matter?" asked Esteban.

"Would you be able to turn the gate toward Elmifel? There's a gate under the Holy City. I can take refuge there."

"What about Serra?" The naja motioned to the limp pixie at his hip.

"When I go through to Thessalin, you can turn the gate for Fae'ren. I'm sure someone at their gate can help you find the Deep Wood better than I can."

"If they don't run screaming in terror." Esteban scratched his scaly green snout. "Also, I don't feel right about sending you through a warping gate without knowing what is on the other side. I promised Jeth two things: To revive his fairy *and* ensure your safe travels home. Besides, I will have a hard time turning that thing by myself, even with naja strength. It requires at least three men to push. I know because I was here when they built it."

Zephira was taken aback. "Y-you worked for Gavarr?"

"For a time." The naja presented himself with his arm. "And what you see before you now was my reward."

"I'm sorry." Zephira lowered her eyes to the ground.

"Don't be. Had I not agreed to go on that fateful job, we could not have found this place . . . or you."

"That's why I'm sorry," she whispered.

"What was that?"

She shook her head and stood up. "Never mind. In that case, we go to Thessalin together. You can see me into ashray care before going to Fae'ren from there."

"I like the sound of that plan much better."

"Good," Zephira said. "Since there needs to be someone to allow us through, I can contact the ashray now and let them know to have their gate ready."

The naja tilted his head to look at her sidelong. "How do you propose to contact them from here exactly?"

"It's hard to explain. But I'll need the ocean."

"After you." He waved her onward.

They made their way through the jungles toward the sounds of the sea. The closer they got, the more the dense fog congregated around them, but it did little to dishearten Zephira this time.

Esteban stopped at the warping gate to put the stone in the cubbyhole while Zephira continued toward the beach. She couldn't wait to feel the saltwater over her skin, for it to cleanse her body of the foul tar she wore and to carry her mind far and away. Her only worry now was whether she would remember how to scry after so long.

Her feet had barely touched the sand before she caught sight of the black dog standing erect near the shore. Partially turned away from her, it cast its elongated snout to the sky.

Zephira warily followed its red gaze. Dark figures disturbed the fog, dozens of giant vultures soared overhead. Nyr snarled at the swarm as they descended, a hundred yards from where Zephira stood.

She could feel Nyr's force threaten to crawl back up her throat in her moment of confusion and terror, but she pushed it back down with all her might. It wasn't until the first winged creature found ground that Zephira realized they were not birds at all.

Esteban bounded onto the beach next to Zephira. "The stone's in place. Now help me turn the gate."

There was no time. Zephira pointed helplessly at the winged women. "Harpies." Her voice cracked. "Hide!"

The sun at the harpies' backs cut through the gray swirling mists. A dense green island emerged from a cradle of fog, so small they could have flown right over it.

"Cordos, due north," Vidya called to her winged team of fifty.

Vidya, Phrea, and Daphne made the first dive. They rode the wind on a downward curve, punching a hole through the mist, then followed the rolling waves rushing up to the rocky shore.

The three harpies came to ground on the gravel beach, fifty more Primaries following. Each of them shuffled hesitantly about the sand. The fog shrouded the rainforest in an eerie shadow, the vegetation lush and yet somehow wrong. Most disconcerting to Vidya, however, was the silence. Not even a seagull squawked.

She called to her team, "Lieutenant, take thirty to search the beaches and form a perimeter around the entire island. Report to me when you find the warping gate."

Malantha nodded and gathered thirty of her command. They took to the air and fanned out.

"As for the rest of you," she said to those still on the ground, "we move inland." Vidya leaped into the air and flew straight over the thick greenery.

Harpies spread out over the island to find small clearings to explore further. It didn't take long before Vidya spotted an abandoned settlement littered with corpses, and she signaled for others to follow her down.

Upon landing, the harpies ransacked the abandoned Rangardian abodes while Vidya inspected the strange bodies splayed out on the ground. From above, she had assumed they were humans, covered in dirt, limbs torn off, and heads smashed in. Now close up, she realized they were all deformed. Some were eyeless or toothless, more creature than person.

Daphne bent down, poking a finger into the deep gash across one's torso. "Looks like these wounds were inflicted rather recently."

"How recently?" asked Vidya.

Daphne shrugged. "A day or two."

She frowned at the bodies. A few had been put in a pile at the village's northern edge as if someone had started to clean up but was interrupted.

A twig snapped, followed by rustling in the bushes nearby. She spun around, looking for the source of the sound, but the jungle fell silent.

"Vidi, come look," Phrea called. Vidya returned her attention to the village just as Phrea sauntered out of a cottage. She tossed her a tin can marked with Del'Cabrian script. "Military rations."

"He was definitely here," said Vidya. "He must have spent a few days here until these *things* attacked. But where did he go?"

"I'm guessing this way." A harpy pointed to a series of tracks leading down a forest path farther west. One set could have been made by Jeth, but the other alongside his was pointed with four elongated toes.

"A naja?"

"That would explain the severity of some of these wounds," said Daphne, studying one of the headless corpses. She sliced off a sample of the humanoid's rotting flesh and placed it in the satchel at her hip.

Vidya called to the other harpies to keep searching the village as she and her two commanders proceeded on foot down the path, her hands hovering over her flintlock pistols the entire way. The footprints stretched farther and farther apart as they went; they had been running and fast. They led to a drop-off. Anything beyond was shrouded in mist.

The shadow harpy materialized on a tree branch just below, facing the same direction. *"There's something here that shouldn't exist."* She pointed down into the fog.

Vidya extended her wings and glided down.

"Vidi, wait up," Phrea called after her.

Towering black rocks encircled a foul pool of muck. Most odors didn't bother Vidya, but there was something about this one that made her positively ill. She instinctively refrained from touching it. Moments later, Phrea and Daphne were at her side.

"What is with all this mist?" Daphne asked.

"I haven't the *foggiest* idea," Phrea chortled.

Vidya spotted a long piece of wood floating slantways in the gook. Careful not to step in it, she swooped over the pool and fished the object out. It was a bow, its string broken and caked in the tar-like substance.

Now Vidya's pulse hastened, wondering what could have happened to the bow's wielder. "Blessed Yasharra, where is he?" she whispered.

"Eww." Phrea plugged her nose. "Do you think the poor boy drowned in this shit?"

"What about these rocks?" Daphne wondered aloud. "Obsidian?" She rubbed her hand against one of the dark stones, staining her fingertips. "Interesting."

"Wait, look over here." Phrea went to another rock with hairline fractures revealing a different color beneath the black. She scraped the stone with the edge of her forearm blade, taking off several black flakes before blowing them away and revealing yellow iridescence beneath.

"Warp stone?" Vidya touched the hard, yellow rock for herself.

"In its raw state," Phrea said with an air of triumph.

"The island must be full of it for there to be chunks this big," continued Vidya. "Do you think the Rangardian settlers built this henge?"

"Don't know, but I wager we'll find Jeth's body under here." Daphne removed her forearm blades, marched right into the muck with barely a flinch, and started sifting through it with her bare hands.

"Good thinking, Daph." Phrea plugged her nose and actively backed away from the pool. "Keep doing what you're doing."

"Anassa. Commanders." Malantha appeared above, the mist swirling around her flapping wings. "We found the gate."

"Lead the way, Lieutenant." Vidya gladly turned away from the goop and nodded. "Daphne, you stay here. Phrea, come with me."

"Oh, thank goddess," Phrea muttered, clearly not wanting to help her friend search the foul pool.

The two harpies followed Malantha to the northeast side of the island, several yards from where they had made their first landing.

There was kicked-up gravel and flattened vegetation around the gate's base, evidence of a struggle. A harpy at the steps held up a brown sack. "We found this resting against the base." She turned it upside down and dumped the contents: Uneaten military rations, a first aid kit, a few tools, a spare bowstring, and a filthy suede shoe—one a Del'Cabrian noblewoman might wear.

Vidya's heart skipped a beat. The shoe was definitely small enough to fit the dainty foot of an urling female. "He found her."

"Alive or dead, I wonder," said Phrea.

"Doesn't matter. We need to get to her before the King is notified one way or another. We can pretend she's alive for as long as necessary." Vidya walked up the base and inspected the dais. It pointed in an eastern direction as she expected but not north enough to be the Herrani or Elmifel gates and far too north to be the Crede gate. "He took her to Fae'ren."

"Unless it was pointed in that direction when he got here," said Phrea. "Maybe Nas'Gavarr went to Fae'ren from here once."

Vidya shook her head. "Unlikely. Though I was half-conscious at the time, I'm fairly certain Nas'Gavarr brought me straight to Fae'ren from Credence. Not to mention, if he had magi looking after the princess all this time, they would have had the gate pointed to Herran so they could resupply. It seems more plausible that Jeth came here, found the princess, or whatever's left of her, then went home." That also meant Thessalin's gate was still non-operational since that would be the quickest way back to the Capital.

Vidya looked down at the goop-smeared bow still in her hand. She found it hard to believe the archer would leave it behind just because of a broken string that he could have easily fixed with the materials he had brought. He was clearly running for his life.

Vidya went to turn the crank, but as she passed by the cubicle on the floor, she found it lacking a certain yellow sheen. "Wait a minute, how . . . ?" Dried blood and smears of black tar lined the cubby.

Stepping up next to her, Phrea said, "There had to be a stone there before. Otherwise, how in Yasharra's might did he get here in the first place?"

"It most definitely was here," said Vidya.

"But it's not possible to take the stone out from the other side, is it?" Malantha asked.

Phrea shook her head. "We've all seen what happens when a pathway closes on an appendage."

"Unless that person has inhuman reflexes." Vidya ground her teeth. "To protect his home from anyone or anything that would follow him back through, Jeth would take that risk, and he might just be quick enough to pull it off." Vidya was more eager than ever to get off this island as quickly as possible. She'd try the gate first in the off chance Jeth didn't shut down Fae'ren's gate on the other side. Otherwise, they'd have to rest here for the night and make the long flight there in the morning, giving Jeth and the princess a massive head start.

She walked off the platform, forming a fist around the case of black powder at her hip satchel. *There should be enough among us to blast a piece of warp stone loose,* she thought.

"Let's get this gate back up and running. We're paying a visit to Fae'ren Province."

35
Compromising Position

Vidya walked through the warping gate's liquid energy, emerging into a small forest clearing. She had been in a daze when Nas'Gavarr brought her through this gate the first time, but the scent of pollen and the choir of birds all around her were a stark reminder of that day and the feelings of betrayal and helplessness that came with it.

An elderly fae stood at the crank, his short, choppy hair sticking straight up, matching his shocked expression at the twenty winged women marching through the gateway.

"Expecting someone else?" Vidya asked with a smirk.

"H-harpies." He tottered backward on the platform, nearly tumbling off the edge.

Phrea flew around the base and caught him. "Don't worry, I got you."

She lifted him high above the gate, causing him to drop his cane and release his bladder. "Please . . . let me go."

"Not sure that would be wise from up here."

The creak of bowstrings interrupted the harpies' cackling. Vidya looked around, but all she saw was the breeze rustling the leaves.

Slowly, several figures emerged from the foliage, clothing, and face painted as green as the ferns, their hair thick like tree roots. Each of them carried a hammer or an axe. Several more men balanced on the winding oak branches, pointing more than enough arrows to take down every harpy present.

Vidya gulped.

"Put him down and carefully," the tallest and blondest Fae'ren man demanded, one throwing axe in his hand, another hanging off his belt.

Vidya nodded to Phrea to do what he said. She wasn't in the mood to terrorize elderly men at the moment, particularly one undeserving of the Harpy's Punishment . . . *today*, she thought with the gory image of Lys's sliced throat still fresh in her mind.

With a pout, Phrea gently returned to the ground but did not release the old man.

Vidya stepped down from the base as eight of the skirt-wearing men cautiously approached. She picked up the old man's wooden cane and handed it back to him—a gesture of good faith for the time being. "Let him go, Commander."

As soon as Phrea did so, the man hobbled as fast as he could down a deer path and out of sight, the pungent stench of urine going with him.

They stopped square in the center of the clearing. The tension of the archer's bowstrings mirrored that in Vidya's gut. There was no telling how many more were hiding in the bushes. "We did not come here to harm anyone. We only require information."

"State your business," the tall man said.

Vidya bit her lip in annoyance. If these men were any bit as skilled as Jeth, she could lose her one and only remaining life right then.

"I am the Anassa of Credence and am looking for Jethril. I assume you guard this gate at his behest."

"Aye." The man eyed the Harplite warily. "But we haven't seen him, not that you lasses would believe anything we tell you."

The shadow harpy, standing next to Vidya, whispered in her ear, *"He speaks true, unfortunately."*

Phrea spoke up, "We have good reason to believe he came through this gate rather recently, so do not insult—"

Vidya raised a hand to stop the commander's tirade. "He's not lying."

"What, you think he's still on Cordos somewhere?"

"No, he's definitely here, but clever enough not to let his own people find out, lest they be put in this compromising position."

A scrawny Fae'ren wearing a foxtail hat stepped up beside the tall one. "We've been watching this gate ever since you chased those desert folks through here." A gold and silver wolf appeared at the boy's hip, and he rested his hand on its head. "If Jeth came through since then, we'd know it."

"Don't say anything more, Tom," the leader warned.

"Perhaps I should speak to the Del'Cabrians on his team. They came through here with the rest of the desert folk, did they not?" Vidya pressed.

"And there was a sorceress with some naja, where might she be?" Phrea added.

More Fae'ren emerged from the forest, further outnumbering Vidya's modest contingent.

"You're too late. They continued on," said the leader.

"Now that's not entirely true," the shadow harpy crooned. *"One of them remains here. Jeth may be persuaded to reveal himself for the life of a dear friend."*

But would he risk the princess and his pardon for that friend? Vidya wondered.

She sighed, wishing she could just start breaking bones. "I'm afraid it may be *too late* for Jeth." She reached into the bag she had found in Cordos and took out the tar-stained bow.

The boy named Tom rushed up and snatched it out of her grasp. "Dayne, this is—this is Jeth's." He shot an accusatory look at the harpies. "Where did you find it?"

"On the Island of Cordos, where he went to search for the Princess of Del'Cabria. He found her and has since disappeared." Vidya worked to force concern into her voice.

"What do you know of the princess?" Dayne asked.

"Just that she is in grave danger, as is Jeth. I understand you have no reason to trust me after what happened in the oasis. A regrettable misunderstanding, I assure you. But Jeth and I are on the same side, just as we've always been. We both wish to see the princess returned to her kingdom. The Crede-Del'Cabrian alliance depends on it."

A few Fae'ren muttered amongst themselves while maintaining their defensive stances. "Horseshit!" an archer said from atop a tree. "You nearly paralyzed him over a year back."

The wolf beside Tom bared its fangs, a growl rumbling deep in its throat.

The heat of frustration rose into her temples. "What else did he tell you? Did he mention that it was *me* who prevented the demise of your Mother Oak, not him? I am the reason the forest you live in still grows!"

Dayne raised his voice, pointing to the knife at her hip. "And it's your blood and that dagger that almost destroyed it in the first place."

Vidya reflexively took a step back, putting her hand on the dagger's bone grip.

"That's right." Dayne nodded. "He told us all about your ambitions back then, and his task force has informed us of your current plans. So, you best go on back through that gate before our archers' fingers get tired."

Vidya regained her stance. "We aren't going anywhere. To ensure the safety of the princess, my Harplite will remain here to guard this gate. The harpies you see here are a fraction of our force. It would be unwise to antagonize us."

Dayne reaffirmed his grip on his throwing axe. His Fae'ren fighters didn't move an inch, and neither did the harpies.

Vidya's heart rammed against the inside of her chest. Either Jeth was somewhere in this forest or still on Cordos. One way or another, she had to secure all the gates to find him, but the last thing she wanted to do was start a war with the Fae'ren people to do so. It wasn't time for them yet.

The gate's energy rippled in Vidya's periphery as someone new came through. "Yasharra has rewarded us once again!" Malantha cheered, dragging a naja behind her. Tar coated nearly all of its light green scales. Its jaws were clamped shut, its arms, legs, and even tail bound in twine. "Look what we found sneaking around the gate." She dropped a chunk of warp stone beside him. "And he was carrying this."

"So that's where it went," said Phrea. "Nobody snatched it from the other side after all."

"Jeth could still be on Cordos," Vidya muttered. *Or dead,* she thought.

"I don't think we need to worry about him anymore." Malantha let go of the helpless reptile and stepped aside.

Daphne appeared behind her, dragging a filthy young girl by the arm, the tips of her ears barely poking through the mats of her tar-slathered hair. "Anyone looking for an urling princess?"

Harpies filed through the gate, filling the tight forest clearing as Zephira struggled against her captor. The woman twisted her arm and forced her to her knees before a tall, curly-haired harpy with bronze-plated armor.

Her massive umber wings cast an ominous shadow over Zephira. She recognized the woman as the harpy that had accompanied Jeth in the Holy City. Jeth had mentioned her name in the Skour . . . *Vidya?*

"Praise Yasharra for this fortuity. Thank you, Commander Daphne."

"She practically crawled right into our arms," the harpy named Daphne said, keeping her firm grip on Zephira's shoulder.

The harpy beside Esteban added, "This naja attacked the guards at the gate. And this little girl thought she could sneak right on through without being noticed."

Zephira stared down at her bare feet in shame. She was a fool to think they could pass through the active gate, hoping the harpies on the other side would be too preoccupied to spot them. She surreptitiously lifted her free arm, running her hand through her matted tresses to check that Serra had survived the tussle and was still there, disguised as nothing more than a clump of leaves in her hair.

The Champion of Yasharra reached down and took her by the chin, lifting her face, so Zephira had nowhere to look but directly into her deep-lined scowl. "Such a scrawny thing. Hard to believe this is really her."

Zephira steeled her jaw and jerked away.

"She's an urling on an island that Nas'Gavarr built a warping gate to access. That's evidence enough," said Daphne.

Esteban struggled on the ground, and the shaven-headed harpy kicked in his snout with her boot heel. A bloody welt of torn scales appeared in its place.

"Don't hurt him!" yelped Zephira.

Vidya asked, "Why not kill the beast, Lieutenant?"

"I was going to, but then discovered it's one of those talking ones. Thought you'd want to see it for yourself, Anassa."

A jolt hit Zephira. She had seen that word written in the ancient texts she'd studied in Thessalin. 'Anassa' was an old Crede term for a sovereign, the last one being the harpy queen one thousand years ago whose fall preceded Credence becoming a republic of sirens. If harpies ruled there again, then that would not bode well for Del'Cabria.

The Anassa hunched over Esteban and severed the twine around his jaws with the edge of her left forearm blade.

"What do you want with her?" he rasped.

She stood back up. "This one is reformed."

"Then we should keep it alive," said a heavy-set harpy with black hair. "He could lead us to his sorceress." She cracked her fist in her palm.

"All in good time, Commander Phrea." Vidya turned to Zephira again. "Stand her up." Daphne yanked her to her feet with one thin arm. "Now release her. We don't wish to cause her any more bodily harm."

Zephira's shoulder throbbed as the commander slowly lifted her hand. She now stood fully, taking in more of her surroundings. These woods were as foreign to her as Cordos had been. It was so bright, her dilated pupils could hardly focus on any one thing. Besides the crowd of winged women, a group of men with matted hair and skirt-like apparel stood in the thickets beyond. Some balanced atop branches, arrows nocked, but none made a move to stop the proceedings. *Are they here to help?* She wasn't sure if the harpies were aware of them, so she tried to keep her eyes squarely forward.

"There's no need to fear, Princess." The Anassa's tone noticeably softened. "I am here to take you home."

"Do not lie," Zephira replied without a flinch. "I know who you are and presumably what you're after."

Vidya huffed through her nostrils. "No lies. I intend to take you home, just not to the one you grew up in."

Zephira swallowed down her wrath and remained expressionless, just as she had been taught to do all her life, only now it was much harder with Nyr violently crashing against the inside of her chest.

"You'll learn to like Credence in time," Vidya continued. "No stuffy old men telling you what to do. Even under our watchful eye, you'll know freedoms you have never before experienced." The harpy's warm smile gave Zephira chills. "I'm taking you to live in a woman's paradise. The Harpy need not be your enemy."

Not a muscle in Zephira's face twitched as she continued to stare straight ahead. "I don't believe you."

A shadowy black canine weaved amongst the harpies, gazing up at them with hungry red eyes. It vanished into the crowd as quickly as it appeared.

"No matter," Vidya muttered. She called out to the harpies nearest to the warping gate. "Is everyone through the gate?"

"All present, Anassa," said a spiky-haired harpy standing on the platform.

"Then prepare the pathway to Credence."

The young harpy pulled the gate in a clockwise direction without assistance.

The sudden crack of the gate's energy collapsing made Zephira's heart skip. Her clotted gash burned in recollection of what Jeth had said in the pit. *'There's no going back.'*

"Princesa," Esteban croaked from the ground. "Do not go with them. You made a promise."

"Shut up, beast!" The lieutenant gave him a hard kick in the abdomen.

"Promise to whom?" Vidya asked.

Zephira bit her lip, not intending to answer her question.

"Jeth . . ." came a young male voice. The harpies turned to a skinny adolescent wearing a fur cap over a tail of ashen locks. "Did you see him, Your Highness?" He edged forward, holding out a dirty bow towards Zephira. She supposed the wooden weapon belonged to Jeth, but she had only remembered him wielding the dagger in the Skour.

A large blond man put out his arm to caution the boy's continued advance.

"Excellent question." Vidya turned back to Zephira. "Why is Jeth not with you? We know he was on Cordos."

Zephira's eyes darted between Vidya's scrutinizing gaze and the Fae'ren's pleading stares. She opened her mouth, but no words dared to emerge.

"Anassa, does it really matter where he is now?" said Daphne.

Vidya put up her hand to silence her commander and didn't take her eyes off Zephira. "Did you see him or not?"

Zephira gave her a silent nod.

"Well? Where is he?" Vidya waved her hand, goading Zephira onward.

She shot another glance to the Fae'ren, rapt to her every word. "He lives."

The ebony dog flashed in her periphery, wagging its tail expectantly.

"So he lives. Big deal." Vidya snapped her fingers in front of her face, jolting her attention away from the shadow of Nyr and back to the harpies. "Where. Is. He?"

There was nothing Zephira could tell them that wouldn't be met with animosity or disbelief. All she could do was remain tight-lipped and take the suspicious and accusatory glares in stride. It was far better than any of them learning the truth. *Our creator wants to take back humanity with Jeth's unwilling assistance.*

"Please, Your Highness," the fox boy begged.

Zephira timidly met the boy's pleading gaze. "I'm afraid . . ." *'No, wait! Ellion—!'* Jeth's last words rang in her mind like a bell toll. She bit her quivering lip and faced Vidya. "I do not know."

The Anassa's fists clenched as if she wanted to strike Zephira at that moment. The splash of liquid energy bouncing back into the ring broke the tension.

Vidya growled in frustration. "Fine. Wherever he is, he won't be able to reach you anyway." She turned back to her flock. "Who among you still has black powder to spare?"

"I do." The lieutenant put up her hand.

"Good. You will remain behind and destroy this gate after we've all gone through. Then fly back on your own."

"Yes, Anassa."

Vidya took Zephira by the arm and walked her toward the gate. The gaggle of harpies closed in around them. Nyr padded along at Zephira's side, unseen by all except her.

Nyr's essence clawed the back of her throat as they neared the swirling energy within the granite ring. A sinister howl drowned out the droning hum. The ravenous black dog at her heels told her one thing: If she crossed that threshold, she would never set foot on Del'Cabrian soil again.

There had to be another way. She just needed to access a body of water, call the ashray, get through a warping gate . . . *Just don't let Nyr overtake you again. Anything but that.* She clutched her brooch so hard the silver frame cut into her fingers. *Esteban, Jeth . . . you should have left me where you found me. Your sacrifices were all for naught.*

⌘

"Stop right where you are," Dayne bellowed. "The princess stays with us." The groan of more bowstrings halted Vidya's pace. Harpies swarmed their Anassa, ready to take an arrow for her.

"Our business here is done," Vidya said, digging her fingers into her prisoner's arm. "She is no longer Fae'ren's concern." She turned her back to the fighters once more and strode swiftly toward the gate. They could release as many arrows as they wished; they'd all be home safe before anyone lost a second life.

Harpies covered their heads with their wings as they rushed forward. A sharp twang of a bowstring followed by a female grunt left an opening next to Vidya. She picked up the pace, dragging the princess by her bony arm.

As more arrows ripped through the air, harpies sent out powerful wind gusts to push them away. Archers lost their balance and fell from their perches. Just up a few stairs, and they'd be thousands of miles away. Except Vidya had underestimated the amount of Fae'ren fighters in the clearing. More archers scuttled along the winding branches above the gate, a couple jumped down onto the granite ring, giving their arrows the perfect downward angle to the top of Vidya's head.

They released a second later. There was no time to cast a gale to protect herself. *No, not this way, not now . . . Spyros, Alonz . . .*

"Vidi!"

Phrea sprung overhead, arrows ricocheting from her forearms blades as she blocked the assault.

Vidya reaffirmed her grip on the princess and pulled her back down the stairs. Her legs shook as her trusted Primaries moved in to cover her.

More arrows rained down from the trees, feathers swirled about in the air. Harpies collapsed to the ground while others pulled them back up.

Vidya fumed, she and her Harplite would not be made fools, and not by these tree-swinging primates!

"Take her." She handed the princess to Phrea and summoned a dome of storm winds above them. The winds pushed outward until the arrows stopped.

"Forward!" Vidya called, and her entourage took one step toward the gate.

Angered screeching sounded around her. Snarling, spitting growls came from all directions.

"Anassa!" A harpy barreled into Vidya from behind, knocking her face down to the earth. Malantha landed on top of her. She screamed as an enraged naja grappled with her, its weight pushing both harpies deeper into the dirt.

"Run, Princesa. Run!"

Vidya pushed herself upright by her arms with all her might, causing the two other bodies to slide off her back. Malantha flipped around, blood dripping down her spine from a gash between her dark brown wings.

Fae'ren fighters scattered into the bush as harpies swarmed around Vidya, blocking her view of the raging reptile. But that wasn't the only thing she couldn't see.

"Forget the naja!" Vidya growled. "Find the princess."

The Primaries backed away from the naja and spread out. Once the beast realized the harpies' attention was no longer on him, he bounded into the bush and disappeared. Vidya stood up and scanned the battlefield.

"Is everyone all right?"

"Mostly minor injuries," Daphne landed, panting. "A few life-threatening ones, but they'll heal. No deaths."

Vidya called out to the injured. "For those of you who can't fly, return to Credence. The rest of you join the others in searching for the princess. She could not have gone far. She only has legs; you have wings!"

Harpies vacated the clearing, either through the gate or into the sky. Malantha approached, her brown eyes wide and worried.

"Apologies, Anassa." She bowed her head in shame. "I saw you were in danger, and I left the naja unattended."

"It doesn't matter," Vidya said coldly. "Just find the urling girl. I don't care if you have to kill every Fae'ren to do it. If they get in the way, they die. Understand?"

The three harpies exchanged glances then nodded earnestly. "Yes, Anassa."

"Good. Now fly!"

36
A Promise

Zephira tripped over a tree root shrouded by thick foliage. Flailing, she came down hard on her hands and knees. Her legs ached, her forearms scratched to oblivion. She groaned. One more fall and she would surely lack the strength to get up again. She staggered back to her feet and ran through a cluster of spindly branches, chunks of dirty hair catching and ripping from her scalp.

She scampered through the moss and clambered over roots until her legs gave out. Resting against an oak stump to catch her ever-elusive breath, she reached up, relieved to find the fairy still in her hair. That relief quickly turned to dread at the seemingly insurmountable task in front of her. *Where's the Deep Wood?* She had hoped to find a Fae'ren to guide her if only she'd been able to sneak through the gate without getting caught. Now, she was alone in a whole new wilderness, large enough to fit twenty-five Cordoses, with no sense of east or west. *Esteban, please find me!*

Distant female voices and the flap of wings reached her ears, reminding her that none of that would matter if she didn't keep moving. The harpies wouldn't give up. Zephira couldn't either.

She needed to contact the ashray and get them to come through the gate. She could leave Serra in the capable hands of a Fae'ren before being ushered to safety. They'd know better than her what to do for the poor pixie. A small hope peeked its way into her heart with the new plan.

Forcing herself forward, Zephira continued stumbling through the woods, eyes and ears open for any sign of water, a creek, or even a puddle, anything that would lead her to a body of water large enough to scry the ashray.

The dog's red eyes stared at her from the shadows, but it stayed far enough back that she could ignore it. One thing at a time.

After a while, the gentle babbling of a brook caught her attention, the sound as triumphant as a symphony orchestra. She veered off to the right, and before she knew it, cold rushing water met her calloused toes. Despite the water coming only up to her ankles, every inch of her body sang.

She fell to her knees and splashed as much of the creek onto herself as she could, quickly scrubbing the thick tar off her face and arms. She wondered if there was enough water to scry from here.

She quickly began to trace the *Veil of Elmifel* on her forehead. She had yet to finish the dots when something splashed into the stream behind her. She spun around, finding the black-winged harpy an arm's length away.

Zephira gasped and fell into the creek with a splash.

"She's here!" Phrea called out, then hefted a massive poleaxe off her back. "Attempt to run, and I'll take your little feet off. You royals hardly need to use them anyway."

Zephira dove to the left and crawled toward the bank.

Phrea swung the axe, the blade scraping the stones under the water. Zephira kicked up water into the harpy's face and dashed into the bush. "Come back here, urling bitch!" Phrea growled from behind her.

Glancing back, Zephira couldn't see the harpy anymore, but that didn't mean she was free of her.

The princess ducked around a massive oak trunk. Catching her breath, she looked up at the dizzying treetops spinning above her. *Keep moving, you dolt!* Her mind begged her to run, but her body stood paralyzed with fear, knowing if she moved, her harpy pursuer would find her, but if she didn't, the result would be the same.

Two arms, wrapped in animal hides, snatched Zephira from behind and a filthy hand clasped around her mouth to smother her cries.

A young Fae'ren pulled her down into a crouch alongside him and put a finger to his lips, then led her down into the earthy tree well where Zephira's humming heartbeat could find some semblance of a normal rhythm.

The boy, his fox hat askew, held her fast as Phrea's armored boots appeared above them.

Zephira held her breath. The boy was as still as the roots they hid beneath.

Another harpy landed. "You saw her, Commander?"

"I had her," said Phrea. "But the brat slipped away from me."

"Well, if we don't find her, she'll die of exposure in these woods. It's far colder here than Cordos."

"The Fae'ren will surely find her before that happens," replied Phrea. "Keep looking if you want Credence to remain under harpy rule."

The harpies continued to wander about, boots passing and pausing inches from where Zephira and the Fae'ran boy crouched. Any moment, one of them would bend over and see them.

Zephira shut her eyes. *Deities That Cannot Be Named, send these heathens away, I beg of you.*

The Fae'ren shifted beside her, drawing her attention. He made a few pointing hand gestures to someone unseen. A few seconds later, a flash of silver fur darted past their line of sight, disturbing the bushes to the south.

"Over there!" Phrea jumped up and careened toward the distraction with a burst of wind. They could no longer see the other harpy, but that didn't mean it was safe to emerge. The boy held her there for what felt like several more minutes.

"What is your name?" she whispered after a time.

"Tomas. Now keep quiet."

She did what she was told, watching a fat earthworm burrow into the soil in front of her. Her stomach growled. Tomas cast her an annoyed glance before climbing to the lip of their den to peer out. When he wasn't looking, she tried to grab the worm, but it escaped into its tunnel. She thought of digging for it, but Tomas nudged her arm. "I think they're gone."

They carefully crawled out from under the roots. With a hand guiding her back, Tomas led her through the underbrush, peering around every tree and listening for every twig snap.

"Wait, the brook. We should go back." Zephira tried to pull him in that direction, but he resisted.

"It's too open. Do you want to get spotted again?"

Reluctantly, she shook her head and let herself be led through the woods. They eventually came out onto a deer path.

"You there!" the harpy with spiky hair shouted at them. She spread her tawny wings and sped toward them.

"Shit." Tomas pushed the princess ahead. "Run!"

Zephira pumped her legs as fast as she could, the harpy gaining on them quickly. She felt the urge to dive to the side, but Tomas kept her on the trail with a firm hand.

Just as the woman was seconds from their backs, Tomas dove forward, taking Zephira down with him. Her arms buckled beneath their weight as their pursuer zoomed past. A second later, the woman screamed and cursed.

Zephira lifted her head slowly, working to still her racing heart.

The harpy struggled to escape a net rigged between two branches on either side of the trail. The twine used was so thin, it was nearly invisible.

The captured harpy quickly began cutting the twine with her forearm blades.

Without hesitation, Tomas threw a knife straight into the side of her left breast.

"You blasted little . . ." Her eyes rolled back in her head, and her body went limp in the net.

Tomas stood there, breathing hard, brow furrowed, yet he looked unaffected by what he just did. *The resolve this Fae'ren boy possesses could give any urling a run for their dels.*

The bushes rustled, and Zephira tensed, but it was a naja who stumbled onto the path. "Esteban!"

"There you are. I knew the smell of blood would lead me to you somehow—Gah!" He jumped back at the sight of the dead harpy hanging between two trees.

Tomas took out another knife. "I should cut her down so the others won't find her and know we were here." He approached the harpy, first yanking his other knife from her side, then wiping and sheathing it.

Before he could reach up to cut her down, she jerked awake, taking in short, choking breaths. "You . . ."

Tomas lurched just out of reach as she grabbed for him. The harpy's wound had somehow sealed itself with only the bloodstains left as evidence that it had been inflicted at all.

"Let's go!" Esteban rasped, starting to run.

Tomas stood frozen. His knife-wielding hand shook as he stared, wide-eyed, at the harpy.

Zephira lunged forward, grabbing his arm. "Hurry."

The boy stood rooted to the spot, petrified.

The harpy cut through the last of the net and tumbled to the ground.

She spread her wings, preparing to launch herself toward them.

Zephira tugged on Tomas's arm, still unable to get him to move.

A wicked grin crossed the harpy's face.

An arrow ripped through the foliage and impaled her neck. She collapsed onto her face as a spry man with short brown locks and a beard hopped down from a low branch.

"Gern!" Tomas sputtered.

The man took Tomas by the shoulder, jolting him back into action. "Get moving. Before she gets up again."

Zephira bolted into the trees, the naja and two Fae'ren close behind.

Off the beaten path, the four bushwhacked for several minutes while winged shadows passed overhead. Tomas found a large hollow under an uprooted tree where they could collect their bearings. With his quiver half full and bow over his shoulder, Gern scuttled up another tree to keep watch.

Intermittent cries and grunts echoed off the old oaks as they hid. Perhaps harpies getting caught in traps or Fae'ren fighters getting pummeled into the forest floor. Each noise in the woods was another jolt of adrenaline that sent Zephira grasping for her brooch, and with it, her sanity.

What if it fell off, and she lost herself? As it was, she could feel Nyr's sticky tendrils reaching up the back of her throat. Deity forbid she do something terrible to the boy helping her now . . . or Esteban.

If only she had not tried to sneak through the gate. The harpies would have left Fae'ren without incident and continued the search in Cordos. They would have taken her straight to Credence from there, and no one else would have gotten hurt. Esteban could have stayed behind and gone to Fae'ren afterward to fulfill his promise. Everyone would have been better off.

She decided she had to say something to ease her heavy conscience. "Why are you helping us, young Tomas?"

Keeping his full attention on the woods beyond their hiding spot, he replied, "Jeth risked everything to get you here, and we follow Jeth." She noticed that his answer didn't include 'Because you are the princess and we serve the King.' Then again, why would she expect that answer from someone like him?

"Well, I owe you my life."

Esteban patted the boy on the back. "Mine as well. Thanks for cutting me loose back there."

Tomas gave no reply this time, just watched the woods, like a hunter patiently awaiting his prey even though *they* were the prey.

"If we can find a body of water far from these women, I can request help from the ashray."

Tomas scrunched his nose. "Huh?"

"As the Champion of Elmifel, I can use water to connect to them, but it has to be a substantial amount. If the stream back there is too open, then . . ."

Tomas scratched his head under his cap, thinking hard. "I can probably get you to the Glacier River farther north, but that'll be quite the hike, and I have no traps set up that way. If we travel at night, it will make us harder to see from above, but we risk other dangers lurking in the dark."

"I've grown accustomed to the dark," Zephira agreed. "Esteban, is it correct to say that naja have good night vision?"

"Sure, but"—he shook his head—"we need to find the Deep Wood first."

Tomas opened his mouth to reply, but a passing harpy flying low drew his attention to the woods once again. When the beating of wings faded in the distance, Tomas looked thoughtfully at the two of them. "Fairies won't let you venture there, especially a naja.

"I don't think that will be an issue in our case." Esteban nodded to Zephira's hair. She unraveled the knot holding Serra in place and showed her to Tomas.

The boy pulled off his hat and squeezed it in both hands. "Mother Oak, is that a fairy? I've seen maybe one in my lifetime, but none that small."

"We don't know how long she has," said Esteban. "But I made a promise to Jeth."

Swoosh. Another harpy flew by, causing the three to drop their heads until the woods were silent once again.

"Alright, it's not far, and there's plenty of water there too."

Zephira and Esteban exhaled with relief. Both of their promises were nearly fulfilled.

Tomas crawled halfway out and looked around. "It's clear." He signaled up to Gern with one hand and beckoned Esteban and Zephira with the other. "Follow me."

37
Grateful

Zephira trudged through the forest behind Tomas for what felt like hours. Esteban's heavy footsteps crunched leaves and twigs at her back. Gern darted in and out of underbrush that was so dense each step was agony for Zephira. Twigs and thistles scraped her legs raw, old sticks popped her blisters, sending waves of pain to her very bones. Esteban eventually offered to carry her on his back, which she welcomed wholeheartedly.

At some point during their trek, a wolf bounded up beside Tomas.

The harpies, it seemed, hadn't caught their trail. With the thick umbrella of leaves above them, Zephira could barely see the sky, and so, she thought, the harpies would have an equally hard time spotting them from above.

Close to an hour later, they stopped to drink at a small stream. Zephira traced the *Veil* on her forehead, but no tiny threads appeared with which to scry ashray. She needed more water.

The black dog sat down beside her. Startled, she shot to her feet. She hadn't seen it since she found that first creek and had let herself hope that she'd lost the thing in the woods for good.

"Are you all right, Princesa?"

Before she could reassure Esteban that nothing was the matter, low growls rumbled out of Tomas's wolf. It bared its teeth at Nyr.

"What's wrong, Pup?" Tomas put a hand on its back.

From everyone else's perspective, it appeared as if Pup were growling at Zephira alone, prompting a more immediate response from Tomas. "Pup, stop it, now!"

Nyr growled back at the wolf, baring its own canines, which vastly outmatched Pup's. The wolf stepped back, tail tucked between its legs, crouching low.

Tomas shrugged apologetically. "Not sure what his problem is."

As Pup put his head down, Zephira said, "Quite all right. No harm done."

"The quicker you can wash up, the better. It's probably all that black mud you have on you."

Zephira wrapped her arms around her front and moved away from Tomas a few paces. For the first time since she left the Skour, Zephira felt ashamed of her presentation.

Gern finished filling his waterskin and stuffed the cork back in. "You three can follow the stream. The grove is just a little farther."

"What about you?" Tomas asked.

"I'll gather the others, set up a perimeter, and make sure no harpies sully this place." The Fae'ren bowed his head subtly to the princess and disappeared into the thick underbrush.

"Pup, you too. Find the others." Tomas made a few hand gestures, and the wolf put his nose to the ground and followed Gern into the forest.

Zephira, Tomas, and Esteban picked their way along the stream until the waterway converged with several others, and ahead, she could hear the rush of falling water. A waterfall cascaded over a rocky bluff, feeding a lazy river that branched around a lush, green clearing. At the center of the graceful streams was the largest oak tree Zephira had ever seen, a breathtaking forest all on its own.

"Welcome to the Grove of the Crannabeatha," said Tomas as they climbed down a series of rocks embedded in the earth, acting as a natural staircase.

After having lived in a misty rainforest for so long, she was awestruck by the warm mosses and comforted by the sweet smell of flowers and tree sap. "Is this where you all come to worship?"

Tomas nodded. "Yes, well . . . not so much. Fairies get testy if humans overstay their welcome."

"It's beautiful." Zephira stood before a deep cradle of thick roots, her gaze following them up the length of the massive trunk and getting lost in the endless canopy of leaves.

Tomas stepped up beside her. "Just last year, this entire grove was leveled by Nas'Gavarr's fire magic."

Zephira trembled in recollection of the burning chapel back home. It felt like a lifetime ago—like it had happened to a different girl.

"It was Jeth who stood against him in this very spot and won." Tomas released a small grin from the side of his mouth.

Zephira snapped her head toward him. "Jeth killed Gavarr himself?"

"He'll never say it, but it doesn't matter. The Crannabeatha still grows here because one cursed Fae'ren did what no other has done since the Great Gershlon. He stood up for us."

Zephira's stomach felt as if it were hollowed out by a trowel. The night Gavarr died was the same horrific night the snakkurs pulled her into the Skour. While she lost what was left of her identity, these people celebrated the conservation of theirs.

"Orphans from Fairieshome heard what happened from those evacuating Lanore." Tomas pointed to the cradle of roots before them. "They came and found Jeth lying right here, covered in burns, barely breathing. As if the Overlord hadn't hurt him enough, that harpy Vidya beat him to a bloody pulp. But a Herrani Flesh Mage showed up and healed him. He broke his own spine to repair Jeth's even though many of his own bones were already shattered. Our new protector Daynerel burned his own ear so the Flesh Mage could repair Jeth's. Gerndal took a wallop to the ribs so Jeth's could be put back together, and his woman, Henna, singed her arm to make his burns disappear."

"And you?" Zephira asked.

"Oh, I wasn't there. I didn't give him anything. I've yet to do anything for him."

"I'm sure that's not true."

"I've been alone since . . ." He wiped his nose with the back of his hand to hide a sniffle. "I figured I'd die in the southern woods with only Pup to mourn me. Then I heard about a commune that accepted the cursed. And who do I find to be living there, but Jethril of the Deep Wood himself, training the next generation of Fae'ren fighters. I'm not sure you realize how profound it is to know that we cursed don't have to be that way anymore. We can fight. We can live . . . together." Tomas sniffed again. "I need to know, Your Highness, is Jeth coming back or not?"

Zephira forced herself to meet Tomas's watery gaze. "I do not know."

"Is he in pain? Does he need our help?" His voice cracked.

"I'm sorry, Tomas, truly." Zephira placed a hand on his fur adorned shoulder. "Pray to the Deities—your Mother Oak—and someday perhaps he shall return."

Tomas jerked away from her touch. She took her hand back, hating herself for giving him false hope. The Fae'ren's orphan hero was gone, but she dared not say it out loud.

"I-uh . . . I'll be right back." He quickly turned away and headed toward the bush, wiping his face with the back of his hand.

"Don't go far," she called after him, but he didn't look back.

Esteban gently placed Serra on the giant oak's mossy root. "Do we just leave her here and hope this tree magically revives her?"

Zephira stared down at the tiny forest creature. The power that came off her in the Skour was frightening. She had sacrificed everything to get Jeth out and ensure Zephira stayed behind. Now she had to save the pixie that hoped for her demise. Zephira didn't exactly blame her.

Rapid whispers danced through the leaves. A distinctive splash came from the pond to their left. The water rippled as something much larger than a fish dunked below the surface.

"What was that?" Zephira took slow steps toward the pond, only for Esteban to yelp at the rustling leaves above him.

A head peeked out from the greenery. Its short, matted hair branched from her head like spindly twigs, her brown skin creased like bark. "You're right, Ami. It's definitely a naja."

"And it's about to eat a poor little fae girl," said an identical creature sitting on the branch straight across from the one that first spoke. She squinted down at Zephira. "Wait, never mind, her ears are too long. She's an urling. It's about to eat a poor little *urling* girl."

"Who are you calling poor?" Zephira huffed under her breath.

Esteban put up his scaly palms in his defense. "I don't wish to eat anyone."

The other creature crawled along the branch and sniffed the air. "I smell the blood of harpies. Mother doesn't like harpies." Esteban looked down at his claws, still caked with the blood of the harpies he slashed.

Water splashed again. A soaking wet woman sprang out of the stream, stretching translucent fins that caught the light like a rainbow of colors dancing over an oily surface. "Don't get too close, Thara. Neither urling nor naja belong here."

Esteban stepped aside to reveal Serra lying on the tree root. The water fairy gasped and ran over to her. "Dear me, it's Serra. Ami, Thara, get down here!" The twin fairies floated to the ground, flapping their wood-brown wings as thin as parchment with swirling tree ring designs.

"What is it, Sky?"

Sky lifted Serra to her chest and turned a vicious eye to Esteban. "You did this?"

Esteban shook his head. "No, no. We're allies. She exhausted herself in battle. Jeth told us to bring her here." The naja's eyes drifted to the ground with remorse. "But I fear she may already be dead. She has no pulse."

Sky put her short, pointed ear to Serra's lifeless body. "Mmm, no heartbeat, but there is a morsel of spark left."

"Spark?" Zephira said, remembering that's what Nyr had referred to. "That bright substance you emit . . ."

One of the wood fairies took Serra from Sky and brought her down to the oak's massive roots. "She shrunk in size to conserve it while she was so far from Mother's care."

The other wood fairy continued, "Every time she would have used her spark out there, it would have depleted her life force."

Esteban nodded. "And she used every ounce to save us. To save Jeth."

Sky's large blue eyes darkened. "He is not with you. Does that mean Serra failed?"

"She did not fail." Zephira's reply came out sharper than she intended.

"Then our pixie has done her duty." Sky nodded. "The Crannabeatha will replenish her life force, and she may continue her duty to this forest for millennia to come."

"You are all fairies, but not pixies, is that correct?" Zephira asked.

"I'm a water sprite," said Sky. "Thara and Ami are wood nymphs."

Thara and Ami placed Serra deep between the Crannabeatha's network of roots and scooped the soft soil over her body.

"How long will it take until she's well again?" Esteban asked.

Ami bit her lip. "Hard to say. A month—a year. Depends on how much life force Mother chooses to spare. We must leave it up to her now."

Once they finished burying Serra, the wood nymphs scampered up the Crannabeatha's trunk, and the water sprite made her way back to the stream. "In gratitude for bringing our pixie back to us, you may rest here for a time. But your presence will bring misfortune."

"We shan't stay long," Zephira said as she eyed the misty waterfalls behind the great oak. The sprite dove back into the stream just before Zephira said, "Thank you."

The stories had never painted fairies as trusting creatures, and being in their sacred wood made Zephira understand why. The unrestrained beauty made her want to run far from this place—to save it from the taint of her presence.

Esteban lay down upon a bed of moss to catch the sun's rays at his front. "That's one promise fulfilled. The next is getting you home."

"If this goes as I hope, we will have a league of ashray here within hours." Zephira stepped into the pond opposite of the one Sky had returned to. She didn't waste another moment in tracing the *Veil* to her forehead once again.

Watery vines sprouted from her head, followed by dozens upon dozens of micro threads almost too faint to see.

She coaxed herself toward the indistinct streams. Her mind was muddled and slow, like it was covered in cobwebs, but with enough time and patience, the phantom rivers eventually whisked her away from the forest and to the glacier springs of Elmifel.

She emerged in a shining quartz hallway, wearing the blue and white robes of the ashray. *"Help! It is Elmifel's Champion requesting your aid. Point your warping gate toward Fae'ren Province. Find me in the Deep Wood. It's urgent."*

In moments, thoughts not belonging to her formed in her mind. *"Princess, you're alive—it has been over a year since we were able to scry you. We feared you had perished by Gavarr's hand."*

"I was lost in a world separate from our own, but I've returned. Please hurry; Yasharra's Champion is near. It is not safe to travel on our own."

Zephira felt a pull in the ashray's gut. Every ashray in the Holy City stopped what they were doing, all with the same aversion. *"Something is wrong. You are not alone . . . a foreign presence resides within you."*

"I know, but I have the blessing of Saint Orester. All will be fine if you—"

"An urling saint's blessing cannot help you. This force is too dangerous. We're grievously sorry, but as Elmifel's guardians on this plane, we cannot allow it to spread any further. You should return from whence you came."

"You'd have me return to the Skour?"

"Leave this world as soon as you can. Keep it away. We pray your suffering will

end soon, Princess."

"*No-No, you can't do this!*"

"*Never scry again!*"

As if slapped in the face by an ocean wave, the ashray cast her back into her own reality. Her chest burned in anguish—she was drowning. It wasn't until Esteban fished her out of the pond and dragged her back to dry land that she realized she had fallen under.

She choked up water onto her soiled shirt and took in ragged gasps. "They can't do this. I'm their Champion!"

"Princesa." Esteban patted her on the back, coaxing the rest of the water from her lungs. "What happened?"

"The ashray . . ." She coughed into her sleeve. "They aren't coming."

"Then we must find a way back to the gate and go to them."

"No." Zephira shook her head. "They will not let us through. It's over. There is nowhere left to go."

"It is far from over." The naja looked at her with his sympathetic reptilian eyes. "We hide out here for a while. I'm sure the Fae'ren are sending word to your father as we speak. He'll come with the whole cavalry."

"That will take weeks. We don't have weeks." Zephira pushed herself up, wrapping her arms around her stomach, and paced.

"Then we do what Tomas suggested. Travel at night, hide during the day, and eventually, we'll find a place where you can enlist some soldiers."

"You don't understand." Zephira's empty stomach twisted. "The ashray won't help because of Nyr. I'm a danger to Elmifel and, therefore, Del'Cabria. Serra knew it too. I should never have left the Skour."

Esteban stood up, looming several feet above Zephira and halting her pacing. "You made a promise. Where I come from, we'd sooner die than go back on one. Jeth risked everything to get you out of that place, and you will do the same and go home."

"I'm sorry, Esteban, but there will be no home for any of us if I don't heed the ashray's warning. They know better than us."

"Where will you go, uh?" Esteban asked heatedly. "The pathway to Cordos is severed. There's no going back."

She mirrored the words Jeth had spoken to her before. "'Sometimes that's the only direction left to go.'"

"The ashray don't know everything. They can't see you as you are now. You are no danger to anyone, least of all the entire kingdom."

"You saw it on Cordos, the beast that hid warp stone in a corpse, the thing that forced you into the Skour." Zephira gulped. "You saw what it did to Serra. Nyr is here." She pointed to her chest. "I feel it every second. If I were to lose control for even an instant in front of my own people, they'd stick me with their swords before ever realizing they could bring me back." She cast her eyes down, but Esteban lifted her chin to him again.

"Then don't let that happen."

She squeezed her brooch at her chest. "This is all that stands between Nyr and the world. How do you expect me to—"

Esteban cut her off. "You don't think I know what it's like to have an insatiable beast inside, constantly fighting to be unleashed?"

"But you're free of Mage interference. Your mind is yours alone."

"The mind and body are not as separate as you think." He tapped his smooth, green head with the tip of his claw. "My mind may be my own, but the monstrous urges are ever-present. Unlike you, I remember all of it, everything I did in the name of those twisted Mages. I don't deserve a shred of mercy for the barbarism these claws have committed. And yet, instead of being put down by those I viciously attacked, they gave me a second chance. A chance to rediscover the man I once was . . . the man I would have become."

Zephira hugged herself tighter. "But surely your struggle has lessened since the Mages' deaths."

He shook his head with a dark chuckle. "Not at all. I struggle even harder. And for that, I am truly grateful."

"Grateful?"

"So many people succumb to the monsters inside them with hardly a fight." Esteban turned over a flat rock. "You should be wary when the struggle lessens. It means you've already lost." He grinned at the grubs scuttling to escape the light. "Ah, dinner!"

He took a couple earthworms and dropped them down his gullet. He then nabbed a fat beetle between his claws, about to toss it in his mouth when he caught Zephira's hungry gaze. "Sorry, but the beast in me must eat. I can do it somewhere else if you prefer."

Her stomach roaring, Zephira snatched the beetle from his hand and threw it into her mouth.

Esteban's eye-slits widened considerably.

She swallowed, then shrugged. "Princesses must eat as well."

Esteban let out a raucous guffaw then went back to turning over rocks. "Then we feast."

Zephira didn't object.

"How long have you served Jeth?" she asked while catching an earthworm before it could burrow into the soft earth. *Now, I've got you.*

"Served? Oh no." Esteban chuckled. "I've only known him for a few weeks. He's just someone who needed my help."

"Oh. The way you speak of him makes it seem as if you'd known each other much longer than that. Your devotion is quite admirable." She slurped the worm through her lips. It tasted so much better than anything she'd found in the Skour.

Esteban crunched another beetle. "Perhaps the same foolhardiness that led me to my naja fate may also be how I live with it now."

"How so?"

"If I focus on a task, help where I'm needed. I can overcome this ravenous affliction for a time. You can too. What happened to you was beyond your control. Focus on what you can control. That's all any of us can do."

Zephira felt the pull of a smile on her face. "Yes. Focus on a task." Her faint grin quickly deteriorated. "Yet, I can't think of what to do in my current state. It's been a long time since I've had control of anything . . . if I ever did." *Only those pesky human emotions,* she thought, her bitterness rising.

"If you weren't in your current state," Esteban said between chews, "what would you do?"

After swallowing another juicy earthworm, Zephira replied, "Well, that's easy. I'd return home. Hug my father. Spend more time with my mother. Write to my brother in Thessalin."

The memories of Rubin's funny face warmed her heart. She never thought she could miss the little brat more than she did right then.

"Alright, but what will be your first task?" Esteban pressed.

"I suppose, informing the Kingdom of the harpy threat . . . and, of course, Jeth's sacrifice."

"You mean, Jeth *isn't* coming back?"

She looked up to see Tomas perched on a raised root, eyes red raw from crying.

Both Zephira and Esteban dropped the bugs and stood up as the young Fae'ren hopped down. "No, that's not—"

"He's dead, isn't he?" Tomas raised his voice. "Why did you tell us he was alive?"

Before Zephira could begin to formulate a response to the distressed adolescent, a forceful wind slammed against them. Birds fluttered in a mad rush to escape. They drew everyone's eyes up to much larger winged creatures swirling above the trees.

Vidya landed first, flattening the flower beds. Phrea and Daphne floated down soon afterward.

"There you are. I had a gut feeling you'd be here." The Anassa scowled, feathers bristling as she looked about the grove. "There's a false belief in these parts that this place is sacred and therefore safe . . . yet it's anything but."

The princess tautened her spine and steeled her jaw. "Your plan to take me hostage is useless."

Vidya continued forward. "And why is that?"

The girl fiddled with a cameo brooch pinned to her baggy, stained shirt. "I have no value to the Kingdom, and thus my death would serve it better. The only way I'm going to Credence with you is as a corpse."

"Princesa, don't say that," her naja bodyguard protested.

Malantha and a few other harpies landed in the grove, covering all escape paths.

The young Fae'ren named Tom stood frozen a few feet away, eyes glued to Vidya. She maintained her gaze on Zephira but didn't let the boy out of her periphery.

"It is my duty as Anassa to protect the island that Yasharra birthed for us. You are key in fulfilling that, dead or alive. However, it is not the harpy way to harm women for any reason."

A steady growl rumbled in the naja's throat as he stepped forward. "Then find some other way to protect your island and leave her be."

Phrea gripped her tabar in both hands. "One more step, and I'll separate your neck from your puny lizard brain."

Daphne cocked a pistol and pointed it squarely at Esteban.

The naja stilled but didn't give up ground.

Vidya smirked.

With a powerful gust of wind, Vidya launched herself toward the terrified Fae'ren and snatched his arm. He attempted to grab a knife from one of his many sheaths, but she tore his scabbard off his torso before restraining him in a headlock. She placed the barrel of her pistol to his temple.

He choked and kicked, but his struggle was futile against the equivalent strength of three grown warriors. She pushed down her rising guilt. He looked no older than fourteen, barely a man, but certainly not an innocent child. He was likely planning to pepper Vidya with knives at the first opportunity. Like any other male, he defied the Harpy and would receive her punishment. Better some insignificant tree-hugger gets hurt than the Princess of Del'Cabria.

"Let him go!" the naja roared. He barreled for Vidya.

A deafening boom from Daphne's pistol sent the reptile flailing to the ground. He grasped his bleeding arm and rolled about in the grass.

"Stop this," Zephira cried.

"I'll gladly take a corpse back to Credence, preferably not yours. Choose wisely."

The Fae'ren shook his head, his frantic breathing moistening Vidya's arm. She only tightened her grip and pressed the barrel more firmly to his temple.

Zephira stood there, squeezing her brooch and staring down at the Fae'ren boy's feet. Stiff and unresponsive.

"So be it." Vidya cocked her pistol.

The black dog stood next to Tomas as he struggled in Vidya's grip. It pawed at his pant leg and cast pleading looks to Zephira. Nyr wanted in. The Primitive Force pulsated in her temples, deafening.

The click of Vidya's pistol snapped something in Zephira's mind.

"No!" Her ears rang from the vociferousness of her own voice.

The green trees around her and the blue sky above melded together in shades of red. The next thing she knew, she was right behind Vidya, wrenching the gun from her hand.

The Anassa spun around, and Tomas, now free, scrambled out of harm's way.

Vidya yanked the gun back out of Zephira's grasp and turned it on her.

The gun flashed. A deafening boom bounced off the trees with a crack.

The red in Zephira's vision turned black.

Then nothing.

Zephira crouched in front of the pond as if she hadn't taken a single step toward Vidya in the first place.

A woman groaned in agony a few feet away.

"Daph!" Phrea ran to the thin harpy commander lying on her back, a gaping hole scorched through her chest, spurting blood.

Vidya looked down at her smoking barrel, mouth agape. She looked back to Zephira, just as confused.

Zephira touched her stomach and turned over her shaking hands in disbelief. There wasn't a speck of fresh blood or black powder to be seen. The gun had been pointed right at her. It should have torn through her, not Daphne behind her. And yet here she stood, unscathed.

Vidya looked down at Daphne again then angrily pointed her second pistol at Zephira. "You . . . what did you do?"

"I-I didn't . . ." stammered Zephira. She backed up against the Crannabeatha's roots, cowering before the enraged harpy queen. "I don't know how." It couldn't have been Nyr, she was still wearing the brooch, and she experienced it all firsthand, unlike the times Nyr had taken control before, and yet she felt Nyr's power coursing through her in that moment.

"Fine." Vidya's voice hardened. "You want to go to Credence as a corpse? Let's do it your way." She stalked towards Zephira, ready to fire her second pistol.

"Put down your weapon!" a male voice bellowed. A drove of Fae'ren fighters emerged from the thick underbrush, arrows nocked, swords and axes drawn.

Vidya stayed her trigger finger. "I told you this is not your concern. If you insist on getting in our way, we will take it as a declaration of war."

"If that's the way you want it." Dayne raised his throwing axe behind his head. "Men, attack!" Before the full order left his lips, his axe left his grip. It spiraled through the air, straight for Vidya's head.

She fired her last round at it, blowing apart the wooden handle and throwing it off its trajectory, but the axe blade still struck her. She grabbed the left side of her face and staggered back. When she removed her hand, a river of blood fell from her left brow, dripping over her intact eye.

"Harplite! Leave no man standing!" she roared.

A mass of feathers and steel filled the forest grove from above. Arrows whisked through the air as harpies deflected them with their forearm blades. Men attempting to bury their axes into arms and torsos were thwarted by armored corsets and well-timed parries. The Fae'ren fighters skirted follow-up blows just as competently.

Zephira tried to stand, but her legs refused to carry her. They dropped her down to Esteban's side instead. Blood surged from his shoulder, making his green scales glisten orange. "Find a way home . . . without me," the naja rasped.

Tomas crawled over, ripping a piece of his fur sleeve off and quickly binding the naja's wound.

"Don't worry about me, boy. Just get the princesa to safety."

Tomas met Zephira's eyes, his brow cinching. He held out his bloodied hand and nodded back toward the path from which they arrived.

She looked to the battle. At least three harpies lay wounded or dead. Men screamed, tossed into the air and away, only to charge right back into the fray, holding their arms or limping.

"Quickly," Tomas urged. "Let me hide you."

Accepting his help would mean leaving his people at the mercy of harpies about to rise from the dead and overwhelm them. The harpies would then track her down and take her to Credence anyhow. Even if she managed to escape, she couldn't forget the ashray's warning.

She couldn't go home, and she could never return to the Skour.

There was simply nowhere left to go.

A vicious scream rang out. Hurricane winds blasted leaves off trees and violently pinned fighters to the ground. Dirt and grass swirled into a towering vortex that surrounded the small harpy contingent.

Pup raced to Tomas's side, biting his coat sleeve and dragging him towards the Crannabeatha, the only thing large enough to protect them from the gale. Zephira followed, pulling Esteban, and they took cover within the Crannabeatha's cradle of roots. She opened one eye a mere slit, trying to determine the source of the madness.

The vortex grew, spreading across the grove. The Anassa was at the center of it all. Her contingent clustered tightly around her, adding their power to the maelstrom.

Fae'ren held onto whatever they could as the winds relentlessly assaulted them. Bits of grass and twigs shredded their skin with shallow cuts. Branches split, and men flew through the air and smacked against tree trunks.

A shadowy canine trotted toward Zephira, passing unaffected through the cyclone. Its red eyes shone through the chaos, vibrant and hungry.

"What's happening? Why won't it stop?" Tomas cried out in terror, burying his face in Pup's fur.

Zephira stared at the enraged mistress of winds while clutching her brooch so hard blood trickled down to her elbow. *It's never going to stop. Not until she gets what she wants.*

The dog reached the edge of their hiding place and grinned.

She knew the choice she had to make. If she were as tainted as the ashray claimed, she might as well unleash it all. The harpies would soon slaughter every man here. At least this way, they would take some damage too.

Congratulations, Nyr. You finally get your way.

Zephira leaned against Esteban, dug her heels into the earth, and slowly stood up. Fighting with all her strength against the pelting winds, she ripped her brooch from her shirt and let it fall to the forest floor with hardly a sound.

Her vision burned crimson.

38
One Little Girl

Vidya had had it with this place.

She hated this forest.

She was the pestilence that devoured the living and that *life* flourished in this grove.

So wrapped up in her tempest of destruction, she forgot about the princess. She forgot about everything and everyone around her, even Daphne, still bleeding to death on the grass, shielded by Phrea's great black wings. She could barely make out whether any Fae'ren were left alive. She didn't care. They should not have gotten in her way.

A twinge in her gut brought Jeth to mind. Despite everything, she could never forget how they fought here side by side to take down Nas'Gavarr. She could not have done it without him.

As the winds howled, she wondered what happened to the Crannabeatha's Champion. The fastest and toughest man Vidya had ever known, thwarted by a bubbling tar pit? Nonsense. He was somewhere, waiting to strike. Biding his time before he flew out of the bushes and launched a well-aimed arrow to her heart, taking her final life.

She almost wished he would.

What are you waiting for, Jeth? I'm ripping your people to shreds. Show yourself!

The shadow harpy darkened the sky, rattling off with a sick delight, *"Punish them. Punish them all!"*

She didn't understand why the shadow wished for this. Perhaps it wasn't from the shadow at all but Vidya's own heart. She lessened her control of the winds a touch, allowing her to see the upturned earth and broken trees. Men were out cold on the ground; most were nowhere to be seen. Grass and leaves continued to spiral across her vision.

She turned to the great oak. The bleeding naja lay huddled with the wolf boy. The princess, however, was gone.

Vidya spun back around, ready to order her harpies to search once again, but someone—or something—stood right in front of her.

Her bones nearly jumped out of her skin, and her control of the winds faltered.

A strange shape of a girl, who eerily resembled the princess, stood hunched, unaffected by the storm winds. Black veins branched across her porcelain white skin. The air around her fell into a vacuum of shadow, consuming the forest light. A ferocious red shone out of her eyes.

"Yasharra's might," Vidya gasped.

With uncanny speed, the shadowy princess kicked Vidya in the armored chest with both feet, knocking her down hard on her backside.

The winds ceased.

Malantha lunged to restrain the girl, only for her to vanish in a swirl of dark mist.

Vidya felt a jolt run up her spine.

"Where did she go?" Malantha growled.

Phrea slowly rose from where Daphne lay, breathing in short, nervous bursts. A dark figure suddenly appeared at her unsuspecting back.

For a split second, Vidya thought it was the shadow harpy about to rub it in that she lost the princess yet again, until Daphne, her wound fully sealed, sat up and pointed. "Behind you, Phrea!"

The demonic urling creature snatched the tabar from Phrea's back.

Phrea spun around and blocked the next blow with her arm blades. She grabbed for the girl's throat on the upswing, but the dark princess disintegrated again, letting the axe drop to the ground.

"Hey!" Phrea picked up the axe and rubbed her fingers together. "It's wet . . . ?"

The thing was now crouched on a low branch of the Crannabeatha, eyes burning.

"Retrieve her!" Vidya ascended with a flap of her wings and hovered in place while harpies formed a ring of protection around her.

The frenzied woman leaped from the branch, grabbed hold of a harpy's ankles, and yanked her down. She dissipated before she hit the ground.

Harpy screams sounded behind Vidya. The thing had reappeared, ruthlessly attacking the harpies on the ground, snatching their knives from their scabbards, slicing through them, and leaving nothing more than dark mist in her wake.

She appeared out of every conceivable place—on the ground, in the trees, the brush. No one could anticipate which branch, root, or rock the shadow princess would appear on before leaping into the storm of panicked, fluttering wings. It was all her harpies could do to defend themselves against the onslaught, but none could land a single blow upon her, just like the round that should have gone through her and not Daphne. *It's a trick of the light, a spell!* There was no other explanation.

A few still-conscious Fae'ren clustered together, watching in horror as they slowly slinked back into the underbrush.

Vidya pushed her way through the chaos, determined to end the girl's rampage once and for all, but every time she caught sight of her, she disappeared in a cloud of black mist, and the harpy nearest to her fell to the ground, blood spurting from multiple wounds. *It's all right, they'll come back shortly,* she kept reminding herself.

She landed, and a dark figure materialized in her periphery. Vidya turned. The princess stood there, knife in hand. Wet, blonde ropes hung in front of her face, and her tiny chin was tucked into her chest as her bulging red eyes burned into Vidya's own.

Another shadow dashed past and sliced through a harpy's gut. Another one leaped off the Crannabeatha's trunk and kicked down Phrea from the air. *Multiples . . . illusions.*

She felt rooted to the earth, her heart hammering in the chest as she stared into the princess's red eyes. All Vidya could do was whisper, "What are you?"

The creature standing in front of her didn't move.

Malantha shouted, "Anassa, look out!" In another act of heroism, the lieutenant swooped between Vidya and the red-eyed princess. She took the princess by the arm and lifted her off her feet.

The nimble urling kicked off a tree trunk and flipped onto Malantha's back while she was in the air. She twisted Malantha's arm behind her so hard, Vidya could hear it pop from where she stood.

As Malantha spiraled downward, the princess forced her arm blade to the back of her neck. The harpy wailed, and she and her rider careened for the Crannabeatha. Malantha's face impacted the great trunk and her own forearm blade sliced through her neck from behind.

The blade scraped the bark, splintering off chunks. Harpies watched impotently as Malantha's severed head tumbled down the length of the mighty oak, bounced off the roots at its base, and came to a rolling stop on the moss.

The princess slid off Malantha's back and landed in an animalistic crouch on one of the oak's giant roots. The headless corpse fell next to her with a dull thud a second later.

"Mal!" screeched Phrea. The rest of the harpies froze in terror.

Tremors ran through Vidya in time with the final spurts of arterial blood from the lieutenant's neck. Flashes of the bathtub from her past. The hypnotic *drip, drip, drip* from the decanter, the clump of flesh on the lavatory tile, all assaulted her mind. She could hardly process the blood-splattered urling girl running her pale fingers up Malantha's recently lacerated back.

"What is she doing?" Daphne croaked in horror.

"Anassa, what do we do?" a harpy next to her cried.

She didn't reply, only stared in shock.

Malantha's body twitched at the princess's touch, then one wing jerked up toward the sky, followed by the other.

Harpies gaped, backing away as the headless corpse rose on all fours. Nobody moved, not even the petrified Fae'ren.

The savage princess hopped onto the back of the reanimated corpse, stuck her fingers through her neck stump, and pulled upward. Malantha's wings pumped furiously, gathering the wind beneath her and lifting both her and the princess into the air. Riding Malantha's body like a headless, winged steed, she clumsily veered west and disappeared over the treetops.

"Lieutenant!" harpies screamed.

"Should we go after her?"

"What just happened?"

Vidya's gelatinous limbs carried her toward the Crannabeatha before collapsing at its base. She lifted Malantha's shaven head from the moss. Her cheeks were caved in, nose flattened from the impact. The flesh was already cold against Vidya's numb fingertips. *All three lives, gone in a flap of a wing.*

"Anassa?" Far away voices called out to her. "Anassa!" They grew louder until they clanged in her ears.

"Vidi!"

She snapped her head around, dropping the one she held with a muted splat.

Vidya pulled herself up onto shaking legs. It was then she saw the full extent of the damage the princess had done. More than half her team lay motionless; others nursed open gashes, writhing in pain. *One little girl did all of this.*

"Not a little girl," said the shadow harpy perched on a branch, wings casting a shadow only perceptible to Vidya over the blood-splattered roots where Malantha's body had been.

"The Champion of Elmifel," Vidya whispered in response.

"Not Elmifel's Champion. It's something else . . . something that shouldn't be here."

"Harplite," Vidya breathed. "Need more."

"Vidi," Phrea's voice was shrill. "Snap out of it and give us some damn orders!"

"Uh . . ." Vidya wiped off the blood still streaming down her forehead. "Daphne, take the dead and injured back to Credence. We need to heal and regroup."

"Yes, Anassa." Daphne quickly enlisted a few healthy harpies to help with her task.

"And what about the rest of us?" asked Phrea.

Vidya didn't reply, only looked at the few frightened Fae'ren left huddled in the bushes, the trembling boy, and the wounded naja, all staring at them, exhausted.

She then spotted the naja holding the princess's brooch in his claws. "You." She pointed to the reptile. "You attempted to take her off Cordos. What *is* she?"

The naja breathlessly replied, "I am as ignorant as you are."

"Bullshit!" Phrea growled, stomping toward him with her poleaxe in hand. "This is your sorceress's doing! Where's the real princess?"

A high-pitched squeal filled the grove, interrupting Phrea and making them all look up. A fairy with her hands clasped over her mouth hovered in front of the blood trailing down the giant oak's trunk.

An identical fairy shot out from the leaves, shouting as she engulfed Phrea in a net of golden sparks.

Phrea fell to the forest floor, cursing in pain. Vidya quickly went to her, knowing full well how much those sparks could sting.

The fairy landed in front of the naja and the boy, scowling. "You defile this sacred grove with Yasharra's violence," she hissed. "Begone, pestilence!"

Two blue fairies emerged from the streams, and several green ones flew out from behind the wind-blown ferns.

"Did you not see what that creature did to your Mother Oak? She is violence incarnate!" Vidya seethed.

"You lasses best heed the fairies' warning and get gone," Dayne warned, streaks of blood caked to his chiseled brow.

Vidya clenched her fists, annoyed by the arrogance of these forest dwellers, outraged by their idiocy, so blinded by their devotion to Jeth they would risk it all to protect a demonic princess whose father didn't give two royal shits about them in the first place.

"You don't know what you're protecting," Vidya said. "She may look like the Princess of Del'Cabria, but she is something from the dark depths. From what you just saw, do you really believe she told the truth about Jeth being alive? The reason he is not here with her is because she killed him."

"You best leave her to us then," said Dayne.

The fairies began to close in as others appeared seemingly out of thin air.

Vidya remembered how it was fairies that drained the life force from Nas'Gavarr using the forest itself. They were not to be trifled with.

The shadow harpy harrumphed and sprang into the air, the sky absorbing her seconds later.

Vidya looked at all the tense faces around the grove. It was over. She failed.

"You have made a grave mistake," Vidya warned.

"We'll see," Dayne replied.

"We're not going to let that *thing* get away with Mal's body, are we?" Phrea protested.

"Mark my words. She will pay dearly for this." Vidya returned with ferocity. "But I will not lose one more harpy to do it."

"We can't leave her here to rot—"

"We will find her body and deliver her through the gate," offered Dayne. "And you will leave the princess be and never darken Fae'ren skies again."

Vidya wiped the steady trickle of blood off her forehead and swallowed hard. "Fine. She's your responsibility. But if she so much as sets one foot outside this province, she's ours. Any pigeon flying these skies will be intercepted. If the King receives one clue that his daughter is here, then my Harplite will rain down upon this very grove and finish what Nas'Gavarr started." She wrapped her fingers around the Bloodstone Dagger at her hip. "You will have war."

Neither the Fae'ren leader nor the increasing number of fairies surrounding them gave an answer.

Vidya didn't wish to test them further and decided to leave it at that.

She and what remained of her flock launched themselves into the sky in a swirl of wind.

A cold metallic sensation stung Zephira's chest. Treetops slowly came into focus above her as red drained from her vision. The dark sickness sank down deep inside her, where it formed a tight ball behind her sternum. She took deep, ragged breaths until the forest around her steadied and her heart slowed.

The aching of her limbs alerted her to the twin wood nymphs pinning her down and pressing her precious heirloom to her chest. She sucked in air, ready to scream, but one of the fairies clasped her small hand over her mouth.

"No need to fret, wee urling girl, you're safe now."

Zephira's wits returned to her like a crimson fog lifting from her mind. She recalled the two nymphs' names were Thara and Ami. She nodded, and they soon released her, allowing her to exhale in place of the shriek she had waiting.

"What happened?" she croaked, refastening her broach to her shirt with quivering fingers. Her blood-soaked hands smeared across the sardonyx shell. Her shirt stuck to her, soiled deep red over the streaks of black tar.

"Your lizard companion told us that thing would bring you back," Thara pointed to her brooch.

"Esteban. Is-is he still alive?"

Ami shrugged. "Last we saw."

"Why isn't he here?"

"Wouldn't have mattered even if he were at peak physical strength," answered Thara. "Only someone with wings could have reached you."

"Wings?" Blood dripped onto the fallen log next to Zephira. Her gaze followed the droplets upward to a twine net tied between branches and a harpy suspended within. Her heart froze. The harpy had no head. Warm bile rose up into her throat, forcing her to cover her mouth with both hands lest she spew her meager insect dinner over her lap.

After swallowing down her nausea, Zephira stammered, "What . . . ? Who? Did you do that?"

The wood nymphs followed her gaze up to the headless corpse then shook their heads immediately. "Nope, that was all you," said Ami.

Zephira began to hyperventilate, but Thara put out her arms to steady her. "Don't worry about it now. The harpies have gone, and the others will soon find us."

As Zephira struggled to calm herself amongst flashes of blood and feathers in her mind, the black dog jumped up onto the log, panting as if it had just come back from a vigorous run. *What in the Deities' lack of name did I let you do?*

The fairies stayed with Zephira for several minutes until a wolf came up behind her. She was startled for a moment before recognizing it was Pup. He sniffed her, then skittered just out of her reach, eyeing her and the black dog warily.

Before too long, Tomas emerged from the underbrush, followed by several blood-drenched Fae'ren fighters. Each of them stared Zephira down as if she were a dangerous animal separated from the pack.

"Thank you, fairies," said the tall man with the blond locks. "We will take it from here."

Thara or Ami, she couldn't tell who, nodded and turned to Zephira. "Thank you for bringing Serra back, but we ask that you and your naja never return to these woods."

Zephira nodded solemnly. "We understand."

She looked around for the naja in question, praying he was near. She wanted to run to his aid until she noticed the several Fae'ren eyes fixated upon her, freezing her in place.

The tall man approached, casting his long shadow over her. He secured his axes at his hip, took to one knee, and bowed his head. "Your Highness. I am Daynerel, Protector of Lanore. Allow us to take you back there, where you will be safe."

Zephira blinked. After what he had undoubtedly witnessed, in conjunction with her ghastly appearance, she couldn't believe they still treated her as royalty, especially a people she wouldn't expect to bow in the first place.

"A-and my companion as well?"

He nodded, his expression warming. "Of course. We'll take you both to the healer."

39
Of Little Faith

A few hours after the forty-nine harpies returned to Credence, Malantha's body was brought through the warping gate and laid to rest, joining her head in the mausoleum beneath the Citadel. Funeral arrangements would soon be underway. In the meantime, Vidya and Phrea met Daphne in the laboratory to lick their wounds.

"Welcome to the second lives club, Daph," Phrea grumbled as she collapsed onto the sofa.

Daphne sighed and shrugged. "Too bad I didn't get a chance to observe my gunshot wound before it healed."

"Of course, *you'd* worry about something like that, not—I don't know—the thing that cut Mal's head off and flew away on her reanimated corpse?"

"Oh, I do. I wager there is a connection between the princess's warrior state and Cordos." Daphne lifted two vials of thick black liquid from her satchel. "These samples from the henge may shed light on what we're dealing with."

"Good luck with that," Phrea groaned. "My coppers are still on that Ingle witch having something to do with this."

"Phrea, stop obsessing over that damn sorceress. It wasn't her." Vidya pulled out a chair from the table littered with Daphne's chemistry paraphernalia and sat down.

"How do you know? The bodyguard was one of her naja."

"Because she wouldn't harm Jeth. She burned you alive to protect him, remember? Daphne's right. It's something on that island."

"Who's obsessed now?" Phrea scoffed. "Who cares about that idiot man?"

Vidya banged her fist on the table, shaking the test tubes so violently, Daphne threw her arms out to steady them before they fell off the edge. "That *idiot man* has never lost a single life to Nas'Gavarr, where I've lost two. He's been stabbed, burned, broken by my hand, and still, he comes back stronger and faster. You can't sneak up on him, you can't catch him, you'd be hard-pressed to best him in a fight even with the strength of three men. That thing we saw back there . . . how it moved, how it slaughtered us in mere moments." Vidya shook her head. "It is the only thing I can see that could end a man like that."

"So, you're saying there's no hope in avenging Malantha?" Phrea asked bitterly.

Vidya put her hand to her throbbing forehead then winced as she accidentally touched the still seeping wound at her brow.

Daphne pulled a needle and alcohol from her satchel and went to tend to it. "Of course, we will avenge her," Vidya said in a more controlled tone. "But we need to learn more and prepare for the inevitable Del'Cabrian backlash."

"Not if those filthy Fae'ren keep the princess hidden like we warned them."

"They can't hold her, even if they wanted to. We can send every spy to watch every road and circumvent every pigeon. Sooner or later, she will get home, and then Yasharra, help us."

Silence enveloped the laboratory for several agonizing minutes until the door swung open, startling them as it banged against the wall. Cosima traipsed into the room, wagging a letter in the air. "Message from your doting husband, Anassa."

With a scowl, Vidya tore the letter open. In a hand she didn't recognize, it stated simply: *'The Emperador has fallen ill. Your presence is required as soon as possible.'* Vidya didn't need any more details. She knew the nature of this sudden illness because she had caused it.

Her gut twisted in panic. The first part of her plan was in motion, but she failed to retrieve the one crucial element needed to see it through. It was too late to backtrack. She had to keep Rangardia on their side a little longer and pray that, in the meantime, the wrath of Del'Cabria could be avoided.

She turned to her friend, resting Ash's poleaxe on her lap and staring into space. "Phrea, how many volunteers are waiting for their wings?"

"Last I checked, about two hundred."

Vidya gulped, recalling how quickly one urling girl tore through fifty of her Primaries. "That's half of what we'll need."

As if reading Vidya's mind, Phrea responded, "That royal bitch only managed to permanently kill one of us, and it's not likely the King would allow his daughter to fight anyway. We can still hold off an attack with our male army and the three hundred harpies we have now."

"Two hundred and ninety-nine," Daphne corrected as if reciting off numbers in a mathematics class.

Vidya glared at the medic before the needle poked through her swollen skin. "Provided the Rangardian Armada comes to our aid when the Royal Navy retaliates," she said.

"And why wouldn't they come to our aid?" Cosima asked.

Vidya shoved the notice into her satchel. "I'll head to Rangardia first thing tomorrow. As soon as I get back, we will perform a ritual. Phrea, prepare the sacrifices while I'm away and send the Tertiaries to recruit more women. I want one thousand. Let them know that it is every able-bodied woman's duty to protect Credence from the mainlanders who will stop at nothing to enslave us."

Phrea nodded indolently, stood up with a groan, and left the laboratory without a word.

Cosima stared after Phrea, worry lining the corners of her mouth. "Are you going to tell me what happened out there?"

"I'll fill you in later. I need you to have every last ship guarding our shores for the coming weeks."

The supreme commander's already thin lips disappeared in her grim expression. "Alright . . . ?"

"It's just a precaution. Also, double security at the squab estates."

"Right away, Anassa." Cosima turned and walked out of the laboratory.

"We still have the plague. And the cure," said Daphne once the two of them were alone. "Just give the order, and those pointy-eared bastards will fall dead before they reach Crede shores."

Vidya bit her lip as Daphne pulled the stitches closed and tied them off. "Hold on for now. As long as we can count on Rangardia, we should have no need of it."

Before sundown, Zephira and her Fae'ren guides reached a small, barricaded commune hidden within a snug clearing. Zephira rode next to Esteban, slumped over the back of a horse while its Fae'ren master walked in front. Two gatekeepers rolled the heavy log doors open and closed them behind the riders.

The modest village was swarming with people. The most noticeable among them were dark-skinned women wearing white robes. A scrawny boy with messy hair tugged on one of their sleeves and silently pointed at the blood-splattered procession. The hefty woman stared at her in awed silence.

As they continued past, the loud ring of a smith's hammer on an anvil resounded in Zephira's ear. Iron cooking pots sizzled somewhere beyond, and hens cawed, darting underfoot. She had always thought the Fae'ren people lived quietly up in tree houses; she wasn't expecting all the bangs, clangs, and chatter.

"It's so crowded," she muttered.

Daynerel, walking just in front of her pony, replied. "Most people here migrated from other communes, ones that fell to the plague recently. We remain uninfected . . . for now."

"Elmifel's grace, the plague still exists?"

Gern grunted from beside her. "You've been away a while, Princess."

Each person they passed stopped to stare at the wide-eyed urling wretch and the wounded naja. Children running up to greet the fighters halted their frolicking steps and backed away cautiously. Zephira couldn't imagine what they were all thinking, what they had been told—if they knew she was their princess or thought she was a demon from the woods.

The people moved aside as the party continued to a quaint log cabin nestled between two sprawling oaks. A woman wearing a belt of fur pouches around her waist and a green kerchief over her thick fairy locks came out to meet them.

One look at Zephira, descending from her mount, and the woman's cheeks blanched. "Where did *she* come from?"

"She's the Princess of Del'Cabria," replied Daynerel in a hushed voice.

"Oh . . ." She dipped her head, eyeing Zephira up and down.

Daynerel turned to Zephira and Esteban. "This is Henna, one of our healers. Hen, this naja is like the others who follow Jenn. He's been shot by a pistol."

"Send him to Leena around back."

"Thank you kindly." Esteban rasped. "See you soon, Princesa." Zephira nodded to Esteban as Gern led the horse out of sight.

"Who else needs tending?" Henna continued. "You boys look like you've been walloped half to death."

"We can mend our own for now."

"Where's Jeth?" Henna asked, craning her neck to look around Zephira's pony. Zephira averted her gaze, swallowing her guilt. *This must be the Henna Tomas mentioned; Jeth's woman.*

"Listen . . ." Daynerel gently took Henna by the arm and led her inside the cabin. Low utterances soon followed, too quiet for Zephira to hear.

"He can't be gone!" Henna suddenly screeched.

The pain in her voice was a dagger to Zephira's gut. She wrapped her arms around herself and leaned against the side of the cabin to keep from collapsing.

"Are you not up for taking care of her?" came Daynerel's more subdued voice.

There was a long pause.

"I-I can still do my duty."

"Let me know if you need anything, alright?" Daynerel's heavy footsteps neared the door.

"Wait." The footsteps stopped. "Fresh water, please. For a bath."

"Aye." He lumbered back outside to start the task.

Henna stood at the threshold with her arms folded in front of her. "Well, come on in, Your Highness. Let's get a look at you."

Zephira nodded graciously. "Thank you, Miss Henna."

The healer wiped her face with her sleeve and led Zephira inside the log structure. It smelled of strange herbs, something Zephira may have found offensive at one time, but after leaving the stench of the Skour, the new odors danced in her eager nostrils.

"Shoot me out of a whale's blowhole. He actually found you!" A man with a red mustache, bandaged head, and an arm in a sling wobbled down a ladder from an upper loft.

"I beg your pardon?"

As soon as the man's feet hit the floor, he took to one knee and bowed his head. "Forgive my manners, Your Highness. Olivier of

Ludesa at your service."

"Pleased to make your acquaintance, sir." She folded her hands at her stomach in an attempt to appear regal, if she could even remember how. "You were also sent by my father to find me, I presume?"

"That's right. I got held up recovering here a few days, but I'm well enough now to see you the rest of the way home, don't you worry."

Zephira feigned a smile. Could she really go home with Nyr still inside of her?

"Neither of you are in a state to travel. You should be resting that noggin of yours, and the princess needs some tending." Henna shooed the ginger man back up the ladder.

He turned and bowed once again. "It's a welcome sight to see you safe and sound. Take all the time you need, and I'll be ready whenever you are."

Once Olivier disappeared onto the floor above, Henna led Zephira to an outdoor veranda, shielded from possible onlookers by tall hedges and quilts hung to dry.

Henna quickly lit the hot coals under one of the clay tubs then went to cut up some leaves on the counter. Without a word, she crushed them in a mortar bowl, causing the sharp herbal odor to tickle Zephira's nose. "What are you preparing, Miss Henna?" Zephira sat down on a wooden bench in the corner.

"Comfrey. A little in the bathwater can help with any scrapes and bruises you may have."

Several minutes of silence later, a line of men traipsed into the cabin with barrels of water on their shoulders and filled the tub nearly to the brim. They nodded politely to Zephira and filed out.

Henna took Daynerel's hand to prevent his leaving. "Dayne."

"Yeah?"

"I should thank you . . . for being here."

The man's complexion went noticeably redder. He simply nodded and proceeded to exit.

Henna sniffed, standing at the doorway for a few more moments before going to stoke the coals. While waiting for the water to warm, Henna went back inside the cabin and tinkered with jars. She came back out with a wet cloth and a wooden stick oozing with a golden-brown liquid. From its sweet smell, Zephira realized it was honey. "Allow me to treat that neck of yours." Zephira nodded, and Henna wiped the dried blood off her skin, its sting a stark reminder of what she had nearly done to herself in the Skour.

Zephira closed her eyes and tried to overcome the nausea rising from her stomach as Henna applied the honey to her cut. When she was done, she let Zephira rest on the bench for a while. Several minutes later, the healer's voice startled her back to attention. "Your Highness, your bath is ready."

Zephira first removed her brooch then held it in her hand as she pulled her shirt over her head. After tugging down her ratted magus robes, she dipped her toes in the warm water. Her skin sang with glee as she sank into the liquid's warmth. *How quickly the body forgets the luxuries it had once enjoyed. Luxury in Fae'ren Province of all places.*

Henna picked up the soiled garments from the floor. "This is a man's shirt."

Zephira's chest tightened. "It belonged to Jeth," she confessed.

"I know." Henna swallowed. "I remember him wearing it the day he left. Though it was much whiter."

She carefully placed it on a pile of used towels in a bin along with Zephira's bottoms. She then grabbed a pitcher from the table and filled it with bathwater. Zephira reached her free hand out to take it. "You need not bother yourself, Miss Henna. Allow me——"

Henna dunked the water over Zephira's head before she could finish, drops beading over her tangled mass of hair. "It's all right. Just keep your head back." Henna raked her hands over her wet mop, removing clumps of blood, dirt, and twigs.

"You and Jeth were——are married," Zephira peeped.

For several seconds Henna didn't respond, then she said, "Whatever counts as married in these parts, I suppose."

Zephira didn't know what else to say to the woman washing her, the woman Jeth was so eager to return to. She simply wanted to close her eyes and scry rather than be present in this moment. She was about to trace the *Veil* on her forehead with a wet finger when she caught sight of Nyr lounging on the bench. Its red eyes burrowed through her exposed form. *'Never scry again!'* the ashray's painful warning still echoed in her mind. She slowly let her hand drop back under the water.

It was then Henna saw the brooch in her other hand. "Let me lay that down for you somewhere."

As Henna reached for it, Zephira snapped her arm tight to her chest. "That's quite all right."

An annoyed breath escaped the fae woman. "As you wish, but

nobody around here has use for a treasure like that, so there's no need to worry."

"Oh, I didn't mean to imply . . ."

Henna filled the pitcher and dunked it over her head once more. The second time shocked her more than the first. Without another word, Henna started scrubbing Zephira's back with a sponge.

Desperate to not let the conversation die on such an awkward misunderstanding, Zephira said, "Jeth mentioned you."

The sponge stilled for a moment. "Oh? What did he say?"

"He said . . ." Zephira gulped. "He'd do whatever it took to get back to you."

"Hmm, yes." Henna wet the sponge again and slapped it against Zephira's back as she scrubbed more forcefully. "His men reported similar things: How he longed to come home and such. Yet he was the only one among them who didn't return. Lift your arm, please."

Zephira complied, and Henna scraped the sponge under her arm and down her left ribcage, each stroke rougher than the next, bringing her closer to the state of physical purity she had once known. However, she knew that all the sponges and all the comfrey in the world would not be enough to cleanse her of the Skour.

She shut her eyes tight while Henna asked her to lift her other arm. Her scrubbing picked up in severity to the point Zephira couldn't ignore it any longer. "Pardon me, Miss Henna, but have I angered you?"

Henna wrung out the sponge as if strangling someone's neck in her shaking fingers. "You need not bother yourself with it, Princess."

Zephira turned around and placed a hand on Henna's to stop her from scrubbing further. "Do not think of me as a princess. I certainly don't feel like one at the moment."

She let Zephira take the sponge away to continue using it on her more intimate areas. Henna sat there, fiddling with her fingers on her lap. "Then as someone who's *not* the princess, may I be candid with you?"

"Please."

Henna rose from her stool, walked over to the bin, and stared at the bloody shirt. "Dayne said you kept silent on Jeth because you didn't want to let the harpies in on what you know. But now that it's just between us lasses . . ." Henna lifted up Jeth's shirt and turned back to Zephira. "What happened to him?"

The bathwater suddenly felt cold against Zephira's skin, and she began to shiver. "It's difficult to explain."

Nyr grinned from its seat as if mocking Zephira for not being able to tell the truth.

Henna stepped closer to the bath, holding Jeth's shirt out. "Try. You're the last person to see him, just tell me—tell me where he is. Please." She swallowed a sob as Zephira desperately tried to keep her own at bay.

Henna dropped the shirt to the floor, her arm falling limply at her side. If Zephira had to tell someone the truth, it should be the woman that loved him most.

"He's where I was for the last year. Trapped by a primeval force . . . and I cannot say if he'll ever come out of it."

Henna weakly sat down on the bench, displacing the black dog she couldn't see and shaking her head. "You're wrong. Whatever's going on, he can handle it. He will come back. He has to."

Zephira shook her head. "Not from this."

"You made it out."

"And had he not come for me, I'd still be there."

Henna rushed to the tub and crouched down to Zephira's level. "Then we need to go get him."

"It can't be done."

"What do you mean it can't be done?" Henna gripped the sides of the tub. "How can you sit there so calmly, telling me the man I love is trapped by some unnamed force, then offer no solution?"

"I can only offer the truth."

Henna shot up to her feet. "What truth? You've hardly told me anything, and I think I know the reason." Zephira took a deep breath, willing her heart rate to slow its humming pace. "You left him there to save yourself."

"No."

"He gave you the shirt off his back, and you ran with it, didn't you?"

The accusation was a dagger lodged in Zephira's heart. "I would have gladly stayed in his place. I was prepared to take my own life, then he'd return to you, empty-handed, but he'd return." She carefully touched the honeyed cut on her neck.

"Then why didn't you?" Henna wiped her rivers of tears and walked away from the tub. "Why is it you in this room and not him?"

Zephira stood up with a start, water beading down her skin as she stepped out of the tub. "Because he wouldn't allow it!"

Henna crossed her arms. Her steeled jaw loosened, and she scoffed. "Sounds like him." She took a soft woolen towel from the hook and handed it to Zephira. "Keep you from killing yourself so he could die instead. He finally got the punishment he's always wanted."

Zephira wrapped the towel around herself, letting it warm her chilled skin. "Punishment. For his crimes against the Crown?"

"Mother, no. For the death of his son. The others don't see it, but I've known it for a while. He blames himself. I try to help him, but he keeps slipping away from me . . . from all of us." She sighed and nodded through her tears. "This is what he wanted."

"You're wrong," said Zephira.

"Oh?" Henna huffed. "And what insights have you gathered of the man you've known a few days that I haven't in over a year?"

"I do not claim to know him better than you, Miss Henna," Zephira said, reaffirming her grip on her brooch and towel with the same hand. "But the man that came for me was not a man who yearned for punishment. He told me he'd do anything to get home, and he tried. He fought harder than I ever thought possible for a human . . . a man."

"But you don't think he'll make it out."

"Admittedly, I'm of little faith at the moment, but I'm certain he is not, and he'd not want you to be either."

Henna stood there in silence for a time, chewing the inside of her cheek and avoiding Zephira's apologetic gaze. "I forgot the extra clothes in the loft. I'll go get them."

As Henna turned to go back inside the cabin, Zephira blurted a name she hoped would give the healer some solace. "Ellion."

Henna's head snapped back around, her jaw trembling. "What did you just say?"

"Was that the name of Jeth's son?"

"No." She took a few steps forward. "It's the name of mine. He mentioned him to you?"

"It was the last word he said before he . . ." Zephira swallowed her words to prevent upsetting the healer further. "He must have meant a lot to him."

Tears dribbled down Henna's cheeks. "Yes. He was abducted not too long ago. By a nobleman."

"A nobleman?"

"Who happens to be his father." Henna wiped her tears and sniffed.

"There's an advocate in Deltashire who was supposed to help, but nothing's come of it yet. Jeth hoped that if he completed the mission to find you, the King would pull some strings to get him back."

"I see." Zephira looked down at her now clean toes. "I'm unsure what even my father could do in such a situation."

"But if you return home, you can make sure he makes good on the deal in Jeth's absence."

Zephira met Henna's pleading gaze. "But if I leave this forest, the harpies will attack the commune. I'm not sure I can ever go home." More guilt tugged at Zephira's gut. She had no intention of going home, but what did she intend to do instead? Stay in Fae'ren forever?

Henna waved her arms back and forth, shaking her head. "Forget it. I keep expecting justice despite never having experienced it. When will we Fae'ren learn? I'll get those clothes for you. You're shivering like a wee mouse."

With that said, Henna left Zephira standing there in her towel, the now cold water dripping off her body and soaking the worn wood boards at her feet.

40
At Your Heel

Jiménez led Vidya through the polished marble halls of the Emperador's coastal palace. The floor was hard and cool against her soft suede sandals. She put away the boots and armor for the occasion and wore a breathy gown. Her hair was only partially held back by silk bands woven throughout her curls. She needed to show her softer, more feminine persona. It was time to play the part of concerned wife.

"He's been asking after you ever since he regained the ability to speak." Jiménez opened the heavy double doors, flecks of gold accents in the female imagery sparkled in the morning sun. Vidya paused, unable to enter the room she had once shared with the man inside.

"Go ahead, Emperatriz," Jiménez urged. "I'll leave you two alone."

"Thank you, Capitán." She stepped onto the plush red and gold rug, blinking away the flashes of bloodstains, her prone body scraping across the fibers that popped into her memory unbidden.

A warm island breeze swept through the open balcony, unfurling embroidered curtains to present an ocean view. *So many times, I contemplated jumping off that,* she thought. *Now . . .*

"V-Vidya." A wheezing moan from the bed pulled her out of her dark reveries.

There he was, the one who had once incited so much terror, now unmoving and helpless once again. The last time he looked like that, Vidya had been in control. After her dismal failure in Fae'ren, she never felt less in control of the paralyzed man before her. *'A dangerous man who knows his place . . . at your heel.'* But what was his place now?

"Husband." She rushed to his bedside and took his deadened hand in hers. "How could this happen again?"

"Poison," he rasped through motionless lips.

She feigned shock. "Who poisoned you?"

"The investigation is ongoing," said a man from the doorway. It was Ricardo. Although he was finely dressed as always, his hair was disheveled and goatee untrimmed.

"You must have some leads by now," replied Vidya.

"There are a few." His dark eyes ignited with a wrathful fury that only Vidya could see, given that Agustin was unable to turn his head in his brother's direction. Ricardo pointed to his left brow. "You've been in a few bouts, I see."

Vidya touched the still tender stitches marring her forehead.

"Know this, Husband." Vidya squeezed Agustin's hand. "My spies will uncover whoever did this, and I will scatter their entrails across the sea."

Agustin released a moaning sigh. A sad rage burned behind his irises.

"Leave him be. He does not wish for you to see him like this. Come. I'd like to discuss what we have learned so far." Ricardo's temperate voice held a razor's edge.

Vidya's stomach churned. She knew what was coming.

He took her by the arm, and not wanting to make a scene, she allowed him to lead her onto the balcony and close the glass doors behind them.

Once out of sight and earshot of Agustin, Vidya snatched her arm away.

"You won't get away with this," hissed Ricardo. "Not this time."

Vidya placed a hand on her hip and leaned against a pillar. "Are you accusing me of something, Ricardo?"

"Enough with your deceptions!" Spit flew out of the man's mouth, almost landing on her bare shoulder. "We both know what caused this."

"Curare gourd. Just like the ones you used to grow in your little herb garden."

"What do you expect to gain from this, uh? If he dies, our alliance dies with him. You know I'm next in line to rule."

"That's why you poisoned him." Vidya laced sorrow into her voice, staring at her husband through the glass panes. "With me coming back into his life, you had to act. You'd help him make the connection that I was to blame. He'll end our alliance, turn away from this silly war you clearly don't support, and you can lead his empire in the meantime, maybe even do away with him altogether." She turned back to Ricardo with a smirk.

His brow pinched. "He'll never believe I did this to him."

"Are you sure about that?" Vidya gored him with her eyes. "He could find out how you lied to him in the past. About his boys. About me."

Ricardo scoffed. "Anything you tell him will only cast you in a worse light. If he had to choose, it would be his loyal brother, not his murdering whore of a wife!"

"Perhaps, perhaps not." Vidya was bluffing. Although Daphne had already planted the curare gourd in Ricardo's garden, there was not much else to prove he actually used it on the Emperador. She hoped she'd have the princess to use as leverage, preventing Ricardo from acting long enough for her to gather more evidence of his many other misdeeds. Agustin would have no choice but to turn on him. The humiliation and betrayal would be impossible to ignore.

"You are mad." The administrador shook his head in awe.

Vidya rolled her eyes. "The only truly mad one here is your brother. It's why he has to go, isn't that right? Now, if you'll excuse me, I must return to my husband's side."

As Vidya approached the door, Ricardo said, "He told me you were searching for the Princesa of Del'Cabria." Vidya's spine tautened as she turned back around. "He also told me that you wanted to keep it between you two." Ricardo walked around her and leaned against the door with his arms crossed. "You taking the King's daughter ransom would make my negotiations with him pointless. I would have wasted a trip at best or be taken prisoner at worst."

"We planned to tell you before you left. Now Credence has her, the King will agree to our terms, and the war in Odafi will soon be won."

"I see," Ricardo's black eyebrows raised in disbelief. "Though, it's strange that Del'Cabrian ships have only increased in the gulf, and I've just received a royal letter detailing when I am to meet with him. Is the King unaware you have his daughter?"

Vidya gulped. "My supreme commander is working on that correspondence as we speak."

"I don't think you have the princesa," Ricardo smirked, then put his hand on the doorknob. "So, let me tell you how things will play out. I will meet with King Tiberius as planned, and I will tell him Rangardia will pull out of all Odafi ports in return for an alliance."

Rage rose into Vidya's temples, making it difficult for her to keep her voice at a low enough register for her husband not to hear. "Agustin will never allow it!"

"I am to act in his stead until he recovers. But not to worry, Señora. You have the princesa, so that gives you all the leverage. Might be a good time to use it, no?"

Ricardo smirked again before turning the knob. Vidya grabbed him by the scruff, dragged him across the balcony, and dangled him over the balustrade. "I should just kill you!"

The man hardly flinched. "Go ahead. Drop me to my death with your paralyzed husband just inside. Maybe he'll believe I jumped. Maybe not. Do you want to be the one to explain it to him?"

"What can he do to me?" Vidya felt her grip waning. How badly she wanted to see the pathetic Rangarder fall the five stories and splatter to pieces over the marble statue below.

"It won't be just his wrath you'll invite, but six more brothers. Kill me, and vengeance against Credence will be swift."

Vidya brought Ricardo back over the balustrade with a frustrated growl and threw him carelessly to the ground.

He rose to his feet with a groan, brushed off his coat, and headed back to the door. "You better hope my brother recovers soon as his love for you may motivate him to stop me. In the meantime, you should return to your Harplite and prepare for war."

Vidya watched the administrador go back inside and sidle up to his brother's bed. Her skin flushed with anger. At Ricardo, at the demon princess . . . at herself.

"Now look what you've cost us," the shadow harpy hissed. *"You've provoked the wrath of a man who commands the second-largest army in the world and is about to ally with the first. You will never be able to make enough harpies in time."*

"Had we taken the princess, none of this would matter."

"You moved on Agustin far too soon. Those men are not about to turn on each other now. I warned you about this!"

Vidya snapped her head around to face the creature perched on the balustrade, blotting out the setting sun sinking beneath the waves.

"You don't think I know that?" She hurled herself against the balustrade and gripped it firmly. "I can fix this. We can intercept his ship on the way to the mainland, create a storm. They'll never know we did it."

"Then Tiberius will simply negotiate with the next brother in line." The shadow brought her sunken face right next to Vidya's left ear. *"Your failures are beginning to mount, Daughter of Sarta."*

"I've done everything you've asked," she snapped. "I took back Credence from the sirens, our harpy numbers continue to swell, the desert tribes are all but decimated. What more do you want from me?"

"Prove you're worthy of the Harpy's strength!" the shadow fired back. *"That you will not be fooled by men—not allow your women to be enslaved by men!"*

"That's what I'm doing!"

"Rangardia will be ours, this I promise you, but not until Del'Cabria falls. Only then will I be satisfied. If you are not up to the task, say so now, and I will find another to take your place."

Vidya stepped back from the railing in shock. "Who are you to say that to me? This is your fault. You wanted me to go after the princess, then you left her behind. You push me to make war with the male-ruled nations, and now you chastise me when they make war upon us! You tell me to punish men who protect those they love while expecting me to ignore the rapists and child murderers!" Pointing a shaking hand at the door, she railed, "That man in there slit Alonz's throat and drowned Sypros in his brother's blood!"

"And what of my children?" The ferocity of the shadow's voice made Vidya's heart leap into her throat.

"Your children?"

"My Harplite. They ruled half the world, and where are they now? Beaten back by Elmifel's mortal brood. I didn't get to avenge them. No. My own sister made a deal and agreed to have every last one of them destroyed. No new harpy was ever born again . . . until now." The shadow harpy slinked down from the balustrade. *"Your pain called to me, and I answered. From the loss of your first child to your final two, I was there, mourning with you—raging with you. But it was the death of your mother that brought us together at last."*

Vidya found herself backing away until her hip bonked against the balustrade. "You're not just the Harpy within *me*, are you? You're the Harpy within us all."

"I've waited one thousand years to punish the ones who took my children from me, and I will not allow you, my representative on this plane, to ruin that for one man. You took the first step in removing my sister from power. The next step is the systematic annihilation of every male-ruled nation, and to do that, Credence must

come first."

"Everything I do is in service to Credence!" Vidya screamed.

"That paralyzed Rangarder in there is evidence to the contrary. Because of your lack of restraint, you have damned Credence to a fate of rape and death at the hands of those buffoons! They should be subservient to you, and here you weep like a little boy. You have forgotten who and what you are!"

Vidya's wings unfurled with a snap. She glared at the hostile goddess before her. "I am a harpy! The first in a thousand years!"

"Then prove it. Crush the enemies of Credence and do it now!"

"It's too late. Without the princess, we do not stand a chance. If she returns home, it won't matter what Ricardo does. War is coming to Credence."

"War is inevitable where men are concerned," she tittered, a phrase often repeated by her shadow. Vidya thought she understood it before, but now that she was talking to the actual wayward daughter of Yasharra, the Harpy herself, it may as well have been gibberish. Why should war always be inevitable? *"Let the princess go home."* The Harpy hopped back up onto the railing, her back to Vidya, but her head craned to face her. *"We already know what devours men from within."*

"Pathogens," Vidya whispered.

Her ethereal grin stretched from ear to ear—if she even had ears—Vidya had never been able to see them through the shadow beneath her dark, stringy hair. *"And the greatest pathogen of all is about to walk straight into the heart of her own kingdom. All us harpies need do is provide it the environment in which to fester."*

Slowly, an idea formed in Vidya's mind. A desperate plan, to be sure, but one that would halt Ricardo's machinations and potentially weaken Del'Cabria at the same time. One that didn't require a thousand harpies today, a royal hostage, or mass genocide . . . at least not yet. And all without taking her revenge off the table. Everything would fall into place. It was so simple she felt embarrassed for not thinking of it earlier.

The backlash would come to Credence eventually, either from their enemy, their former ally, or both. But she could buy some time. Enough time for thousands of squabs to grow their wings. Then all the armies in the world would be useless against them.

Vidya rose to her feet, spread her wings, and leaped off the balcony. She plummeted toward the palace gardens and swooped up at the last minute, pumping furiously into the orange sky.

If Ricardo and Tiberius wished to bring war upon them, so be it. For she would bring them *pestilence*.

Zephira sat cross-legged in the Elders' Hut the following morning. The Elder Midwife, Twilla, who had invited her to stay in her roomy cottage, for the time being, sat next to her.

Among the other elders encircling the unlit fire pit sat Daynerel, the commune's protector, and Olivier of Ludesa. Even Henna attended the meeting, leaning against the wall near the doorway to listen in.

Daynerel just finished relaying what had happened at the gate and in the Deep Wood while conveniently leaving out the moment when Nyr took control, preventing Zephira from piecing together the events for herself.

"The harpies were wise enough to retreat when the fairies came," Dayne said, coming to the end of his report. "But not before threatening to rain terror down on us if we allow the princess to leave Fae'ren."

"And why again do they want her so badly?" asked Elder Abel.

Olivier replied, "It's not too clear, but I reckon it's the same reason Nas'Gavarr took her in the first place. To keep Del'Cabria from intervening in their plan to overrun the desert tribes."

"This is not about the desert," Zephira piped up.

"What have you learned, Your Highness?"

"I overheard one of the commanders say that their harpy rule depends on finding me. The Champion of Elmifel played a role in the Harplite's fall one thousand years ago. I am the Champion now, and the harpies have returned . . ." She paused, hoping Olivier would catch on.

He nodded immediately. "And they won't be stopped this time. Credence wants to invade Del'Cabria again."

"Or prevent Del'Cabria from invading them," Elder Leena chimed in.

"In any case, we need to find a way to get you home, Princess, or otherwise warn the King."

"But what if the harpies attack again?" She looked to all the Fae'ren in the hut. None would meet her eye. None except Daynerel, the only one there who had witnessed Nyr's carnage. He knew as well as she did that it wasn't entirely a question of what the harpies could to do them, but what Zephira could do to them if she lost control again.

"It seems to me," said Twilla, "we have two options: The princess remains in Lanore indefinitely to placate the harpies, or we finish what Jethril started and see her home, safe."

The hut erupted in a hushed discussion about Zephira's fate, making her feel as if she were a ghost looking in on her own funeral.

"If you take the underused paths, is there a chance you can get her home without them being aware?" asked a male elder.

"They'll find out sooner or later," a female elder rejoined.

They looked to their protector, who loomed over the group even while seated. "Dayne, can your fighters hold off the possible retaliation?" Abel asked.

"The harpies may retaliate regardless," Daynerel glanced at Zephira once more, then quickly averted his gaze. "It's not safe to keep her here."

"I agree," Olivier jumped in. "The longer she stays, the more time the harpies have to regroup. As soon as she's behind castle walls, His Majesty will reward our task force, clear Jeth's name, and send soldiers to defend you."

As the murmurings continued, Henna quietly huffed and left the hut. Zephira wanted nothing more than to do the same.

At that thought, she noticed all eyes were suddenly upon her, finally confirming her corporeal existence.

Twilla placed a soft hand on her knee. "What do you think is best, Your Highness?"

"I . . ." Zephira gulped, realizing this may have been the first time anyone has asked for her input on anything regarding her own fate. She felt paralyzed.

Returning home would seem to all present as the most obvious course of action, but she couldn't get the ashray's warning out of her head. *'An urling saint's blessing cannot help you. This force is too dangerous.'* Little did the elders realize there was a third option: Neither stay in Lanore nor return home. Find a cell, a mountaintop, another uninhabited island, it didn't matter where, as long as it was as far from civilization as possible.

Nyr sat straight across from her, eyes glowing, gleefully awaiting that moment of weakness when she'd let it take over again.

Brushing Twilla's hand off her knee, Zephira stood up. "I don't know. I'm not sure I can—I need more time."

"Take all the time you need, lass," the midwife said concernedly.

Nyr pounded against her sternum from the inside. She rushed out of the hut, walking briskly across the commune with her hand on her brooch until the Primitive Force stilled . . . for now. The only one she could talk to about this was recovering in the healer's cabin.

Once inside, she called out for Henna. Finding that she was not there, she climbed the ladder to the loft. There, Esteban lay splayed out on the floor below a faint sunbeam coming through the circular window.

His bandages appeared clean, the smell of infection having considerably lessened since the night before. Her conflicted heart warmed to know her heroic reptilian was pulling through.

The creaking old planks made Esteban's eyes snap open, and his vertical pupils narrowed. "Is that you, Princesa?"

"Can you not recognize my scent?"

"Scent?" He chuckled then sat up against the wall. "Unless you're covered in blood or viscera, you may as well not exist. In fact, you are peculiarly devoid of any odor."

Zephira scrunched her face. "Is that so? I suppose I'll take that as a compliment." She sat on the bed closest to Esteban's.

"Were it not for that trinket"—he pointed to her brooch—"I wouldn't recognize you at all."

She looked down at it briefly then sighed. "I'm glad to see you're healing."

Sniffing his shoulder wound, he replied, "It takes a lot of force to penetrate naja skin. But those rounds . . . I'm not used to this kind of pain. Thank goodness for Fae'ren herbal remedies. Now, I hardly feel a thing. What about you? How did the Elders' meeting go?"

"The consensus is that I should return home as soon as possible."

"But you still have doubts."

"Who wouldn't have doubts after what I did?"

Esteban gasped. "You remember?"

"No." Zephira shook her head. "But . . . you saw it. No one else will tell me what happened. I don't blame them. They must be terrified. So much so, they'd risk the harpy's return rather than keep me in their presence another day." She rubbed her fingers together on her lap until they burned from the friction. "Tell me the truth, Esteban. Were the ashray right? Am I a monster?"

Esteban sighed heavily and looked down. "Any sane man who bore witness to what occurred in that grove would answer yes to that question." Her heart sank, and a single tear trickled down her cheek. "Those men would take one look at me and think the same. What matters is what you believe you are."

"I did not ask what some men might think. I asked you."

The naja looked Zephira straight in the eye and said, "No, you are not a monster. You're a good woman with a monster inside her just like everybody else."

She was taken so aback she nearly released a sob. "Then how do you manage to keep the monster inside?"

"Not sure what you mean. As you can see," Esteban pointed to himself with both hands, "I don't so much keep the monster inside me as . . . well, beside me. Out in the open, where it can be seen at all times."

"Are you saying I should allow Nyr to take control?"

"No, no, no. Not inside or outside. Beside. Like it or not, it is a part of you now. The only way to control it is for *it* to become you before you become *it*."

Zephira looked to the ceiling, pondering the naja's wisdom. It made her wonder what kind of man he was before his transmogrification. "Have you always been this wise, Esteban?"

The naja chuckled. "I don't know about me, but my father never wasted an opportunity to impart his wisdom on us whether we wanted it or not."

"Us?" Before Zephira could ask him more about his family, a shuffle from the ladder made her turn around. Olivier's bandaged head poked up into the loft.

"Oh, Your Highness. Didn't expect to find you here. I was just going to grab a few hours of shut-eye."

She stood up and smoothed out her apron. "I will leave you to your slumber, kind sir."

"Don't worry about it." He climbed the rest of the way up the ladder and walked into the room. "Once you've made your decision, come wake me up. I won't mind."

As Olivier pulled aside the covers of his bed, Zephira looked back to Esteban. He smiled and nodded in encouragement. She could sequester herself to obscurity or take her own life, making the efforts of Jeth, Esteban, and all the Fae'ren worthless, or she could move forward. She could be the one thing standing between Nyr and the rest of the world. Only she knew the nature of the force she carried inside her. She was responsible for it now.

"Actually, I *have* made my decision."

Olivier looked up in surprise.

Taking a deep breath, she nodded. "Fear does not serve in times of need. Only duty."

"Uh . . . good." Olivier scratched his mustache. "So that means . . . ?"

"It means." Zephira blinked slowly. "I'm going home."

41

Every Single One

Jeth awoke in pure darkness. Warm, fleshy walls encased him. Snakkurs dug into his back, holding him in place. The throb of a thousand heartbeats echoed all around him in macabre harmony.

He was one of them now—one small organ in a much larger animal. The cradle of roots from the Spirit Chamber had become a prison of sinew in his new demented reality. Hopelessly stuck once again.

Branches of arms and legs protruded below him, upside-down faces hung above him, and all manner of teeth and hair were in his periphery. It was enough to make him throw up had he anything left in him to regurgitate.

His stomach was a gnawing vortex about to suck his entire body into the abyss. He was so ravenous, he thought about biting down on one of the fingers dangling in front of his face if only he were able to move.

As Jeth struggled futilely against his fleshy restraints, he heard shuffling, but from where he couldn't pinpoint. His once impressive sense of direction was useless here.

The shuffling turned into footsteps, muffled by the pit of bodies. It grew louder—closer. Jeth continued to struggle, but there was no strength left in his limbs.

Soon, a full-figured woman formed out of the shadows. He could not make out her face, only the long white hair cascading over her naked shoulders. "Jethril, you're awake."

His gut churned at the familiar, sultry voice that lapped around his full name like a gentle wave.

Once she came less than a foot away from him, there was no mistaking her gorgeous face. Among all the unfamiliar and incomplete human shells around them stood Anwarr. Every supple curve of honey brown skin was molded to perfection.

Jeth shut his eyes, trying to turn his head, but it was held fast.

Her smooth fingertips caressed his cheek. The next thing he knew, his eyes were open, and he was staring straight into those piercing frost-blue eyes.

"I told you once I had a good sense about people, and I was right about you. You're truly unbreakable."

"How stupid do you think I am?" he croaked. "I know you're not her."

She smiled that captivating smile and giggled in that irresistible way. "But I am. This is her exact form." She waved her hand to the side. The sinew loosened, releasing Jeth from its grasp. He landed on the crushed bone below with a grunt. He was suddenly cold. A painful tingling sensation ran through his arms. His attempts to lift himself were thwarted by his incredible weakness. The snakkurs, still attached to his back, pulled him upright to his knees.

"Spirits can't be replicated," he wheezed.

"Hmm . . . that may be true." Her eyes filled with Nyr's red glow. "Reused and repurposed, but replicated"—she wagged her finger down at Jeth—"No. Once absorbed into the Spirit Realm, the Anwarr you knew effectively returned to the pot of souls to be stirred up and served into existence as something new."

Nyr bent down and brought Jeth to her perfect bosom. Her sweet scent took him right back to Anwarr's room on the spice shop's third floor. It comforted him and trapped him. "No one said reuniting with your creator would be easy."

His arms were too weak to push her away, but he could find the strength to scream. "Get off!"

Her full lips formed into a pout. "I thought you'd respond more favorably to this form. She was your first love, after all."

Lifting his heavy head, he glared at the red-eyed version of Anwarr backing away into the shadows. "I didn't know what love was when I was with her."

Only the glowing red eyes were visible now. "Of course, you didn't, poor boy," she cooed. "You had no one to teach you how. Perhaps I was wrong to come to you this way."

The red glow disappeared, and the figure crouched down. A sickening, sloshing noise emanated from where Nyr had been standing. The putrid stink of black muck engulfed the last of Anwarr's sweet scent.

Nyr stood up once again and walked toward him. "The time has come for me to reunite with my children and end their enslavement to their false gods." She spoke with a Fae'ren dialect. He made out an outline of voluminous hair, a full hourglass shape . . . *Henna?* But the voice wasn't quite right. Jeth felt an overwhelming urge to run, but his legs were useless slabs beneath him.

"If you think I'll listen to you looking like my Hen, you'll be sorely disappointed. I listen to her even less."

The woman was closer now. It wasn't Henna, but someone he'd never seen before, and yet she was somehow familiar. An abundance of twisting locks tumbled over her shoulders and down to her knees, hiding her nakedness.

She chuckled jovially. "So much levity even in the darkest of hours." Nyr was close enough that Jeth could make out its whole new form. "Just like your father."

Jeth suddenly couldn't find the air to breathe. The woman kneeled before him, concerned round eyes full of compassion. Hazel. Just like his own.

He jerked his head to the side, refusing to look at the woman before him, the mother who abandoned him in the woods then succumbed to the plague shortly after, or so he assumed. He never let himself give her a face. She had never been real to him then, and she certainly wasn't in this moment.

"It's going to be all right, my son."

"I'm no one's son."

"To Kassandra, you are."

He closed his eyes, shaking his head back and forth. "Stop . . ."

"Open your eyes and look at the woman who birthed you."

With his eyes clamped down tight, he felt her gentle hand graze his head—how he imagined a mother would touch her son to comfort him—but there was no way for him to know what that felt like.

Salty tears wet his face. "Why are you doing this?"

Nyr cupped his face in her cold hands. "I need you to learn what's at stake . . . on behalf of all my children. They know not what they have lost. The Conduits must be removed from your world so they can remember where they came from."

"Something tells me they want to forget," Jeth said.

Nyr stood up and looked down on Jeth with disappointment and contempt. "I gave you a chance to forget, let you find peace in the Spirit Realm, but you insisted on remaining tethered to this mortal coil. Now, you will see what I've seen. Feel what I've felt. Then, through you, all my children will know who they truly are."

A snakkur shot out from the wall and embedded itself on the back of Jeth's head. The suction yanked him down flat on his back.

The proto-human cavern faded into a blur of vibrant color.

Jeth blinked, suddenly transported to a field of dry, brown grass. Rain splattered over his bare skin as he stood up on reinvigorated legs. He looked down into a valley from atop a grassy hill. Thousands of gray-skinned people, filthy and dazed, marched in several lines down a muddy trail.

Some were tall, others short, thin, fat. Some old, many young. A few children. No one appeared to be leading them. Just droves of naked, blank-faced men and women, boys and girls wandered in the same direction, all the way into the violet horizon.

Nyr, still in Kassandra's form, appeared next to him. Now clothed in traditional Fae'ren attire, she wore a short dress, apron, and beads woven throughout her rich brown locks. She stared at the endless caravan, arms crossed, lips pursed.

"What is this?" Jeth asked.

"You're looking at the reason for human existence," she stated darkly. "This nameless lot is being delivered, feeding mouths that can never be filled."

"The Skour?"

"No. The Skour is my domain, where I fulfill my purpose: To create an endless supply of flesh casings to appease the rulers. You call them Conduits. I call them tyrants."

More people than he had ever seen in one place continued to march by. "You created humanity to be slaves? That's our purpose?" Jeth felt sick. . . . it was impossible, yet he felt the truth of it as sure as his own heartbeat. Nas'Gavarr had discovered the secret of humanity's origin, not in Thessalin, not on Cordos, but right here. Jeth now believed that this very sight was what put him on his path of destruction. *Did you just take his place?*

Nyr nodded solemnly. "The ones you've seen so far are soulless shells, extensions of my own flesh as your eyes or hands are to yours." She pointed to the droves. "These ones are different. Our rulers grow more demanding, their appetite insatiable. I had to give these ones their own sentience."

"Souls?" Jeth gasped, turning toward her.

"No more than that of an animal. They're not capable of critical thought, self-actualization, or even language. Not these ones anyway."

He could hear cries of women in the distance and the pain-filled bellows of men, but the passersby were blank, expressionless. The screams were coming from somewhere else.

"But they can feel pain," continued Nyr. "They can laugh, cry, even scream. And . . ." Tears pooled in her hazel eyes.

". . . I hear *every single one* of them."

End of Book Two

CONTINUED IN…

Book Three of *The Bloodstone Dagger*

MAGIC TERMS

Aura - The energy that makes up each of the six essences (see Essence Mage).

Blast gel - Clear, highly explosive gelatinous agent enchanted by fire magic and discharged from a small dispenser.

Bloodstone Dagger - an ancient dagger made of bloodstone used for ritual sacrifice and blood magic. The stone can absorb and store blood of one being and return one hundred times that amount.

Dulsakh's Sarcophogus - A coffin believed to hold the remains of the ancient leader of the Najahai.

Emerald of Dulsakh - An emerald that houses the spirit of the ancient leader of the Najahai.

Essence Mage - A Mage who manipulates the six essences of wind, light, water, earth, fire, and life force.

Flesh Mage - A Mage who manipulates the physical tissues of living organisms.

Flesh whip - Whip wielded by Snake Eye, made of enchanted leather that can take the form of human skin.

Gizelle's Sapphire - A sapphire shaped like an antelope owned by Snake Eye used for storing large amounts of aura.

Ice powder - Granular substance that freezes anything not warm blooded. It is useful in putting out fires and making objects more brittle.

Maga(s)/Magae(p) - A long lost female-only order who primarily worship Salotaph. They have made a resurgence since the Burning

Waste became an oasis, and thus named it the Gift of Salotaph. High-standing members specialize in water magic.

Mage - A person, also referred to as a witch/wizard/sorcerer, who can manipulate one or all three components of existence: Essence, Spirit, and Flesh.

Magitech - Items that a Mage has enchanted with magical properties for the use of people without magic abilities. Examples are: Blast gel, flesh whip, ice powder, and wind blades.

Magus/Magi (plural) - An male-only order of the former Death tribes who primarily worship Sagorath with the Immortal Serpent as their exalted master. Its high-standing members specialize in fire and water magic.

Naja Handler - a Spirit Mage who controls an individual naja contingent.

Priming - The process in which a Spirit Mage readies a subject's spirit for manipulation (see Spirit Mage).

Spirit Mage - A Mage who manipulates spirit, the energy that makes all living creatures sentient.

Wind blade - A round throwing blade enchanted by wind magic to allow the wielder to control its trajectory.

NATURAL SUBSTANCES AND THEIR USES

Cael petals - Flower petal that resemble lillies and used for recreational purposes. It heightens sense of touch to make certain sensations more pleasurable, and pain more prominent.

Fae grass - Umbrella term for a group of plant leaves that are smoked recreationally and medicinally in Fae'ren Province. Effects vary from plant to plant and person to person.

Khat leaf - a gnarled plant grown in the dry Tezkhan plains that acts as a stimulant for those who chew it. Has a strong and unpleasant odor.

Naja blood - contains the antidote for naja venom born out of their saliva.

Rangardian drops - A mysterious liquid used recreationally by Rangardian men to increase feelings of vitality and virility. Long term use is thought to cause bouts of confusion, impotence, and violent mood swings.

Rangardian tea - A mysterious tea that originated in Rangardia, though is used by women worldwide as a form of birth control and an abortifacient.

Valerian - flowering weed extract used as a powerful sedative.

Vera - Gelatin contained in leaves used in Fae'ren to hasten healing of flesh wounds.

CONDUITS AND ANCIENT BEINGS

Verishten
Ancients: Golems
Location: Volcano of Verishten, Deschner Mountain Range, Ingleheim
Role: Foundation of life
Dominant essence: Earth
Weakness: Itself *(The foundation collapses and all fall with it)*
Champion: Siegried

Spirit of Elmifel
Ancients: The ashray
Location: Sacred Spring, Holy City of Thessalin, Elmifel Province,
    Del'Cabria
Role: Source of life
Dominant essence: Water
Weakness: The Serpentine *(The rivers run dry)*
Champion: Zephira

Crannabeatha (aka Mother Oak)
Ancients: Fairies and ogres
Location: Grove of the Crannabeatha, Deep Wood, Fae'ren Province,
    Del'Cabria
Role: Nurturer of life
Dominant essence: Life force
Weakness: Yasharra *(Pestilence devours the living)*
Champion: Jethril

Yasharra with Daughters the Siren and the Harpy
Ancients: Harpies and sirens
Location: Grand Altar, Citadel, Credence
Role: The suffering of life
Dominant essence: Wind
Weakness: Elmifel *(Pain is washed away)*
Champion: Vidya

Serpentine (Sagorath and Salotaph)
Ancients: Naja and their progenitors (Najahai)
Location: Temple of Sagorath/Gift of Salotaph, Herran, Desert Tribe
    Lands
Role: Death of life
Dominant essence: Fire
Weakness: Crannabeatha *(Ruins become overgrown)*
Champion: Snake Eye

BOOK ONE CHARACTER REFERENCE

<u>From Credence</u>

Althea – Mistress of Law & Order
Ariston – Supreme Commander of the Crede forces
Calisto –Mistress of Treasures
Camdus – Demeter's breeder
Daphne – Infantry medic, friend of Vidya
Demeter –Mistress of Foreign Relations & Trade, sister of Vidya
Lysandros (Lys) – Spice shop owner and member of the thieving crew
Maramus – Infantryman sacrificed to the Harpy (deceased)
Penelope – Mistress of Markets
Phrea – Infantry spy, friend of Vidya
Rufios – Demeter's second breeder
Sarta – Former Mistress of Foreign Relations & Trade, mother of
    Vidya and Demeter (deceased)
Vidya – Harpy, Champion of Yasharra
Xenith – Archon of the Siren Council (elected leader of Credence)

<u>From Del'Cabria</u>

Del'Cabria Proper:
Baird – Urling spearman (deceased)
Faron – Urling swordsman, Major.
Loche - Urling swordsman, navigator
Tiberius – King of Del'Cabria
Tobin – Urling spearman (deceased)

Elmifel Province:
Garwin – Ashray monk

Fae'ren Province:
Ami - Wood nymph
Ellion – Henna's young son

Henna – Fae orphan
Jethril (Jeth) –Fae'ren orphan, bowman, Desert War Traitor,
    Champion of the Crannabeatha
Serra – Forest pixie
Twilla – Midwife of Lanore

Ludesa Province:
Hanalei – Daughter of Talbit, former flame of Jeth's
Olivier – Bowman, medic
Roscoe – Horse master and cook
Talbit – Owner of ranch where Jeth used to work

From Desert Tribe Lands

Ankarr:
Khiri – Pickpocket and freed slave

Herran:
Anwarr – Thief, former wife of Nas'Gavarr, mother of Jeth's unborn
    son (deceased)
Ashbedael (Ash) – Thief, ex-member of the Bahazur
Nadila – A Herrani warrior general
Nas'Gavarr – Former Overlord of Herran, the Immortal Serpent
    (deceased)
Saf'Raisha – Daughter of Nas'Gavarr
Saf'Ryeem – General of the Naja Horde, son of Nas'Gavarr
Snake Eye – Ashipu, Flesh Mage, sibling of Nas'Gavarr, Champion of
    the Serpentine

Odafi:
Ezrai – Treasure Keeper of the Merchant Council
Istari – Thief and coin stasher, Light Mage
Sahadina – Woman at the Lunahalah

Sunil:
Yemesh – Servant of Snake Eye

Tezkhan:
Genkhai – A Tezkhan raider chief
Ukhuna – Former Chief of the Tezkhan Raiders (deceased)

<u>From Ingleheim</u>

Heinrich – Former Führer of Ingleheim (deceased)
Jenn – Essence and Spirit Mage, liberator of naja
Melikheil –Essence and Spirit Mage, the Raven Sorcerer
Siegfried – Kaiser of Ingleheim, Champion of Verishten

<u>From Rangardia</u>

Agustin – Emperador of Rangardia, husband of Vidya
Alonz – First born son of Vidya and Agustin (deceased)
Jimènez – Capitán General of the Rangardian army, brother of
   Agustin and Ricardo.
Ricardo – Palace Administrador, brother of Agustin and Jimènez
Spyros – Youngest son of Vidya and Agustin (deceased)

About the Author

K.E. Barron wanted to be a writer her entire life but chose to be an accountant instead. Now she divides her time between writing books and balancing them. She grew up in Fernie, British Columbia and now lives in Red Deer, Alberta, working as a financial analyst and writing fantasy books in her spare time. Her interests are vast and varied, ranging from the aesthetics of eighteenth- and nineteenth-century period pieces to the scholarly realms of evolutionary psychology, anthropology, economics, and religion. These eclectic inspirations are all part of the magic and culture of *Queen of the Skour*, her third publication.